THE
DISAPPEARANCE
OF
CRISTEL EPPS

MATTHEW LINK

WESTBOW
PRESS®
A DIVISION OF THOMAS NELSON
& ZONDERVAN

WestBow Press books may be ordered through booksellers or by contacting:

WestBow Press
A Division of Thomas Nelson & Zondervan
1663 Liberty Drive
Bloomington, IN 47403
www.westbowpress.com
1 (866) 928-1240

ISBN: 978-1-9736-1505-7 (sc)
ISBN: 978-1-9736-1504-0 (e)

Print information available on the last page.

WestBow Press rev. date: 1/26/2018

CONTENTS

Chapter One 1
Chapter Two 33
Chapter Three 55
Chapter Four 71
Chapter Five 93
Chapter Six 115
Chapter Seven 129
Chapter Eight 147
Chapter Nine 169
Chapter Ten 179
Chapter Eleven 199
Chapter Twelve 217
Chapter Thirteen 235
Chapter Fourteen 251
Chapter Fifteen 263
Chapter Sixteen 287
Chapter Seventeen 301
Chapter Eighteen 329
Chapter Nineteen 343

CHAPTER ONE
DARYL EPPS

1.

If you follow our road into town, you'll eventually find a 7Eleven on the corner with the highway. The corner by the 7Eleven is the last place anyone saw mom. The cops think a truck driver picked her up. They tell me she stood at the curb, her thumb out, the convenience store parking lot in back of her and the stop light in front of her. Waiting for a trucker from New York or Florida or California to pop the cab door and beckon her in.

If I close my eyes, I can picture her right now. She's wearing that super short denim skirt I never liked and those high stacked shoes that make her legs tense up. See those shoes as they climb the tall steps into the cab – one, two, three. Behind the wheel sits some greasy driver with a ponytail and a gut. The door slams, and off she goes with a hiss of hydraulics. Down Highway 32 to Charleston, to Chicago, to who knows where, out of my life forever. Sometimes I think if I just wish deep enough, if I could just concentrate hard enough, I could wind back time to that moment, and stop it playing out that way. Maybe I could convince her to come back to her family, to make another go of it with Dad. Or convince her to take me with her.

So far, my wish hasn't come true. But I keep wishing. And right now, sitting in the yard behind the trailer, I draw pictures in the dust with my finger. This line, that's the road mom took. Here are the trees and mountains she passed. And here she is now, sitting in a room somewhere thinking about me. Deciding to come back and get me.

Scraggly pines line the yard, pointing at the gray, sunless sky. The grass is patchy down here behind the water tank. I can dig or draw in the dust and they can't see me from the trailer. Even so, I can hear Eminem telling most of River Rapids what his name is from my room. My room and Ken's room, that is.

Well, Eminem, *my* name is Daryl Epps, I'm nine years old, and I hate you. Don't go thinking you're special, though, because I hate everyone. I hate Dad, I hate Ken, I hate Cristel. *Sometimes* I hate Cristel. And I really hate that Debra. Once, I called her a bad word and Dad knocked my tooth out. Debra just laughed. But I don't care.

This, this is the car that mom is going to drive to get back to me. It will have a roof and windshield and four wheels, just like this. And that there, that is a door handle, do you see it? It's a nice car. Plush seats. Electric windows, CD player. And, oh look, I nearly forgot, this is the convertible roof. One push of a button and it folds away, and me and mom will cruise the highway with the wind in our hair. We'll go to Los Angeles and Disneyland and build sand castles on the beach, like a vacation that never ends.

2.

My best friend is Nathan Dicken and the first thing you need to know about him is that everybody at school calls him chicken, because, you know, that rhymes. If Nathan could change his name, he would, because that's the only thing wrong in his life. If it weren't for his name, I would trade places with him. If a genie appeared when I rubbed the broken gas lamp on our porch and granted me three wishes, my first would be *change Nathan's name* and my second would be *change me into Nathan.* Nathan can do anything. His grades are always top of the class, he's the best Fourth Grader at football, baseball *and* basketball. He can already bench seventy pounds even though he's still nine, and all the girls love him. They follow us at recess and accidentally bump into us and try to get him to kiss them. Nathan is awesome and he's my best friend. Ken says he's only friends with me because I make him look good, but Ken's jealous because he's got no friends apart from Dale and Hayley and she looks half dead.

The best thing about Nathan is that he doesn't care what the kids at school call him. They can call him Chicken and he shrugs and tells them their mom is so fat when she jumped on a rainbow, Skittles fell out. If I was called Chicken, I would get so mad my head would hurt. I would get so mad, I would want to kill them. Especially fatso Dirk with his piggy little eyes and those cheeks like chipmunks.

The other best thing about Nathan is that he always knows what to do. Every recess, every time we play out in the evening or at weekends, Nathan knows what to do. Last week, we made a hideout in the woods behind his

3

house, and nobody knows it's there. It's hidden deep in a thicket and you can only get inside if you crawl through a tunnel. Nathan found an old tool box of his pa's in his basement, still with a key in the lock, and we took it to the hideout. Getting it along the tunnel was hard, because branches kept scraping the sides, but it was worth it. Nathan keeps the key, but we can both put things inside. Precious stuff, like the ostrich feather I found caught in the bandstand rail on the Green last summer. Or the pennies we lay on the tracks behind Main Street, flattened when the train went over them. Or the sword we found in the dump behind Harry's Mercantile, which only fits in the box if you put it in sideways.

Nathan and I sit in our hideout for hours sometimes. Especially after school when Ken's being a moron and trying to hurt me. Or if Dad is drinking. It's better than being at home. Even when it's cold, we sit in our coats until dark. Nathan goes home sometimes when he gets too cold or hungry. In the summer, it's better. We sit and play for hours.

Sometimes in the winter, we go to the library instead, because it's warm, they have comic books and a vending machine where you can get Reece's Butter Cups and peanut M&Ms. Sometimes me and Nathan go there after school and sit in the corner where adults read the newspapers. If it's quiet, Brenda even lets us play Angry Birds on the computer.

Brenda is the lady in charge of the library, and sometimes I wish she were my new mom. Never tell her that. But I know that if Brenda lived in my house, Ken wouldn't dare beat up on me, and Dad wouldn't lie on the sofa all day watching daytime soaps. Brenda is fat in a good way and always smiles. She loves to look up books on her computer and keeps telling me and Nathan to ask our friends to come to the library too. 'Got to keep up the numbers,' she says. But I'll never say anything about the library at school. All the kids would laugh at me if they knew I hung out at the library. And anyway, it's mine and Nathan's place and anybody else would spoil it.

Nathan likes the library because he gets lots of ideas from the books. Not long ago, he chanced on a book all about code-breaking, and we spent the next two weeks inventing secret codes and encoding messages to pass to each other in class. We even thought of a way of saying simple sentences to each other in code. We put the sound *lay* before and after every word. It was great while it lasted, but it didn't last long. It was just too difficult and boring to have to say, 'Layarelay layyoulay laycominglay layoutlay laytolay layplaylay?' to ask a simple question. But it drove Ken mad the whole time we did it, so it was worth every second.

Before that, Nathan read somewhere that dinosaurs had lived in West Virginia. I tried to imagine one getting a Slurpie at the 7Eleven at the end of our road or driving to the hatch at the MaccyD drive thru. Nathan shook his head and showed me a photo of a smiley archaeologist with her hair tied back brushing dust from bones. The photo was in a history book of the local area, and the caption read, *Dinosaur remains found near River Rapids, WV in 1979.* Nathan found shovels in his Dad's shed and for two weeks we dug up Nathan's backyard, an area of the woods behind his house, part of our own hideout and an area of the schoolyard looking for dinosaur bones. 'If we find a skeleton, we'll be rich!' Nathan said, and he spoke of little else. The hole we dug next to the swing set in the schoolyard was probably a step too far, especially when Amelia Michaelson put her foot down it while chasing Nathan and went crying to Miss Villareal. Of course, we never found a single bone.

You never knew what Nathan was going to come up with next, and I guess that was one of the reasons why he was my best friend.

3.

My Dad is fat, and not in a good way like Brenda at the library. He's fat because he eats too many pizzas, hot dogs and fried chicken dinners. He sits on the couch in front of the TV so much that it has molded itself to the shape of his backside and he wears it like clothes. Like the gray stretch pants or the *Mountaineers* T-shirt he always wears. His name is Donald Epps, although he is always called Don, and he proudly informs everybody that he has never worked a day in his life, 'and never will, and there ain't nuthin' the government can do about it!' He says it as though he is single-handedly championing freedom for the working man, and not idling his life away with sloth and gluttony. The only time he heaves his rear end off the couch is when he parks it on the toilet. Or on the seat of his junker of a Ford on the way to stock his fridge with Budweisers from Walmart or the 7Eleven. The only time he speaks to me is to yell at me, call me stupid, or demand I bring him another Bud from the fridge. If I ran away tomorrow or fell under the wheels of a bus, he wouldn't turn away from *The Bold and the Beautiful* long enough to shrug.

The biggest mystery about my Dad is what Debra sees in him. Debra is at least ten years older than him and stick thin. Nobody seems to know exactly where she came from, but she started hanging with my dad a few months before mom disappeared. Mom didn't like her, of course. Mom told her to get out of her house once. Debra screamed, face millimeters from my mom's, spit flying, until mom pushed her out the front door and slammed it in her face. Dad let her straight back in. Now that mom's gone, she lives here all the time, emerging from Dad's room like an Egyptian mummy at two in the afternoon, covered in makeup and perfume, barking orders at me if I'm there. So I just make sure I'm never there. She is so thin her bones poke against her skin so she is covered in sharp edges. Sharp elbows, sharp fingers, sharp wrists. Even her face is sharp. She looks like a witch.

Our home is a trailer on the edge of town, and it's not large. Dad's TV is nearly as big as the room it's in. There are three bedrooms: the den from which Dad and Debra emerge each day (if Dad made it off the couch the night before, of course), Cristel's room (which is so tiny the door bangs into the bed and the bed is the only piece of furniture in there), and the room I share with Ken. Actually, share is the wrong word. Ken is sixteen and I'm nine, so it's Ken's room and I sleep on a camp bed in the corner. Ken spreads his things over the whole room: his way of marking his territory, like cat pee. His dumbbells take up all the floorspace not covered by his clothes (mostly black jeans and T-shirts, and crusty boxers). His TV takes up the whole table space, and his posters cover the wall space. He keeps me up all night while he watches late night movies. Or he puts death metal or rap or hip-hop on his stereo at top volume, ignoring Dad's yells to turn it down. I can't say anything because he'll beat me. He is proud of his arms, honed from hours of moving his stupid dumbbells up and down and down and up, and loves showing me the way his biceps pop out and ripple under the skin. 'Don't make me angry, Daryl,' he says, 'or you'll feel this fist pounding your weakling baby face.' He means it too, as he has happily demonstrated more than once. His girlfriend, Hayley, loves his arms too, and the two of them spend hours on his bed giggling while she feels his muscles and I'm banished from the room on pain of a severe beating.

So I spend as little time in this room as possible, and in the trailer in general. Nobody seems to care where I am, which suits me. I swear I could stay out all night and only Cristel would notice.

Cristel is my little sister. She's six, and the only member of my family I like. Sometimes. She was mom and dad's last attempt to make a go of it and fix their marriage. It didn't work, because three years after Cristel was born, mom ran away with a truck driver. According to Dad and the cops.

Cristel screams a lot because nobody looks after her. She is thin and has dark circles around her eyes because Dad and Debra don't give her enough to eat. And she's small for her age. Most people think she's three or four and are surprised when they find out she's going to be in First Grade this year. Not that she goes to school much. Some days, if I wake up in time, I take her to the school bus with me. Most days we don't make it, because Ken's kept me up all night and I sleep in. Dad and Debra are never anywhere to be seen and there's no food in the kitchen.

8

Some days we eat Dad's pizza left over from the night before. Or there'll be some cold chicken or a handful of uneaten Doritos. Any breakfast is better than none. But by the time I've got Cristel up and dressed, and we've eaten whatever we can find, I look at the time on the microwave and it's nine or ten and the school bus has long gone.

I make it to school maybe three days a week. Mondays, forget it. Ken will have been up all night playing Grand Theft Auto, or Dad will have spent the night yelling at the TV or at Debra, or both. They usually fall silent around four in the morning, and by that time I can forget making it to school the next day. Tuesdays are better. I'm usually asleep by midnight, and if the alarm goes off, I can get Cristel to the corner of the street in time for the bus.

It's not like I hate school. Actually, I like it. I get away from Dad and Debra and Ken and Hayley, and I get to hang out with Nathan. Most of the kids and the teachers are okay. Even Miss Stevens doesn't shout all the time. Sometimes I catch her looking at me and I know trouble is on the way.

'Daryl, would you stay behind for a moment at recess,' she says.

I know what she wants to talk about, and already I'm thinking of ways to reassure her. She'll tell me she's worried by how much school I'm missing, and that I'm falling behind. She'll tell me I don't do much homework, and she's noticed that I'm wearing the same clothes as yesterday, and is Dad at home? And I'll tell her that things are difficult since mom disappeared, but Dad's doing his best, and thanks for her concern, but I'm fine, I really am, and then she'll put her hand on my shoulder and look into my eyes and tell me that she just wants what's best for me, and I'll squirm at that because I don't know what to say, so I'll just say nothing at all, and look at her, until she looks away, sighs, and tells me to run out to recess. And I'll go and find Nathan and hope that nobody turns up at the trailer this evening to take me and Cristel away, because if there's one thing worse than living with Dad and Debra and Ken, it's living with strangers.

Then Nathan tells me about the mushrooms he's found behind a tree in the schoolyard that he's convinced are poisonous, and maybe we can pick some and scare girls with them, and within moments I forget about being taken away, and nobody ever comes anyway.

The only kid at school apart from Nathan who's my friend is Amelia Michaelson, the nicest of Nathan's fans. She lives in the better part of town, and, as she frequently reminds us, will leave us in River Rapids Elementary for Appalachian Elementary on the other side of town just as soon as a spot opens up. Appalachian is where the rich kids go, but Amelia's been saying that since Kindergarten, and she's still here. She's one of the few nice girls in River Rapids. She doesn't wear pink and she doesn't mind playing in the dirt. She hangs out with us because she likes Nathan, but I like having her around. The only place she never comes is our hideout. She's not allowed there. That's just for me and Nathan and nobody else. Often the three of us will ride our bikes downtown or along the Clayton River in the creek bed. We will be gone all day, living on candy bars and chips and whatever else we can afford from the gas station with our measly pocket money.

Out beyond County Line Road, the old cannery is another playground. Nathan showed me where the fence has come away and kids can squeeze through. It's supposed to be dangerous, but that's why we go there. Why go at all if it's not dangerous? The place closed down like fifteen years ago and the big fence went up, complete with the signs. One of them has a skull and crossbones on it, like a pirate ship. Another has a zigzag lightning bolt and *DANGER OF DEATH* written on it like it were true. We ignore all of them, of course.

Inside, the huge warehouse is like a video game. We imagine bad guys with guns are hiding behind the crumbling pillars or broken windows or rusting machinery, ready to jump out and spray us with bullets. Unless we get them first. Piles of broken cans lie in puddles of rainwater, waiting for kids like us to kick them around and climb on them. The old machines that filled the cans and put the lids on look like deathtrap James Bond contraptions, dripping in grease and bristling with whirling blades to chop off your head. We could spend hours in the old cannery, lost in a fantasy world.

Better than the real world, that's for sure. Especially after Cristel disappeared.

4.

I guess I have to get to this sooner or later. This is what put my family in the papers. Dad even appeared on the local news on PBS. People hung out at the end of the drive, yelling at us whenever we left home, wanting to know what had happened to the little girl whose elementary school picture appeared in full color on the front pages week after week. This is how our family's guilty little secrets became public knowledge all over the country.

Saturday August 20th, 2011. No fear of forgetting that

date. I spend Friday night at Nathan's house on a sleepover, and we wake up early the next morning so we can go play. Nathan's mom gives us bowls of Coco Puffs, his favorite, and we sit at his clean kitchen table to eat them. When we finish, we leave the bowls in the dishwasher and bolt outside with a quick wave to Nathan's mom. I love sleepovers. For one morning, I can pretend I am a real kid.

The temperature is in the eighties, we are in shorts and T-shirts, enjoying the shade of the criss-crossing branches overhead after feeling the sunshine burn our arms and legs brown. Days stretch out long and inviting and school is so far away thinking of it seems blasphemous. We ride Nathan's bike, me perched on the handlebars, and hang out in the hideout for a while. Then Nathan's belly growls so loudly it cuts off our conversation and sends us both rolling in the dust in uncontrollable fits of laughter. 'Man, I could eat a hippo!' he says, and agrees to meet me back here in an hour. Enough time for us both to go home and raid our respective fridges. It is an appointment I am never to keep.

Dad is watching some cheap daytime game show when I get home. An enormous woman in huge, dangly earrings has just won a yacht. The fact she comes from Iowa doesn't seem to concern her at all. Dad pops another beer and says not a word as I open the fridge. On the way home I had dared hope he had managed to squeeze a visit to Walmart into his packed schedule, but the empty fridge dashes my hopes. Two frozen microwave dinners and half a bottle of flat Dr Pepper will do nothing for my hunger. Anger flares inside me and I slam the fridge door. Once again, I'll have to beg food from Nathan.

'What's your problem, runt?' says Ken's voice, so close

that I jump. He is standing just inside the kitchen, one hand wedged into a packet of Cheerios. He wears one of those tight T-shirts he likes so much, the ones that show off his muscles. This one has a cartoon silhouette of a bodybuilder lifting weights on it, and the address of the downtown gym Ken spends his time in rather than looking for a job.

'I'm hungry,' I mutter, not daring to catch his eye. I can tell by the way he stands that he wants trouble. Although I hate myself for it, fear makes saliva flood my mouth. I gulp it down and try not to let my brother know I am scared of him. He knows anyway.

Ken pulls his hand from the Cheerios packet and crams a handful into his mouth. 'Oh, you want some, runt? Here!' He spits them at me. Most fall to the floor between us.

I try to step past him, but he puts out an arm to block me. I know better than to try to get past. 'Pick 'em up and eat 'em,' he says. 'Do it.'

And I do it. One by one, fluff and dirt and Ken's spit and everything. Until they are all gone. At least I manage to keep the tears from my eyes while he watches me do it. When I stand after eating the last of the little sugary rings, that is when I see Deputy Fincher get out of the squad car on our drive.

5.

Deputy Johnson Fincher is a man I have encountered before. A few months ago, I stood in the line for the counter at the 7Eleven, a bottle of Dr Pepper in one hand and a box of Junior Mints in the other. Three people waited in

13

line ahead of me: a guy in a beanie hat and a Metallica T-shirt; a woman with a round, acne-covered face and two buckets of popcorn clasped to her bosom; and a kid with a skateboard under his arm buying milk for his mom. Metallica T-shirt was already tapping his foot impatiently, and acne-face was staring around trying to catch an eye but not quite daring to. The hold up was because the teenager behind the counter (a skinny guy with a prominent collarbone and a button reading *Shaun – Have you tried our 2-4-1 promo on sodas?*) kept glancing out of the window at the group of young people gathering in the parking lot. Trouble was brewing between two gangs, and I was beginning to wonder if a Dr Pepper and a box of Junior Mints were worth the risk of getting caught up with whatever was going on out there. Shaun and I were both relieved when a squad car pulled into the lot, lights chirruping.

Most of the troublemakers melted away at the first sign of the cop car. Some stayed, leaning on the railing that lined the handicapped-access ramp, clearly intent on fronting it out with the cops. I could easily imagine them using the 'no law against standing here' line.

The cop car came to a halt in the middle of the lot, straddling the exit and effectively blocking the parked vehicles in. I was convinced that had not happened by accident. I watched the parking lot through the window (the same parking lot from where my mom disappeared, insisted a voice within my head), as the squad car door popped and Deputy Johnson Fincher stepped out. He was probably somewhere in his mid thirties, but I couldn't be sure. To me, all adults look pretty much the same from age twenty to about age fifty. So split the difference and call him mid thirties. Although not out of shape, I could see his belly was starting to put extra pressure on his belt, something his beige uniform shirt couldn't quite disguise. But he was a large, imposing man, and his presence alone was reassuring. He yelled something about breaking it up and going home or he would take great pleasure in running in every one of you young punks, or similar words to a similar effect. After moments of yelling and grumbling, the parking lot emptied.

Deputy Fincher took off his hat, scratched a head of thinning hair, replaced his hat, sniffed, and made his way toward the store. The bell rang and every eye in the place watched him enter. He nodded at us, wandered along the aisle devoted to chips and dips, grabbed a large packet of chili hot Doritos and Jack Link's Beef Jerky. Without hesitation, he walked past the line, dumped his purchases on the counter and handed Shaun a twenty dollar bill. Shaun handed him his change, he picked up his goods, and walked unhurriedly back to the squad car. The doorbell rang as he left.

And nobody, not Metallica, not acne-face, and certainly not skateboard kid, said a word in protest. That was Deputy Johnson Fincher. Not a man anybody messed with.

And here he is walking up to the trailer door and pushing our doorbell with a fat finger. Ken forgets me and skitters into the living room, calling, 'Dad, it's the cops!' in an exaggerated comedy whisper. Through the kitchen door, I see Dad sit up suddenly, the fastest he's moved in several days. I keep back from the window so the Deputy doesn't see me. His wide arm pounds on the door.

'Open up, Mr Epps, this is the police!'

Ken runs around the living room, scooping up half smoked joints, cigarette papers and bits of unsmoked weed.

'Open up!'

'I'm coming!' yells Dad. He heaves himself off the couch, waddles to the door, scratches his backside through yellowed underpants and cracks the door an inch. Ken disappears into the bathroom.

'Yeah?' says Dad.

'Mr Epps, is your daughter at home?'

'Who?'

'Your daughter. Cristel.'

'Cristel? Yeah, she's here.'

'Bring her to the door, would you?'

'What's this about?'

'Just get her, Mr Epps.'

'She's in her room.' He turns his head to yell along the trailer's short corridor. 'Cristel! Come here!'

I expect the door to Cristel's room to open, or at the very least to hear her voice, but when there is no response, Dad yells again.

Eventually, Dad yells, 'Daryl! Daryl, go get your sister and tell her she better hop to when I call.'

I try not to catch the Deputy's eye as I sidle past the couch and along the short corridor to the bedrooms. I can feel Johnson Fincher's eyes on my back the whole way. I am sure he knows all about me. I am sure that the Epps family is well-known in the River Rapids Police Department as one of the trouble making families of the county, especially considering the amount of times Ken has been hauled into the police station downtown. A repeat customer, they probably call him, and there's his little brother Daryl who'll be just as bad in a few years.

Cristel has the tiny room at the end of the corridor. It contains only a narrow bed and a heap of clothes on the floor. I can tell at a glance that Cristel is not there. I yell to Dad and hang out of sight in the corridor to listen to what happens next.

'She's not there,' Dad tells the Deputy. 'She's probably out with her friends.'

'You don't know where your six year old daughter is, Mr Epps?'

'She's out! How should I know where she goes?'

'When was the last time you saw her?'

'I don't know! This morning!'

Dad is lying. I haven't seen Cristel all day. It is now three o'clock in the afternoon, and looking back, I can't remember having seen her since before I left for the sleepover at Nathan's. That was nearly twenty-four hours before. We all kind of assumed she was in her room the whole time.

Dad is getting mad. 'Listen, Deputy, tell me what this is about, or get off my property!'

'Mr Epps, the Police Department received a call from a concerned citizen at twenty-six minutes past seven this morning. The woman in question reported seeing a little girl, no more than six years old, wandering by herself along the side of the freeway. By the time we got there, the girl was nowhere to be seen. We have spent the rest of the day visiting numerous families with little girls, trying to ascertain her identity. At what time did you see Cristel this morning?'

Dad hesitates. His voice has changed. From where I stand out of sight, I know he is beginning to realize he could be in serious trouble this time.

'I.. I'm not sure. Maybe it was last night.'

'Mr Epps, I shall work on the assumption that your daughter is missing and set up a search immediately. Officers will be here within ten minutes to search for clues to her whereabouts and to take a statement from you regarding when you last saw her, what she was wearing etc. I strongly advise that you co-operate fully if you want to see Cristel again.'

Deputy Fincher returns to his squad car, already issuing orders into his radio. Dad doesn't move for several seconds. I peek at him, standing there framed in the doorway in his shapeless, yellow underpants and tank top, below which his hairy belly jiggles. Then he curses and bellows, 'Ken! Daryl! Get here now!'

And that was how the nightmare started. Within moments, the trailer is crawling with cops. They go through everything in Cristel's room. They turn over the living room. I see the way they wrinkle their noses at the leftover pizza and moldy coffee cups and the dust bunny collection under the couch. More than once they direct pitying looks at me where I sit in the corridor trying to look small. Ken tries to bar the door to his room. Our room. He yells abuse and something about rights and freedom and warrants until Dad tells him to shut up. He grabs his leather jacket and departs moments after that, his motorbike protesting as loudly as he as it disappears down the drive. I wonder if he's managed to dispose of all evidence of his drug-taking. Probably not.

Dad gives them photos of Cristel, although he has

none very recent. The best he can find is a photo from school. He has no idea what she was wearing. He has no idea who her friends are, or indeed if she has any friends. I know that she plays with a girl from school called Frannie, but I can't tell them where she lives. The police woman I speak to says she will get in touch with Cristel's teacher and find out from her.

That evening, the TV is off for the first time I can remember. Dad and I sit around in silence, hoping that Cristel will walk through the door at any moment and everything will return to normal. Debra turns up around the time it gets dark. The banging of the screen door makes me think that Cristel has returned after all. The sight of the bony witch elbowing her way in sends my spirits plunging again. She plunks herself down on the couch next to Dad without even saying hi, and lights a cigarette from a brand new pack of Marlboros. She takes a deep drag and blows the smoke right at me.

'Little minx got herself lost, did she? One less mouth to feed.'

I don't understand why Dad doesn't throw her out right now. I would. Then I would throw all her worthless possessions after her. And I would pour paraffin over her and them. And I would light her on fire with one of her own cigarettes. And watch laughing as she burned up like a dry leaf right there in front of me. How can Dad not understand that Cristel is worth ten Debras? A hundred. A million!

Instead of throwing her out, he smirks, takes one of her Marlboros and lights it. 'Don't let the cops hear,' he says, releasing a foul cloud in my direction, 'or they'll think you took her.'

'As if I'd want the little puke stain.'

I wonder what she had been doing that morning when Cristel went missing. Where had she been? I picture my sister locked up in some dank room at Debra's apartment right now, crying in a corner, wondering what's going to happen to her. I know where Debra lives. I can find Nathan and we can go there right now. I can rescue Cristel and take her away from this poisonous family in this trashy trailer. We can hitch a ride from a trucker at the 7Eleven and go find mom. Find our happy-ever-after in LA or San Francisco or wherever she is waiting for us.

'Where do you think you're going?' Dad growls. 'You think I'm gonna let you out of my sight after today? I lose another kid, the cops'll put me away for ever.'

Debra sniffs and takes another drag. 'Too bad it weren't this one got taken by some pervert. Just too fugly. Look at that face like a donkey chomping thistles!'

They both laugh like it were the funniest thing they ever heard, honking and snorting like pigs. They start popping Buds soon after, and then the TV goes back on. Some late night movie about gangsters shooting up Chicago. The next time I stand and walk away, they say nothing. But this time I am merely going to bed.

6.

Sunday August 21st 2011

I wake when it gets light. Ken lies in bed in his undershorts, snoring, but at least he's alone. If Hayley had spent the night, I would have been kicked out to sleep on the sofa. That's two nights in a row I've had my own bed, something of a record. I push open the door to Dad's room as I pass, hoping the squeaking hinges won't wake him. No, he is passed out in bed, snoring, with Debra's skinny arms draped across him. I gag and walk on past. I don't even pause to scavenge leftovers from the living room or the kitchen. Today, I just have to get out of here, and as quickly as possible.

I hold my breath as I close the front door behind me, and guide the screen door into place so it doesn't squeak or slam. I still hold my breath as I run silently past Dad's truck and along the gravel drive to the road, expecting to hear a yell behind me at any moment. I am prepared to hightail it if I have to, and face the consequences later. When I pass behind the stand of pines screening the trailer from the road, I finally release my breath. There will be consequences, I am sure of that, but not right now.

The road beyond the pines is a two lane blacktop. On this side, trailer homes of different shapes and sizes are spaced on plots of land, connected by electrical wires looped across the tops of telegraph poles. Opposite, Jefferson's Woods stretch to a creek bottom, where a shallow river bubbles over rocks, another place where Nathan and I sometimes hang out, especially in summer. When the temperature hits the nineties and makes a concerted effort to break three digits, stripping down and splashing in that cold water feels like heaven right here in West Virginia. Half of me wants to head on down there right now and while away the day as though I can somehow kid myself that nothing has happened and that will make it right.

Instead, I run along the edge of the road toward town, feet slipping in the cracks where the edge of the tarmac crumbles, moving quickly but not so fast that I draw attention. After only a few seconds, I hear a vehicle approaching and quickly hide among the tall grass at the side of the road. It doesn't do to be seen out alone this early in the morning. I watch Deputy Fincher's squad car speed past me and turn into our drive. I let out my breath. Just in time. When the squad car is out of sight behind the pines, I emerge from hiding and hurry away.

We live on the edge of town, just a few hundred yards before the town limit sign if I had taken the other direction. Even moving quickly, it will take me thirty-five, maybe forty minutes to get downtown. I envy Nathan his bike, knowing that Dad would never get me one. Fortunately, I am not going all the way downtown. Follow the road until the Freeway and the 7Eleven, cross the Freeway without killing myself, hang a left until the Old River Road, then a right and the little bungalows of green-gray siding start to crowd in. Two blocks further and I am in River Rapids proper, passing the Dairy Queen and the Texaco, and right there on the corner by the stop light is the apartment block where Debra lives. When she isn't hanging around our trailer stinking the place out with Marlboros.

The block is an ugly concrete box, built way before I was born. Just rows of identical windows in a blank, gray wall, frames peeling, glass cracked. Our trailer isn't much, but it beats this depressing building. I can't see why anybody would want to live here. Most of the windows seem to be cracked, the parking lot out front is studded with potholes, weeds, and broken pieces of brick and roof slate, and most of the street lights don't work. I wouldn't want to be here after dark, that was for sure. Man, I don't want to be here now!

Do I really think I'll find Cristel in this dreary building? Do I really think Debra has her inside somewhere, gagged and bound to a radiator? Short answer: no. But some part of me knows I have to do something to find my sister, and this is the only thing I can think of. I don't plan ahead. I don't try to foresee different eventualities. One thing at a time. I have made it here. Now I have to get inside.

The door is locked. One of those electromagnet locks that only disengages for residents when they hold a fob up to the plate. No way I am going to open that. I hang out near the entrance door, crammed into a crack between two dumpsters. One thing I've learned from avoiding Dad and Ken is if a kid keeps quiet and still, most adults won't even notice he's there. I can turn invisible if I want to. Just tuck in close to the dumpsters, look at the ground and don't move. Instant invisibility, and when the door opens to emit an old man with one of those basket-on-wheels things that all old people seem to have, he has no clue I am standing within arm's reach of him. He doesn't notice me slip through the gap before the door closes. He has no idea I even exist as he totters along the sidewalk.

The lobby is gray and smells of cat pee. Pizza menus are scattered across the floor, many with footprints on. More are stuffed in the mail slots against the left hand wall. Two choices: corridor or stairs.

Next problem: which apartment is Debra's? Solution: there is her name above the mail slot for apartment 415. I take the stairs to the fourth floor.

Each floor up seems worse than the one before. Darker, damper and smellier. The paint is more chipped, the walls more stained, the floor dirtier. 415 is at the far end, where the corridor ends in a grimy window. I can see the rooftops

23

of downtown River Rapids, the abandoned theater, the municipal park with the dilapidated bandstand where I found the ostrich feather last summer, and just peeking around the corner, I can see the end of the Police Station. RRPD. Where Deputy Johnson Fincher and his men are no doubt doing everything they can to find my missing sister.

I know Debra isn't here, so I crouch and try to see through the crack beneath the door. Shadows, dust. Nothing moves. I put my ear to the door. If I listen hard enough, maybe I will hear my sister grunting behind her gag, trying desperately to attract somebody's attention. Or maybe she can tap the radiator pipe with her feet in Morse code until her rescuers come.

I push the door with all my might, but it is never going to yield to a nine year old like me. I yell Cristel's name through the crack, but of course no reply comes. But can you imagine if she really was there? I would tell her that help is on the way, and then I would run out of here and find a policeman and rescue her and I would be the hero older brother with my picture in the papers, and how would Ken like that?!

But it doesn't happen like that. I lean against the door and slide down until I hit the floor. So what now? I turn around and slink back home, powerless to find my sister and once more at the mercy of Dad and Debra and Ken? Or I go find Nathan and see what ideas he has. He always knows what to do.

I hear voices as I jump to my feet, and I freeze. Two voices coming from the stairs, from the only way out. I skid away down the hall, but there is nowhere to hide, not even a shadow to crawl into. If I keep back against the wall and don't move, maybe I can turn invisible again.

Super-Daryl, the Boy with the Power of Invisibility. I hold my breath.

Deputy Johnson Fincher turns the corner onto the landing, big, powerful, the picture of authority in his tan uniform and wide brimmed hat. He talks to a thin, weaselly man with no hair and a thin nose, keys in his hand.

'I can't open the door for just anyone, Deputy.'

'I'm not just anyone, Mr Swicks, I'm the police. If you can't trust the police, who can you trust?'

'Not even for the police. My tenants have a right to privacy and...'

'A little girl is missing, Mr Swicks. She's six years old and she is probably in a good deal of danger.'

'You need a warrant...'

'I can get a warrant, Mr Swicks. But it will take several hours and by that time the little girl could be dead. Do you want to be responsible for that? How will that sit on your conscience, Mr Swicks?'

'I don't think...'

'Then quit complaining and open the door!'

Still muttering, the weaselly guy – Swicks – jams a key into the lock of Debra's front door. He leads the way in. Deputy Fincher stops on the threshold and looks right at me. My heart thumps in my chest as our gaze locks. Then he enters the apartment and is gone.

I breathe again. My powers worked! Super-Daryl, the Invisible Boy, has come through! Or had the Deputy really seen me? Had he recognized me from the trailer yesterday? Maybe he thinks I live here.

I wait no longer. I run along the hall, down the stairs, and through the front door. The warm sun hits my face, birdsong drops from the trees, on the opposite sidewalk a woman walks her dog, and Deputy Fincher's squad car waits at the edge of the parking lot. I run to find Nathan.

7.

Nathan lives in a big, clean house just like the ones you always see on sitcoms on the TV. It was built probably in the nineties, the gray siding is beautifully finished, without a splatter of bird poop, the windows are clean and edged with tidy net curtains. The front yard slopes just right and the grass is the perfect shade of green. Beds of flowers run along the edge of the sidewalk, all prim and pretty. A basketball hoop hangs above the doublewide garage, a lawnmower is propped against the wall, and one of Nathan's toys sits on the lawn, an imperfection so tiny it makes the whole picture even more perfect. All it needs is a white picket fence.

Inside, it looks even more like a sitcom house. The living room is huge and full of things without looking cluttered or untidy. Everything has a place, from Nathan's board games and jigsaws, to his mom's library of romance novels and his dad's collection of fishing magazines. Up two steps is the kitchen with its central island, where the family eat, and the countertop where the microwave, the juicer, the knife-sharpener and the potato peeler all have designated spots to sit. The enormous fridge, with its water-chiller and ice-maker, hums softly to itself next to the back door, with just enough space next to it for the family to place tidily their outdoor shoes.

The wide staircase turns two corners as it rises to the second floor, and the TV, widescreen and flatscreen, fits perfectly in the corner, surrounded by shelves of alphabetized DVDs, not always on, not always off.

I tell you all this just so you know I've noticed.

When Nathan's dad answers my knock wearing a robe, I remember how early it still is.

'Can.. Can Nathan come out and play?' I ask.

Nathan's dad pulls the robe tight around himself and ties the cord. 'Daryl, do you know how early it is?'

I don't, so I shake my head.

'It's almost nine in the morning. Sunday morning. Don't you ever sleep?'

I sleep sometimes on my camp bed, but mostly Ken throws me out of the room and I end up on the couch, and I don't sleep there. I think about telling Nathan's dad that, but I don't think he wants to know. I try to think of something else to say, but I can't, so I just stare at him. After a couple of seconds, he sighs, and says, 'You better come in.'

I sit on the couch while he tramps slowly up the stairs. I hear a murmur and he replies, 'It's Daryl, that's all.' Doors slam upstairs.

I swing my feet against the couch. I like the thumping noises they make. *Thump, thump, thump.*

At last, Nathan jumps down the stairs. 'What's up?' he says. He doesn't care how early it is, and I knew he wouldn't. Only grown ups care about things like that. He's wearing a cool Spiderman T-shirt and band aids on his knees where he scraped them in the cannery yesterday.

'Coming out?' I ask. 'Wanna spy on Ken?'

He grabs a backpack and stuffs a huge pack of Doritos into it. Two bars of Hershey's Cookies and Cream follow the Doritos, plus a bottle of root beer. This is how great

Nathan is. He'll let me have most of these things. He knows without even having to ask.

We leave without yelling goodbye. We hop and skip along the road. I feel great. Right now, far from Dad and home, running along the sidewalk with my best buddy in all the world, all the scary things in the world can't touch me. I know I should tell him that we can't find Cristel. I know that. But why should I spoil things? I want this time to stay perfect just a little longer.

We go find Amelia Michaelson. She lives in a house even bigger and, if possible, more perfect than Nathan's house. Her mom never wears pants and always wears a necklace. Her dad works in a law firm in Charleston. He always smiles because they always have lots of money. He loves telling jokes, even jokes that aren't funny. He says *Hey kid, what do you call a man with a shovel on his head? Doug!* And then he creases up as though he has never laughed before. He always kisses Amelia on the top of her head whenever we go out to play, and he always says *Don't get up to mischief.* We don't know what mischief is, but Nathan says it means doing things that adults don't do anymore since they stopped being kids.

We say goodbye to Mr Michaelson and make our way along Amelia's street. She is wearing a dress with purple flowers on it because her mom won't let her wear pants, but she doesn't care if it gets dirty. 'We're just being kids,' she tells her mom when she comes home with mud on her clothes and leaves in her hair, and her mom sighs and smiles and says, 'I just wish you could be a nice, clean kid,' and puts the clothes in the washer.

'I wanna spy on Ken,' I say, and Nathan and Amelia nod happily. Spying is fun, and they both know my family is weird and Ken deserves it. I know I should tell them that Cristel is missing and I want to know if Ken knows where she is. But Nathan and Amelia don't ask why, so I don't tell them. They don't need a reason. They know I hate my brother and that is enough.

We make our way downtown to Ken's gym. The signs say that River Rapids' downtown area is 'historic' and 'part of a special regeneration program sponsored by Mayor Bob Vance designed to reposition the downtown area as a vibrant shopping and eating destination'. Robarts Street must be waiting for its turn to come, because right now all the buildings are empty apart from Frank's Gym. Large windows reflect the sunshine into our eyes, but if I push my nose against them I can see inside and the stores are empty and dusty. Some have old pieces of furniture jumbled everywhere, display cabinets that used to hold racks of Goodwill skirts and blouses. In others, old cardboard boxes spill papers onto the floor. Nathan and I have talked many times about trying to get into one of these old stores, but so far we have not found the courage.

We huddle in a doorway across the street from the gym. A notice in the window next to me thanks customers for their loyalty for more than twenty years. *Maybe one day we will have the pleasure of serving you again*, it finishes. Next to it a bill for a boxing event peels from the glass. I wonder if some of the boxers frowning from behind poised gloves trained at the gym across the street.

Nathan passes around the Doritos. I eagerly cram some into my mouth. I realize I haven't eaten at all today.

Amelia crunches chips. 'Any idea how long we'll be waiting?' she says.

'He always goes to the gym as soon as he wakes up,' I say.

Nobody cares much. We may as well hang out here as anywhere else. Soon Nathan has transformed deserted, rundown Robarts Street into a busy New York boulevard and we are private eyes hired to spy on a notorious gangster who's been running rings around the police for months. He's Dick Spencer, grizzled former police detective now on the verge of alcoholism, I'm Robin Bruce, teenage assistant, handy with my fists and handier with the girls, and Amelia is the gangster's moll, tired of violence and ready to go straight. Together we'll keep the streets safe for the law abiding public of New York City.

For a time, Dad and Ken and Cristel fade from my mind.

Until Ken's Harley roars around the corner from Main and comes to a halt outside Frank's. We press into the shadows of the doorway. If Ken sees us, he'll go berserk.

He pulls the helmet from his head and struts into the gym.

I let out the breath I didn't know I was holding.

The windows of Frank's Gym are blacked out and the brief glimpse through the door when Ken went in is not enough to satisfy our curiosity. I imagine a dark, dank room, full of sweaty, over-pumped men in wifebeaters, grunting to each other. The smell of testosterone and metal. Comparing sizes to see who has the biggest arms.

'I'm going in!' says Nathan, suddenly.

I stop, a handful of Doritos an inch from my mouth. 'You're not serious?'

'I'm Dick Spencer, private eye,' he says. 'And there's only one way to find out what goes on behind those doors.'

'What will you say?' asks Amelia.

'I'll pretend to be you, Daryl,' he says. 'I'll say I have a message for my brother.'

'He'll beat the life out of you,' I say, eyes wide, Doritos still held in suspense.

'Only if he catches me,' says Nathan. 'I do this for the benefit of young brothers and private eyes everywhere. I am prepared to risk all for our cause.'

He thumps his chest over his heart, leaves our hiding place in the empty doorway and cruises the street to Frank's Gym. Amelia and I watch, fists in mouths, as he pushes the door open and disappears inside. I expect the guy at the door who checks membership to boot him onto the sidewalk on his backside. But a moment passes and then another and nothing happens. Has the guy swallowed Nathan's story about carrying a message for his brother? I am just thinking that maybe Nathan truly can do anything when the door bursts open and Nathan runs into the street, eyes wide, a huge grin stretched across his face, yelling, 'Run!' as loud as he can. Amelia and I watch, dumbstruck.

Until Ken bursts through the door behind Nathan, red-faced and yelling something about kicking his behind.

Nathan runs past us and we follow, sneakers slapping against the concrete sidewalk of Robarts Street, past empty stores to the end of the block. Then right on Main, no clue where we're going, high and screaming on the adrenalin of the chase, the *thump, thump, thump* of Ken's training shoes on the sidewalk behind us reminding me of the sound my heels made against Nathan's mom's couch hours and hours ago.

Right again and now we're behind the stores on

Robarts, among dumpsters and abandoned cars and dog turds. We slide into a space between a wall and a dumpster, sweaty and giggling, even Amelia, trying to stifle our noise so we don't give ourselves away. Moments later Ken's heavy footfall approaches.

'It's disgusting in there!' whispers Nathan. 'Smells like old man farts and window cleaner!'

I smirk.

'Shhhh!' hisses Amelia.

Ken shoves the dumpster aside with one arm like it weighs nothing. The brick wall behind me presses into my back. 'My snot-nose brother and his snot-nose friends,' he says. 'You spying on me, that it? Your sister goes missing, you still playing your stupid games?'

'What?' Nathan says. 'Your sister's missing?'

'You didn't tell your little buddy?' says Ken. He smiles and punches my nose. Pain explodes in front of my face and my nostrils fill up. I scream.

'Get out of here, runt,' Ken says. He cuts his eyes at Nathan and Amelia, gobs spit on the ground and stalks off. Nobody moves or speaks until he has turned the corner.

'Are you alright, Daryl?' says Amelia. She puts her arms around me and hugs me tight. Usually, I would pull away, disgusted, especially with Nathan standing right there, but this time is different. This time it feels nice.

A tear squeezes from my right eye but I blink it away.

CHAPTER TWO
JOHNSON FINCHER

1.

Saturday August 20th, 2011

Johnson Fincher squeezed, pushed, prodded and poked the narrow overlap of flab at his waist, contorting it into different shapes like a partially inflated party balloon. But no matter what he did, it always *flupp*ed back into place over the top of his belt, obstinate and eternal. *A bit like God,* he thought, and then felt guilty and apologized to the Almighty for comparing Him to flab. He was pretty sure God *did* have a sense of humor, however, despite rumors to the contrary. He certainly hoped so, anyway.

Forty-two years old and gaining weight was as easy as breathing. Not so long ago, he could have washed down an entire steak at Kelly's with a root beer float, then belched, and ordered another. Now just walking past the diner on Main added pounds to his waistline. Susan had noticed, he was sure, although she hadn't said anything. He was turning into the cliché of a donut-guzzling cop.

Outside the tiny bathroom window, the sunlight

gathered strength behind the stand of trees screening Conway Crescent. It was going to be another beautiful day. Days like this convinced Johnson that staying in small town WV and keeping the good folks of River Rapids safe had been the right choice for him, and for Susan and Millie. Never mind Charleston, Huntington, or, God forbid, DC, Philly or New York. This was where he could do the most good. This was where warm summer sunshine first thing in the morning made him feel glad to be alive. Flab or no flab.

The bed was empty and he could hear Susan in the kitchen, firing up the coffee machine. Any moment now, the radio would go on (*WKWV, West Virginia's premier morning station – guaranteed to get you up and away!*) and the delicious smell of cinnamon bagels would waft up the stairs. Johnson could already picture Millie pushing out her nose from under her comforter and scanning her pink room with its jumble of toys and books, ready to dip her toe into the new day. Of course, it was Saturday, and still a week from the end of summer vacation, so she could afford to take her time. *Some of us,* he murmured to himself, *have to get to the office and earn a crust of bread.* For now, though, a cinnamon bagel would do.

Susan was in her robe, hair floaty and sleep dust in her eyes. She kissed him when he walked into the kitchen, still attempting to find the most comfortable hole in his belt. The bagel sat on the table next to a glass of orange juice and a huge mug of coffee.

'Thought I might go into the shop for a couple of hours today,' she said. 'Get some of those invoices done. Might even get on top of them this time.'

'Fine,' he said.

'Millie's going to Becka's. Becka's mom can find me at the shop if she needs me. Be a good opportunity.' She sipped coffee opposite him. 'Should be a nice, slow day. The weather's lovely. Who would think of committing crimes today?'

The squad car, a 2008 Ford Crown Victoria that could reach sixty mph in five seconds (so Johnson was told – he had never put the claim to the test) slid off the drive and onto the tarmac of Conway Crescent with scarcely a bump. Conway Crescent, an elegant curve of widely spaced single-level homes with carports, lovingly crafted in the early nineties, was one of the more upmarket communities in River Rapids. Johnson was well aware that many of his neighbors – lawyers, doctors, surgeons, even a psychiatrist and a high-court judge – earned more than he did, but the house came with the job. As his boss, Sheriff Millstone, put it, 'We law enforcers need a bit of distance from the crims,' and as long as Johnson held down the job of deputy, he could enjoy living in a nice neighborhood. Johnson put the Crown Victoria in gear and drove carefully past the neat front lawns and picket fences.

The River Rapids Police Department was housed in a low concrete building that had been put up in the early seventies and so far escaped redevelopment. Although the ceilings were low, the windows small and the architecture uninspiring, Johnson loved the place because of its cozy familiarity. He pulled into his parking spot (right next to Bill Millstone's), popped the door, heaved his bulk from the driver's seat and ambled into the building. The clock on the courthouse across the square read dead on seven thirty.

Carole Jeffrey, River Rapids' one and only daytime dispatcher waved a paper at him as soon as he walked in. 'Don't get comfortable, Johnson,' she said. 'This just in. Little girl seen walking along the shoulder of Highway 32. Chief wants you to check it out. Good morning, by the way.' Carole was in her late fifties, although kept herself looking ten years younger, liked to wear trouser suits at the precinct, and had been doing this job for more than twenty years. She likely knew more about the people of River Rapids and their family histories than anybody else in the building.

'Morning to you too, Carole.' He swiped the paper, performed a comedy about-turn maneuver, and hurried back to his car without quite breaking into a run. Johnson turned on the Ford's flashing red and blues, but decided against the sirens. It was early, and most of the roads were still clear. River Rapids was coming to life slowly this lazy summer Saturday. He took Main until Jefferson, hung a left without waiting for the stop light to change, and roared along the southbound carriage past the Sonic drive-through, Dollarite mall, the H&R Block offices and onto the Highway 32 entry ramp. The dispatch had reported the little girl – probably no more than five or six – wandering along the edge of the southbound lane between junction 4 (downtown) and 5 (Clayton Creek Mall), dressed in pajamas and perhaps barefoot. The lady who had reported the sighting, one Georgina Campbell, couldn't be sure.

The obvious conclusion was that the little girl was a runaway, but if so why had no children been reported missing? It was still early on a Saturday morning. Was it possible that the girl's parents simply hadn't yet realized that their daughter was not tucked up snugly in bed clutching her teddy and sucking her thumb? Johnson tried to imagine not checking on the exact whereabouts of little Millie every morning, and shook his head in frustration. Surely the first thing any decent parent would do of a morning would be to check on their kids?

The squad car cruised along the highway for seven or eight miles before Johnson used one of the police-only U-turns to head back to River Rapids. No way could a little, possibly barefoot, girl walk that distance along the freeway without being spotted. Johnson kept his gaze fixed firmly on the hard shoulder on the opposite carriage as he drove back to town, with no more success. Of course, it was possible that she had turned away from the freeway, but the land on either side was dense with prickly gorse and other shrubbery. If she had stumbled into that, days could pass before she was found. Johnson shuddered at the thought that some dog-walker or hiker could stumble across a child's body in a week or longer.

The third possibility was that a car had stopped and picked her up. Maybe a kindly stranger was already returning her home, or perhaps on their way to drop her off at the police station. At any moment Carole's voice could crackle through the radio, telling him that the little girl was safe at the station and he could come back in. Or, and this was a possibility that Johnson didn't like to think of, she could have been picked up by some pervert and driven off to God knew where. Or maybe the whole thing was a big mistake and the caller hadn't really seen what she thought she had seen. Johnson was well aware that witnesses to crimes often swore that they had seen a gun when CCTV footage showed a knife, or insisted that the thief drove away in a van when the video showed a truck. And even after seeing the evidence, some witnesses would rather claim the footage was tampered with than concede that they had been mistaken. In short, eye-witnesses were often unreliable. Perhaps the whole thing would blow over within an hour.

After cruising up and down the River Rapids stretch of Highway 32 for nearly two hours and seeing nothing remotely connected to a little girl in her pajamas, Deputy Johnson reported that he was returning to the station, and pulled his Ford Crown Victoria onto the exit ramp. He rolled through a number of blocks of overgrown lots and neglected one and two level homes, each of which seemed to have at least one rusting old hulk parked up on the drive, usually on piles of bricks. Junk was strewn liberally across these front yards, usually a toilet or a sink, half covered with grass and weeds.

Drapes or blinds always blocked the windows of these homes. Johnson was sure most of these living rooms hadn't seen natural sunlight in months. God knew what lay hidden on the other side of those flimsy siding or plasterboard walls. And God was welcome to that knowledge: there were some things that Johnson simply didn't want to know.

River Rapids was not a large town, but enough little girls lived hereabouts to make tracing one a difficult job, especially when he had only a sketchy description to go on. Johnson had already asked Carole to send a police artist to witness Georgina Campbell's address to get a likeness made. The next job would be to circulate the picture to the principals of the local elementary schools, River Rapids and Appalachian, see if there was a match.

If there were, Johnson was willing to bet it would be from River Rapids Elementary rather than Appalachian. *Just saying*, he thought.

2.

The picture produced a list of possibles from both schools, but no instant match. Johnson discreetly asked the principals to put names at the top of the list if they were from families that were perhaps more of a concern. Third from the top was Cristel Epps, and so at just before three o'clock that afternoon, Deputy Johnson Fincher pulled his Ford Crown Victoria to a halt in the driveway of the Epps' family trailer.

This was an interesting one. Three years ago, the mother, Yvonne, had disappeared without a trace. She remained missing to this day, her file languished embarrassingly in the *unsolved* category in Carole's file cabinet back at the station. So the family had a history with missing persons, and Johnson knew from experience that similar crimes seemed to strike similar people.

As Johnson raised his fist to knock on the trailer's screen door, he thought he saw a kid - a boy - staring at him through the window.

'Open up, Mr Epps, this is the police!'

Johnson thumped the door hard.

'Open up!'

'I'm coming!' yelled somebody. The door opened a crack.

'Yeah?' said the guy who had to be Donald Epps.

'Mr Epps, is your daughter at home?'

'Who?'

'Your daughter. Cristel.'

'Cristel? Yeah, she's here.'

'Bring her to the door, would you?'

'What's this about?'

'Just get her, Mr Epps.'

'She's in her room.' He turned his head and the door opened wider. Johnson saw a dirty living room, strewn with fast food wrappers, and a dark corridor leading further into the trailer. Donald Epps was a doughy man in faded undershorts and a tank top with more hair on his arms and legs than on his head. 'Cristel! Come here!' he yelled. When nothing happened, he yelled again. 'Daryl! Daryl, go get your sister and tell her she better hop to when I call.'

The boy Johnson saw through the window sidled off along the corridor. He poked his head through a door and yelled back, 'She's not here!'

'She's not there,' Donald Epps said, as if Johnson had not heard. 'She's probably out with her friends.'

'You don't know where your six year old daughter is, Mr Epps?'

'She's out! How should I know where she goes?'

'When was the last time you saw her?'

'I don't know! This morning! Listen, Deputy, tell me what this is about, or get off my property!'

'Mr Epps, the Police Department received a call from a concerned citizen at twenty-six minutes past seven this morning. The woman in question reported seeing a little girl, no more than six years old, wandering by herself along the side of the freeway. By the time we got there, the girl was nowhere to be seen. We have spent the rest of the day visiting numerous families with little girls, trying to ascertain her identity. At what time did you see Cristel this morning?'

The truculence disappeared from Donald Epps' voice.

'I.. I'm not sure. Maybe it was last night.'

'Mr Epps, I shall work on the assumption that your daughter is missing and set up a search immediately. Officers will be here within ten minutes to search for clues to her whereabouts and to take a statement from you regarding when you last saw her, what she was wearing etc. I strongly advise that you co-operate fully if you want to see Cristel again.'

Johnson returned to the Crown Victoria, shaking his head. No idea where his daughter was. No idea she was missing. And he had the nerve to lose his temper with an officer of the law. Johnson decided he would do his utmost to make Donald Epps' life as difficult as possible from this moment on. He called for backup.

In less than ten minutes, two more squad cars pulled up at the trailer. Donald Epps grudgingly allowed the officers access. The living area of the trailer, dominated by a sagging sofa and an enormous TV, smelled of cold pizza and cannabis. Johnson saw a pumped up teenager scowling on the sofa. The guy clearly spent way too long in the gym. Probably lived on a diet of creatine shakes. When Johnson opened the door of the second bedroom, the teen jumped up and started yelling about his rights and privacy until Donald Epps yelled, 'Ken, shut up!'

Johnson led the search of the trailer. He found almost nothing belonging to a little girl. Dirty clothes were bundled under a tiny cot bed in the smallest bedroom.

A few crayons and scribbled pictures lay on the bed. A copy of *Children's First - The Three Little Pigs,* with *This book belongs to River Rapids Elementary, River Rapids WV* stamped on the inside cover, was jammed into the crack between the bed and the wall.

Donald Epps finally found a photo of Cristel from her school picture day. Her blonde hair was pulled into bunches. A huge gap-toothed grin covered her face like a smiley face marker-penned onto a balloon. Donald Epps grunted when Johnson asked permission to take the photo away.

3.

Georgina Campbell's tidy detached villa was packed with china teapots. China teapots huddled in the shelves between books. The books were mostly recipe books and travel guides and the teapots were mostly little thatched cottages and castles, European style, Johnson noticed. More teapots crouched on the sideboard, these mostly in the shape of telephone booths and motor cars. Even more teapots crowded the cabinet around the 42 inch TV, tucked between DVD box sets of *Murder, She Wrote* and *Columbo.* As he sat in a soft arm chair that dumped him closer to the shaggy carpet than he'd like, Johnson wondered how much money had gone on the china teapot collection. Mrs Georgina Campbell, retired school teacher and widow, somewhere in her early seventies, wearing a dress-suit combo straight out of the nineteen-eighties, and sporting a pair of reading glasses, sat opposite and stared attentively at him, clearly enjoying the opportunity to entertain an officer of the law in her house.

'May I offer you an ice tea, Deputy Fincher?' she said. Her voice was calm and controlled and made Johnson think of his father.

'No, thank you, Mrs Campbell...'

'Lemonade? Freshly made this morning?'

'I really can't stay for long. I wanted to show you a photograph.'

He watched Georgina Campbell move her glasses onto her impressive coiffure (which didn't budge an inch), squint at the photo, move her glasses back onto her nose, squint again, and finally attain an optimum reading distance. She triumphantly handed the photo back.

'That's her, Deputy Johnson. That's the girl I saw on the side of the Freeway this morning.'

Johnson radioed the station right away. 'ID confirmed,' he said. 'We have a missing six year old girl. Start a search operation.'

His wish for a quiet summer Saturday in River Rapids was not going to be granted.

4.

Bill Millstone was Sheriff of River Rapids. He had been part of the River Rapids PD for more than twenty years, and Sheriff for the last nine. For many people, he was not just the face of law and order, he was synonymous with the town itself. River Rapids was his, and everybody knew it. His face was seen regularly around town, at community events and council meetings, at the courthouse and at River Rapids Methodist Church, and it was seen smiling benignly at passers by from the wall of the police station, the latest in a long line of portrait shots of past Sheriffs.

The fact that the picture was twenty years old, and Sheriff Millstone had clearly aged quite considerably since then, mattered not in the least. In fact, thought Deputy Johnson Fincher as he walked past it that afternoon, the old photograph spoke of dependability and continuity. Bill Millstone's craggy features from twenty years ago were reassuring. And right now, Johnson was pleased that Bill was taking the lead on the missing person case. This one had all the potential to blow up into something huge.

Bill had called in backup from Charleston, including sniffer dog teams, and the station was heaving with people. Johnson couldn't remember the last time the modest River Rapids Police Department had been so busy. A huge West Virginia State Police people carrier straddled at least four parking spots outside, the tiny conference room was full of men in hi-vis jackets pulling on boots and checking radios. As Johnson walked into the main dispatch room, he counted no less than five Bloodhounds, all barking all of the time, all straining against leashes. And in the middle of it all, somehow exuding an air of ordered calm, stood Sheriff Bill Millstone. He motioned with his head for Johnson to step into his office.

Once the door closed, Bill Millstone said, 'I want you to go with them, Johnson. The state guys are all for doing this themselves, wanting to walk in and take over. But we need a local touch, and that's you. The Epps family may not be model citizens of River Rapids, but they are local. Just make sure it stays real, will you?'

Johnson nodded and hurried to join the search teams. He hoped this assignment was Bill Millstone's way of demonstrating confidence in him and not merely a way of distancing himself from an investigation he was convinced would turn sour. Johnson thought highly of the Sheriff, but Bill Millstone had always been better at the politics than Johnson had. Perhaps that was why Johnson was still Deputy.

Head of the search teams was a serious looking guy from Charleston called Wolensky, who snapped off orders in a clipped voice and expected instant obedience. If the guy were as experienced in searches and rescues as he claimed, he could be as terse and humorless as he liked, Johnson thought, especially if Cristel Epps could be returned safe and sound to her family later that day. Wolensky assigned Johnson a group. Johnson pulled on his hi-vis jacket, made sure his flashlight was clipped to his belt, checked his radio was working, and offered up a quick prayer.

They rolled out shortly after. Wolensky had decided to start the search at the area of Freeway where Cristel Epps had last been seen, and subsequently spread out from there. The Freeway snaked through a sparsely populated area as soon as it emerged from downtown River Rapids, cutting a line through a forest dense with pine, maple and beech. The odds were that Cristel would be in there somewhere, lost or asleep. Probably scared and alone. The area was vast, and even with the Bloodhounds, it would take all day to search. Johnson realized there was little chance of him seeing Susan or Millie that evening.

Not unless there's a miracle, and we find the little girl safe and well in the next hour or so, he thought. But when did that ever happen? How often did this kind of story end well?

Johnson was the first to pile out of the people carrier when it pulled to a stop on a highway turnout a short distance from where Cristel Epps had last been seen. A Buick whizzed past, the driver staring at the search team as he passed. The vehicle's slipstream sent an empty Lays packet tumbling. The sun was low, angling through the trees in sharp bursts. There couldn't be more than a couple of hours of sunlight left and when it got too dark to see, they would all have to pack up and go home until first light the next morning, even if Cristel had not been found. Despite the sunshine, Johnson shivered. He didn't fancy a six year old's chances of spending a night lost and alone in these woods. He imagined Millie in the same situation, and shocked himself when tears pricked the corners of his eyes. Thank God she was safe with Susan in their comfortable home, probably watching Nickelodeon or The Disney Channel at that very moment, preparing for bed.

'We're burning daylight,' yelled Wolensky. 'So let's move out!'

The search party had organized themselves into a long line to sweep through the woods, by far the best plan, but still not foolproof. Johnson could see the next guy ten feet or so to his left, and another to his right, their hi-vis jackets a burst of color in the undergrowth. But a little girl's body was a tiny thing, and she could so easily slip through the gaps. Johnson moved methodically through the undergrowth, watching for a scrap of clothing, or a leg protruding from a tangle of shrubbery, maybe a shoe still on the foot. He kept level with his co-searchers on either side, simultaneously hoping that the body would be found and resolution achieved, and praying that Cristel was still alive and would be found safe and well. The two hopes co-existed unhappily in his head. He half-hoped, half-feared that he would hear a call that something had been found.

Dusk was a few minutes before ten o'clock that evening. Shadows gathered over the woods. Johnson's radio crackled at his belt and Wolensky's voice came through, calling the search off. Nothing had been found. With a heavy heart, Johnson retraced his steps to the people carrier. By the time he pulled himself wearily inside, darkness had fully fallen. He sat silently beside the other searchers. Nobody spoke for the entirety of the ride back to town.

Johnson called Donald Epps to tell him that the search would resume first thing tomorrow morning, although he had a strong suspicion that he wouldn't care much. Bill Millstone sighed and ran his hands over his impressive jowls. 'We'll try again tomorrow,' he said, leaving unsaid what Johnson already knew: that each passing hour reduced the chances of Cristel being found alive. 'And Johnson,' Bill said, 'first thing tomorrow, bring Donald Epps in.'

The digital alarm clock on the bedside table read 11.52 when Johnson slid under the comforter and put his arm around Susan's sleeping form. She muttered in her sleep and leaned into him without waking.

5.

Sunday August 21st, 2011

Johnson's fist hammered against the door of the Epps family trailer a few minutes past six the next morning. The sound ricocheted from the line of pines screening the trailer from the road, and bounced back and forth. No other sounds could be heard. No birds sang, no dogs barked, not even a plane leaving a vapor trail overhead.

'Mr Epps, open up, it's the police!' Johnson yelled, feeling guilty at breaking the tranquility. The echoes faded away and Johnson hammered again.

At last, movement came from within. The door opened and a kid in his boxers stood there, brushing sleep dust from his eyes, hair in a mess. The same teenager Johnson had seen yesterday, the one who had protested about his privacy. The guy was probably sixteen, seventeen, and had the look of a bodybuilder: shoulders hunched with muscle, thick arms heavy with biceps, and a six pack of abs that contrasted unfavorably with Johnson's own gut straining against his belt. Johnson remembered looking in the bathroom mirror the previous morning – was it really only yesterday morning? – ruefully watching his flab as it *flupped* over his belt. The kid cursed and muttered something.

Ken, the older of the two brothers, Johnson thought. The one who spent his life in the gym and thought he was a tough guy.

'Tell your dad I need to see him,' Johnson barked.

'He ain't here.'

'What, you're telling me Don Epps, that fine, upstanding citizen of River Rapids County, has already left for church this fine Sunday morning? Get in there and wake him up, or I'll do it.'

Ken cursed again, and wandered away, scratching his backside as he did so. Johnson watched him pound on a door and yell, 'Pa! Cops are here!' Ken disappeared into the bathroom. The sound of pee hitting the bowl reached Johnson's ears seconds later, shockingly loud this early morning.

Don Epps emerged from his room, yanking a T-shirt

over his hairy belly. Johnson caught a glimpse of Debra Faulkner pulling the comforter over her head before Donald closed the bedroom door. 'What the...?' Donald said. 'What time do you call this?'

'This is morning, Mr Epps. This is when the rest of the world starts their honest day's work. In fact, a party of thirty men have been up since daybreak searching the woods for your daughter. They've been at it for,' he glanced at his watch, 'nearly two hours now.'

'Right. Yeah.'

'I thought you might be interested, Mr Epps. And maybe you'd want to help us out.'

'In the woods?'

'No, I was thinking at the station.'

'Are you arresting me?'

'Do I need to?'

Don said nothing.

'Get dressed, Mr Epps.'

6.

Don Epps was silent all the way to the station. He sat in back of Johnson's squad car, sometimes scratching his belly, sometimes pulling the hair on his legs where they dangled from his shorts, sometimes running his hands over his stubble. Johnson pulled up in the parking lot and opened Don's door. 'Watch your head,' he said, automatically.

He led Don in the back way, the way usually reserved for criminals and felons. No harm in making the guy think he was under arrest, or at the very least under suspicion. Maybe then, he may start to give a dingo's kidney about his daughter.

Johnson led him into an interview room and told him to sit. Outside, Johnson found Bill Millstone. He nodded at the interview room door. 'Got the father in there, Sheriff.'

'Let's get to work,' the Sheriff said.

Johnson let Sheriff Millstone take the lead. Don Epps leaned back and forward in his chair, clearly uncomfortable, unsure whether to feign nonchalance or concern.

'I need coffee and a cigarette,' he said.

'Your daughter's safety should be your number one concern right now, Mr Epps. You know where she is?'

'No! You think I'd be sitting here if I knew where she is?'

'Is she alive, Mr Epps?' the Sheriff said.

'How should I know? Some paedo has her and you're questioning me? What are you doing to find her?'

'When was the last time you saw her, Mr Epps?'

He looked away, eyes focused on the ash tray. 'I don't know. Day before yesterday.'

'Why was she walking along the Freeway early yesterday morning, Mr Epps?'

'How should I know? I thought she were asleep in her room! I can't be held responsible for her every movement, can I?'

'She's six years old, Mr Epps, and you're her father. If you're not responsible for her, then who is?'

Nothing.

'Where's Cristel's mother, Mr Epps?'

'What?'

'You remember. Your wife, Yvonne. Where is she? What happened to her?'

'That broad ran off, okay? She could be in Dickshooter, Idaho for all I care.'

'People seem to have a habit of disappearing around you, don't they, Mr Epps?'

'What about your new lady friend, Mr Epps?' asked the Sheriff, as if it had just occurred to him. 'One Debra Faulkner, right? Will she disappear, do you think?'

Don Epps glowered at the Sheriff and refused to answer. Bill Millstone had made an enemy in that moment. Not that the Sheriff cared.

They couldn't keep him without sufficient evidence. And he wasn't technically under arrest. Johnson filled out the form and let Don Epps go some two hours after they had brought him in. He ignored Don's request for a ride home. The man could get a cab or walk for all he cared. 'We'll see him again, that's for sure,' said Sheriff Millstone, as Cristel's father disappeared across the parking lot toward Main Street.

'I want you to check out the girlfriend's apartment,' Bill said. 'Debra Faulkner.'

'You think she's involved?'

'I want to make sure Cristel's not there. Just check it out, will you?'

'Sure thing.'

7.

The caretaker, a rat faced man called Swicks, made a half-assed attempt to obstruct access, but Johnson brushed his objections aside and got him to open the door to Debra Faulkner's apartment. She lived in a down-at-heel block on the edge of town, the sort of place with graffiti tags on the walls and abandoned cars in the parking lot.

Cristel Epps wasn't there, of course – if only it was that easy. The apartment was trashed and Johnson may have wondered if it had been burglarized if he didn't know better. This was just the way a slob like Debra Faulkner lived: clothes strewn over the floor, coffee mugs choked with mold, spilled Cheerios mingling with dust bunnies on the carpet. Even the TV screen had something encrusted on it.

There was nothing to see here, but just as he had entered the apartment, he had felt eyes on him, and seen a kid pressed against the wall of the corridor outside. Eight or nine years old, eyes wide and fearful, watching his every move. Johnson had taken a moment to place the kid. *It was the other brother,* Johnson thought. *Daryl Epps. Another kid caught in the middle of this mess.* The one he had glimpsed in the Epps' trailer the previous day.

But what, he wondered, *had the kid been doing here?*

8.

Johnson had followed the Sheriff's instructions and come up empty. As soon as he returned to the station, he returned to what he really wanted to do: be part of the search party. Wolensky and his guys had been out in Jefferson's Wood since daybreak and Johnson was convinced that the best thing he could do was add his local knowledge to the mix.

The search party had made good progress, covering much of the area from the highway back toward the town. But as Johnson arrived on site, he could tell that morale was flagging. Wolensky, who had seemed so matter of fact the evening before, now seemed tired and depleted. His eyes were bloodshot and stubble prickled his jaw. Johnson wondered when he had last slept or eaten.

'Last year,' he said, taking a small breather, 'we found a little boy in the foothills of the Appalachians after three days. Miracle, it was. Dehydrated and sick from eating berries, but basically okay. There's still hope.'

Wolensky's eyes told a different story, however, and Johnson realized he was trying to convince himself as much Johnson. The reality was that the chances of finding Cristel alive and well were fading with every passing hour. The reality was that Cristel had not simply got lost in the woods. Something had happened to her. Somebody had her stashed in a basement somewhere. Or had probably already killed her. Johnson felt a knot of tension clench somewhere at the back of his head and quickly squashed it.

The line of men resumed the search, sweeping through the woods like the antidote to a virus. Many, Johnson included, beat the undergrowth with a pole, simultaneously hoping and not hoping to feel resistance beneath the surface. Nobody spoke. The only sounds were the crashing of booted feet and the beating of poles.

And these were the sounds Johnson dreamed of many hours later when he finally eased between the sheets, trying not to wake Susan, and fell quickly to sleep.

CHAPTER THREE
GEORGINA CAMPBELL AND BARBARA BRUCHNER

Saturday August 20th, 2011

1.

Georgina Campbell felt water enter her nostrils. She felt it surge along her nasal passages and reach her lungs, filling every tiny space, until no room remained for air. Cold, fetid water, it was, the kind you might find in a pond, covered in algae and dead things. Georgina's heart strained in her chest, swelling, swelling, in a desperate attempt to find air. When she jolted awake, it still pounded, pounded, as though it too struggled to separate dreams from reality.

Georgina lay in bed, gulped down air. Her throat was parched and the alarm clock read 5.11. Beyond the drapes, the world was already bright and welcoming. Georgina whispered a prayer of thanks. *But why, Lord? Why these dreams? What are you trying to tell me?*

Slowly, her heart rate returned to normal. Times like this, she missed Ardal. She missed somebody being there, reassuring and dependable. Somebody to notice if she wasn't well. Somebody to notice if she didn't wake up one morning.

She could phone Barbara, but Barbara had her own problems.

She was wide awake now. No chance of any more sleep. May as well get up.

Georgina pulled on her robe and slippers and padded into the kitchen, past shelves of china teapots. Everything was in its place, everything right and proper. The flowery cushions on the sofa. The pictures of cute dogs on the wall above the imitation fire. The DVD box sets on the shelves around the TV: *Colombo,* her favorite, and that new British series she liked. The British always did crime series so well. Maybe because of all those stately homes they had over there.

Oh yes, everything was exactly as she wanted it, exactly as it had been since Ardal had died, so why did she suddenly feel she wanted to get away? Why did it all seem so small and unremarkable all of a sudden?

The street was already sunny. Summer in West Virginia. The paper called it an August heat wave. *Enjoy it while you can,* the paper said. *The good weather should last until at least Labor Day.* The fall rains would come soon enough.

A wall of water flashed into Georgina's brain again. Towering, threatening. Overwhelming. And then it was gone.

That was it. She needed to get out of the house. A drive into the hills would clear her head. Perhaps to the rest stop on the Freeway and back. Get some fresh air. Enjoy the sunshine. And then she could decide what to do with the rest of her day. Maybe call Barbara, maybe not.

The roads were beautifully clear this time in the morning. Almost like she had River Rapids to herself. *Because most sane people were still in bed, enjoying sleeping in on their Saturday morning.* Still, enjoy it while you can, the paper had said, and Georgina intended to do just that. She pulled her Nissan onto Columbia Avenue next to the Virginian Bank (*Friendliest Tellers in Town!!!*, ran the crawl across the electronic sign), and joined Highway 32. The highway was so clear of traffic she could zigzag across it like a race car driver. She could do handbrake turns and really burn some rubber. Leave circular stains on the tarmac and pieces of shredded tire by the roadside. Georgina shook her head at the crazy images passing through her brain. What was wrong with her? Dreams of drowning and now absurd fantasies about breaking the law!

She guided the Nissan safely along the slow lane at a steady sixty-five miles an hour. Past Applebee's and Arby's. Past the drive through Starbucks and the bagel place. Past Dollarite and the huge Goodwill place on the corner of Gunther. Up ahead was the exit to County Road Six with the 7Eleven on the corner. Locals teens hung out in the 7Eleven parking lot most days, but not this time in the morning. Georgina had never seen the town look so fresh and new. *Without people to clutter and spoil it,* she thought.

The buildings were more spaced out now. Bigger homes in bigger grounds out here. And suddenly the buildings were gone altogether. The town of River Rapids ended as suddenly as it began. *A wide spot in the road, wasn't that the expression? A podunk town in West Virginia, but somebody had to live here, right? Be it ever so humble.*

And then Georgina saw the first person she'd seen since the 7Eleven. Right there on the shoulder, alongside Jefferson's Wood, a little girl in pajamas. She held her head low, trudged her feet through the long grass at the side of the blacktop. She was alone.

Why was she out here by herself at this time of the morning? The electronic clock read 7.21. Georgina braked and pulled into the shoulder.

The Nissan chimed when she opened the door. *Ding, ding, ding, ding!* The door was open but the key was still in the ignition. Whatever computer brain there was built into the Nissan didn't like it. The thing didn't like it if she drove away without buckling her belt either. But it was okay because she was just getting out to see the little girl. Ask her if she was okay. If she needed help. *Ding, ding, ding, ding.*

But the little girl was gone.

She must have stepped into the woods. Or maybe... *or maybe she'd never been there and you were seeing things, Georgina, you ever think about that? Ghostly little girls by the side of the Highway. You'll be seeing dead people in mirrors next.*

But no. She *had* been there, Georgina was sure of it.

Ding, ding, ding, di-. She got back into the car, pulled her cell phone from the glove box, and dialed 911.

2.

Barbara Bruchner, nee Campbell, looked at the Greyhound Station at Richmond, Virginia and wondered if it were the most depressing place on Earth. If it weren't, it had to be in the top five. A colorless concrete block, it managed to be cold, unwelcoming, damp and dirty all at the same time. A skinny guy in a dirty wifebeater seemed to be trying to break into one of the bank of left luggage lockers against the far wall, many of which were already battered and dented. A Greyhound employee, lazily pushing a mop over the floor tiles, watched him but did nothing about it. A woman laden with bags yelled into a payphone, the end one of a long line, something about wanting her money or she would call the cops. Barbara didn't think anyone used payphones anymore. A long line of people stood at the ticket counter, some wanting to know why only two spots were open. And over there, next to the restrooms, an old guy with a streaky dog kicked a vending machine with his Doc Martens. These were the transients of America, Barbara thought. The people most people never saw. The people of No Fixed Abode. People Barbara never thought she would identify with.

And yet here she was, sitting on an uncomfortable metal mesh bench hoping nobody would notice her and hoping her bus would arrive on time. Hoping she wouldn't have to sit next to a weirdo all the way to River Rapids.

Hoping she wouldn't burst into tears in front of everyone.

The old man with the dog stopped attacking the vending machine and sloped off. Barbara dragged herself to her feet and dug in her purse for change. She fed a dollar bill into the slot and punched the numbers for a KitKat. For a second, it seemed the chocolate was going to catch on the end of the spiral mechanism holding it in place, and not tumble into the vending tray, which would surely have triggered the tears, but at the last second the candy fell and public meltdown was avoided for now. Barbara gratefully withdrew her purchase and returned to the uncomfortable metal bench.

Traveling Greyhound was perhaps not the wisest choice for a lone forty-something woman, especially one in the midst of a disintegrating marriage, but she had little choice. The worst she'd had to contend with on the journey from DC had been lascivious stares from the fat guy sitting two rows behind. If that was the worst of it, she could cope with that. Just as long as nothing else happened on the final leg to River Rapids.

Again she thought of phoning her mother. Letting her know she was on her way was a good idea, but right now a conversation with her mother was the last thing Barbara wanted. She knew how it would go. Disapproval and disappointment would ooze from every syllable her mother said. The subtext was clear; it always was. You should have tried harder. She should have given it another chance. You should have done whatever it took. Instead, you quit. And Barbara just couldn't take another second of that tone right now.

And yet you want to go live with the woman? Barbara thought. A recipe for disaster if ever there was one. *But what choice do I have? What possible other choice do I have?*

She almost missed her bus when it was finally called. If she hadn't noticed the handful of passengers shuffling to the exit gate, tickets ready, she may have ended up sitting in Richmond Greyhound Station, top five in the list of most depressing places on Earth, for a heck of a lot longer. Instead, she handed her case to the fat, sweaty guy who slung it roughly under the bus, and gratefully climbed the steps onto the bus.

3.

The lemonade needed perhaps a touch more sugar, but all in all, it was pretty good, if Georgina did say so herself. She carefully covered the jug in Saran wrap and set it in the fridge next to the ice tea. Two hours of squeezing lemons had helped keep her mind from her nightmares and from the little girl she had seen at the side of the Highway.

She had spoken to a nice lady called Carole at the Sheriff's Department, who had promised to send an officer to look into it. And although her nerves were still jittery from the combined effect of the nightmare and the ghostly child, she was in fact looking forward to having an officer of the law in her living room. She seldom had visitors these days, and never anybody as important as an officer of the River Rapids Police Department. She could barely imagine what Janice across the street would think. She would be dying to pop over and find out. Georgina could get at least a week of interest out of this if she played it right.

The living room was spotless, as always. The cushions were plumped, the teapots dusted, the coffee table gleaming. The whole room smelled of furniture polish. And now she had perfected the lemonade, she was ready. Georgina sat in a chair with a view of the front lawn and the road, and waited.

Twelve minutes later, she started when a police cruiser pulled up outside. She clutched her armrest and watched a deputy emerge from the driver's seat, adjust his pants, and walk up the path toward her front door. He was resplendent in his nicely-ironed beige uniform,

RRPD stitched onto the shoulder, gun belt slung around his hips.

Georgina waited until she heard the doorbell before she stood, walked to the door and opened it. By this time, she wore an expression of delighted surprise.

The deputy had already produced his ID and was holding it up. Not that Georgina could read it from this distance. Not without her glasses anyway.

'Deputy Johnson Fincher,' he said. 'Mrs Georgina Campbell?'

'That's right.'

'I'm here in connection with the little girl you reported seeing this morning, Mrs Campbell.'

'Please, come in, deputy. Make yourself comfortable.'

She led him into the living room.

'May I offer you an ice tea, Deputy Fincher?' she said.

'No, thank you, Mrs Campbell...'

'Lemonade? Freshly made this morning?'

'I really can't stay for long. I wanted to show you a photograph.'

They sat, she on her favorite armchair, he on the sofa. He pulled a photo from his shirt pocket and passed it to her. Georgina picked up her reading spectacles from the little table at her elbow, opened the bows, settled them on her nose, looked at the photo, perched them on her forehead, looked at the photo again, replaced her glasses, took another look. She really had to make an appointment to see Jared Gotiet at the optometrist's one of these days. Finally, she focused on the picture enough to hand it back and pronounce confidently, 'That's her, Deputy Johnson. That's the girl I saw on the side of the Freeway this morning.'

The deputy with the surname for a Christian name couldn't leave quick enough after that. He thanked her, said he'd get in touch if there was anything else he needed to ask, declined an offer of ice tea one last time, and hurried down the path to his cruiser. Georgina watched the vehicle disappear around a corner at the end of the road. It was a shame he hadn't had any lemonade, but his very presence would be enough to make Janice envious. Georgina could almost feel Janice's eyes on her right now, and if she looked across the street, she was sure she'd see Janice's nets twitch. Instead, Georgina closed the door and wondered how long it would be before Janice's curiosity got too much for her and she would find a pretext to drop by.

She returned to her armchair and settled herself down, groaning at the ache from her bones. Even using her own living room was becoming a chore these days, especially when she hadn't slept well. She felt strangely distant from the world, as if the whole world had taken an unexpected turn and she had been left behind.

Almost without realizing what she was doing, she rose and made her way up the stairs. It was slow going these days. She tried not to go upstairs until she was ready for bed, but sometimes she needed something from up there, and sometimes there was just no choice. She walked into the spare room and stood there in the center of the floor, blinking.

Then she opened the closet and stared at the jumble of toys piled on the floor inside. There were balls and jigsaws and color paints, but more than anything else, several little girl's dolls, all in different outfits, wide-eyed and smiling up at her.

4.

When the doorbell went just over an hour later, Georgina looked up from the latest issue of *House and Garden* and glanced at the clock on the mantle above the flame effect fire. She was surprised Janice had waited this long. She must be bursting by now.

Georgina opened the door to find Barbara standing there with a large suitcase. Her face froze.

'Hi, mom. So glad you're home.'

'Barbara, what are you..?'

'Are you going to let me in? Because I've been holding it in since five minutes after the bus left Richmond.'

Georgina stood to one side and watched her daughter struggle to maneuver her case over the door step. By the time Barbara emerged from the restroom, Georgina was back in her favorite armchair, *House and Garden* back in the rack and forgotten. Barbara sank into the sofa, in exactly the same spot Deputy Fincher had occupied a little over an hour previously.

'I have ice tea or lemonade,' Georgina said.

Ten minutes later, coffees made, Georgina said, 'So. Lovely as it is to see you...'

Barbara took a long gulp of Nescafe.

'It's over, mom. I've left him. For good this time. And you know what, I'm too exhausted to go over all the details right now. I just need somewhere to stay. And I need a mom who'll support me.'

'Of course, Barbara dear. You're always welcome here, you know that. But what about the paper? Please tell me you didn't just up and leave without telling anybody.'

'Of course not, mom.'

'Of course not, she says. Like she's never done anything like that before. Does Tim even know where you are?'

'You don't get it mom. This isn't some row. I've left him. There's no coming back from this. I'm never going to see that deadweight again, and good riddance.'

'You can call him later, when you feel better. Talk things over.'

'No, mom. Listen to me. It's over between us. You'd think I'd spend a night on the sodding Greyhounds if I didn't mean it?'

'But darling, you're married! It's not that simple. You can't just run away and say that's that...'

'You know what, I can't deal with this now. I've been up all night chugging Advils. I'm going to get some sleep. We can talk about this later.'

'Of course we can, darling. And I'll get baking. See if I can get a nice dinner ready.'

Georgina watched her daughter angrily drag her case up the stairs to the spare room, to the room that had actually been hers way back when she been a teenager. Getting on for thirty years ago, Georgina realized suddenly. How time had flown. And now, out of the blue, her daughter was back.

And much as she loved Barbara, Georgina could see only trouble ahead.

5.

Barbara's case wouldn't fit through the door of her room. First it caught on one door frame, then the other. Then one of the wheels ran painfully over her foot. Then the corner jammed against the door, yanking the pull-handle from her grasp. The case fell and hit the polished floorboards with a *crack!* so loud that dead people probably turned in their graves throughout River Rapids County. Barbara tilted her head to the ceiling and cursed loudly.

She took a deep breath and forced herself to calm down. She hoped her mother hadn't heard her outburst, whilst being simultaneously sure that she had. Mom was probably downstairs right now clicking her tongue, shaking her head, and taking it as yet another sign that she was right about her daughter being unable to cope.

Barbara shoved the suitcase in front of the closet and closed the door. The bed, single mattress sized and pushed up against the wall, was the very same bed she had slept in as a girl. But she wasn't going to lose herself in the past, not now. She was exhausted and emotional. All she was going to do was pop a Valium and catch up on lost sleep. And do her very best not to think of you know who.

By the time her head hit the pillow, the pill had started to dull her senses into a pleasant haze. Now it was just a matter of whether sleep came before the tears.

She woke to see a figure in her room and let out a scream. Her mother turned, startled, from where she had been rummaging in the closet. She had some objects in her hands.

'Mom? What're you doing?'

'I was just clearing some things out of the closet. Err, making room, you know, so you can hang your clothes.'

'Mom! Please! I'm trying to sleep! Do that another time.'

The closet door had not opened fully because Barbara's suitcase blocked it. She couldn't quite see what her mother was doing in there.

'Yes, you're right, darling. I'll come back later.'

It was only after her mother had left and shut the door that Barbara tried to remember what she had been holding. But the room was dark and Barbara hadn't really noticed. Things she had taken from the closet, presumably. What had been so important that it couldn't have waited?

Barbara swung aside the comforter, planted her feet on the floorboards - the very boards she had barfed on the first time she had come home blingo'd, aged fifteen - and pulled open the closet door, scraping it along the side of her suitcase.

Inside the closet was a pile of toys belonging to a little girl. She saw building blocks, paints, a tea set, and several dolls. One was dressed as a princess, another a nurse, another wore a ballerina's tutu. Puzzled, Barbara picked up the little ballerina. Wide blue eyes gazed at her from within a cute, shiny face. A *wooden* face. These toys were *old*.

And the strange thing was, these toys had never belonged to Barbara. She had never seen them before. Somebody had loved them and played with them, but it hadn't been her. Maybe she would ask mom at dinner.

Barbara replaced the little ballerina, closed the closet door and climbed back into bed.

6.

Dinner that evening was strained. Mother and daughter sat opposite each other at the kitchen table, the room so still and quiet that the occasional clatter of silverware sounded like an intrusion.

Georgina had prepared a chicken dinner. The gravy

came from a packet, but it tasted great to Barbara. Barbara had slept until mid afternoon, and now regretted it. She felt jet lagged and she'd only come from DC. Sodding overnight Greyhound bus. She wasn't sure quite how much of this chicken she was going to get down, and yet mom would take it personally if she left so much as a morsel. *Another of the small ways she manipulates everybody around her.*

'So, what have you got to tell me?' Georgina said as she straightened her knife and fork.

'Do we have to do this right now, mom?'

'You'll have to tell me sooner or later, so it may as well be sooner. You and Tim had a fight?'

Barbara sighed and threw down her fork. 'He's drinking again, alright? Too much, as always. Comes home hammered every day. Can't even speak to him. How many times have we been around this block? Thursday night, he didn't even get back from work until two in the morning. I had no idea what had happened. No call, no message. Could have been dead in an alley for all I knew. So I told him, give it up or this marriage is over.'

'You told him that?'

'Too right I did.'

Silence. Georgina fetched a spoon to dish out homemade rice pudding.

'I know you don't approve, mom. I can see it in every move you make. Even in the way you hold that spoon! But I don't care, right? I didn't come here for your approval. I just need somewhere to stay for a few weeks until I sort something out, okay?'

'Of course it's okay, darling. This is your home, you know that.'

Georgina ladled strawberry jam onto the rice pudding. The smell of hot milk filled the kitchen, giving Barbara another flash of nostalgia.

'I thought I might head down to the *Recorder* offices in a few days. The *Recorder's* still going, right? Try to get a little work. Maybe volunteer until something else opens up.'

'Expect you'll find it all kind of tame out here in the boonies. Lost dogs and church fetes. Not exactly big city news.'

'Just want to keep my feet under the newsdesk. Bring in a little cash if I can.'

Georgina pushed out her lips, a habit that Barbara knew too well from years of teenage disagreements. Her mother disapproved again. Although how the idea of getting out of the house and bringing in some money could possibly earn her mother's disapproval was something she couldn't begin to understand.

'It'll all blow over in a week. Tim will phone and apologize and moments later you'll be on that bus back to DC.'

'No, I won't, mum. And he won't be on that phone. He doesn't know I'm here, and he's not going to know.'

'You shouldn't have said that to him. The drink or you. That's no way to speak to your husband. And Thursday night, he was at a work party, celebrating a new commission.'

'There's always a reason! Wait, have you spoken to him?'

Georgina stood suddenly and started loading the dishwasher.

'You did, didn't you? You phoned him! While I was sleeping!'

'I was only thinking of you, Barbara darling.'

Barbara felt anger fizzing in front of her eyes like bright lights. Tears of frustration blurred her vision.

'How could you do that, mom? I came here to get away from him! I came here because I needed your support! And instead you betray me!'

Georgina kept loading the dishwasher. Plate, knife, skillet, fork.

'Come on, Barbara, my darling. Don't you think you're being a tad melodramatic? He's your husband. He has a right to know you are safe and sound.'

'No, mom, no! Why can't you understand? *I've left him! He's not my husband anymore! I'm going to start divorce proceedings. Do you understand, mom? You will be mother to a divorced woman! And you have no right to interfere!'*

Barbara could hear her voice becoming a shriek and she hated it. She hated the way her mother could still reduce her to the level of a petulant, screaming teenager. Even now, after all these years. And what else could she do but leave the table, run upstairs to her room, and slam the door?

It was only later, after she had calmed down some, that she remembered she hadn't asked her mother about the little girl's toys in the closet.

CHAPTER FOUR
DARYL EPPS

1.

Amelia has to go home for lunch or she'll be in trouble with her mom. She gives me another hug and hops and skips away, leaving me staring after her. Nathan nudges me and says, 'She's a nice girl, dude.' I, of course, immediately turn bright red. Nathan laughs. It's okay for him. He's the one Amelia likes. No way would she hang out with me if he weren't here.

'Come see my palaeolithic bones,' he says.

I've no idea what he's talking about, but if it means going back to his house, that's good for me. I'm hoping his mom will give me something to eat.

Later we sit in a dust bowl four or five feet wide in the shade of the line of pines at the side of his back yard, shovels in one hand, magnifying glasses in the other. His face, T-shirt, and shorts are all smeared with dust, and I guess mine are too. He brandishes a bone at me. 'A fibula!' he says. 'Finally, proof positive that paleolithic man lived in America!'

It looks more like a chicken bone to me, but I nod

enthusiastically and start digging. I realize he's trying to keep my mind off things at home, but right now that's fine by me.

Nathan's mom comes through with PB&J sandwiches and lemonade just as we unearth the remains of the jawbone of a Neanderthal warrior, as I knew she would. She clicks her tongue and rolls her eyes when she sees the state of our shirts and fingernails, but she doesn't say anything. Nathan doesn't know how lucky he is. We guzzle the lemonade, which of course has exactly the right amount of sugar in it, and cram the sandwiches down as though we hadn't eaten an entire bag of Doritos that morning.

We leave our excavations and go to the hideout shortly afterward. A narrow track runs between two of the pines at the back of the yard, which we are convinced nobody else in the world knows about (not even Amelia Michaelson) and through an area of tall, snake-infested grass to a copse of trees. A crawl along a tunnel of thorny branches brings us to a clear space in the center of the undergrowth. We sit in the shade, panting from exertion in the summer sun.

Nathan opens the treasure chest and produces the ostrich feather and the sword we found behind Harry's Mercantile. He lays the fibula of paleolithic man and the jawbone of the Neanderthal warrior alongside them. 'These must be worth a fortune,' he says. 'I bet the Natural History Museum in New York would kill to get their hands on this fibula. If they knew we had it, they would send their agents to get it from us!'

'The Natural History Museum has agents?'

'Of course! Sent all around the world to find rare

animals and birds. The dodo bird from the Caribbean. The griffin from Amazonia. The basilisk from Mongolia. And I've heard rumors of a land of dragons hidden in the middle of Antarctica where no human can reach them!'

'Wow!' I say, and try to think of something else to say. It's hard to be excited about griffins and dragons when my sister's missing. Maybe it's because my belly is full, maybe because I know I can't keep pretending, maybe because I have to know if she's been found, but something churns my stomach. I don't want to bring PB&J sandwiches up over my shoes.

Nathan seems to realize this, and says, 'You wanna go look for your sister?'

I nod, and suddenly the tears I've been damming since Amelia went home for lunch, burst forth and run down my cheeks. Suddenly they are here, cascading down my face and dripping from the end of my nose, and now Nathan will laugh at me and call me a baby, and I'll have to run someplace else.

But Nathan does something different, something I will never forget. He scrambles across the dirt of our hideout and wraps his arms around me and rocks me until I have no more tears left. When, finally, my eyes are dry, he says, 'Let's go find Cristel, Daryl,' and I want to tell him I love him, but I don't because it would sound weird.

We didn't know at the time, but the copse that contains our hideout is connected to the woods, some three or four miles to the south, where the search party is still holding out hope that they would find Cristel. I half-expect that we would join in somehow, but Nathan has other ideas. 'She was seen walking along the Highway, right?' he says. 'So she must have gotten from your house to the Highway somehow. We should trace her route and look for clues.'

He's right, of course. He's always right. But neither of us wants to make the journey all the way back to our trailer, especially if Ken is back from the gym and looking for somebody to beat up on. The closest we dare to go is the 7Eleven at the end of our road, and start from there. Nathan grabs his bicycle, I squeeze on the saddle behind him, and we are off. Wind runs through my hair, I am with my best friend, and I am doing my part to find my sister. I haven't felt this good in ages.

We skid to a halt at the 7Eleven, Nathan's back wheel describing a circle over the parking lot tarmacadam like the hero of an action movie at the wheel of his muscle car. Three teenagers leaning against the rail of the handicapped-access ramp snicker but don't care enough to remove the Dunhills from between their lips. We ignore them anyway. Cars and trucks thunder by on the Highway. Warm wind pulls at our hair and T-shirts. A red DVD rental box sits outside the main entrance, screen silently repeating scenes from the latest releases. Across a scrappy grass verge sits a motel office, a Coke machine humming to itself outside. Beyond that is a liquor store with bars on its windows.

'If she was coming from your place, she would have walked along here,' says Nathan, indicating the sidewalk along the front of the store. 'She may even have stopped in.'

'She didn't have any money,' I say.

'She could have asked directions. Asked to use the phone. Even used the restroom.'

Three possibilities I haven't considered, but none seem likely to me.

'They may have her on CCTV,' continues Nathan.

I shrug. 'They won't show us. We're only kids.'

A truck rattles past, the words *Hoult Bros Cannery* written on the side. I try to see where it's from, but the license plate goes by too fast. I like to see where the big trucks come from and imagine how it would be to live on the road, moving from one exotic city to another. Miles from dad and Ken. Every day a new horizon. A familiar thrill goes through me. One day. One day I will hit that wide open road and never come back.

I suddenly realize that Nathan is holding something between his fingers and thumbs, snapping it to and fro in front of my face. A piece of paper. A twenty dollar bill.

Nathan has twenty bucks.

'Where did you get that?'

'Earned it delivering papers.'

'Seriously?'

'Come on.'

A skinny teenager slouches behind the counter, wearing the custom green and orange 7Eleven T-shirt and a button reading *Fred, How can I help?* Red spots pockmark his face and his collar bone sticks out. He watches us as we walk along the aisle between the cookies, nuts and jerky, and past the counter with the soda fountain and Slush Puppie machine. I hang back and let Nathan do the talking.

'Hi there, Fred,' he says. 'Nice place you have here.'

Fred stares at him, jaw slung low. He stops chewing whatever he was chewing.

'Er, I was wondering if you could do me a solid. You know, as one upwardly mobile, aspirational young man to another.'

The jaw drops lower.

'As a matter of interest, Fred, where do you see yourself in, say, five years? Regional manager? State Manager with the whole of WV under your control? Or, why stop there? Why not raise your sights and aim for the whole east coast slash mid west region?'

Dribble teeters in the corner of Fred's mouth.

'Something to mull over, perhaps. I'll tell you why I'm here. My friend and confidant, Daryl, here, has ambitions too, one of which is to find his mysteriously-disappeared sister, and here's how you could help, Fred my friend. Said sister must have passed this way sometime early yesterday morning, and if you could just dial up the right time on that CCTV screen of yours, you could help assure the safety of a six year old in distress. What do you say?'

I keep still, waiting for the response. I always suppress the urge to laugh when Nathan starts talking like that, but it invariably produces one of two responses. He either gets his way or he gets punched in the mouth.

Finally, Fred says, 'Huh?'

'Let me put it another way,' says Nathan and slides the twenty dollar bill across the counter. 'We want to see your CCTV for yesterday, between say five and seven am.'

Fred sniffs, leans forward, resumes chewing, puts one dirty, skinny finger on the bill and pulls it toward him. He raises a bony elbow and turns a screen next to the cash register so we can see it. 'I can turn back the clock in steps of one hour,' he says. 'You want the camera facing the street, right?'

I smile for real for the first time in two days.

We find her. Fred has to break off every so often to serve a customer and to threaten to kill us if we tell anybody he let us do this, but at last we find her. My heart lurches in my chest as I see a white blur move slowly across the parking lot, lit by the floodlights. She first comes into left of frame at six minutes to six the previous morning, a tiny scrap of a thing made even smaller by the grainy, black and white image. I am shocked anew by how small she is when seen alone and unprotected. The tiny steps she takes and the way she constantly looks behind her speaks of how terrified she is. But what was she doing outside at such an hour anyway? What had made her leave her home – such as it was – at that time in the morning and make her way past the 7Eleven, and along the Highway? She hadn't even stopped to put outdoor clothes on. She must have been freezing, even in the summer.

I watch her walk slowly across the frame. A car goes by. A fat guy in a baseball cap emerges from the store, walks right past her, and roars away in a pickup. Doesn't stop, doesn't seem to wonder what a six year old girl is doing there in her pajamas before six o'clock in the morning. Probably doesn't care. And then, in the space of a few seconds, she walks out of right of frame. Gone. Something had happened to her shortly after that. Somebody had taken her, she had had an accident, got lost. Something. And whatever it was had happened after she had walked slowly past the 7Eleven.

We thank Fred and wander out to the side of the store, where Nathan has leaned his bike. Here, weeds grow through the cracks between the paving stones and old, faded chip packets collect in the corners. We sit on the curb.

'My mom disappeared from here too,' I say. 'First mom, now Cristel.'

'We ain't done yet,' Nathan says. 'We'll find her. We just keep following her trail, that's all.'

We spend most of the day trying to pick up Cristel's trail, but even Nathan has to admit defeat in the end. Two nine year old boys are never going to succeed where a police search team has failed. We walk along the side of the Highway, even the dangerous part with no sidewalk and try to find the spot where Cristel had last been seen. The town buildings soon fall away, and the woods crowd in, right up to the side of the Highway, and there is no telling where Cristel could have gone. No obvious trails lead into the undergrowth, at least none that Nathan and I can find, and we are worried about getting caught up in the area the police are covering. In the end, I have no choice but to bid my farewells and head home, wondering if the police have taken Dad in, and whether I will have anything to eat tonight. Wondering if maybe the police have found my sister, and maybe she'll be sitting at home waiting for me to return.

The trailer is dark when I arrive. Dad sits asleep in front of the TV, crushed Budweiser cans strewn willy-nilly. Ken is gone, probably staying the night at Hayley's. I hope so. I want the bedroom to myself tonight. Because there is a good chance I will cry again.

2.

Dad wakes me by grabbing my ankle and dragging me from my bed. My tailbone bumps painfully on the floor. I yell, but Dad yells louder.

'Get up, you lazy kid! We're going to the supermarket.'

The clock reads *11.35*. At night. And Dad wants to go

to the supermarket. 'Leave me alone!' I yell, brain still swamped with sleep. 'I don't wanna go!'

'You'll do as you're told!' Dad yells. 'The police are stickin' to me closer than fleas to a dog, and I ain't leavin' you here alone. And I need you for the fetchin' and carryin'.'

'Go in the morning!'

'We're going now!' he yells, and that is that. And I know why. He's woken up out of beer. Nothing but a midnight beer run is going to pacify him. I jab my legs into my jeans and squirm into a T-shirt. Seconds later, he has me by the scruff of the neck, pulling the T-shirt up painfully into my armpits, and shoving me into the passenger side of the pickup. I wonder if he's right about the police watching his every move, and what will happen if I yell, 'Help!' at the top of my lungs. They'll have to come running, right? I can tell them that he's abducting me just as he abducted my sister and probably my mom too. And they will put me in a home someplace, or with some other family I don't know.

So I don't yell. I huddle into the passenger bucket seat, hug my knees, and try not to shiver when the cold brings gooseflesh up all over my arms. We pull onto the main road, the pickup's twin beams picking out mysterious shapes between the trees that are never there in daylight.

Within moments, the lights of the 7Eleven come into view ahead, and I wonder if Dad will stop there, but no, we sweep on past and take a left onto the Highway. The journey that takes me an hour or more on foot takes moments in Dad's pickup. We take the exit for the out of town mall and pull into the enormous, and almost empty, parking lot. Dad leaves the pickup parked diagonally across two spots, drags me from the seat, and shoves me in the direction of the *24HR EZ-MART.*

This is the largest supermarket in town, a huge warehouse stuffed full of everything an inhabitant of a small town in West Virginia could ever possibly want. During the day, the place seems to be full of fat families with fat babies who never stop screaming, and now it seems eerily empty. The harsh strip lighting is harsher still at night, and the aisles seem to be wider and longer. At first I think the whole place is empty, as though the zombie apocalypse has happened while I slept, but then I glimpse movement and see a pale-faced man listlessly push a cart of boxes of diapers past. Other men – they are all men, for some reason – fill shelves with shampoo bottles and baby food and hair dye kits and a million other things. One more guy sits hunch-shouldered at a checkout counter. I wonder what sort of customer prefers to do their shopping at midnight, and seconds later I find out. Guys not a million miles removed from my father, it seems.

One pimple-faced guy stands in the snacks aisle, filling up a cart with bags of chips, popcorn and frozen pizzas. Another fills a cart with box after box of cans of Coors. Two more stand at the magazine rack, leafing through issues of *Guns and Ammo* or *American Truckers*. One stares at a picture of a woman with spread legs giving birth to an alien on the cover of *National Enquirer*, and I think of Nathan and his crazy ideas, and wonder if he gets them standing in line for the checkout at *24HR EZ-MART*. And then my eye falls on the latest edition of *River Rapids Recorder* and the blurry picture of my dad under the headline *HUNT FOR MISSING GIRL CONTINUES: DAD QUESTIONED*. My heart beats double in shock and my vision swims.

For several seconds I can't form a clear thought. The possibility that my dad – anybody from my family – would ever feature on the front of a newspaper in the supermarket, is so beyond ludicrous that I can't believe it is happening. Newspapers are always full of terrible things that happen to other people, and some part of me never properly connects the pictures from the papers with real, living people whom I may walk past on Main Street. And yet, here it is, right here, my dad in the newspaper, right there so anybody in this supermarket and in stores all over town, can look at him and reach down and read all about what's happening to my family.

The picture had been taken outside the police station, and zoomed in from some distance away. Dad is clearly unaware that he is being photographed. I can see Deputy Fincher out of focus behind him, opening the door and leading him in.

Arm shaking, I pick up the top copy and begin to read. *The hunt for missing local girl Cristel Epps stepped up today. Fears are growing for the safety of the six year old, who has been missing since early Saturday. In a new turn of events, Deputy Johnson Fincher of the River Rapids Police Department this morning questioned Donald Epps, father of the missing girl, raising the possibility of Mr Epps's involvement in his daughter's disappearance. Local crime expert Mabel Merryweather said, 'It is standard in missing child cases of this sort to suspect family members, especially the father.' She further went on to say that the chances of finding Cristel safe and well are dropping by the hour. 'Statistics show that missing persons are more likely to be found alive within the first forty-eight hours after disappearance. Time is running out for Cristel Epps.'*

A meaty hand rips the newspaper out of my grip. Dad's yell dies when he sees his own pixelated face on the page in front of him. I dare not move. I wait. The color has drained from his face.

He stuffs the paper into the rack. 'What are you looking at?' he yells at the guy reading *Guns and Ammo*. 'Come on, Daryl,' he says, clamping my bicep painfully and dragging me away. The guy reading *American Trucker* stares at us. So does the guy with the frozen pizzas. So does the podgy guy with the thinning hair sitting behind the only open checkout. 'What do you think you're looking at?' Dad demands. The guy just shakes his head and looks away.

Dad pushes me through the doors and into the parking lot. His fingers still grip my arm painfully. He shoves me toward the pickup. 'Get in there,' he says.

We end up at the 7Eleven after all. Dad puts two twenty dollar bills into my hand and tells me to get two boxes of Budweisers. I walk across the parking lot and up the handicapped-access ramp against which we had propped Nathan's bike earlier that day. I wonder if Fred will still be standing behind the counter, but no, his shift has clearly come to an end, and a fat woman with long hair that was dark at its roots and blonde at its tips sits on the stool, idly picking off her nail polish. She watches me open the cooler containing boxes of Budweisers, and struggle manfully to heave two onto the counter. *Raquelle* reads her name button. *Here to help.*

'You don't think I'm letting you walk out of here with those, do you?' she says.

'Please. My Dad's out there in the pickup and I just wanna go home to bed.'

'Then you just get out there and tell your dad to get in here, 'cos I ain't sellin' beer to an underage kid, not with CCTV watchin' my every move.'

Wearily, I turn my feet toward the door, already imagining the yelling I am going to receive. But if Dad wants his beers, he's going to have to get them himself. Muttering and grumbling, he pushes open the door of the 7Eleven and yells, 'Just sell me some friggin' beer, would ya?'

'I know who you are,' Raquelle yells back. 'Even before you were in the paper. What did you do to little Cristel? You some sort of pervert? A paedo, is that it? Your own daughter! You disgust me!'

'I ain't done nothin'!' Dad yells.

'Cops think you 'ave! S'always the dad! Where've you hidden her, eh? Buried her under your trailer, that it? Up to me, you'd fry in the 'lectric chair!'

Dad slings the twenty dollar bills at her, takes the cases of Bud, and leaves the store, yelling and swearing as he goes. He is silent all the way home, but as soon as we are inside, he punches me in the mouth, splitting my lip. The second time a member of my family has punched me since Cristel disappeared.

I squeeze the pain away, run to my room and slam the door.

3.

The search continues the following day. It's Monday, August 22nd and River Rapids Elementary opens its doors for the new school year. Needless to say, I don't go. Instead, I go down to the woods and watch the search party advance slowly through the undergrowth, yelling Cristel's name and beating the shrubbery with sticks. Big dogs with lolling tongues sniff the ground, but none of them seem to have caught a scent. I wonder how much longer they will search. *First forty-eight hours,* said the crime expert in the paper. And then the chances of finding Cristel alive and well drop right off.

I sit with my back against a tree and draw patterns in the dust with a stick. Where is Cristel right now? Is she alive? Has somebody taken her? I think of her bound and gagged in a tiny, darkened room, a dark, shapeless figure watching over her. She is crying and wondering if her father or her brothers would come for her, or if she will stay there in the dark forever. Tears prickle my eyes suddenly, but I force them down. I had cried once and that was enough. I had cried in front of Nathan and that was okay because he was my best friend. But no more, and never in school.

Perhaps she has run away. Perhaps she has gone to find mom. Maybe she isn't in a darkened room, but instead she's sitting at the breakfast table in mom's apartment in Los Angeles or Austin or San Francisco, eating Cheerios and laughing as mom kisses her. Maybe they are thinking of a way to come get me. And I can leave dad and Ken forever.

I draw spirals in the dust.

Perhaps I should run away too.

Boots step into the dust in front of me, not quite stepping on my spirals. Big, brown, police boots. I scramble up, preparing to run, already expecting the cop to ask why I am not in school.

'It's Daryl Epps, right?' says Deputy Johnson Fincher.

I don't move. The sun is right behind him. I squint.

'I've been meaning to talk to you.'

Still I don't move or speak. What should I say? My mind is empty. Not a word occurs to me.

'I'm sorry about your sister. But we're doing everything we can to find her.'

I try to swallow, but my mouth is dry.

'Don't say much, do you? Well, I just wanted to say that if you need to talk about your sister, I'll listen, okay? I get the feeling your dad ain't one for lots of words. So, anytime you want to talk, stop by the police station and ask for Deputy Fincher, okay?'

He squats, bringing his face in line with mine. 'How did you get that split lip, Daryl? Huh? Somebody hit you?'

Yes, sir, my brother did it because I followed him to his gym. Or my Dad did it, because the lady at the 7Eleven made him mad. My Dad and my brother always hit me for no reason, sir, please arrest them and sling them in jail. Find my mom and send me to live with her and we'll all live happily ever after.

I stare at him, my brain fills with words, but none of them come out of my mouth.

'Well, you can't stay here, can you? I guess I can overlook you taking the day off school, considering what's happened, but how about I give you a ride home in my squad car? I can talk to your dad while I'm there, make sure he's clear about a coupla things. What do you say?'

I say nothing, because I can still think of nothing to say. He puts his hand on my back and leads me through the woods to where his squad car is parked on a turnout, right in front of a police van, which, I realize, must have brought the search party here this morning. He opens the back side door for me and I scramble obediently in.

This isn't the first time I have been inside a squad car. With a family like mine, rides in squad cars are not altogether uncommon. But I still feel a churning in my stomach. The interior is not so different to Dad's pickup, apart from the grille that separates the front seats from the back. *That's to make sure the bad guys can't get the driver,* says an authoritative voice inside my head. The upholstery is a brown plastic vinyl of some sort, and squeaks when I move. I imagine all the criminals and bad guys who have sat on this bench seat before me: murderers and bank robbers and thieves, and I hope that Deputy Fincher will remember that I am not one. I'm a little boy he's giving a ride to.

The tires crunch and then we are on tarmac and heading back to town. Soon small bungalows in overgrown yards replace the pines, and before long the sidewalks and telegraph poles of the town have appeared from nowhere. We turn by the 7Eleven, and I'm sure I glimpse Fred back in his place behind the counter. And then we are heading out of town again, along County Road Six, where the lots get bigger and the houses get smaller, until suddenly, only trailer homes remain. In no time at all, we are turning into our drive, and my thoughts turn to how Dad will react to another visit from the Deputy Sheriff.

Ken answers the door, wearing sweatpants and a loose, sleeveless shirt that puts his humungous biceps on show. Sweat drips from his hair onto his face. He is clearly angry at having his workout interrupted, but Deputy Fincher doesn't seem to care. He asks Ken where Dad is.

Dad heaves himself from the couch and makes it to the front door. I quickly slip inside and find an unobtrusive spot where I can hear what is said. Ken's best buddy Dale sits on the armchair, twisted round to take an interest in the conversation. And if Dale is here, Hayley probably is too, although I can't see her right now.

One thing I have noticed about Dale from the very first time Ken started hanging out with him was that he is almost identical to Ken. His hair is perhaps a little lighter, and cut in a round boyish style that looks odd on an adult. And maybe his shoulders aren't quite as wide as my brother's, his arms not quite as thick, but they can't be far off. He has the same blank expression – *stupid,* insists a voice in my head – not helped by the fact that his eyes are just too far apart. I always think of an ape when I see him. He sits there in the armchair, Bud can held in one fist temporarily forgotten as he listens intently to the conversation at the door.

I listen too.

'Mr Epps, I thought I would return another of your lost children. I'm afraid I can't bring you happy news about the one still missing. The search is continuing today, but is due to be called off at sunset.'

'You can't call it off!' Dad says. 'She's out there somewhere! She's only six.'

'I'm fully aware of that, Mr Epps, but we can't search forever. It seems increasingly unlikely that Cristel is in the woods. Maybe she never was. We have other lines of inquiry to pursue, and we need the manpower for that. Unless you have anything more you want to tell us?'

'What do you mean by that?' growls Dad. 'You still thinkin' I got her stashed somewheres? You're a sick man, deputy.'

Ken stands in the kitchen, just out of sight of the door. He's listening to every word, clenching and unclenching his fist, and watching the muscles move under his skin. He looks like he wants to punch somebody. And I have a good idea who will end up on the receiving end.

'Not at all, Mr Epps, I simply wondered if you had remembered anywhere she likes to go when she's with friends.'

'I told you, she don't have no friends.'

'That's right. She's practically a shut-in, isn't she? Doesn't even make it to school most days, isn't that right?'

'You been checkin' up on me, deputy?'

'That's right, Mr Epps, because that's my job. Well, you think of anything, you know where to find me. You just go right on ahead and give me a call. And I'll keep you posted of any developments.'

Deputy Fincher puts his hand out to prevent the door closing.

'Oh, and one more thing, Mr Epps. I shall be keeping a very close eye on you and this family. You won't be able to turn around without seeing me right there. And if I see another mark on your little boy, I shall run your fat, lazy keister into the station faster than you can chug another Bud. I hope I'm clear, Mr Epps.'

And then he's walking to the squad car, and the door slams shut.

After a moment of silence, Dad swears and kicks the wall. He stomps into the living room and upends the table, sending cans spinning and the TV smashing to the floor. I run for the bathroom, slam the door after me and shoot the bolt with trembling fingers. I stand in the corner with my back against the wall. Somebody yells my name and the bathroom door shudders. My eyes zero on the bolt, suddenly realizing how flimsy it looks. I wonder if I should yell for help. Perhaps Deputy Fincher is still outside. Perhaps he hasn't yet pulled away. He could be sitting out there on his radio and all I have to do is yell and scream.

But then the bolt cracks and the door bursts open and I am too scared to yell and scream.

It's Ken. He clamps a fist around my shirt and hauls me off my feet. He holds my face an inch from his and I can smell his breath, mixed with the metallic odor of male sweat. I fight to keep my face straight. My heart pumps madly. I wonder if this is it for me. Lights out, goodnight. The world will have to continue without Daryl Epps in it. I find time to wonder if this is what had happened to Cristel. Had Ken killed her and hidden the body somewhere?

'You pathetic little runt,' Ken hisses. 'You been hangin' out with your cop buddies, have you? Been tellin' them all about us? About your own family?'

He shakes me so hard my teeth rattle and my neck cracks.

'Ken, leave 'im.' Dad stands at the door. He seems to have calmed down a little, spent his rage on smashing the TV.

'He needs to be taught a lesson, pa,' says Ken, spit flecking my face. Again, I don't react.

'You heard what the cop said. I ain't goin' to jail for 'im. Leave 'im!'

Ken stares at me, eyeball to eyeball, and I can see he would love nothing more than to use me as a punch bag. At last, he shakes me again, and hisses, 'You go near the cops again, I'll break your arms and legs, you hear me?'

I nod. He drops me in a heap on the scummy bathroom mat. And I am alone.

4.

I go to school the following day. When I get up, Dad sits at the kitchen table with a bowl of Cheerios in front of him and a can of Coors Light in his hand. 'Eat your breakfast,' he says.

Ten minutes later, I am on the school bus. The bus monitor, a fat old lady with gray hair and breakfast stains on her cardigan, looks at me and blinks, and wordlessly gestures to a seat. Only two other kids are already on the bus, kids who live even further out of town than I do, and neither of them make eye contact. I vaguely remember their faces from before the summer, but I can't remember their names. I sit by the window and watch the road rumble by.

By the time we pull into the bus parking lot at River Rapids Elementary, the bus is full of screaming, yelling kids. The bus monitor gives up even trying to keep us quiet. They shoulder backpacks with Disney princesses, boybands, or superheroes on them and meander into the yard. I suddenly feel stupid, standing there with no backpack, no bag, nothing in my hands. Not even a pencil. It also occurs to me that as I missed the first day of school yesterday, I don't even know which class I am in. It's with huge relief that I spy Nathan approaching. He has Amelia Michaelson with him. I clap him enthusiastically on the back.

'What happened to your face?' Nathan says.

'Dad hit me,' I say, seeing no reason to lie.

'Did they find Cristel?' asks Amelia. She has had a haircut for school. I can imagine her mom sitting her on a chair in the middle of the kitchen and snipping away with scissors. Now her small, round face is framed with red hair that curls under at the ends. She has a cute way of wrinkling her nose when she speaks. I already mentioned that, right?

I shake my head my head in answer to her question. Amelia looks away.

'You're in my class,' says Nathan. 'Miss Stevens. She's okay.'

The whistle blows and I follow Nathan and Amelia into the building. I know some of the kids are talking about me because they look at me and stop talking when I get near, but I don't care. I'm with my friends, and who cares what dipstick kids think anyway?

The day would have passed okay if it weren't for Drew Hartman. Miss Stevens, a young teacher who has only been at the school for a couple of years, sets aside an hour to talk about rules for Third Grade. 'Rules,' she says, 'are important so that we can all work together and look after each other. Daryl Epps, why is it important we look after each other?'

Suddenly, twenty-four pairs of eyes stare at me and moments tick past while I think of something to say. Drew Hartman speaks a second before I do. 'Don't ask him! He can't even look after his own sister!'

Drew Hartman is a wimpy kid who always has snot glistening in the corner of his nostril. He comes to school with his sandy hair carefully combed into a side parting, but by recess it's always a mess. He's never on the school bus, because his mother always drives him to school, and she always wears designer dresses and high heels when she does so. We all know he will be gone as soon as a spot opens up in Appalachian Elementary. The sooner the better.

'Now, Drew,' says Miss Stevens, 'we use kind words in this school. It's not Daryl's fault that his sister is... is, er, lost.'

'No, it's his deadbeat dad's fault. My mom says the police are gonna lock him in jail, and about time too. She read it in the newspaper.'

My face burns red. Every kid stares at me, waiting to see what I will do. Even Miss Stevens doesn't know what to say.

So Nathan stands up and tells Drew to shut his mouth because he can't even look after his own boogers. The whole class falls about laughing and Nathan is sent to the principal. But I swear I see a ghost of a smile on Miss Stevens' face when she sends Nathan away.

Drew Hartman blubs for an hour, which only serves to spread snot further over his face.

That, right there, is what a best friend is all about.

CHAPTER FIVE
JOHNSON FINCHER

1.

Monday August 22nd 2011

We won't find her, thought Deputy Sheriff Johnson Fincher of the River Rapids Police Department, West Virginia. *Not here, not like this.*

He stood beside his squad car in a turnout in the woods, driver's door open, radio in his hand. But he couldn't give the good news he wanted to. He couldn't put the microphone to his lips and tell Carole Jeffrey that Cristel Epps had been found safe and well. Because she wasn't here. He was sure of that. She wasn't in these woods. She had got into a car on the Highway, spirited away by some predator. Which meant she may never be found. And the days would go by, the newspapers would tire of the lack of developments and turn their attentions elsewhere. And Cristel Epps would become just another statistic, another barely remembered name languishing in a file labeled *unsolved.*

And what if it were Millie? Would you let it go at that if

Matthew Link

it were your own daughter in the clutches of some faceless pervert? What are you going to do about it, Deputy Johnson Fincher? What are you going to do?

Johnson tossed the radio into the car and slammed the door. The sound ricocheted from the trunks of the pines and silenced the voice in his head, at least for a while.

Fact was they had no leads at all. And the only suspects were the father and the big brother, Donald and Kennedy Epps, and possibly the father's girlfriend, Debra Faulkner, and they had zip with a side of squat on any of them. The search of the woods was due to conclude at the end of the day, Wolensky would take the extra men and the bloodhounds and disappear back to Charleston, and Johnson was stumped over what to do next.

And then he spotted the boy under the trees, drawing patterns in the dust with a stick.

'Daryl Epps, right?'

The kid squinted at him. He seemed to be here alone. No dad getting in the way. Maybe this was the break Johnson had been hoping for. He sent a quick prayer of thanks up to God.

'I've been meaning to talk to you. I'm sorry about your sister. We're doing everything we can to find her.'

The words came out easy enough, but Johnson wasn't even sure they were true. *Were* they doing everything they could? Or just everything they could think of? And while they were going through the motions, the kidnapper could be tiring of having to feed and guard a little girl, and be preparing to kill her.

The kid said nothing. He just kept staring as though he had been struck dumb. The effect of the uniform, thought Johnson.

'Don't say much, do you? Well, I just wanted to say that if you need to talk about your sister, I'll listen, okay? I get the feeling your dad ain't one for lots of words. So, anytime you want to talk, stop by the police station and ask for Deputy Fincher, okay?'

The kid just kept staring with wide, unblinking eyes. Johnson crouched to be more on a level with the boy and noticed the kid's split lip and a smear of blood across his chin. There were even signs of a black eye starting to come up. Suddenly, irrationally, without warning, rage boiled through Johnson's veins. The deadbeat had lost one child and reacted by beating up on the other. He imagined what he would do if Donald Epps were right here, right now, in the privacy of Jefferson's Woods, away from prying eyes where Johnson could teach him a lesson he wouldn't forget.

Failing that, he would just have to talk to him.

He took young Daryl home. He couldn't leave the kid in the woods, and at least he could speak to his father at the same time. Give him a warning. Johnson pulled the Ford Crown Victoria into the increasingly familiar driveway belonging to the Epps family trailer and brought it to a halt on the gravel. Old bits of furniture and unwanted bucket seats lay strewn among the unkempt grass. A plastic slide lay on its side and an old paddling pool now collected rainwater and mud.

The older brother, Ken, opened the door again, the one who thought he was a hoodlum from the hood. He stood in the doorway, covered in sweat, chest heaving, apparently mid-workout. Daryl slipped past him, and Johnson noticed how the kid seemed to be scared of his big brother. Another teenager, presumably Ken's buddy, sat on an armchair inside, almost as large, with eyes so far apart Johnson wondered if he could see sideways like a fish. He decided to find out who this guy was as soon as he could.

Donald Epps waddled reluctantly to the door, looking at Johnson as though *he* were the fat bum who neglected his kids, rather than the local law enforcement keeping River Rapids a decent place to live.

Johnson delivered his warning and managed to keep his temper under control. He meant every word. He would keep a close eye on Daryl Epps and if the boy exhibited any further signs of physical abuse, he would have Donald Epps in a cell and Daryl placed in care quicker than Ken Epps could spell 'dumbbell'.

He got into the squad car, slammed the door, and pulled away in a spurt of gravel. As he turned onto the road, he looked back at the trailer, wondering what was happening behind those curtained windows, and whether he had taken the right decision bringing Daryl back here. But then all thoughts of Daryl temporarily left his head when the radio chirped to life and Carole Jeffrey reported that the search party had found a body and Johnson was to get back down there just as fast as he possibly could.

2.

Yellow crime scene tape had been strung around four trees, cutting off the rectangle of long grass between. Johnson was reminded of the bucket seats and children's slide lying discolored and forgotten in the tall grass at the Epps' home. Only this time it was not old furniture tossed out to rot, but the body of a woman.

'White, maybe early thirties, strangled with electrical wire,' Johnson told Bill Millstone. 'Still clothed, no immediate signs of sexual assault.'

The body was right there, half-glimpsed among the tall grass, half-covered with trash from a burst garbage bag. Just the suggestion of milky white skin and faded denim. Johnson had already taken a look and felt no requirement to take a second one. Crows and rooks had pecked away the eyes, leaving gooey sockets that made the face skull-like even though the flesh was still present. The mouth hung slack, leaving yellow and black teeth exposed, so there was a good chance of identification. This part of Jefferson's Woods was dense with undergrowth and far from well-used paths, which may, Johnson thought, explain how it had clearly remained undiscovered for some time.

'Any ideas?' asked Sheriff Millstone.

Johnson watched the scene of crimes people tiptoe around the body, taking photos. He had always found those guys a little sinister. Maybe it was the disposable coveralls they wore, like the whole world was toxic but them.

'One,' said Deputy Fincher.

3.

Tuesday August 23rd, 2011

For the umpteenth time that week, Johnson Fincher hammered on the door of the trailer belonging to Donald Epps. Don opened the door himself this time, but left the screen door closed between them.

'Have you found her?' he said.

'May I come in, Mr Epps?'

'No, you can say whatever you need to say right there.'

'We haven't found Cristel, Mr Epps, but we have found the body of an older woman.'

That got his attention. He stopped chewing whatever he was chewing.

'What's that to do with me?'

'I think it may be your wife, Yvonne, Mr Epps. I'd like you to come with me down to the hospital to make an ID.'

'Yvonne? You've found Yvonne?'

'That's what we need to ascertain, Mr Epps.'

'But she ran off. What, three years ago?'

'Will you come with me, Mr Epps?'

For a moment, Johnson felt sure that Donald Epps would refuse. Then he pushed his way through the screen door. Johnson followed Donald Epps to the squad car. He popped the rear door and closed it behind him.

The vehicle bumped off the gravel and onto the road into town. Of course, if the body were that of Yvonne Epps, what did that mean for Cristel? It meant, thought Johnson bitterly, that Cristel was probably dead too, and if Yvonne's body could moulder undiscovered in Jefferson's Woods for three years, then so could Cristel's. Somebody had murdered Yvonne Epps, strangled her with electrical wire and dumped her body, and got away with it for three years, and maybe, probably, her killer was sitting in the backseat of his car right then. And if Donald Epps had killed his wife, he had probably killed his daughter too. But could they prove it? If they could just find a lead, maybe some evidence on the body. A fingerprint, something to tie Donald Epps to the body, that was all they needed.

'Daryl make it to school today, Mr Epps?' Johnson said as he pulled the car into the Medical Center parking lot.

'Yeah, he's at school. Not that it's any of your business.'

River Rapids Medical Center was a squat, brick building put up in the mid eighties. It had low ceilings, small windows, and a flat roof, and despite several paint jobs over the years, it always seemed to look past its prime. Johnson came here regularly for cholesterol tests and tried hard not to see the building as a metaphor for the state of his own life. *And body,* he thought as he caught a glimpse of his reflection in the automatic doors. He glanced at the man walking beside him and thought, *Still, could be worse.*

Donald Epps clearly did not want to be here. He kept looking over his shoulder as though he thought somebody were chasing him. Or he expected to be arrested at any moment. *And this is only the medical center,* Johnson thought. *What would he be like if I had asked him to come to the station?*

Johnson called hello to Pauline on reception. She waved back cheerily, but Johnson caught the momentary look of disapproval she aimed at his companion. Donald Epps seemed not to notice and continued slouching warily after Johnson as he led the way to the tiny mortuary at the rear of the building. At a certain point, the noise and bustle of the building fell away leaving only a background hum and a smell of disinfectant. Johnson paused at a narrow door inset with a small frosted window.

'You should know,' he said, 'that she's been exposed to the elements for the best part of three years. You should prepare yourself.'

Donald Epps probably didn't care, especially if he were responsible for her condition in the first place, but

Johnson felt obliged to give the warning nonetheless. He led the way into a small tiled room containing a large ceramic table, and a wall of numbered doors. An immobile form lay on the table under a sheet. Johnson took a breath, and carefully folded back a portion of the sheet, exposing the face.

The mortician had done her best in the short time since the body had been moved. She had cleaned the skin and removed much of the detritus from the eye sockets and ear canals. The straggly remnants of hair had been washed and tidied. She looked much better than she had when Johnson had first seen her, dumped twisted and broken in a tangle of thorn bushes. But the eye sockets gaped empty, and yet were still able to give the impression they were staring right at you. And the skin around the nostrils and mouth was discolored and broken.

Johnson watched Donald Epps look at the body. He saw the man's Adam's apple twitch once, twice, and then he said, 'Yeah, that's her. That's Yvonne.'

Johnson took him to sign the papers. When the formalities were taken care off, he left the man in the parking lot. He protested about the lack of a ride home, but Johnson had better things to do, and he was sure he would see a good deal more of Donald Epps over the coming days. For now, he could make his own way home. Johnson pulled the Ford Crown Victoria out of the parking lot, shaking his head. The man had just been presented with the body of his long missing wife, and all he could think of was the inconvenience of getting home. As Johnson pulled the squad car onto Appalachian Boulevard he realized that he was developing a healthy hatred for Donald Epps.

4.

Johnson realized how late it was when his stomach growled as he pushed open the door to the precinct. Glancing at the clock mounted above the reception desk, he saw that it was nearly two thirty. And all he'd eaten was a cream cheese bagel at six that morning. And then he saw the donut and coffee sitting on his desk. 'Carole, you are an angel!' he called.

'Tell me something I don't know!' she said. 'Doctor Schwartz is on the phone.'

Jeanette Schwartz split her time between the medical center and the police station, conducting autopsies and analyzing forensic evidence. Johnson picked up the phone hoping for good news. Jeanette was from Tennessee, and told gory stories of the horrific injuries she dealt with in her line of work in a southern drawl that made her words even more ghoulish. Johnson thought she was hilarious.

'Carpet fibers and blood, Johnson,' she said, 'and frankly, you're lucky to get that after three years.'

'DNA?'

'I hope so. Already sent the sample to the lab. You know the drill, maybe a day or two. I hear the Epps guy made the ID.'

'It's her. Went missing in oh eight. Guessing the body was stored until after the search, then dumped in the woods. What can you tell me about the carpet fibers?'

'Short, wiry. I'm guessing from a vehicle, maybe a pickup.'

'The vehicle they used to transport the body.'

'That's my guess.'

'It's a lead. Thanks, Jeanette.'

'Always a pleasure, Johnson.'

Johnson let Bill Millstone know. Sheriff Millstone instantly ordered that Donald Epp's pickup be searched and a sample of the carpet fibers taken for comparison.

'His DNA on file?' he asked.

'No. We've never been able to pin anything on him.'

'No point asking him to volunteer it, I guess?'

'I can ask,' Johnson said, 'but I know what he'll say.'

Sheriff Millstone leaned back in his chair, hands behind his head. He closed his eyes. 'Even if they match, the carpet fibers won't be enough on their own. We need the DNA, Johnson.'

For the second time that day, Johnson drove to the Epps' trailer, this time with Phil Logan in the passenger seat. Phil was a local boy, ex-quarterback for the River Rapids High Cougars. He had joined the River Rapids Police Department the previous year as a trainee, and still looked a little uncomfortable in his uniform. Still, he was a big lad, and just the sort of wing man Johnson needed if Ken Epps or his father got nasty.

Bill Millstone was right, they needed the DNA, but there was no way Donald Epps would supply it voluntarily, even if he were innocent. If he could get a warrant to search the trailer, he could find DNA easily – hairs from a brush or a shower drain were obvious sources – but if it were obtained without Epps' knowledge, it would be inadmissible. Was it possible that Donald Epps would wriggle his way off the hook once again?

And don't forget, Johnson told himself, *you still have a missing six year old to find. Now is not the time to take your eye off the ball.*

'You expecting trouble, Deputy Fincher?' Phil Logan asked as the Crown Victoria passed the 7Eleven.

'Maybe, Phil. I don't know. Depends on whether his bodybuilder son and his buddies are there. And on how many Buds he's snaked back today. Whatever happens, he won't take kindly to us impounding his truck. Just be prepared, that's all.'

Johnson remembered when he was new to law enforcement, barely out of cop school, going into every situation blind. Ten, no *twelve* years ago now. Bill Millstone had been deputy then, and old man Dedham had been the sheriff, just a couple of years out of retirement. Johnson hadn't dared call them by first name either, despite exhortations to do so.

Johnson found a moment to smile at the memory of his first day as a serving member of River Rapids Police Department. The sheer wide-eyed bewilderment of it. He'd been called to a domestic assault, not too far from where he was headed now, come to think of it. A guy beating up his wife because he couldn't afford the mortgage repayments, same old story. By the time he'd got there, the guy was gushingly apologetic, the wife tearfully insisting that he wasn't usually like this and he loved her really. Johnson had left them with a stern warning and had been halfway back to the station when he'd received the call to turn around and go right back. Tempers had flared again and a neighbor had called an ambulance this time. Not, perhaps, the most successful first day ever. But always unpredictable and always exhilarating. In some respects, he envied Phil. Still finding everything new and interesting, and with his whole career ahead of him.

Donald Epps' pickup, a battered Ford that had started out dark green, stood on the gravel outside the trailer. As Johnson made for the front door, he cast his eyes through the cab window, looking for carpet. *Something* lay down there in the footwells, but it was so stained and covered in mud and dirt that he couldn't tell what color it was. Certainly looked like it had been there for three years.

Before he could rap on the door, it opened. Daryl stood there, staring through the screen door, eyes hopping from Johnson to Phil and back. Johnson crouched to the kid's eye-level. He was determined to get a response from the kid this time.

'Hey Daryl, I'm Deputy Fincher, remember me?'

A nod.

'So, you made it to school today?'

No response. The kid was probably scared of getting into trouble. *Try a different tack, Johnson. Show the kid you care.*

'You doing okay, Daryl? Nobody hurt you today?'

'No, sir.'

'Good, good. We want it to stay that way too. Will you tell your daddy I'm here?'

'He's asleep.'

'Is he now? Well, we'll go right on and wake him in a little while, shall we? First, Daryl, I want you to tell me all about your sister.'

Johnson's knees were killing him after crouching for this long, but no way in God's beautiful backyard was he going to miss this opportunity to talk to the kid. Especially now the kid was actually talking.

'Who's Cristel's best friend, Daryl?'

The kid shrugged. *No, no, Johnson, keep him talking.*

'I bet Cristel was kinder than your big brother, am I right?'

'Cristel never hurt me,' Daryl said. 'She was too small.'

Johnson noticed he used the past tense. *Keep him talking.* 'Did anybody hurt her? Your dad? Your brother?'

Daryl looked at the floor. 'Dad paddled her sometimes. When she was bad.'

'Was she bad a lot of times?'

Shrug.

'Did Cristel love your dad, Daryl?'

A Harley bike pulled to a halt in a fan of gravel. Johnson stood, pleased to straighten his knees, but sorry that his conversation had been interrupted. Ken Epps pulled off a cycle helmet with cartoon flames along the side. The type of helmet only a sixteen year old would find cool, Johnson thought.

'What's going on here?' Ken demanded. 'You can't talk to him without an adult!'

'We were just asking him where his daddy is, Kennedy, that's all.' Johnson felt a guilty stab of pleasure when he saw how mad the use of Ken's full name made him.

'Where is he?' Ken demanded of his brother.

'He's asleep,' Johnson said. 'Make yourself useful and tell him to move his lazy self. Tell him Deputy Fincher needs to see him right now.'

Ken scowled and pushed his way into the trailer, shoving Daryl to one side as he did so. Too bad the big brother had turned up. Donald Epps alone may not have created a scene over the confiscation of his pickup. But Ken almost certainly would.

Donald Epps appeared at the screen door. Ken stood behind, brow ruffled, one meaty hand rubbing the back of his head. The motion made the teenager's biceps jump, and Johnson again felt thankful for Phil Logan's solid presence beside him.

'What do you want now?' Don grumbled. 'Can't you leave me alone for five minutes?'

'Donald Epps, we're here to impound your pickup as evidence. I need the keys.'

'You can't do this! You need a warrant!'

Johnson pulled a wad of paper from his breast pocket. 'I have all the necessary documentation right here, authorized by Sheriff Millstone of the River Rapids PD. Either you hand me the keys, Mr Epps, or I will run you in right here and now.'

Donald Epps swore. Ken yelled something about a free country and getting off his father's property. Donald told him to shut it, and Ken yelled something about 'fascist pigs' and 'constitutional rights,' after which Donald pushed open the screen door enough to throw a set of keys through, and finished off by telling the cops on his doorstep to leave him alone because this was harassment and he'd make a complaint.

The trailer door slammed.

Daryl had long since disappeared.

Johnson scooped up the keys from the dirt. 'Could have been worse,' he said. 'You do the honors, Phil.'

5.

Phil Logan drove the Epps' pickup back to the station in downtown River Rapids, leaving it parked in a secure compound out back. Within moments of it arriving, a forensic team swarmed over it. All they needed was one piece of carpet fiber that matched the fiber found on Yvonne Epps' body. One piece of evidence and they could start to build a case. Johnson had doubts that anything would remain after three years, but unlikelier things had happened. Donald Epps was not a man who cleaned. He probably hadn't even run a vacuum over his truck in three years. The long shot was worth it.

Johnson sank gratefully into his chair and stared blankly at his computer screen. He pulled up the report of Yvonne Epps' disappearance from 2008. The details were scant, which was unsurprising. Yvonne had worked at a hardware store on Framlington, selling pots of paint and discounted skillet sets to the DIY obsessed River Rapids homeowners. Then, one day in May 2008, she had left work at her usual time of six o'clock, and had never been seen again. A witness came forward to say that he had seen a woman of Yvonne's description climbing into the cab of a long-distance hauler in the parking lot of the 7Eleven. But no amount of appeals or CCTV footage scrutiny had yielded any leads. The truck, if it had ever existed, had not been traced, and no sign of Yvonne Epps had ever been found.

Until today, when her broken remains had been found mouldering away in Jefferson's Wood.

So the long-distance hauler had likely never existed. And their fruitless inquiries in California and New York and Illinois surely had been a waste of time. She had been right here in River Rapids the whole time.

But Jefferson's Wood had been searched back in oh-eight. Johnson knew that, because he had been one of the men doing it. He had spent close to seventy-two hours beating that undergrowth with a stick and several dozen other men. Indeed, doing the very same this week for Yvonne Epps' daughter had brought back unpleasant memories from three years ago. And, it would seem, the same unhappy result. But if the body had been there back in oh-eight, they would have found it. Which meant that it had been stored somewhere until after the search had been called off, and then dumped.

So, where had it been stored?

And how had it been moved?

Donald Epps' pickup could provide the answer to the second of those questions. And a thorough search of the Epps' trailer could provide the answer to the first. He would get Bill Millstone to authorize a search of the trailer first thing tomorrow.

Johnson paged through the report. A photo of Yvonne caught his eye, taken outside Kelly's Diner, a couple of blocks further down Main Street. It had to have been taken at least ten years ago, because Kelly had taken down the old neon sign and smartened the place up a bit since then. In the photo, Yvonne stood with a root beer float in hand, lips puckered to the camera, Donald Epps' meaty arm encircling her. He wore a low-slung wife-beater and looked just the same as he always did. Just as fat, just as bald.

What had a girl like Yvonne Epps ever seen in a loser like Donald?

And if Donald had killed her, what was his motive? *Because he didn't want to be married anymore*, Johnson thought. *Because he didn't want to pay alimony for three children. Because he wanted to be with Debra Faulkner instead.* Was that motive enough? Would a man like Donald Epps consider that enough to murder?

The report finished by detailing efforts being made to find Yvonne in California, New York and Illinois, but reading between the lines, Johnson could tell that the inquiries were formalities. No leads had shown up and three years had passed. After all, Yvonne Epps was a grown adult, and sometimes grown adults did things like run out on their family, right?

But no, not this time. Because Yvonne's dead body had been found in Jefferson's Woods and somebody had put her there.

It was getting late. The sun was low outside, slanting through the slats of the window blind and hitting the far wall. Johnson wandered out to the parking lot, more for a breath of fresh air and to clear his head than anything else. The search team had mostly departed for Charleston, the final stragglers heading for their vehicles right now. Wolensky came over and shook his hand.

'I'm sorry we didn't find her,' he said. 'Anyone goes missing, it's a terrible thing, but a little girl, that's somehow worse.'

'We'll keep looking,' Johnson said. 'It's not over yet. And the search wasn't fruitless. We found Cristel's mom, and at least we have some workable leads.'

Wolensky nodded. 'Keep in touch,' he said. He disappeared inside the State Police people carrier and Johnson waved them off. The parking lot seemed strangely quiet once the convoy of vehicles had disappeared from sight along Main Street. Johnson took a deep breath before heading back inside. There *was* still hope, but if he were honest with himself, he was beginning to wonder if anybody would see Cristel Epps again.

He felt strung out. He felt that he had given everything

he had and got nothing to show for it. He felt that if he saw Donald Epps again that day, he may just pop him one on the nose. Time to go home and spend some time with his family. The Epps family and their troubles would still be there in the morning.

6.

Johnson Fincher stopped thinking of himself as the Deputy Sheriff of River Rapids County when he hung his hat on the stand in the hall. There was something symbolic about it, he thought. Something symbolic about hanging up your troubles and letting them rest a while. Now he was a husband and a father, and after having neglected his family over the last two or three days, he had some time to make up.

Susan sat on the couch, her legs folded under her, half watching some medical drama on the flatscreen. The lights were low and the drapes were drawn. She patted the seat next to her and Johnson didn't need asking twice. He sat and pulled her to him, kissing her tenderly.

Johnson asked how her day was because he didn't want to talk about his day. His day and the details therein, did not belong in this house, in this cozy room, on this comfy couch. Here was where he could get away from all that.

'Another day at the shop,' Susan said. 'Nothing special. Oh, Judith Krantz told me say hello to you. She brought round some of her special fruit cake.'

'Special in the sense that...'

'You need a meat cleaver to cut it, yes. There's a slice for you in the fridge.'

'Thanks, hon.'

'No problem. Don't forget to tell her how much you liked it next time you see her. It means more coming from the Deputy Sheriff.'

A pitter patter of tiny feet paused the conversation. Susan said, 'What's that I hear coming from the stairs? Could it be fairy footsteps?'

A giggle came from beyond the door.

'Or could it be my very naughty little girl who should be in bed?'

Millie appeared at the door, hair astray, thumb hovering near her mouth, sleep in her eyes. Disney Princesses smiled from her pajamas.

'Mommy, I can't sleep.'

Johnson patted his lap. 'Come here, cinnamon bun. Come say hi to your tired daddy, and then we'll take you back up to bed.'

Millie skipped and clambered onto Johnson's lap, and Johnson realized that he had fallen for her cuteness again. 'I should be cross that you're out of bed,' he said, 'but I guess you're just too cute to be cross with, cinnamon bun. Just like your mother.'

Susan rolled her eyes, but Johnson knew that little comment would keep him out of trouble with Susan later for not sending Millie straight back to bed where she belonged at ten o'clock in the evening.

'Daddy.'

'Right here, sweetness.'

'I'm not a cinnamon bun.'

'What? Are you sure about that?'

'Yes!'

'But you're full of sweetness, soft in the center, and...'

he licked her nose, '... you taste great! You must be a cinnamon bun!'

'Silly daddy!'

'Huh! Did I just hear right? Did I just hear Millie Fincher call her daddy silly? No! No! Right! There's only one thing to do! I shall have to tickle her to death!'

After two minutes of squirming, giggling and squealing, Millie's head drooped. Johnson took her hand. 'Come on, cinnamon bun. Upstairs to bed.' Glancing at Susan, Johnson led his daughter up to her bedroom and helped her climb into bed.

'Story, daddy.'

Johnson opened *Horton Hears a Who!* but long before Horton finished splashing in the pool, Millie's eyes had closed. Johnson silently replaced the book, pulled up Millie's duvet, and brushed a strand of hair from her face.

What if Millie had been out there on the edge of the Highway at six o'clock in the morning? What if Millie had disappeared without trace, probably lying dead somewhere in the woods or on a concrete floor? What would you be doing right now, Johnson, if your daughter were out there somewhere, missing and defenseless?

Johnson turned out the light and closed the door until it was ajar.

Downstairs, Susan was still watching the medical drama. Johnson knew he had to try harder.

7.

Next morning Johnson thumped his desk in frustration and burst into Bill Millstone's office.

'We have to do something! It's been four days since anyone saw Cristel Epps!'

'What do you need?'

'Authorization to search the Epps' trailer!'

'You got it.'

'What? Do we have probable cause?'

'Leave me to clear it with the DA. I'll find a way. Just get in there and find that little girl, Johnson.'

CHAPTER SIX
DARYL EPPS

1.

I step off the school bus and watch it chug away until the corner swallows it. To my left, the line of pines screens the trailer, but through the gaps I see the dirty beige slats, the picture window of the living room, and the enormous satellite dish mounted on the roof. I see how the rain has left stains on the walls and wonder why I have never noticed that before.

I stand on the side of the road and ask myself whether I want to walk up that driveway and let myself into that trailer. Instead, I could run into the woods across the road and paddle in the stream. Or go play cops and robbers at the cannery. Or turn up at Nathan's house for PB&J sandwiches and ice cream. Nathan's mom would never refuse me, not with Super-Daryl's mind control powers!

But Dad would be mad. Really mad. Because he knows the police are watching him, and if I go missing too... I don't even know what would happen. But it would be bad, that's for sure. And whatever has happened to Cristel, I don't want the same thing to happen to me.

I shoulder my backpack and walk up the drive to the front door. At least, that's what I planned to do. But suddenly a woman stands in front of me, and I don't know who she is or where she came from. She's fat, with curly hair, she smiles at me like she's not used to smiling. Her smile is false and crooked, like a witch's smile. She wears a huge T-shirt with *Size Matters for Big Girls* written on it, and a camera dangles around her neck.

She blocks my way into the drive.

'You're Daryl, right?'

I stare at her, trying to think what to say. Some age-old instruction about not talking to strangers runs through my head.

'Do you know where your sister is, Daryl?'

I shake my head but still can't manage words.

'She's been missing for three days, right? Your dad know where she is?'

She lifts the camera and a flash puts spots in my eyes.

'Tell your dad that if he wants to put his side of the story, Rowena's right here, okay? All he has to do is step outside. Rowena, that's me.'

I still can't think of anything to say. She steps aside and I run up the drive to the trailer.

Somebody – Dad or maybe Debra – has tried to tidy the living room. The TV is back in place. A jagged crack runs down one side, but it's still working: Debra sits on the sofa watching a show about rich Californians arguing and calling each other names. She doesn't even look up when I enter and that's fine by me. The coffee table is clear of pizza boxes and beer cans, most of which are bagged and stacked by the garbage can in the kitchen.

Dad emerges from the can, belching. When he sees

me, a look flickers across his face, almost as though he has forgotten who I am for a second. Or he has been caught red-handed at something. I try to enter my room, but he puts out an arm.

'Daryl, wait, I want to talk to you.'

'I got homework...' I don't even consider telling him about the woman at the gate. Rowena. I don't talk to my dad if I don't have to.

'Daryl, will you listen for once? I gotta talk to you! It's important.'

I sling my backpack on the floor and stand there, in the middle of the living room, head hanging. On the TV, some orange-skinned woman tries to yank out another orange-skinned woman's hair.

'I got some bad news for you, son. The cops have found your mother's body in the woods.'

My brain takes a few moments to realize what he has said. I had thought he would say something about Cristel, that they had found her, that she was okay, that she was dead. But whatever it was, I expect to hear *Cristel*. For a handful of moments, I think he really had said Cristel. Then my brain processes the words properly, and I feel blood drain from my head and legs.

'But... but... Mom?'

He's made a mistake, surely? He meant to say *Cristel* only it had come out wrong, right? Right? Because mom is out there in California or New York or somewhere, living a great life, and just waiting for the right time to come and get me. Any day now, she'll appear at the front door, or at school, in a swanky car with the engine revving and the door open, beckoning me inside, and then we'll be gone, disappearing along the Highway with River Rapids in our rear view mirror and Dad and Debra and Ken nothing but bad memories.

That's the way it's gonna happen, right? Not a body in the woods. There has to be some mistake.

I run. My brain is frozen, but not my muscles. I duck Dad's arm, run into my room and slam the door. I dive under my duvet and cry into the Batman sheets, oblivious to the musty stink.

I don't know how long I stay there. All I know is how grateful I am Ken is at Hayley's, or somewhere, and not filling the room with his demands and sweat. I stay there until night falls and I fall asleep.

It's light outside when I wake up. I hear a rapping on the front door.

I sit up. My stomach growls painfully.

Only the police hammer like that. Perhaps it's Deputy Fincher, come to tell me that there had been a mistake and the body in the woods isn't mom after all, but some other woman who looks like her, and it's all a false alarm.

But then I hear shouts and yells, Dad screaming at somebody to get off his property, and Debra screeching curse words in her witch-like voice. Other footsteps thump along the hallway. I watch my bedroom door spring open.

Deputy Fincher stands there.

'Hiya, Daryl. Nothing to be scared of, we're just searching the trailer. Some of my officers will come in soon and search the room, but you just stay there on your bed and stay calm and everything will be fine. Okay?'

My brain is too far gone to put together a response. I just stare at him.

Two officers come in wearing disposable gloves. They open every drawer and go through my shorts and T-shirts.

They even go through my underpants. They move Ken's weights and look behind them. They pull out old shoe boxes of photos and letters from under the bed. They flick through Ken's magazines of naked ladies that he thinks I don't know about. They open the closet and toss out my old books and comics. They even pull the sheets and duvets from the beds, and pull the furniture out. Dust swirls and spirals.

Deputy Fincher sits beside me the whole time. Seeing him sitting on my Batman sheets is weird. He tries to explain that they are looking for clues to where Cristel might be, but I know she isn't in my bedroom. How can the cops not know that? I wonder how smart they are. Even Nathan had better ideas about where Cristel might be. I remember his idea of looking for her on the CCTV footage at the 7Eleven and wonder if the cops have done that yet. Should I say something? What would Dad do to me if I did?

I keep my mouth shut. Keeping my mouth shut is a strategy I follow often, at school when Miss Stevens asks me a question, at home when Dad and Ken are mad at me, most always when an adult talks to me, and it never fails to work. They eventually give up and go away, sometimes calling me dumb or stupid, but I don't care. I hate them all anyway, don't I, Eminem?

Even Deputy Fincher, who lets his men come into my bedroom and search through my underpants.

Whatever they are looking for, they don't seem to find it. Deputy Fincher's lips are set hard and his eyes glare when he finally leads his men out of the trailer. Dad yells about knowing his rights and they'd better have top lawyers because he's going to sue, and Debra curses and curses, calling the police fascist pigs until Deputy Fincher seems to have had enough. He marches over to Debra and at first I think he's going to punch her in the mouth and I feel like cheering him on, but instead he gets in her face and says, 'Maybe we found nothing here because everything incriminating is at your cesspit apartment, Miss Faulkner, what about that? Maybe we should go riffle through your pantie drawer next, what do you say, eh?'

I just have time to remember standing in the stinky corridor outside Debra's apartment four days ago, watching Deputy Fincher persuade the landlord – Mr Swicks, his name was Mr Swicks – to let him in to poke around. I wonder if the witch Debra even knows that Deputy Fincher has already been in her cesspit apartment, and then my jaw drops when she hawks a loogie and spits in his face.

Deputy Fincher doesn't pause. He twists her arm behind her back and says, 'Debra Faulkner, you're under arrest for assaulting an officer of the law...' Everything else he says is drowned in filthy screams and curses. Debra stretches her scrawny neck just like a witch and her face gets red as she screams obscenities at Deputy Fincher until two officers drag her from the trailer.

I run back to my room, sure that I've just seen the best episode of TV ever and it was right there live in the living room.

I hope Deputy Fincher slings her in jail and never lets her out.

2.

Miss Stevens says God knows what we are thinking. He knows if I call Debra a witch in my head. He knows if

I want her to die in jail. He knows that I want Amelia Michaelson to put her cherry flavored Chapstick on and kiss me with it. Miss Stevens says there's nothing God doesn't know about.

But if that's true of every human on the planet, God must know hundreds and hundreds of secrets. How does he keep track of them all? I mean, I know he's God and everything, but that's an enormous number of secrets, and some of them must be very dull.

God knows what happened to the *Mary Celeste* and Amelia Earhart and all the ships that disappeared in the Bermuda Triangle. He knows what *croatoan* means and who killed the Princes in the Tower. He knows where Cristel Epps is right now and whether she's alive or dead. Why should he care if I call Debra Faulkner names in my head and wish she were dead?

I think we've got God all wrong. We think he's up there in heaven, looking down on his creations, keeping a checklist of all our rights and wrongs, like Santa with a list that lasts longer than a year. We think he balances them up, and when we finally croak we get summoned up there and all our darkest secrets are laid bare. But what if God isn't creating a list? What if he's looking down on us and laughing at all our silly foibles and crazy ways? I think he's up there right now, thinking, *Of course I don't mind that you said that bad word about Miss Stevens, young Daryl Epps, or you thought that unkind thought about Debra, or you lie in bed at night thinking about Amelia Michaelson kissing you with cherry flavored lips. I'm God! I've got the whole universe to take care of!*

This is important. This could change everything. This could mean everything about our lives could be different, and I need to find the answer. The next time I pass Our Lady of the Sacred Heart on Elm, I'm going right in there to talk to the priest about it.

You see what I'm getting at, don't you? If God really only cares about the big stuff, that would explain so much. That would explain why somebody can take Cristel away and get away with it. It would explain how mom can wind up dead in Jefferson's Woods. It would explain why the world is the way it is.

I saw something else in the CCTV video of Cristel walking past the 7Eleven at seven o'clock in the morning last Saturday. I saw something important when Fred turned his screen to show me. But it's taken me three days to realize it. Three days in which my sister could have been taken even further away. Three days in which she could have died wondering where I was and why I didn't come to rescue her.

What did I see?

The camera is mounted on the exterior wall of the 7Eleven. Its purpose is to monitor the parking lot and the vehicles that turn in and out of it. This means it is pointed toward the road. Toward Highway 32, which is always full of traffic zipping past, bypassing downtown River Rapids.

Except that time, right then. That early morning last Saturday when my sister walked past the camera. Just this once a car does not zip past on its way someplace else.

Right beside her, on the Highway, a vehicle keeps pace with her stumbling walk. Crawling, crawling. Following her every step of the way as she passes the front of the 7Eleven. And in that car is the person who must have taken her away.

3.

What do I do?

Easy, I hear you say. You go out there and tell the police. Tell your new friend, Deputy Fincher, Daryl, even if he did let police officers go through your underwear. Go find him, or call him, and tell him to go look at the CCTV from the 7Eleven. Tell him to run the footage through the latest video enhancing technology so they can pause it at just the right time to glimpse the pervert who abducted little Cristel. Then the cops can swoop, because they're good at swooping, and maybe find your sister alive, locked in a closet under the stairs or in some crawlspace, and you'll be her hero and you'll be on TV and everybody will think you're amazing. That's what you must do, Daryl. Of course, it is.

But it's not that easy. It's not easy at all. Dad, terrified of losing another child and having to take blame, won't let me out of the trailer. And even if I do get out, Dad or Ken will kill me if I talk to the cops. And even if I do find my way to the station, Debra the witch is there right now and she'll see me.

There's only one way this might work. I need Nathan and Amelia. I need Dad to think we are only going out to play.

Dad won't let me get a cellphone, but I have Nathan's phone number stored in my head. We have a special code. Three rings is the emergency Bat Signal. If I can get to the phone in the living room, where Dad and Ken are yelling at each other right now...

Dad called Ken right after Debra was arrested and made him come home, but all they've done since Ken burst through the door in his motorbike leathers is argue. Dad accused him of never being here when he was needed. *What's the use of having a son built like a chimney stack if you're never here when I need yer?* Dad yelled. Ken yelled back, *If you got up off your can and went to the gym, you wouldn't need your sixteen year old son to take care of you!* To which Dad bellowed, *Never mind that now! What are we going to do about Debra?* To which Ken made it quite clear how little he cared about Debra and suggested that she could take care of her own scrawny tail.

Now, they are standing by the kitchen countertop, arguing about whether Ken should leave. Dad thinks Hayley can do without Ken for one evening, and Ken forcefully suggests Dad get a life and a grip. Ken gulps glasses of water from the faucet between bellows. He seems to be on his fourth, at least. His attention is focused on Dad and Dad has his back to the phone. I tiptoe silently into the room, eyes zeroed on the wireless phone left face down on the coffee table. Once again, I am Super-Daryl. My powers of invisibility are in full force. They just have to hold up a few seconds more.

Moving slowly, I begin to dial Nathan's number. It rings once, twice, three times. By the time Dad and Ken see me I'm filling a glass from the faucet.

'Get out of here, runt!' yells Ken.

I run back to the bedroom. Right now, Nathan will be asking his mom if he can go out. He knows what three rings means. He'll be jumping on his bike, picking up speed as he rounds the bend at the end of his road. He'll be whizzing along Main Street, wind flicking his hair back. On his way to me.

He makes good time. Thirty-two minutes after I put

the phone down, I hear a knock on the door. The familiar squeak of the screen door, and then his voice. 'Hi, Mr Epps. Can Daryl come out to play? We're just going to the stream for a few minutes, get him out from under your feet.'

Nathan always seems to know exactly the right thing to say to make grown-ups do what he wants. Remember Fred at the 7Eleven? He would never have shown me that CCTV footage if Nathan hadn't been there. It's a knack, he says. I wish I had the knack.

I get out of there before Dad changes his mind. Amelia Michaelson stands on the doorstep beside Nathan, smiling at my Dad. She must have ridden on the back of Nathan's bike. I am pleased to see her. My heart thumps a little, but that's because my Dad could change his mind at any second.

The door slaps shut behind us and we're gone.

Amelia sits on the back of Nathan's bike, and I sit on the handlebars. He has to look around me to see where he is going. Nathan takes a few seconds to get going with all the extra weight, but soon we're flying along the road toward town. I'm not afraid that Nathan will put the front wheel in a hole or skid around a corner and send me tumbling because I know he's too smart to do things like that.

We stop at the 7Eleven for popsicles. We sit on the railing by the handicapped entrance, swinging our legs. I wonder if we could convince Fred to let us see the CCTV again so we can show Amelia, but Nathan doesn't think he can convince Fred twice. 'No,' he says, 'we must tell the cops, and the cops can make Fred show them.'

I have almost finished my popsicle. Grape flavor sits at the bottom of the plastic where the ice has melted, and everybody knows the flavor at the end is the best bit. I tip it into my mouth, the flavor so strong it sends a shiver up my spine.

'My mom's dead,' I say.

'I thought she got into a truck,' says Amelia.

'Dead. They found her in the woods.'

'That sucks,' says Nathan, crunching ice.

Amelia has a cola flavor popsicle. Her lips and tongue are brown. If I kissed her now, would she taste of cola? A treacherous voice inside reminds me that the only reason she hangs out with us is because she likes Nathan. All the girls like Nathan.

We go to the police station and ask for Deputy Fincher. The police station is quiet. I expect people to rush in and out with bad guys to lock up. I expect to hear police sirens all the time. Instead, cops sit at computers and the lady at the counter turns and calls for Johnson.

Deputy Fincher smiles at me. 'Daryl, nice to see you. Who are your friends?'

Nathan tells him about the car on the CCTV footage. Deputy Fincher beckons us to follow him. He swipes a card and takes us through a door into the back of the station. I have never been to the back of the police station before. Nathan grins and gives me a thumbs up sign. Amelia skips as she walks along brown carpet tiles. Deputy Fincher takes us into a small room containing a tabletop of screens and DVD players. We sit and watch him unlock a file cabinet and pull out a DVD in an envelope. The envelope has *Epps* written on it.

It's the footage from the 7Eleven. Just the same as when Fred showed us. I swallow as I watch my sister move along the sidewalk from left to right, looking around her, clearly scared. There's the man getting into his pickup, ignoring the little lost girl. The man who could have saved her if he had thought to ask her if she needed any help. And behind her, the Highway, and the car following her every step, trailing her. The car is little more than a gray blob, and the driver a handful of white pixels.

The driver. The one man who probably knows exactly what happened to my sister. Who knows where she is right now. Who knows if she is still alive.

A handful of white pixels.

'Do you recognize the car, Daryl?' asks Deputy Fincher. 'Any of you? Think carefully. Anyone you know drive a car like that?'

The only person I know drives a car is Dad, and his car is a pickup. And the school bus driver but his car is a bus.

'Do you know where she would end up if she carried on along the highway in that direction?' Deputy Fincher says. 'She would come to Jefferson's Wood. The exact same part of Jefferson's Woods where we found your mom, Daryl. You think somebody told her where your mom was? You think she was trying to find your mom?'

I want to say something, but my mind is blank.

'Who do you think told her where your mom was, Daryl?'

Dad! Ken! Debra! They killed mom! They all did! They must have! Arrest them and take them to jail!

I shake my head and say nothing.

'If you think of anything,' Deputy Fincher says, 'anything at all, no matter how small, you come and tell me. You understand?'

We understand. We walk into the parking lot. Nobody speaks. We sit on the parking lot wall. I wish I had another popsicle. Grape or cola. I wonder if I will ever see my sister again. Or will she end up as another body in the woods, like my mom?

I don't know what to think or feel. I should feel something, right? But I don't know what. I know I should feel happy at birthday parties. I know to feel excited at Christmas. I know to feel anger when Dad beats me. I know what to feel when Nathan and I are playing hide-and-seek at the cannery. I know what to feel when we two sit in our hideout with a new treasure to put in the chest. I can feel all these things, good and bad, no problem. But how am I meant to feel when my sister disappears and my mom turns up dead? I can feel sad, but I feel sad when I flunk a quiz at school, and how can that be the same? They must be different, right? So tell me then, if you know, how can I feel the same thing for both? If you know it all, tell me if I'm missing an emotion. Tell me what I should feel.

I go back home when it gets dark, and so do Nathan and Amelia. I crawl under my comforter and cry for what seems like hours. At some point, Ken bursts in and kicks my bed. He puts loud music on – some LA rapper telling the world how great he is and how much money he has – farts, kicks my bed again, lifts some weights. I pretend I'm asleep, but he knows.

'Little prick,' he says, 'why don't you do us all a favor and disappear like your sister?'

I say nothing. I think of what Deputy Fincher said and wonder if Ken told Cristel where mom was. I wonder if Ken killed mom.

If he killed Cristel.

Whether he'll kill me.

CHAPTER SEVEN
JOHNSON FINCHER

1.

Wednesday August 24th, 2011

Deputy Johnson Fincher watched Daryl Epps and his buddies amble across the parking lot. Daryl kicked a stone and sat on the low brick wall separating the lot from the grassy verge. His buddies, a sturdy-looking kid who could be a match for Ken Epps in a few years and a pretty girl with red hair and a snub nose, sat with him.

What was the kid thinking? He didn't say much, that was for sure. Millie, he knew every thought that ran through her mind, just by looking at her face. It was all right there, writ large. If she was hungry, thirsty, sick, excited, mad, all of it plain. But Daryl, he had looked into that kid's eyes trying to see what went on in there, and all he saw was a brick wall. Sometimes it seemed that he hated his dad and his brother, and wanted nothing more than to help Johnson put them away. Other times, he shut down, as though a lifetime of warnings not to talk to the police had taken root.

Whose side was Daryl Epps on? Did he even know himself?

Johnson watched Daryl and his buddies clamber onto a Schwinn and wobble away along Main.

Inside the precinct, Carole reminded him that they had Debra Faulkner in holding and what did he want doing with her?

Johnson could think of several slow tortures he would love to inflict on Debra Faulkner. He could still feel her saliva dribbling down his left cheek and over his lips.

'Any chance we could keep her until we've searched her apartment?' He knew the search of Debra's apartment would be much smoother if she weren't there. And she wouldn't have the chance to hide anything incriminating.

Carole wrinkled her nose. 'We're talking tomorrow, what with the paperwork, right? We keep her in overnight, we'll have the DA's office down on us like a grand piano. Bill'll never authorize it.'

'So caution her and let her go, Carole. We'll have to take our chances.'

He phoned Jeanette Schwartz, hoping for good news. He knew it was too early to ask her for the test results on the carpet fibers taken from Donald Epps' pickup and trailer, but she had to be able to tell him something. And right now he wanted to hear of any slight possibility that they could tie Donald Epps to the murder of his wife.

'It's not looking good, Johnson,' Jeanette said, and Johnson's heart sank a little further.

'That's not what I want to hear, Jeanette,' he said.

'Hey, you know me, Johnson. No sugar-coating. You want me to tell you maybe? Well, maybe. I don't know for sure until the results are in. But don't get your hopes up.'

He thanked her and hung up. He sat at his desk, head in hands. Dead end after dead end, and the likelihood that Cristel Epps was still alive faded by the hour. Four days into the investigation and he couldn't think of another lead. What had he missed? What vital clue lay buried awaiting his attention?

He realized he had a headache. How long had he had that? Perhaps a cup of coffee would help, even if it were from the machine in the corridor.

When he arrived home several hours later, he sank into the sofa, kicked off his shoes and leaned back. The coffee hadn't helped and his headache had developed into a sharp throb right behind the eyes. On top of that, his back ached, his armpits were damp and sticky and his tongue kept worrying a painful and rapidly developing mouth ulcer.

'I want you to come to church on Sunday,' said Susan. 'You haven't been for several weeks, and I think it will do you good.'

Johnson was about to protest, but stopped. Maybe Susan was right. Maybe it would do him some good. He felt disconnected from God right now and had done for some time. *And face it, Johnson, what can you do on the case that you haven't already done? Sitting in the station Sunday morning staring at a computer screen and beating yourself up would accomplish nothing. And going to church would clear your head some.*

'Good idea, hon,' he said. 'I'll be there.'

'Here.' Susan handed him three Tylenol, a glass of water, and shot of brandy.

2.

Thursday August 25th, 2011

The results came back negative, just as Jeanette Schwartz told him they would. The carpet fibers recovered from Donald Epps' pickup and trailer did not match the traces found on Yvonne Epps' body. Sheriff Millstone was not best pleased and chewed Johnson out in his office that morning, which Johnson did not think was entirely fair since searching the Epps trailer had been the Sheriff's idea in the first place. Bill Millstone, however, did not appreciate being reminded of that fact.

Eventually, he stopped yelling and stood by the file cabinet, watching Jerry Hartwell park his pickup outside Kelly's Diner and head inside for his daily helping of chicken dinner and home fries. He took a deep breath and ran his hands over his jowly face.

'Okay, okay. I have the DA breathing down my neck, that's all. Talking about civil rights and home invasion and how probable cause isn't going to fly this time. No mention of a missing six year old girl, of course.'

He returned to his desk and sat.

'I'm having a devil of a job keeping this out of the papers, Johnson. Called in favors with that tomfool Gerald Sumner over at the *Recorder*, fielded a number of calls from the *West Virginian*. You tell me, are we going to find this kid? Or is it all going to blow up in our faces?'

'I have no more leads, Bill. It's not looking hopeful.'

'What's your next move?'

'Search the girlfriend's house.'

'Debra Faulkner? Didn't you bring her in yesterday?'

'Assaulting a police officer.'

'And now you want to search her place, with the DA already twitchy? You know how this is gonna look?'

'She spat on me, Bill.'

'Hurt your feelings, did she? You know better than this, Johnson.'

'Do I go ahead?'

Bill Millstone heaved a sigh. 'Yes, do it. But tread carefully. And get me something, or we'll all be neck deep in the proverbial excrement.'

Johnson left the office feeling helpless.

3.

Debra Faulkner was in bed asleep when Deputy Johnson Fincher, officer Phil Logan and two other police officers burst open her front door and charged into her apartment.

Johnson had been here before four or five days ago – it felt like another life – when he had persuaded the landlord, Swicks, to let him in. On that occasion, he had ascertained that Cristel Epps was not in the apartment and had left without disturbing anything. And Debra Faulkner had seemed not to notice that anybody had been in her apartment. Provided Swicks kept his mouth shut, she need never know. *And going by the trouble you're in right now, Johnson, that's probably no bad thing.*

The apartment was exactly as he remembered it: almost empty and yet still somehow a mess. The small living room contained only a futon, an ancient cathode ray tube TV (Johnson wondered if it still worked) perched on a filthy carpet, and a thin covering of debris over the floor. Bills, demands for payment, and invoices mostly.

Johnson's heart leaped when he saw that under the muck the carpet was the same orange color of the fibers taken from Yvonne Epps' body.

The kitchen was little more than a stretch of countertop along the wall of the living room. A food-encrusted microwave sat at one end, its door open and sagging forlornly. A fridge was jammed into a tiny space behind the door. A wedge torn from pizza boxes replaced a missing foot, but even so the fridge canted to one side.

A puddle waited at the bottom of the bathtub, and judging by the tide marks staining the enamel, it had been there for some time. A limescale encrusted shower head poked wonkily from the wall between tiles speckled with mold.

In the bedroom, twisted sheets lay over a mattress on the floor by the window. Discarded clothes covered the floor. Debra leaned against the wall in a hastily-donned gown, shooting daggers at Johnson. He didn't get too close in case she spat again. Her cries of harassment and threats of litigation and promises to make him wish he had never been born had subsided, probably only temporarily.

The apartment was not large and the search was complete after an hour. No indications of the presence of a child, not that Johnson expected any, but carpet samples had been taken and there was still her car to check out. He gave her a few moments to get dressed and then told her to lead them to her car. She told him to perform a sexual act on himself that was probably anatomically impossible. Johnson calmly informed her that if she chose not to cooperate, he would arrest her. Again. And this time a night in a cell *would* be on the cards. After another outburst of yelling and screaming, she snatched up a set of keys and stomped out of the apartment.

Along the narrow corridor that smelled of urine (and where Johnson had spotted Daryl Epps that last time he had been here, he recalled) and down the narrow staircase to the parking lot. Weeds grew between concrete paving slabs and around the tires of abandoned vehicles. Beer cans and Pepsi bottles tumbled. Debra stopped next to an ancient Ford which had once been red but was now edging closer to brown.

Johnson took the keys and popped the driver's door. Hot air and the smell of cigarettes drifted out. He glanced over the scuffed plastic molding of the dash and the worn mats in the footwells. He lifted the lid of the trunk, wincing at the gust of rancid air that assaulted his nostrils. An assorted jumble of trash greeted him: plastic Walmart bags, empty cardboard beer containers, old receipts, a road map of West Virginia dated 2004, and an ice scraper. Buried under there somewhere was another carpet. Something else for the forensics boys and girls to get stuck into.

Johnson told Phil Logan to drive the old Ford back to the station and thanked Debra for her cooperation. She was still screaming at him when he slammed the door of the Crown Victoria and pulled out of the parking lot, but this time a ghost of a smile played around his lips.

4.

A match!

Johnson could practically see Jeanette Schwartz's smile on the other end of the phone.

'I could kiss you, Jeanette!'

'Yeah, so what's new? You're just a fair weather friend, Johnson Fincher. We both know that.'

'Never! Soon as you can tear yourself away from your test tubes, I'll get you a drink.'

'Uh huh. I'm overwhelmed, Johnson. I'll call if we dig up anything else.'

A match! The carpet fibers on Yvonne Epps' body matched the carpet in Debra Faulkner's living room. After a week of dead ends, at last they had something.

'It's not enough, Johnson,' said Bill Millstone.

'It proves Yvonne was in Debra's apartment the day she died!'

'You know what a defense attorney will say. They knew each other. Yvonne could have been in the apartment perfectly legitimately.'

'They hated each other!'

Sheriff Millstone shrugged. 'Irrelevant. What's important is they knew each other and Yvonne could just as easily have been there of her own free will.'

'So why was she on the floor? Carpet fibers, Bill!'

'She slipped and fell. She sat on the floor because there was nowhere else to sit. You say Debra's only got a futon in there, right? She took off her outer clothing because she was hot and left it on the floor. A cat or dog tracked carpet fibers on her. She was sitting on the floor playing with a cat or dog. Or small child. Could be any number of reasons, Johnson.'

He was right and Johnson knew it. If he were honest with himself, he had known it from the jump and had been holding onto the vain hope that Bill Millstone would think differently. If the fibers had matched the carpet in the trunk of the Ford, that would have perhaps been different. That would mean Yvonne had been in the car's trunk the day she died and that very strongly indicated foul play. But the carpet in the apartment? That could all be explained away, leaving Johnson no better off.

'There must be something we can do, Bill.'

'There is. I'm putting Donald Epps on TV, get him to make an emotional plea for the return of his daughter. Get the public involved. There's nothing else to do.'

'They'll want to know why we didn't do this six days ago when there was a much higher chance we could find her alive.'

'I know that, Johnson. Got any ideas what we can say to that? Cos I sure don't!'

Johnson could see why the Sheriff was mad, but as he returned to his desk nursing a fresh headache, he wondered what he could possibly have done differently.

A voice in his head said, *Perhaps, Johnson, you should stop treating this investigation as a missing person case and start treating it as a murder case. Because let's face it, Deputy Sheriff, the chances of Cristel Epps still being alive are practically nil.*

5.

Saturday August 27th, 2011

One week after the disappearance of his daughter, Donald Epps made a tearful plea on national television for the safe return of his beloved little girl. One day later, Donald Epps gave an interview to the *West Virginian* newspaper in which he denounced the River Rapids Police Department as 'dangerous incompetents who waited a week before taking any action. As I see it, Sheriff Bill Millstone and Deputy Sheriff Johnson Fincher may just as well have killed Cristel themselves.'

Anxious for his moment of fame, Ken Epps soon weighed in, loudly decrying the efforts of the police in an article in the *River Rapids Recorder* headlined *HUNKY KEN TELLS OF HIS LOVE FOR HIS MISSING SISTER.* The subtitle read: *River Rapids PD: The worst PD in America?*

Reporters from Charleston newspapers turned up next, shuttling back and forth between the police station and the Epps trailer. Hours later a reporter and photographer from New York City, and another from DC. Before long a posse of reporters and photographers from as far afield as Chicago, St Louis and Tallahassee turned up in the tiny West Virginian town of River Rapids.

'I'm surprised they could even find us,' murmured Carole Jeffrey, darkly, as she fielded yet another call from some reporter trying to trick her into revealing a hitherto unknown nugget of information, or maybe just recommend a decent motel. She looked through the window at the gaggle of camera-toting reporters setting up camp on the lawn. There was even a TV camera out there now from the local PBS station.

Johnson stayed away from the windows. He was unwilling to appear on the local news, especially as a shadowy silhouette in the window. Some papers were already painting him as the bad guy behind the disappearance of Cristel Epps.

'How long is this going to last?' muttered Sheriff Millstone.

6.

Sunday August 28th, 2011

Millie woke him at six minutes to six by yanking on the comforter and demanding juice. By juice, she meant the sugar-crammed concoction with a vaguely orange flavor sold by the gallon in the supermarket. Johnson had hoped to wean her off it, but Susan complained that it was the only thing she would drink and something was better than nothing.

But not at six minutes to six on a Sunday morning. After the worst week of Johnson's career.

'Not now, cinnamon bun. Go back to bed.'

Millie promptly burst into tears. Susan sat upright in bed, hair twisted around her ears. 'What's going on?'

'Daddy won't give me juice!' Millie whined, and Johnson knew he was getting no more sleep that morning.

He swung his legs out of bed, staggered to his feet, and pulled the seat of his shorts out of his backside. Millie stopped crying when he hoisted her up and sat her on the roll of fat just north of his waistband. Some part of him remembered his resolution to get down to the gym a bit more, a fine intention made before any little girls had disappeared and before the Epps family had hoovered up every spare second of his time. Maybe one day.

In the kitchen, he produced a glass, set it on the table, turned to face his daughter riding on his hip, and prepared for fireworks. 'Milk or water?' he said.

'Juice!'

'No juice at six in the morning. Milk or water?'

Millie burst into shrieking tears once again. She squirmed until Johnson set her down, and then rolled on the kitchen floor, screaming for juice.

Johnson steadied himself on the counter and rubbed his eyes. Seemed he could do nothing right.

Susan came down in her robe ten minutes later, by which time Johnson at least had the coffee on. Millie sulked in a corner with a full glass of water close by. Susan flicked on the radio and lowered herself into a kitchen chair.

'Still coming to church?' she asked.

He nodded at Millie. 'I hope so.'

Susan glanced at the clock on the oven. 'She's got three hours,' she said.

Millie stopped screaming when Susan set a bowl of Cheerios in front of her. And milk became acceptable once Susan had stirred in a spoonful of banana Nesquik. Johnson sat at the table watching his daughter dribble milk over her chin and enjoying the peace. Until he caught his name in the news bulletin from WKWV.

'More than a week after the disappearance of six year old Cristel Epps, hopes are fading for her safe return.

The missing girl's father, Donald Epps, of River Rapids, WV, has called into question the competence of Sheriff William Millstone and Deputy Johnson Fincher of the River Rapids Police Department, who have so far failed to comment.'

Susan stood and switched the radio off. The sudden silence was so deep Johnson found himself wishing his daughter would tantrum again.

'You did everything you could,' Susan said, and Johnson caught the past tense in what she said. She clearly thought Cristel was dead, along, it seemed, with most of the town.

'You know he didn't even know his daughter was missing until we told him!' Johnson burst out. 'That Donald Epps! All over the papers and the TV like the sun shines from his keister! Some people shouldn't be allowed to have kids.'

Susan stood behind him and laid her chin on his head. 'None of this is your fault.'

Millie paused with upraised spoon. A Cheerio slid from it and hit the table in a little puddle of milk. 'Don't be sad, Daddy,' she said.

Johnson went upstairs to put some clothes on. Against all the odds, they were ready to leave the house shortly after eight thirty. Millie wore a little flower print dress which even Johnson had to admit was cute, especially when combined with the red ribbon Susan had put in her hair. Susan herself had put on a sleeveless blouse and billowy skirt: just smart enough to make a favorable impression at church without seeming too dressy. Johnson wore sand-colored pants with a gleaming white polo shirt, and it felt wonderful to be going out in something other than his uniform. He had parked the River Rapids PD Crown Victoria out front last night so that they could get the Subaru out of the garage. With Millie in the safety seat in back and Susan beside him, he pulled onto the road. The day was beautifully warm, and with the windows rolled down, a delicious breeze brushed his face. Just the sort of late summer day that made you think maybe true happiness did exist in the world.

Until you think of a missing child. And the fact that everybody seems to think it's your fault.

The lights at the end of the road were red. Johnson hit the wheel with frustration, releasing a honk that caused a passing old lady to turn her head. Susan looked at him, quizzically.

'Statistically, you'd think these lights would be green half the time, right?' Johnson growled. 'But no, every single time red. Red, red, red! How is that even possible?'

The lights changed and Johnson pulled away a little sharply.

'Sorry, sorry,' he said. 'Guess I'm a little wound up right now.'

River Rapids Ecumenical Church was housed in a single level brick building erected at huge expense twelve years ago. The congregation's tithes for five years had been sunk into the new building, along with private backing and a huge loan the church would still be paying off in twenty years' time. To Pastor Freddy and his attendees, however, it was worth every penny, even if the AC bills in summer and heating bills in winter were extortionate, even if weeding the parking lot was a full time job, and even if the window frames were starting to peel and needed freshening up. A shallow pitched roof climbed leisurely to a point from which a large stone cross sprouted. Back-lit letters above the main entrance read *Blessed Are Those Who Enter.*

The Finchers had arrived ten minutes before the service was due to start and the parking lot was already full. Johnson cruised up and down the access roads, looking for a spot. Why were parking lots never big enough? No matter where he went, from church to Walmart to the precinct, parking spaces were always at a premium. Finally, he managed to squeeze the Subaru into a corner spot under one of those trees that always seemed to drip sticky sap. He dare not imagine what the Subaru's roof would look like when they emerged a couple of hours later. But Millie had had enough of sitting in the car and was starting to whine and Susan was insisting that they park somewhere – anywhere – before a full-blown tantrum kicked off. Johnson found himself wondering why everything they did as a family these days always had to revolve around Millie and tantrum-avoidance, and then caught himself because he was stressed out and grumpy and blaming a four year old was not fair. He forced a smile onto his face, tried not to think about sap and poop on his car roof, and led his family into church.

They picked a spot near the front because Millie would scream if she 'couldn't see', which in the language of a four year old meant she wanted a completely unobstructed view of absolutely everything, even if there were absolutely nothing to see. Susan also insisted on an aisle seat, in case Millie started screaming, in which case she could grab her and make as swift and as unobtrusive an exit as possible. Specially useful if Millie kicked off halfway through Pastor Freddy's sermon, which seemed to be the time she usually picked.

Hank Overstreet sat with his family one row back, and he leaned forward to shake Johnson's hand. Hank's brood of four were all over ten years old now and seemed able to make it through the service on Sundays without meltdowns. Johnson looked forward to the time when he could say the same.

'Sorry about all the ding dong,' Hank said. 'You know. I hope you find her, I sure do.'

'Thanks, Hank.' The last thing Johnson wanted to think about right now was work. He wondered how many others would feel obliged to extend their condolences before they could pile back into the Subaru and leave in a couple of hours. He began to wonder if coming to church was a good idea.

A woman with straight cut bangs hanging over her eyebrows spoke into the microphone on the lectern with the easy confidence of somebody who has done this countless times before and knows exactly what she's doing. Johnson knew he should know her name, but he just couldn't think of it right then. Susan would know. She reminded the congregation of the upcoming Picnic in the Park, and if anybody could play a musical instrument, could they please bring it along? They were particularly interested in tambourines, maracas and other percussion instruments. On Saturday, Men's Breakfast was being held at six o'clock in the morning, and would be an ideal opportunity for the Godly men of the church to receive prayer and ministry. 'All done by eight,' the announcer said, 'so, men, you should even be back in time to honor your wives and get the children out of bed so she can have a lie in.' Johnson wondered if men ever got the opportunity to have a lie in, but the woman at the lectern had already passed on to a reminder about the Women's Retreat coming up next month and could all monies be handed to Florrie Bisset as soon as possible. Entrance to the spa and a facial treatment was included in the price and if any woman still wished to sign up, a few spots were available.

The announcements came to an end. Johnson watched the woman resume her seat in the front row, and became suddenly conscious of how tightly wound up he was at the moment. Something had to give or he would end up yelling at Millie or Susan, and not exactly displaying the qualities of a 'Godly man of the church'.

Johnson believed in God, but held the view that he could manage perfectly well without Him. God was fine for Sundays, Christmas, weddings and funerals, and the rest of the time, Johnson was quite okay running his own life, thank you very much. God and religion meant a lot more to Susan, who had grown up with it in a nurturing family environment right here in River Rapids. Truth be told, he was only here in church right now to please Susan.

But maybe this was one time he could do with a little help.

The congregation struck up a stirring rendition of *Amazing Grace*. Johnson closed his eyes and did something he hadn't done for some time. Months. Maybe years. He prayed.

And the moment he did so, tears flooded his eyes. He dropped to his knees in the pew and rested his hands on the top of the pew in front. The polished wood – what was it, pine, birch? – felt sturdy and dependable beneath his fingertips. And right there, in an attitude of supplication to God, he felt the tightly-wound feelings drop away from him and a sense of acceptance take their place.

When he got to his feet he found his wife's hand and squeezed it. She squeezed back.

Pastor Freddy spoke about taking Christ as your example, using a passage from Philippians, and all through, Johnson felt more at peace than he had for some time. And for once, Millie dozed off and did not make a fuss.

'So what did you think?' asked Susan as she strapped Millie into the child seat. Johnson closed the driver's door and fiddled with the AC. Two hours under a tree had not had any noticeable effect in keeping the Subaru cool. *Although it had produced some truly superb sap and poop splatters,* he thought, ruefully. Susan sat in the passenger seat and closed the door.

'I think on reflection, I could be free next week,' he said.

CHAPTER EIGHT
GEORGINA CAMPBELL AND
BARBARA BRUCHNER

1.

Monday September 5th, 2011

Georgina was drowning again, but this time somebody was with her. She couldn't see who it was exactly, what with the thrashing arms and murky water and long hair plastered over her eyes. But somebody was there in the water with her, and it was a little girl.

Georgina twisted and turned, felt her clothes become heavy and cling to her, dragging her down. Her shoes were dead weights, like someone had tied bricks to her feet and she couldn't kick them off. Her arms flailed, catching the arms of the little girl beside her. She opened her mouth to scream, water filled her lungs...

... and she woke in bed, sheets damp with sweat, breath coming in gulps. Georgina traced the patterns in the cracks in the ceiling and forced her heart to calm down. She was too old for this sort of thing. Keep this up and one day she would wake up dead.

There was a knock at her door. 'Mom, you okay in there? Mom?'

Georgina hurriedly yelled that she was fine, knowing that Barbara would push her way in if she didn't, and Georgina didn't want that. This was her room, her private space. Georgina heard her daughter's footsteps recede to her own room. She let out a long breath.

Why were these nightmares coming now? And what did they mean? She had at least three a week. Why drowning, and who was the little girl?

She remembered the little girl she had seen by the side of the Highway just two weeks ago. Little Cristel Epps. Still missing, despite the attempts of that nice Deputy with the surname for a first name. The one who had visited her home, the one that Janice still mentioned every time Georgina saw her in the street or in her yard.

Maybe little Cristel Epps had drowned. Maybe God was telling her that she was dead and she should tell Deputy Johnson. Would he believe her? Georgina stared at the ceiling and wondered what to do.

So she got up, put on her robe, and made coffee.

Barbara was in the kitchen, wearing a smart pant suit and blouse combination, and finishing a bagel. After two weeks of building up to it, she was ready to start volunteering at the *River Rapids Recorder* offices downtown, and honestly, Georgina would be pleased to see her get out of the house. The past two weeks had been strained between them, to say the least. A bit of space would do them both some good.

'What were you yelling about, mom? Sounds like you were fighting in there!'

'Just a bad dream, darling. It was nothing. Don't even remember what it was about. So, first day then?'

'Yes, and I must be going. Make a good first impression. May be only voluntary now, but Gerald promised to give me something more suited to my abilities - his words - as soon as he could. Maybe even cover the Cristel Epps case. Here's hoping anyway!'

She brushed the bagel crumbs from her blouse, grabbed her purse and keys, and made for the door. 'I'll see you this evening, mom!'

Georgina followed her to the front door, but she was already trotting away along the sidewalk toward downtown. Greg Phillips' United States Postal Service van was parked three doors up, and there he was leaving mail in Janice's mailbox opposite. He waved and she waved back, but she didn't want to have a conversation with him while she was in her robe, so she stepped inside and closed the door.

She turned on the shower, and images of water and drowning and a little girl filled her head again.

By the time she emerged from the shower, the mail had been delivered. A Verizon bill, an exclusive opportunity to own a real part of history by pledging $50 a month for a year for a genuine Aztec death mask, a reminder about an overdue library book, and a handwritten envelope with no return address. Georgina tore it open and pulled out a single sheet of lined paper. On it, in uppercase letters, were the words: *I KNOW WHAT YOU DID TO THAT LITTLE GIRL YOU DISGUSTING MONSTER.*

Georgina flung the paper onto the table. Her knees drained of strength. She fell into a chair, which rocked dangerously beneath her. Her breath caught in her windpipe and came out in gulps. Spots burst before her eyes.

2.

The walk downtown took nearly thirty minutes. Just long enough for Barbara to wonder if she should find a car from *Chuck's Autos* or somewhere. Or maybe a bicycle. Or maybe she should just take the exercise and enjoy the walk. This time of year, the sunshine still strong and the depths of winter still some months away, the walk was actually very pleasant, through the good side of town where each home sprawled in its own grounds, surrounded by carefully maintained trees just starting to turn orange at the tips of the boughs.

A short cut across the Green beside the bandstand brought her out close to Main Street, three blocks from the *River Rapids Recorder* offices. She passed Kelly's Diner, took a moment to check in the window that the walk hadn't completely ruined her hair, and confidently pulled open the front door.

The *Recorder* offices occupied one of the brick-fronted two storey buildings that the mayor's office was keen to call *the historic beating heart of River Rapids* in a largely successful attempt to prevent the decline and dilapidation of the downtown area that so many small towns across the state, and indeed the country, were experiencing. Of course, generous tax breaks and peppercorn rents had a lot to do with it. Coffee culture had also started to hit the town, bringing many formerly empty buildings back to life as cafés. Barbara had found time to sample one or two of them had found to her surprise that the coffee wasn't too bad at all. She was starting to hope that she may not miss DC quite as much as she feared.

Inside, the office was exactly as she expected the office of a small town paper to be. Six or seven desks were scattered about, almost buried under stacks of papers, photos, directories and other paraphernalia. Barbara had already met the staff here, at least twice, but still couldn't confidently say who worked where. She knew Gerald Sumner, overweight, smiley, connected to every bigwig in town, and all round big cheese, spent most of his time in the partitioned office at the back. Annette Goodkind, whom Barbara charitably described as roly-poly, southern (Georgia, going by the accent), and always talking about her kids, usually sat at the desk nearest the window, although Barbara had seen her sitting at the desk in back close to the restrooms, and at the one tucked under the stairs to the archives. Anthony Cryer, Gerald's latest recruit, twenty-three years old, nice smile, bit of a charmer, often sat with a paper cup of coffee at one of the desks, feet up on a pile of papers, shooting the breeze with Annette. He was a bit full of himself, and clearly thought he was Clark Kent, hotshot reporter of *The Daily Planet*, but he was harmless enough.

One person who always worked at the same desk was Gerta Trupp. She used the desk closest to the front door, where she could look out the window and see the people of River Rapids go by. Almost the first thing Annette had told Barbara when she first visited was that nobody, but *nobody,* sits at the front desk but Gerta. Not even Gerald would dare sit there. Gerta had been at the *Recorder* almost since day one, she was the fount of all knowledge about the town and its paper, and many people felt that she really ran it, not Gerald Sumner. Short, painfully thin, and of an indeterminate age that could be anywhere between fifty and eighty, but was probably closer to the latter, she was the source of all gossip.

Annette was on the phone when Barbara walked in. She cupped the receiver, nodded at the office and mouthed, 'He wants to see you.'

'He' could mean only one person. Barbara dropped her bag in a niche somewhere and made her way through the desks and organised chaos to the editor's office at the rear. She patted her hair one last time, knocked, and entered when summoned.

Gerald Sumner sat behind his desk, an enormous wooden edifice that surely couldn't have fitted through the office door, with the corner of a napkin tucked into his collar and the rest draped over the blotter in front of him. Sitting on top of it was a plate piled high with a stack of over-easy eggs, cooked tomatoes, home fries and fried toast, clearly just ordered in from Kelly's Diner, two blocks down. A salt pot and pepper pot in the shape of the Statue of Liberty and the Empire State Building sat ready next to his telephone. Gerald Sumner waved a fork at her, which she took as an invitation to sit, and stared greedily at his repast, jowls aquiver. She sat and watched him shovel forkfuls of breakfast down his gullet and felt vaguely sick.

'So, you're here, are you? You're serious about this whole volunteering thing?'

'Never more so.'

'Just because you were a big-shot writer in DC, doesn't mean you'll fit in here, you know. We do things differently here in River Rapids. More traditional in our approach.'

'I know that, Gerald. I'm not looking to change things or muscle in on anyone. I just want to join in, and if you like my stuff, maybe you can use it on a pro rata basis, no strings attached.'

Gerald grunted and crammed another fork of home fries into his mouth. No wonder the guy had put on the pounds, if he breakfasted like this every morning. He must be headed for a coronary. And each home fry brought it a step nearer. Gerald dabbed his lips with a napkin and said, 'I guess you must have heard about this whole business with the missing girl? Little Cristel Epps? Terrible, terrible.'

Of course Barbara had heard about it. The fate of Cristel Epps had been the talk of the town for two weeks now. Every time Barbara had ventured into a grocery store or a coffee shop, she had heard little Cristel's name mentioned or she had read it in headlines, including headlines from the very paper whose editor was currently stuffing his face right in front of her.

'She's big news in this town,' Gerald said. 'Little girls don't disappear in River Rapids. Not as a rule. Jerry Hartwell over at the *Virginian* beat us to the candy store for an interview with the father, the son of a gun. We managed to get the big brother, but you know what would really send those hard copies flying out the door? I want to nail Bill Millstone to the wall. Really hang that boot-licker out to dry. He's messed up royally this time.' He spat little pieces of egg and quickly mopped them up with his napkin.

Bill Millstone was the local Sheriff, Barbara knew that. She wondered why Gerald had it in for him, but knew better than to ask. Instead, she said, 'You're putting me on the Cristel Epps story?'

Gerald barked laughter until it dissolved into a cough. 'Am I heck. Anthony Cryer needs an assistant on the Cristel Epps story, and you'll do just fine.'

Which was no more than Barbara had expected, really. Still, being assigned to the biggest story in town was a great start, even in an assisting capacity. She found Anthony sitting at a desk in the main office, staring at a computer screen. As she approached, he looked up and flashed her that charming young man smile of his. And despite herself, she found she liked that smile quite a lot.

'Seems we're going to be working together,' she said.

'Cool. Welcome to the *Recorder*. Take a seat.'

He wore his hair in a tidy, winsome cut that looked as trendy today as it probably had in the fifties, an open neck, understated shirt, and tight cut blue jeans that again looked like they had warped forward from the fifties. No twenty-three year old should be so appealing to a forty-something soon-to-be-divorcee, but so far she could find nothing to criticise. She sat in the proffered office chair beside him.

'Barbara, right? I gotta ask, you're Georgina Campbell's daughter?'

'That's right.'

'So you could get her to talk to us?'

'My mother? Why?'

'Well, you know. She was the last person to clap eyes on Cristel.'

Barbara blinked. Her mouth opened but nothing came out.

'You knew that, right?' Anthony said.

'Yes, of course. Right.'

But she hadn't. Her mother had kept that little nugget

secret. What else wasn't she telling her? And why, at that very moment, sitting there in front of Anthony Cryer with the cute smile, could she think of nothing but the image of her mother trying to hide the dolls in her bedroom closet? Dolls that belonged to a little girl.

Anthony showed her the file on the Cristel Epps story. The *West Virginian* had scooped them when it came to talking to the little girl's father, but Anthony had saved the day by getting Kennedy Epps, the big brother, to do an interview. 'And when I say big brother, I mean *big* brother,' Anthony said. 'The guy is an amateur bodybuilder. Already won awards in the state under eighteen championships. And you know what? Sales that issue were the year's best so far. Always helps sales to put a buff guy on the cover. The old man was delighted.' Anthony nodded toward Gerald's office.

Anthony was preparing a new piece slamming Sheriff Bill Millstone and the River Rapids Police Department. 'It's been two weeks and the police have got nowhere. No arrests. Not even an obvious suspect. They haven't even found Cristel's body. Gerald's going to write an editorial calling for Bill Millstone's resignation.'

'What do you want me to do?'

'Talk to your mother. See if you can get her to say something critical of the PD. Something we can use. In fact, quotes from any prominent citizen or interested party will bolster the piece.'

Barbara decided to go for the top and spent much of the day speaking to different people at the mayor's department, attempting to convince them that Mayor Vance should give the *Recorder* an exclusive interview. She approached it from the angle of publicizing the mayor's big Fall PR opportunity, the city funded Halloween event to be held by the bandstand on the Green. She could ask plenty of approved questions, all designed to shine a glowing light on Mayor Vance and his office, improve public morale and increase his chances of re-election, and then at the end she would wrong-foot him by sneaking in some questions about Cristel Epps and the competence of the RRPD.

Barbara thought she was getting somewhere with a departmental assistant called Chris, who had at least promised to run it past the Mayor. Another couple of phone calls and she may actually pull this off. She was feeling good - she had missed the buzz of a newsroom since leaving DC, even a small outfit like this - and when they all trooped out to lunch at Kelly's Diner two blocks down Main, Barbara was happy to accompany them.

They squeezed into a booth - Barbara, Anthony, Annette and Gerta - and passed around menus. A specials board (mac and cheese, fried chicken in a Cajun sauce, vegetarian burger) was posted above the counter that ran the length of the rear wall. The diner was busy this time of the day. It seemed that almost everybody who worked in the downtown district, and most of the shoppers spending their money here, had popped into Kelly's for lunch. Most of the tables were occupied, and the diner was full of bustle and noise. Again, Barbara felt like she had rejoined real life and she liked it. For once, he-who-must-not-be-named had no part in her life.

She ordered Kelly's burger - double patty, lettuce, tomato, pickles, eggplant, drizzled in Kelly's unique burger sauce, and famous throughout the state of West Virginia, apparently - Anthony took the Cajun chicken,

Annette ordered a whopping steak with all the trimmings, and Gerta took the homemade meatloaf with gravy.

Gerta took the lead in the conversation, asking if anybody had heard the rumours about Brenda Connelly over at the library getting it together with Harry McCarthy - who runs the mercantile, she helpfully informed Barbara - after a drunken night at the Red Onion Bar and Grill out at the Clayton Creek Mall, *not* a pairing that Gerta would have seen coming in a million years, although she did happen to know that Brenda's bosses at the city's public amenities department were not happy about the liaison and were thinking about reviewing her position. Barbara smiled to herself at small town politics and tucked into her burger, which certainly did seem to be as tasty as promised.

'Does anybody know why Gerald has it in for Sheriff Millstone?' she asked.

'That's easy,' Gerta said. 'Because back in oh two, both of them ran for Sheriff. Bill Millstone won and Gerald's been consoling himself ever since by piling on the pounds. That's the thing about Gerald Sumner: He'll hold a grudge until the day he eats one too many home fries and his ticker gives out. So just you make sure you don't drool on his donuts, that's all.'

Barbara smiled again. Drool on his donuts? She hadn't heard that one before. Although she remembered thinking the exact same thing about the home fries when she had watched him cram his face with them in his office that morning.

Annette received a text message from her eldest, informing her that he was studying late that night and she shouldn't wait up.

'He's such a hard worker,' she said. 'Studies all hours. Do you know, three colleges have offered him a place? Gonna be a lawyer, make his mom so proud.'

Barbara wondered where Annette's son was really spending his evenings that he didn't want his mom knowing about, and then chided herself for being cynical. Maybe the boy was the world's only hard-working teenager, after all.

The conversation drifted on to Annette's younger son, who was top of his class, acing everything that could be aced, and destined for great things. Gerta soon pulled it back to Gerald and his inability to grasp what sold papers in twenty-first century River Rapids, and if only he would follow her suggestions they could reverse the *Recorder's* falling sales and stop it disappearing like so many small town newspapers these days.

'What it needs is dynamic, modern reporting on the issues that matter to the readers,' said Anthony. 'The community's newspaper at the heart of the community.'

'What it needs is to get back to basics,' Gerta said. 'No chasing sensations or jumping on bandwagons. Leave the gimmicks behind and report the truth.'

'We've got to give the people what they want,' Anthony said. 'Make them feel connected to the world even here in the backwoods of West Virginia.'

'Nobody cares what color Kim Kardashian's panties are, and if they do, they won't come to the *Recorder* to find out. We are not a celebrity rag! Low brow celebrity websites are a dime a dozen!'

'Speaking of which, we need to launch an online edition and build up a list of subscribers. Readers want to access content on their computers and Kindles now. If we don't keep up with the times, we'll disappear!'

This was clearly a well worn debate. Annette rolled her eyes and busied herself tucking into her steak. Barbara leaned back and enjoyed feeling part of the world again, even if it were only the world according to the *River Rapids Recorder.*

By the time Barbara had walked home, she felt good. The best she'd felt since she'd walked out on you-know-who. For the first time in a long time, she could see forward momentum in her life. Okay, so this was hardly the big city, but maybe the familiarity and charm of small town America was just what she needed right now. *The Recorder's* readership was a fraction of the readership enjoyed by the human interest/celebrity gossip magazine she'd worked on in DC, but right now that didn't seem to matter at all. The people at the *Recorder* were decent, she enjoyed spending time with them, and best of all, her soon to be ex husband knew nothing about them. She could easily do six months here, get her life back on track, then perhaps move back to the city if she missed it. Perhaps not even DC. She could try Charleston or Richmond. Maybe even Savannah or Chattanooga. Or perhaps Atlanta! That would be something! Barbara Bruchner in Atlanta!

She turned the key and pushed open the front door, cheerily calling, 'Hi, mom! It's me! I'm back! You here?'

She received no response, and so jumped out of her skin when she walked into the kitchen to find her mother sitting at the table, staring out of the window.

'Mom? What are you doing, sitting in here in your bathrobe? Are you ill?'

Georgina still didn't respond. Barbara set her bag down on the countertop. 'Mom, have you been sitting here all day? You haven't, have you? Mom, what's wrong? You're scaring me!'

It was then that Barbara noticed the sheet of paper on the table and what was written on it.

3.

Georgina felt better after draining a huge mug of coffee. The sense of the whole world staring at her faded with her daughter in the room and caffeine in her blood. Especially when Barbara drew the drapes. Of course, Barbara had a million questions (*Who wrote it? Why do they think you had anything to do with the disappearance of Cristel Epps? Oh yes, and why didn't you tell me you were the last one to see her before she disappeared?*) that she couldn't answer. All she could think of was her nightmare. The little girl - Cristel Epps? - struggling in the water, drowning, while Georgina pulled herself out to safety. And now she thought of it, there was a voice. A voice so very distant, begging for help.

'Did you call the police? We should call the police!'

'No! No! I don't want the police! It's just a prank. Somebody's idea of a joke. The police have a little girl to find.'

'But this might have something to do with their investigation, mom! We must tell them!'

'No! I won't waste their time.'

Eventually, Barbara had to settle with a promise that the police would be called if another letter arrived. Georgina watched her daughter stomp off upstairs, clearly unhappy with her mother's decision. Not the first time, and certainly not the last. Barbara had always been headstrong, even as a girl growing up. Would never take advice or listen to anybody else's suggestions. Georgina had had to be really quite firm with her in the past. And even now there seemed always to be a power struggle whenever they spent time together. Of course, if Barbara had listened to her earlier, she would still be happy married and Georgina would have a gaggle of grandchildren to spoil.

Why didn't she want to tell the police? Did she really think it would waste their time? No, that wasn't it. She didn't want to tell the police because she was afraid. She was afraid that she had blocked some traumatic experience from her memory, something involving a little girl.

She was afraid she really did have something to do with Cristel Epps' disappearance and she just couldn't remember. What if it were her fault that the girl was missing?

Her eye caught the letter still lying crumpled on the table. Maybe she really was a disgusting monster.

4.

Tuesday September 13th, 2011

Georgina set the envelope on the kitchen table and considered what she should do. As soon as Barbara got back from the paper she would insist that they inform the police, and Georgina knew she couldn't resist twice. The Sheriff would take a dim enough view as it was. If Georgina didn't report it this time, she would likely be committing a felony or something. Eight days had passed and Georgina was daring to hope the first letter had been a once only anomaly, some kind of sick joke that the prankster had got out of their system.

But that would have been too easy. The second letter was waiting for her in her mailbox that morning, along with an electricity bill, a notification about a forthcoming Neighborhood Watch meeting and an invitation to own a Lord of the Rings pewter chess set for a super low subscription price of $19.99 per piece. She recognized the handwritten capitals and hadn't even opened it. She told herself that Barbara could open it if she wanted, or even the police. She told herself she didn't want to know what it said.

So she made herself a coffee, stirred in the required the teaspoons of sugar, lowered herself into her favorite armchair, read today's verses from *The Scripture for Today* (Matthew chapter three, John baptizes Jesus and the symbolism of the River Jordan) and prayed for guidance.

That done, and feeling much calmer, she put on her coat - after all, it was September now and the weather could get cold any moment - picked out a Gucci bag Ardal had bought her for their thirtieth anniversary, checked she had her purse, keys, glasses, gloves, scarf, lip balm, moisturizer, phone, charger and anything else she may, possibly need, parked herself behind the wheel of her Nissan, clicked the remote on her key chain that opened the garage doors, and started the engine.

She turned right out of her cul-de-sac onto Columbia and made her way toward Clayton Creek Mall on the edge of town. She remembered when the whole area had been farmland, but inevitable urban expansion had set in back in the eighties and now even the roads leading to the mall were packed with outlets: Starbucks, A&W, H&R Block, Chipotle, Sonic, Buffalo Wings and Dips, Quiznos, the list went on and on. But Georgina ignored them and turned into the huge parking lot fronting the Clayton Creek Mall. She parked as close to the entrance to *Clayton Creek Fashions* as she could, idly wondered why there were so many handicapped spaces when they were always empty, killed the engine, beeped the door behind her, and walked confidently to the store.

A photo of Cristel Epps - the same school photo all the papers had - was posted to the window. The word MISSING was printed under it in bright red. Georgina didn't bother reading the entreaties to call the police underneath.

She walked through the automatic doors into the warehouse style space packed full of racks of clothes. She smiled when she saw the ordered neatness and the signs pointing the way to *underwear, casualwear, formal wear, house wear, garden wear* and many others. An associate greeted her and asked if she could help with anything today. Georgina replied that she would love to see a selection of beautiful dresses for all occasions.

Georgina spent the following two hours trying on various dresses, and then various shoes to go with the various dresses, and then various bags to go with the various shoes and dresses, until finally she had made her selection. She accompanied the associate to the cash desk, who carefully scanned the purchases and informed Georgina that the total was $724.25 including tax. Georgina calmly handed over her MasterCard. Another photo of Cristel Epps had been posted behind the desk.

This had a *How You Can Help* list beneath it, which asked the townsfolk of River Rapids to check their outhouses, barns and crawlspaces, to report any neighbor who may have unexpectedly acquired an extra child in the household, report any suspicious behavior, and pray for Cristel's safe return to her family.

Georgina dragged her eyes away from the poster and returned her attention to the girl who was serving her. Her purchases were smartly boxed and brought to her car. Georgina thanked the associate who carried them and generously tipped him.

When she pulled out of the parking lot, she felt better than she had for a long time. Ready perhaps to face whatever curve balls life pitched at her.

Home again, she parked the Nissan, hit the control to lower the garage door, and carried her purchases past the kitchen table, where the unopened envelope still sat, and up to her bedroom, where she opened her new packages and admired them in the mirror on her wardrobe door, the only mirror that always showed her to best advantage. The new dress was a finely-balanced combination of cream and burgundy, embroidered with delicate flower patterns with a hint of China in them. The sleeves finished just above the elbow, the hem reached her calves, just as she liked. And just as she hoped, it looked wonderful. Especially with the matching bag and burgundy shoes. One more job to do and she would be ready.

She unzipped her skirt, and began to change.

Ready at last, confident that whoever was sending her these letters had not ruined her day, or indeed, affected it in any way, she returned to the kitchen, smoothed down her new dress, and opened the letter.

*HOW DO YOU SLEEP AT NIGHT KNOWING WHAT YOU
DID TO THAT LITTLE GIRL? I'LL MAKE YOU SORRY.*

Georgina wept as she sat at the table. Then she walked calmly to the phone and called the police.

A little less than two hours later, Deputy Fincher pulled up in his squad car outside. She remembered him from his previous visit - what was it? - three weeks ago. Then the prospect of a police officer visiting her home had been thrilling. Janice across the street had been jealous for days. Now Georgina could imagine Janice sitting over there shaking her head in disapproval at the goings on, watching Deputy Fincher approach her neighbor's front door for the second time in a month. Georgina quickly let him in.

'Deputy Fincher, thank you for coming again so soon. Despite the circumstances. How are you getting on with finding little Cristel? Would you like a beverage? No lemonade this time I'm afraid, but I can certainly do you some delicious ice tea.'

The Deputy politely declined, as she knew he would. She led him into the living room. His reassuring presence already made her fears seem small. When they were sitting, she handed him the two letters and allowed him time to read them. She tried to read the thoughts on his face, but his expression remained calm. She tried to guess his age and put him down somewhere in his late thirties or early forties. Hair just starting to turn gray above the ears, lines just becoming visible around his mouth. Just about her daughter's age. Only, the deputy would be happily married, of course.

'Nobody has tried to harm you, Mrs Campbell?' asked the deputy. 'You haven't noticed anybody follow you in the

165

street or in your car? You haven't noticed the same car in different places?'

'No, I don't think so.'

'No threatening phone calls?'

'Only the letters.'

'And have you any idea why somebody would associate you with the disappearance of Cristel Epps? Think carefully before you answer, please.'

This was the moment she could have come clean. This was when she could have said, *I think I have gaps in my memory. I think she may be dead. Drowned. And I think I may have drowned her.* She could have unburdened her soul, allowed the truth to emerge, and paid whatever penance she owed. Instead, she said, 'Beyond the fact that I was the last one to see her, I can't think of any reason at all, deputy. I haven't even met her.'

'If any further letters arrive, keep them for me,' he said. 'Record when they arrive. And if anything else happens. Phone calls. You suspect somebody's following you. Record it all and let me know immediately. And try not to worry. Mostly these things turn out to be some sad loner with too much time on his hands and a twisted need for vicarious attention. When things get too hot, they quickly back off.'

Barbara arrived just as Deputy Fincher was leaving. Georgina told her about the second letter. 'You did the right thing calling the cops, mom,' she said. She made coffee and asked her mother about her day, but Georgina seemed to be distracted. She brushed Barbara's concerns aside and said she was going to take a nap. 'I can feel one of my migraines coming on,' she said.

Barbara watched her mother climb the stairs. Barbara

knew Georgina hadn't been sleeping well recently. More than once her mother's screams had woken her in the early hours. She'd rush into her mother's room to find her wide eyed and breathing deeply. She found accounting for her time more and more difficult, her memory apparently full of gaps.

Was it possible that Georgina had been the last to see Cristel alive because she had had something to do with her disappearance?

Was it possible that she really didn't know her mother at all?

CHAPTER NINE
DARYL EPPS

I lose track of days. Tuesday, Wednesday, Thursday. They're all the same to me. School, if I make it. The cannery or our hideout, if I don't. Or maybe the library. I'm risking the library more and more now because it's too cold to be outside all day. But sooner or later, Brenda is going to call the school and find out why I'm not there. I tell her I have special release to research a project on Ancient Egypt or the War of Independence and she kinda believes me, but I can't say that too often. All it takes is for her to amble over to the phone and call the school and I'll be in big trouble and likely banned from the library too. I try to wait until three o'clock before I go, but that makes the day long and miserable and so very difficult to fill.

One Tuesday in October - or maybe it was a Wednesday or Thursday, I'm not sure - I go to the library with Nathan and Amelia. Nathan's got a thing for the Encyclopedia Britannica right now. He takes a random volume from the shelf, and each book is as big as a cinderblock, heaves it over to the reading area and lets it fall open at any entry. Within seconds, he's absorbed in native South American birds or how to mix concrete or the function of blood platelets, or something. He loves it. *Encyclopedia Rouletta*, he calls it. Amelia gets the TV listings magazines and makes a little pile of them to read. I usually head for the Horror section and pick up a Stephen King or a Dean Koontz. Brenda always purses her lips and tuts disapprovingly, but she doesn't stop me.

Today, I sit at a reading desk with a paperback of *Carrie* with a cracked spine, skimming to find my favorite part with the pig's blood. I am kinda aware that Amelia hasn't gone straight for the TV mags like she usually does. She hovers uncertainly. In the corner of my eye, I see her sit beside Nathan and whisper something to him. Whatever she says makes him pull his head out of the Encyclopedia Britannica and stare at her with raised eyebrows. They both look at me and I wonder if they were talking about me. A crazy voice in my head says they don't want me around and they're plotting ways to lose me. I tell the crazy voice to shut up.

Amelia walks over to me, past the science fiction section and a display of books by black writers, past the magazine rack and up to the reading desk where I'm sitting. I lay *Carrie* down.

'I've got something to tell you, Daryl. Some news. Bad news.'

My face tingles. Either I've gone pale or I'm blushing: I can't tell which. What is she going to say? She loves Nathan more than me? I know that already.

'We're moving,' she says. 'Mom and dad told me last night. They've sold our house. We're moving to Tallahassee. That's in Florida. River Rapids isn't safe anymore. Because of what happened to your sister. That's what they say. It isn't the same and it's time to move.'

My chest hurts and I don't know what to say. No words enter my head. None. Only a long loud scream begging to come out. I don't remember running out of the library. My chest hurts so much everything is a kinda blur. I must have run down Main Street, probably startling an old lady or a mom with a stroller. I must have turned left behind Harry's Mercantile and come to a dusty halt by the dumpsters. Cold air wheezes through my lungs, making my chest hurt even more. Breath steams from my nostrils like I'm smoking a cigarette. A cat paws through the mess spilled from the dumpster, darts away when it sees me.

I yell and scream. I kick the dumpster five times - *clang! clang! clang! clang! clang!* I let tears tumble down my face and neck. Then I fling myself into a narrow space against the wall and sob.

Mom abandoned me. Dad and Debra hate me. Ken wants to kill me. Cristel ran away from me. And now even Amelia is leaving me. It's not fair! Why me? Why me? What have I done to deserve this? Now I know I'm right, don't I? Now I know I'm right about what I said about God. He's way too busy to care about me. He's too busy making sure the planets don't crash and the stars don't explode. Even He done gone and left.

I don't know how long I stay wedged into the narrow space round back of Harry's. I lose track of days, I lose track of hours. At some point, I notice my hands have gone blue and numb. At another point, I notice how hungry I am. But there's nothing I can do about either thing, so I just stay where I am. I watch pickups go past on the other side of the vacant lot behind Harry's. I wonder who dumped a stack of tires on the vacant lot, and how long ago. I wonder if I could somehow sit here and rewind time long enough, maybe I would see whoever it was who dumped them and ask him, *Hey, why don't you take your tires to the town dump, huh? Why don't you dump them with all the other garbage, huh? Why do you dump them there, where they're just gonna sit for years until they're covered in weeds, huh, huh, huh?* Behind the stack of tires, the other side of the road where the pickups drive, that's the block where Frank's Gym is. My brother is probably in there right now, curling dumbbells, lifting barbells, doing whatever it is meatheads do. But he won't see me, squeezed in this narrow gap behind Harry's. Here, I'm safe. Safe from big brothers beating me up. Safe from people leaving me.

'I've been looking for you forever!' Nathan says as he sits next to me. 'Been to the hideout, been up the cannery. Thought you'd disappeared like your sister.' He hands me a *Mr Goodbar* candy bar. I tear off the wrapper and cram it in my mouth.

'I see why she disappeared now,' I say between bits of chocolate and peanut. 'Beats staying in this doggone town where everything turns to crud.'

'She doesn't want to leave. It's her stupid parents. It's not her fault.'

I know that, of course. Deep down. Not Amelia's fault, blah blah. But she's still leaving. Going down to Florida where the sun always shines and little girls don't disappear.

'You'll be next,' I say. 'Your mom'll say to your dad, why don't we move somewhere nice? And your dad'll do whatever she wants, and then you'll be gone too.'

'I wish. My ma grew up here. No way she'll go to Florida. And even if she does, I won't go unless we take you with us.'

He puts his arm round my neck and I pull him close, because he's my best friend and he's all I've got left. We still have our arms round each other's shoulders when we get back to the bike rack outside the library. The library is closed now, empty and dark like a graveyard for dead books. We cycle home. At the Cedar Creek turn off, he drops me off, waves and says he'll see me tomorrow. I keep on keeping on along Quaker Mill Lane, then the side of the freeway, then right at the 7Eleven onto County Road Six. I jog, my feet in a rhythm, the tarmac slides beneath my keds like an endless ribbon. Keep following this ribbon long enough, I could end up anywhere. I could go see Amelia in her new house in Florida. I could find mom and Cristel watching TV or playing Monopoly in a perfect little house next to a road somewhere, just waiting for me to come join them. I could go to Hollywood, star in a movie. *Daryl Epps as SuperDaryl, the greatest superhero the world has ever known!* I could watch the sea crash against the shore, get on a boat and sail to Hawaii or Europe. All I have to do is keep running and follow the ribbon.

I wake up later that night when Ken bursts in drunk with Hayley. He throws me out of our room because he wants to have sex with her. I clear a space on the sofa and try to sleep. I think of Amelia and fresh tears fill my eyes. I do not let them fall.

Next day at school, I don't speak to her all day. I know it's not her fault and I don't want to make her feel bad, but I can't think of any words to say. My brain freezes when I think of her mom and dad making plans to leave. Boxing up their things. Booking a U-Haul. Enrolling her in a new school. She's upset, I know, and I want to tell her I'm sorry and I know it's not her fault. I want to, but I can't.

At recess, she sits with Shona and Shaniqua and doesn't look at me.

For three days, we don't talk. Then, suddenly, she's there, sitting next to me and Nathan at the table in the lunchroom, making little stacks of cracker, cheese and ham with her Lunchables, and I give her some mini-pretzels and she gives me some Oreos, and Nathan laughs and everything's good. He picks up a *Baby Ruth* candy bar and says did I know there was a baseball player in the olden days called Babe Ruth, and he hit more homeruns than anyone in the world, like, ever? And suddenly we're talking about the time Nathan hit a homerun at the Little League diamond in Ryland Park and Mr Parker, the ump, had to duck and he got mad and thought Nathan had tried to hit him on purpose, and Nathan's dad got mad and they started yelling. 'Of course,' says Nathan, proudly, 'they didn't know I really *did* try to hit him because he was a bad ump and his kid played on the other team so he wanted them to win!'

Recess ends. In class, Miss Stevens tries to tell us that triangles are exciting and fun because they come in different types. I pass notes to Nathan, who passes them to Amelia, until Drew Goddard rats us out. It's like Amelia never mentioned she was leaving, and maybe that's for the best. Act like it's not happening. Enjoy the time we've got. Cling to the hope that maybe her dad will change his mind.

Two weeks pass and we're hanging out on the bench outside the 7Eleven. It's early, school ended thirty minutes ago, and there's no sign of big kids yet. I keep my eyes open, because when the big kids come, we'll have to leave.

They like to smoke and curse and they don't like little kids in their hangouts.

Nathan sucks the juice out of a grape popsicle. Amelia licks a snow cone. I slurp a fountain Dr Pepper.

'You gonna come say goodbye?' she says suddenly, and it's the first time we've mentioned her leaving in two weeks. 'The U-Haul comes Saturday. Mom and Dad already started packing boxes. You gotta come say goodbye.'

Again, my brain freezes up. But Nathan says, 'We'll be there. Can't miss it. Chance to get in the way, create some chaos. I'm there! And you know what, Daryl, bound to be some quality stuff they're throwing away. Got my eyes on that ice cream maker in the kitchen.'

I nod dumbly. All I can think of is *Saturday*. That's only three days away. Three days and I'll never see Amelia again. I toss the Dr Pepper cup in the trash. Tears are stinging my eyes again, but I can't let Amelia see I'm crying. Not again. I mutter something about seeing them at school tomorrow, and then I'm gone.

But I don't make it to school the next day. Dad is already awake when I get up. He's still drunk from the night before and I don't think he's been asleep at all. He and Debra had a row. They have rows all the time. He tells me to clean up all the trash. I tell him I have to go to school. He slaps me across the face and tells me to do as I'm told. By the time I get out of there, the school bus has long gone, and I can't face turning up late at school with a red face. I think about hanging out at the library again, but it's too risky. Brenda might report me. Instead, I spend the day in Jefferson's Wood looking for Cristel and finding diddly with a side of squat.

Matthew Link

Friday is Amelia's last day at school. I keep my head down most of the day and Miss Stevens doesn't ask me where I was yesterday. We all sign a goodbye card for Amelia. All the kids write 'good luck' in it so I do too because I don't want to be different. But while I do it, I think again of her cherry-flavored lips against mine. I tell myself to get real, that would never have happened anyway. But Amelia is special. And now she's going away forever.

The first thing I think of when I wake on Saturday morning is that Amelia is going away today. I don't want to get up. I think if I stay in bed maybe this day will never happen. Ken is snoring and I pull the comforter over my head and try to sleep, but I can't. I'm desperate to pee, so I tiptoe to the bathroom. Dad's either in bed or he didn't come home last night. The trailer is quiet.

I'm looking for cereal for breakfast when I see Nathan cycle up the drive. My heart leaps. Nathan doesn't come here much, but today he's made the effort. I know why he's here, but it's still great to see him. He sees me through the window and jerks his head: *Let's make like a tree and leave!* I sneak out of the trailer without telling anyone, and seconds later I'm on the back of Nathan's bike, whizzing down County Road Six, cold air on my face and wind in my hair.

We stop at the end of Amelia's road. I see her house on the bend, a U-Haul truck parked on the drive and a trailer attached to their car. The front lawn is full of boxes, every door and window is open. Amelia sits on a box, swinging her legs, watching her parents run this way and that. Looks like they've requisitioned help from somewhere. Likely other family members.

'You're not gonna blub, are you?' says Nathan.

I shake my head.

'You wouldn't have come if I hadn't got you,' he says, and although I hadn't thought about it, I realize he's right.

We ride the rest of the way. Amelia runs up to us as we approach, and I can see she's relieved to see us.

'They're driving me crazy,' she says. 'Everything I do is wrong, everywhere I sit I'm in the way. The house is empty. Doesn't even look like a house anymore.'

Nathan cheerily waves to Amelia's dad, and although he tries to hide it, I can see he's not pleased we're here. More kids getting in the way. Nathan asks if we can help, but Mr Michaelson shakes his head and tells us the best thing we can do right now is to find somewhere far away to play. His face is red and sweat patches stain his underarms. Nathan shrugs and we wander to the grocery store at the end of Amelia's road. Time for one last popsicle together.

Amelia's been crying. Her eyes are red. We suck cola popsicles but none us has much to say, not even Nathan. If Amelia starts crying again, I think I will too.

After what seems like only a few moments, we hear Mr Michaelson calling. It's time to say goodbye. Nathan goes first. He hugs her.

'Don't forget us,' he says. 'As soon as my mom lets me have Facebook, I'll look you up.'

'Me too,' she says. 'You'll be my first two friends.'

She's crying again and so am I. We hug and as we pull apart, I kiss her on the cheek. I didn't know I was going to do it, it just kinda happened. I'm ready to shrivel up and turn bright red like roadkill, but she kisses me right back. I catch a moment of the cherry chapstick she always wears. When I open my eyes, she is already running up the road toward her house.

Nathan and I watch. The last of the boxes have been crammed into the U-haul and the trailer. Mr Michaelson climbs into the cab of the U-haul. Mrs Michaelson and Amelia sit in the car with the trailer attached. We wave. We shout goodbyes and promises to call and visit. The vehicles pull away, honk at the end of the street, turn the corner, and are gone.

And I know that despite the promises to be Facebook friends, to call, to visit, I know that I will never see Amelia Michaelson again.

Nathan and I put our arms around each other's shoulders and stand there on the sidewalk for a long, long time.

CHAPTER TEN
GEORGINA CAMPBELL AND BARBARA BRUCHNER

1.

Monday October 24th, 2011

The *River Rapids Recorder* offices were a headache to heat. Gerald had run to the expense of installing two electric heaters, but all they managed to do was heat a foot of air directly around them, leaving the rest of the high-ceilinged room so frigid Barbara could see her breath. She had taken to wearing a coat at her desk and typing with gloves on: no easy task.

'Of course, he's toasty in that office,' grumbled Annette, wrapping her hands around her coffee mug. 'Exactly the same last year. Wouldn't do anything then either, the cheapskate.'

'What we need,' said Anthony, 'is an interview with the brother. The younger one. Drum up some interest. Say it will jog people's memories, go for that angle. We could make it fly.'

More than two months had passed since Cristel

Epps disappeared and no developments had been forthcoming. Donald Epps had been questioned about the discovery of the dead body of his wife in Jefferson's Wood, but he still hadn't been arrested. There had been no arrests concerning Cristel either. No sightings. No body. Nothing. One Charleston paper, not entirely seriously, had theorized that she had been abducted by aliens. What other explanation could there be for her apparent disappearance off the face of the earth, and the evident failure of the police to find either her or whoever was responsible? Nine weeks in and the inevitable was starting to happen: interest was waning.

And the one member of the Epps family who hadn't spoken to the press was the little brother, Daryl.

'What's the legal position regarding talking to children?' Barbara asked. 'We'd never get permission from the father.'

'So we go under the radar,' Anthony said. 'Run into him on his way home from school. You know, accidentally. Big coincidence. Just chatting, that's all.'

'You talked to any of my kids without me being there, I'd slap you up and down Main,' said Annette.

Two weeks ago, Barbara had bought a used Honda from *Chuck's Autos,* mostly as protection from the cold on her way to work in the mornings. A bent spring jabbed her backside and the right indicator blinked way too fast, but the heater worked a treat and anything that gave her a little more independence from her mother was worth every cent. The first few days she went out for a drive every night, reveling in her newfound freedom and daring to feel like an adult again for the first time since she'd left DC. She had even gone for a spin past the Epps trailer out on County Road Six. She hadn't dared stop and get out, but she had slowed way down and had a good look. The place had looked dark and empty to her. No signs of life at all.

But the school... River Rapids Elementary was an altogether different prospect. Figuring that Daryl Epps likely attended River Rapids rather than the upmarket Appalachian Elementary across town, Barbara pulled the Honda to a stop across the street just before three pm and watched the big, double entrance door.

'I used to go here,' said Anthony from the bucket seat. 'Eight years, Pre-K through sixth grade.'

'Last week in your case, right? I went to Appalachian.'

'Figures.'

'What do you mean by that?'

'We used to cream your preppy hides at football.'

'Yeah? At least we could spell football.'

'You ever regret leaving?'

'River Rapids? No. I've made a lot of mistakes, but leaving River Rapids wasn't one of them. Mind you, here I am, back again like I've never been away.'

'Has it changed?'

'Not at all. The same town, the same people living the same lives. Only change in River Rapids is the malls get bigger. What about you, Tony? You got ambitions for the big city?'

'I don't know. Guess it depends on the right opportunity. The right woman.'

Barbara pressed her lips together and stared at the entrance to the school. She couldn't think of anything to say that didn't sound like some sort of line. More than fifteen years separated them, for goodness sake! Anthony couldn't possibly be interested in her, and it wouldn't work if he were. *You're just feeling lonely because your marriage collapsed, Barbara, so just you leave the young guy alone! And while you're at it, stop reading double meanings into everything he says!* Barbara decided to listen to the voice of reason and focus her mind on the job at hand.

'I wonder if old Mr Davenport still teaches sixth grade?' Anthony was saying. 'He must be close to retirement if he is. Funny old codger. He made chocolates. Truffles, he called them. Always had boxes stashed. Used to hand them out sometimes. I remember once he mistakenly gave us truffles with sherry in them. Got into big trouble over that! And there was Miss Juniper. All the boys fancied her. She used to wear these tight sweaters and... anyway. The things you remember, eh?'

Barbara raised an eyebrow at him, feeling like his mother. 'Two things, apparently!'

She was relieved when a bell rang at the school over the road, and moments later the double doors burst open to emit a crowd of brightly colored kids all with backpacks and book bags, all yelling and pushing and jumping on each other's backs. Many bounced round to the side of the school where several long, yellow buses with *River Rapids Elementary* written on the sides waited with engines idling. Others poured onto the sidewalk and the street, and Barbara suddenly wondered if she would recognize Daryl Epps even if she saw him. She had only ever seen a picture, and many of these kids looked alike with their footballer style haircuts and boyband style clothes. Maybe this wasn't such a good idea after all.

'There he is,' said Anthony suddenly, pointing at a kid crossing the street just ahead. He was a shrimpy looking kid, gangly and bony, looked like he spent most of his days avoiding getting beat up. He kept his head mostly downcast, his collar turned up. His backpack hung listlessly from one shoulder. The boy next to him looked bigger, sturdier, looked like he would be more likely to give as good as he got.

'Come on then,' said Barbara, reaching for the door handle.

'Wait! We'll follow him a ways. Put a bit of distance between us and the school. More chance of getting him alone.'

Barbara was doubtful. They were already courting trouble just talking to the kid. Surely stalking him first would just ice the cake? But Anthony was already complaining that they'd lose him, so she pulled out and negotiated her way between the pickups, ATVs, SUVs and tanks parents drove to school to collect their kids in these days.

Daryl and his buddy ambled to the end of the street and turned right onto Grand. Three blocks down, they turned off the sidewalk onto a trail leading into a section of Jefferson's Wood. Already feeling uncomfortably conspicuous at following a couple of kids down the street (especially in a town jittery about the safety of its kids), Barbara pulled over and popped the driver's door.

'Wait a moment,' Anthony said. 'Where are they going?'

'Does it matter? We don't catch them now, we'll never find them in Jefferson's Wood.'

'I want to see where they're going. Come on, we'll follow them on foot.'

The last thing Barbara wanted was to stomp about in

cold, muddy woods, especially in her best Jimmy Choos, but she found herself worried that Tony would think she was prissy or old. Annoyed at herself for even caring what he thought of her, she kept her lips pressed firmly together and followed him following Daryl along the trail. The sun was already lowering toward the horizon, leaving lengthening shadows and a chilly, gathering mist. *If this were a horror movie,* Barbara thought, *or a TV crime series, this is when the heroic but flawed protagonist would discover the dead body abandoned in the woods. Fade to black with a sting of incidental music, cue commercials. Return to Act Two, with police tape and people in hazmat suits swarming gingerly over the site, and a sheriff shaking his head and wondering how such a terrible thing could happen in his small town.* She found herself half expecting to see the dead face of Cristel Epps peering at her from the undergrowth. With a grimace, she pulled her shoe out of a patch of sucking mud.

'Tony, this is ridiculous. Why don't we just talk to the kid already? How are we going to convince anybody we just ran across him in the middle of the woods?'

'They're going to the old cannery.'

'What?'

'You know, the old factory out on County Line Road. This trail comes out there, I'm sure it does. You never play there as a kid?'

'No, Tony. Because when I was a kid, the old factory was actually still a factory.'

'Right, yeah. Well, we can talk to them there. Perfect place. Nobody will see us.'

They stomped through the woods for nearly forty-five minutes. Barbara fell silent after the first ten, and gave up trying to keep her shoes mud free and her hands warm after fifteen. She was seriously contemplating insisting that they turn back and find somewhere warm for a coffee, and he could pay, when at last the birches and spruces began to thin out and they arrived at a chain link fence. Tony found a section where the links had been detached from the frame and pulled the mesh up, revealing a triangular gap just large enough to squeeze through. Barbara looked doubtfully at the space, saw how mud-splattered her shoes already were and shrugged. Going through was preferable to going back through the mud again, right? But she made Tony hold the mesh while she maneuvered through, to reduce the risk of her clothes catching.

They walked across a cracked parking lot to the smashed hulk of a building. A long time ago, whoever had designed the building had tried to liven it up with a touch of Art Deco, but now the curving windows were broken or missing, and the tall fluting crown above the main entrance had almost vanished beneath peeling paint. The doors were boarded over, but one corner had been snapped off, meaning another undignified crouch and hop to get in, but Barbara had come too far to quit now.

Inside was dark and dingy and strewn with broken furniture, cracked tiles, and piles of Pepsi bottles and cigarette butts. They walked through what had once been the reception area and through a doorway onto the factory floor. The vast open space was empty of the machines and conveyors that must once have filled it, but still contained dozens of pillars, corners and crannies perfect for hiding in.

'Can't believe your parents let you come here,' Barbara said.

'They didn't.'

'I don't see Daryl anywhere.'

Tony suddenly yelled, 'Daryl Epps, we know you're in here! We just want to talk to you, that's all!'

After a moment of silence, two boys emerged from behind a pillar and darted into shadow further back.

'We're not the police, Daryl! And you're not in trouble! We just want to talk to you!'

'It's no good. We'll never catch them like this.'

'We will. This is the only way out.'

'And you had to know that.'

'We'll wait here, Daryl!' Tony shouted. 'Come talk to us.'

Tony sat on the top step of the short flight down to the factory floor, careful not to park his rump on broken glass. Barbara decided to remain standing.

'So what brought you back?' Tony asked.

'My marriage failed,' she said. Why lie?

'How long were you married?'

'Eight years. Three were great, two okay. The rest... Well, I'm back in River Rapids because of the rest.'

'Any kids?'

'No, thank God. He kept putting it off. Should have seen that as a warning.'

'Not too late.'

'I think it probably is.' She shivered. 'Anyway! Enough of the personal questions! Shivering my nose off on the set of *Dawn of the Dead*. Let's get this over with already!'

'*Dawn of the Dead* was set in a mall, not a factory.'

'Shut up.'

'And do you mean the seventies original or the 2004 remake?'

'Shut up!'

A movement made her look up. Daryl Epps and his buddy stood at the foot of the stairs. Both of them were wide eyed and ready to flee.

'Who are you?' said the bigger kid.

'My name's Tony. This is Barbara. We're from the *River Rapids Recorder.*'

'What do you want?' asked the big kid.

'We just want to talk to Daryl here,' Barbara said. 'That's all. Get his side of the story.'

'You really want his side of the story, or just to sell some papers?'

'Both,' said Tony.

Daryl still hadn't spoken. He stared like somebody had asked him to spell 'encyclopedia' or something. Couldn't the kid speak for himself?

Barbara crouched in front of him and held out her hand for him to shake. Slowly, he did so.

'You don't have to say anything you don't want to, Daryl,' she said. 'We only want to help.'

Daryl slowly nodded.

'When did you last see your sister, Daryl?'

'Friday. The day before she left. I went to Nathan's for a sleepover. Never saw her again.'

'Do you miss her?'

He nodded again: large, exaggerated movements.

'What do you think happened to her?'

He shrugged: no words, just a flick of his shoulders.

'Your dad do something bad to her, Daryl?' Tony asked, suddenly. Barbara shot him a warning glance, but he ignored it. 'Or was it big bro, huh? Nasty old Ken do something to her?'

187

The big kid - Nathan? - said, 'Why don't you ask the police? Come on, Daryl, let's get out of here. They don't want to help us.'

The boys brushed past Barbara and Tony and ran for the door. Within seconds they were gone. Barbara stood, knees cracking painfully. She stamped pins and needles out of her feet.

'Seriously? You had to butt in? We'll never catch them now.'

'We got enough.'

Suddenly, Barbara had had enough of him. Without waiting, she stomped over to the gap in the boarded up door and squeezed herself through, no longer quite so bothered about snagging her clothes. By the time she had stalked across the broken parking lot to the chain link fence, he had caught up with her. They followed the trail through the woods in silence.

Barbara's Honda was where she had left it. She slid behind the wheel, absurdly pleased to be comfortable again, and pulled away almost before Tony had landed in the passenger seat. She didn't dare look at her shoes.

When she slowed for the stop sign at the end of the road, Tony cried, 'It's him: look! Wait, what the...?'

Maybe a hundred feet away, Daryl walked along the side of the road, kicking a can and reminding Barbara of the old song by Queen. No sign of his friend, Nathan. Even as she saw Daryl, a motorbike roared up and skidded to a halt in front of the kid, blocking his path. Two older guys dismounted: bigger guys wearing gym clothes designed to display their gym-built arms. One of the big guys said something to Daryl. He turned to run, tripped over something, and sprawled face first into the dirt.

One of the guys picked the kid up and pinned his arms behind his back. The other punched Daryl in the face. Barbara gasped. She watched him punch Daryl again, meaty fist right in the face. Daryl's skinny neck snapped back like his head might actually fall right off his shoulders.

Stop it! Barbara screamed. *Stop it!!* She tried to get out of the car, but somehow the seat belt had got itself caught around her foot and whatever she did just pulled the tangle tighter. By the time she had pulled herself free, Tony was already out of the vehicle and running along the shoulder. Daryl dropped to the ground and lay still. The two guys kicked the fallen boy twice in the side. He didn't move or make any noise.

'Stay away from him!' Tony yelled. 'I'm calling the police!'

The two big guys stared at Tony. He came to a halt. Behind him, Barbara did too. She realized her heart was beating fast, swollen with adrenalin. Fear filled her mouth with saliva. *What if they turn on Tony? What if they turn on you?* These guys were massive, probably spent every waking hour moving weights back and forth in a gym. Tony wouldn't stand a chance, and neither would she.

Nobody spoke, nobody moved.

And then the two guys jumped back on the Harley, and roared away.

Barbara ran to where Daryl lay in the dirt. His breathing was ragged, his eyelids fluttering. His nose dribbled red. 'He's barely conscious!' she shouted. 'The poor kid! Those sickos! He's just a kid!'

Tony lay Daryl in the back seat of the Honda and cradled the boy's head in his lap the whole way to the

River Rapids Medical Center. Barbara pulled to a halt right outside the main entrance and followed Tony into the single storey building. The Medical Center was not large enough to be called a hospital, but they had no choice. Daryl was motionless in Tony's arms. His little arms dangled pitifully.

A nurse whisked him away. Barbara could barely see the form she had to fill out through the tears filling her eyes.

2.

Tuesday October 25th, 2011

Georgina woke late that morning. For some time, she couldn't quite place where she was. Her bedroom seemed somehow different, as though goblins or pixies had snuck in while she slept and changed little details, just to play with her head. When she could face it, she switched on the bedside lamp. The light helped, but even then, her heart pitter-pattered dangerously.

She had been dreaming again. She had had her hands around a little girl's neck, pushing her head underwater until bubbles came up.

Georgina wanted to be sick, but she knew that if she made it into the bathroom, she would only dry heave. So she contented herself with crying into her pillow.

At last, she swung her legs off the side of her bed and pushed herself upright. She pulled on her robe and staggered to the top of the stairs. She needed a coffee, right now, large and strong, if she were going to face the day. Her foot came down awkwardly and she toppled toward the stairs. Heart racing, she pawed the wallpaper, searching for purchase, searching for the bannister, and then, mercifully - *thank you, God, oh thank you, God* - her fingers grasped the wooden rail and she regained her balance.

A tumble down the stairs at her time of life would be the end of her, she knew that for sure. She could just imagine Barbara coming home from the newspaper to find her mother sprawled dead on the floor at the foot of the stairs.

No, thank you, God. Not today.

White-knuckling the bannister, Georgina took each step one at a time until she was safe on the first floor. She turned on the coffee-maker and lowered herself into a chair. The walls were closing in on her. The rows of china teapots, the wooden spoons arranged in a fan above the microwave, the lines of jars of herbs and spices, the shelves of recipe books, all of it stifled her. Perhaps it was this place. Perhaps it was poisoning her. Maybe some odorless, colorless gas was escaping from the water heater and slowly killing her, day by day. She was sure she had read in a magazine about something like that happening. Some housewife in Ohio or Idaho or somewhere. It wasn't impossible. Or perhaps it was asbestos in the ceiling, getting into her lungs, asphyxiating her one breath at a time year after year. Or lead in the paint, that could be it. Toxins in the very air she was breathing.

It had to be something. Because memories didn't erase themselves, right? Something had to be affecting her memory. There was no other explanation for the blank patches. She was so forgetful these days, even Barbara had noticed. She tried very hard not to show she had noticed, but Georgina could tell from the way she looked at her. Like she feared Alzheimer's had finally caught up with her mother.

Maybe it was Alzheimer's. Maybe that was the explanation for the dreams she had of drowning a little girl. The explanation for why she couldn't remember what had happened to Cristel Epps.

The phone rang so loudly and suddenly her hand jerked and she spilled coffee over the table. *Brrrrrup-brrrrrup. Brrrrrup-brrrrrup.* She snatched her hand away, shocked by the instant scalding pain of coffee running over her skin. *Brrrrrup-brrrrrup. Brrrrrup-brrrrrup.* She jumped up and held her hand under the cold tap. The pain ebbed away. *Brrrrrup-brrrrrup. Brrrrrup-brrrrrup.* She gripped the edge of the counter. You know what that was, Georgina? Exactly the sort of thing senile old ladies do. Starting at the telephone. Spilling coffee over themselves. Perhaps Barbara is right, you do have Alzheimer's.

The phone was still ringing. *Brrrrrup-brrrrrup. Brrrrrup-brrrrrup. Brrrrrup-brrrrrup.* Angrily, she snatched up the receiver.

'Yes? What is it?'

Nothing. Just breathing.

'Who is this? What do you want?'

The voice, when it came, was muffled, as though a handkerchief or a scarf had been stretched over the microphone. It was thin and reedy as though an evil goblin or sprite were talking to her, the same one that had moved things around in her bedroom.

'I know what you did to that little girl. You're a filthy murderer. You won't get away with it. You're going to get what's coming to you. You're going to suffer for what you did. You're going to pay-.'

Georgina dropped the receiver. It clattered against the wall, swinging on its cord. The round speaker with its grill looked like a face smiling at her, taunting her, mocking her.

She stared at it for what seemed like a very long time. Then, slowly, she picked it up by the cord and put it to her ear. The connection was broken. The voice was gone. She dialled the police.

'Hi, er, I need to talk to Deputy Fincher, please.'

'I'm afraid Deputy Fincher is unavailable right now. May I take a message?'

'Er, this is Georgina Campbell. I... No, it's fine. I'll call back later.'

She had to get out of here. Right now. She had to.

Leaving the coffee half-drunk, she pushed open the door to the garage. She punched the garage door control and squeezed herself into the Nissan's driver's bucket seat, knocking her hip against the doorframe as she did so. She winced at the renewed shock of pain, but maybe the pain was doing her good. First the scalded hand, now the jarred hip. But she was more alert now, like she had splashed cold water on her face. This was good.

The garage door slid to a stop against the ceiling. The Nissan's engine roared to life and at last she was off, out of the house and into the real world. Barbara had taken the junker she had bought from *Chuck's Autos* to work with her, meaning the driveway was clear for once. Having always to maneuver around Barbara's Honda on the driveway was another one of the little frustrations that came with having her daughter suddenly return home without warning. Another little adjustment Georgina had had to make.

She took the turn onto Columbia too fast, the rear tires making an embarrassing screech. She pushed the accelerator too hard to compensate and the engine over-revved like a kid's wind up toy. Fortunately nobody was walking past, and she was probably too far from Janice's net curtain for her to notice. Probably.

Downtown. She would go downtown. She needed to talk to Deputy Fincher, and if he wouldn't answer the phone, she would just have to corner him in his office. Face to face. Make him listen to her. Get some answers.

And turn herself in.

Past Arby's and Applebee's. Past that Mexican she went to with Ardal that time, just six months before his liver had failed. She nearly missed the Quaker Mill Lane turning opposite the 7Eleven. Zoned out for a second. Almost didn't make it across to the left lane in time. Earned an angry honk from the Volkswagen behind. She just slipped through before the filter arrow flicked to red. Row houses crowded in now she was on Quaker Mill. And the inevitable speed bumps. She didn't notice the first one and nearly hit the roof when the Nissan bumped over it. The junction with Grand was just up ahead. Lights on green. No problem.

Filthy murderer. That's what the voice on the phone had called her. And the voice was right, wasn't it? Why else would she keep dreaming of swimming in a river, her fingers reaching toward a little girl, pushing her under the surface? Here it comes again: the cold, cold water, bubbling around her, glimpses of trees on the bank, clouds in a blue summer sky, and in front of her a little girl, soaking hair plastered over her face, screaming, spitting river water from her mouth, screaming again, eyes terrified because Georgina was pushing her under. And Georgina hated her. *Hated her.*

A loud car horn broke into her thoughts, a screech of tires. She had time to realize she had gone right through the now red lights at the junction with Grand, and a Ford pickup was fantailing toward her. She spun the wheel, flung her arm over her eyes, and plowed the Nissan through a newspaper vend box and into a bus stop. The Nissan rocked gently to a halt and unsold copies of the *River Rapids Recorder* fluttered to rest around it.

3.

MISSING GIRL'S BROTHER: I MISS CRISTEL. Tony tapped the headline and tossed the newspaper onto Barbara's desk. 'Four hundred words. Front page. Check out the byline,' he said.

Barbara had already checked out the byline. *From Special Correspondent Anthony Cryer,* it read. No mention of one Barbara Bruchner of course. May as well not have bothered ruining a pair of perfectly good Jimmy Choos. No need to have spent an afternoon hanging out in a damp abandoned factory chasing a pair of nine year olds.

'That's great, Tony,' she said. 'Good for you.'

'Right? Told you we had enough. The rest we can imply. Suggest. All in the wording. Looks like the kid gave us an exclusive interview.'

Annette bumped her way through the door, packet of Marlboros in one hand, coffee cup in the other, shoulder clamping a phone to her ear. 'Yes, I understand he shouldn't have hit the boy, but he had just called him a - what was it? A dumb weirdo from Dumbville, Weirdonia. So what's happening with the other boy? Well, yes, Miss Franklin, I do think it concerns me. I don't want you picking on my boy just because he... comes from the wrong side of the tracks. No! I didn't say that, but if I have to make my way over to that school, you'd better keep out of my way, hear?'

She cut the call and slung the phone onto her desk. The cigarettes and coffee followed it.

'Where have you been, Annette?' called Gerta Trupp from her desk.

'I needed caffeine, that fine with you?'

'You didn't say. Just disappeared.'

'Listen Gerta, you do not want to mess with me right now, you get me?'

Silence hung over the newsroom. Nobody moved or spoke. Even Barbara and Tony had fallen silent.

Annette sighed.

'Gerta, I'm sorry, okay? Lot of things going on, just cut me a break, would you?'

'Sure.'

A phone rang and Gerta answered it, breaking the tension.

'Gerald's pleased,' Tony said. 'Thinks he's got one up on the *Virginian*. Reminded the public how badly Sheriff Bill Millstone is handling the Cristel Epps case.'

'Good to know, Tony. I'm so pleased everything's working out for you. I phoned Nurse Joyce O'Neill over at the Medical Center earlier. Asked how Daryl's doing, if you're interested.'

'Yeah, right. Course. How is he?'

'His dad took him out of there as soon as he could. Against all medical advice, of course. He had a broken arm, two cracked ribs. Bruising around the face. And now he's back with his father in that trashy trailer, trapped with the very same psycho brother who beat him up in the first place.'

'Okay. Yeah. Not good.'

'And the only people who could maybe protect that little boy from his own family are the police. The police that this little small town rag refuses to support for no other reason than the editor has history with the Sheriff. But Tony Cryer's got his front page byline, so who cares?'

'Hey, look. I'm just doing my job...'

'Oh, shut up, Tony. I mean it this time, just shut up.'

The phone rang again and Barbara gratefully snatched it up.

'Oh hi, could I speak to Barbara Bruchner please?'

'This is she.'

'This is Joyce O'Neill over at the RR Medical Center.'

'Hi, Joyce. We were just talking about you.'

'Really? Well, er, I'm afraid I have some bad news for you, Barbara. I have your mother here. She was involved in a traffic accident.'

4.

Barbara brought the Honda to a halt in the parking lot of the River Rapids Medical Center. It wasn't straight and at least one wheel crossed the line into the next spot, but she didn't care. She hurried into the building, vaguely aware that this was the second day running she had visited the RR Medical Center, and did not like it one bit. The receptionist pointed her to the minor injuries unit.

According to Nurse Joyce O'Neill, her mother had sustained minor cuts and bruising to her face and torso, and a bump on the head that could result in mild concussion. 'But she was very lucky,' Joyce had said. 'Apparently, she jumped the stop light at Quaker Mill and Grand. Could have been a lot worse.'

Barbara found her mother sitting up in bed. Her hair, usually puffed into an implacable bouffant, was wet and slicked back, and her face, usually hidden behind a layer of makeup, was bare and craggy. A large band aid had been taped to her cheek, and a bandage wound across her torso and over one shoulder. Barbara suddenly realized how old her mother looked, and shocked herself by bursting into tears. She sat beside her and took her hand.

'Thank God, mom! What happened?'

'I don't know, darling. One moment, I was fine, the next... But it's good, Barbara, it's good.'

'What do you mean, it's good? How can this be good? I could have lost you today!'

'It's good that I'm in here. Safely tucked away where I can hurt nobody.'

'What are you talking about?'

'Don't you get it, Barbara, dear? It was me. I did it. *I killed Cristel Epps!*'

CHAPTER ELEVEN
DARYL EPPS

1.

The reporters and news crews camped outside our trailer have long gone. Cristel has been gone for two months, and nobody cares anymore. Now the papers are full of the apple harvest and how farms are struggling this year despite Obama's assurances that America is 'pulling the world out of recession'. Nothing about a little girl who went missing in the summer. The summer seems so very long ago. Those blue skies and three digit temperatures feel like another world when chilly winds rush along Main Street, Jack-o-Lanterns sit on stoops, and the teenagers hanging out at the 7Eleven wear padded jackets and blow frosty breaths, pretending they are smoking.

Debra has moved in permanently. Three weeks ago, Dad drove his pickup round to her apartment and spent several hours loading it with her junk. Now, it's everywhere. Every surface in the trailer's living room is piled high with old magazines, dirty clothes and fast food wrappers. Even the floor is ankle-deep in garbage. Dad and Debra have carved spots for their backsides for when they watch TV, and every place else is buried under mounds of garbage.

The kitchen is worse. The countertops are overwhelmed with old cans and microwave meal trays. Last week, I moved a moldy tissue and found a nest of cockroaches in a half-empty can of Campbell's Chicken and Noodle soup. They squirmed and crawled over each other and I felt puke coming, so I ran outside.

Dad never cleaned anything anyway and doesn't seem to care. The toilet has a brown crust around the bowl that gets thicker every day, and the basin no longer drains properly. Yellow towels cover the floor and the stain in the shower cubicle is worse. If I say anything, Dad yells at me to clean it myself.

The rest of Debra's junk was thrown into Cristel's room. The bed has disappeared under a pile of catalogs and thrift store clothes that touches the ceiling. The door doesn't open properly. When I pass Cristel's room, I get so mad, I want to kill someone. It's like Cristel has been erased from our life. It's like I never had a sister. Dad never mentions her, it's like he's pleased she's gone. A little voice inside says I'll be next.

Ken spends most of his time at Hayley's, but that doesn't stop him filling up our room with box after box of *Muscle UP Protein Shake Powder.* And more and more dumbbells. Recently he put a bar across the doorway so he could do pullups on it. That means that the door doesn't shut anymore. All I have left is a tiny mattress crammed into the corner where I can sleep.

The whole trailer stinks of garbage. I spend as little time there as possible.

It's getting too cold to hang out at our hideout but

Nathan and I do it sometimes. I haven't told him much, but I think he guesses that things are bad at home. We go to his house after school most days and that's okay. His mom is nice and gives me something to eat.

But weekends are hardest. Two whole days to fill. Two whole days to keep away from the trailer as much as possible. Mostly, I go to the old cannery with Nathan and we pretend we're running away. We bring bags of Hershey bars and muffins and Nathan brought a compass once. 'We'll need it if we're not going to get lost,' he said. 'America is a big country.'

We talk about running away. We talk about hitching rides to Tallahassee and visiting Amelia, but we will never do it. Nathan never will, and I'm just too scared. I think of all the places I've seen on TV: New York and LA and Chicago. I think of the deserts, the Highways, the endless Greyhound stations. I think of men who do things to boys like me. I think of being alone with no money and no friends and no food, and I get so scared I go back to the trailer every night. If I'm lucky, Dad will toss me a *Stouffer's Mac and Cheese*. If not, I can usually scavenge something from his and Debra's leftovers. And that has to be better than sleeping on the sidewalk of some big city. Right?

I can bear it as long as Ken keeps his cool. One Sunday I wake up when he grabs my T-shirt, yanks me off the mattress, slams me against the wall and punches me in the face. I feel something wet dribble slowly from my lip. He punches me again. Then he slams my head against the wall three times until my vision disappears into blackness, and then he drops me. He kicks me twice in the ribs. I miss school for two days until the bruises fade.

Apparently, he's broken up with Hayley. They are back together two days later.

The worst time is a few days before Halloween. After school Nathan and I go to the cannery. The place is cold and damp, but it's better than going home. And this time of the year, the whole place is usually ours.

Except today. We have just arrived, and Nathan is just telling me of a new game he has invented called *Brain-Eating Zombie Killer Massacre* when we hear a noise. At first, I wonder if the zombies have found us, and then I realize I can hear voices. Grown up voices. The police! They must have found us! They'll arrest us for trespassing and they'll sling our sweet little rear-ends in jail and we'll have to dig our way out using soup spoons. By the time we find freedom, we'll be old and have long, white hair.

And then somebody yells my name.

We freeze. We're in trouble now. We try to run, but there's only one way out. And a man and a woman I've never seen before block the exit.

'What do we do?' I hiss. Suddenly our safe haven does not seem safe anymore.

'We go and see who they are,' Nathan says. 'And if we need to, we can run for it.'

We get close enough to talk to them and far enough to be in with a chance of getting away. The man says they come from the *River Rapids Recorder* and they want to know my side of what happened with Cristel. I don't want to give my side of what happened. I don't want to talk to anyone, especially strange grown ups who've invaded the space I share with Nathan. When the man seems to want me to blame dad, we get out of there, pushing past them and through the broken board that covers the entrance.

We run across the cracked parking lot, through the hole in the fence, and along the track into town before we realize they're not chasing us. Puffing hard, we slow to a walk. My breath steams below my nostrils.

The day is very cold and the sun is dropping behind the trees. I shiver. We have to go find some warmth. I want to go to Nathan's but he has to have a bath, he says. His mom will not take no for an answer, he says, and so I have to go home. We reach the main road close to school and say goodbye. Nathan runs around the corner toward his nice house with his nice mom and his nice dad and his nice, warm bath.

I am halfway home, kicking a can along the roadside, when Ken's bike screeches to a stop in front of me. His friend Dale sits beside him, both wearing tight muscle vests designed to show off their biceps. They don't seem to feel the cold.

'Just who we've been looking for,' Ken says, and one look at his face tells me I am in trouble. I turn and run and might even have got away if I hadn't put my foot down on the very can I had been kicking. My ankle turns and I go down, scraping my knee on the blacktop. Tears prick my eyes, but the pain is nothing like I would have to deal with in a couple of moments.

Ken picks me up by the scruff of my shirt – yes, he is strong enough to do that. I see his biceps ripple under his skin like when John Cena pumps his arms on WWE. Dale holds my arms behind my back while Ken lays into me like a punchbag. He says something too, something about Deputy Fincher running him in for questioning that morning and it's my fault. I hear somebody shouting, *Stop it, stop it, stop it,* but I don't recognize the voice, and it's too far away anyway. All I can hear is a buzzing in my ears. Ken and Dale seem to have gone. Somebody picks me up. Then I'm in a car, watching stars pass by through the window.

I wake in a strange room with a strange woman sitting beside me and my whole body hurts. And I mean *all* of it. My face feels like somebody with a fat rear end is sitting on it. If I move it at all, pain explodes across my nose and mouth. If I try to speak, smile, or eat (as I discover a little later), I cry with pain. Even breathing sends little daggers of pain into my brain. If I try to move an arm or leg, or even a finger, pain swamps my body.

'It's Daryl, isn't it?' says the woman beside me. 'My name's Joyce. I'm a nurse, here at the Medical Center. You're safe now. Everything's going to be okay. I've called your dad and he's on his way.'

I start crying because that is pretty much the only thing I can do.

Nurse Joyce tells me I was brought in by the people from the *River Rapids Recorder*. Must be the same two from the cannery. I don't remember them bringing me. The last thing I remember is Ken hitting me while Dale held my arms. Joyce asks me who did this, and I want to tell her. But I don't, of course, because I can't. When Deputy Fincher arrives, I tell him two guys attacked me and beat me up but I never saw them before. He doesn't believe me, I know. He wants to talk to me some more, but Dad arrives and starts yelling and ordering him away from me and Deputy Fincher has no choice but to leave.

'I'm taking the kid home,' Dad says.

'Daryl has a broken arm and two cracked ribs,' Nurse

Joyce says. 'He must stay here where he can be looked after.'

'I can look after him at home.'

'I don't think that's a good idea, Mr Epps.'

'You listen to me, lady. I didn't ask for him to come here and I'm not paying for what I didn't want. I'm his dad and he's coming home with me right now.'

'And you listen to me, Mr Epps, it's just not possible. Daryl's arm needs to be set and he's still in a lot of pain. We can talk insurance later. There may be something we can do.'

Dad isn't happy, but he doesn't say more. He knows his standing in this town is at rock bottom anyway, and doesn't want more rumors about maltreatment of his kids doing the rounds. He mumbles something and wanders along the corridor, probably heading to the vending machine. He'll want a smoke or a drink soon.

People come and go. They set my arm in plaster, and as soon as they do, it itches like a hundred mossie bites. I swear there's an ants' nest down there. Somebody checks me for concussion. Somebody checks on my painkillers. The rest of the time, I sleep.

When I wake, Nurse Joyce has gone, and Dad stands beside me. 'Get up, son,' he says. 'We're goin' home.'

The painkillers are kicking in and I find I can walk with my arm held awkwardly around Dad's shoulders. He half-drags me along the corridor and into the parking lot. He bundles me into the pickup, slams the door, and pulls out, tires screeching. He runs a light at the parking lot entrance, earning an angry honk from a Ford that has to brake suddenly.

Up Quaker Mill Lane, right onto the Highway, and a left at the 7Eleven. As the buildings fall away around us and the streetlights end, the gathering dark crowds in like fog. I wonder what time it is. I suddenly realize I have no idea how long I spent lying in that hospital bed. Is it still Monday? Is it Tuesday morning by now? Or even Tuesday night? I think about asking Dad, but then he curses. Blue and red lights flash in our rear view mirror. A siren chirps on and off.

Dad pulls over. I look across as a flashlight approaches and shines in our eyes. I can't see the face behind it, but I know the shape. It's Deputy Fincher.

'Get out of the car, sir,' says the Deputy.

'I ain't done nothin' wrong,' Dad protests. 'I know what you're doing, Fincher, and this is harassment.'

'Get out of the car, sir. I won't ask again.'

Dad curses again, pops the driver's door and steps out.

'Over here, sir,' says Deputy Fincher's voice.

Dad moves a few steps away, out of my line of sight. And suddenly I hear the sound Ken's punch bag makes when he slams his fist into it, followed by a groan and a long, retching cough. Something drops heavily to the ground. I hear a whisper, and I strain to hear the words.

'That's for Daryl, Mr Epps. If either you or that meat-head son of yours lays a finger on him again, I'll kill the pair of you. I swear. Whatever you do to Daryl, I'll revisit on you seven times over.'

The sound of boots on gravel, a car door slamming, and the blue and red lights turn and disappear the way we came. I sit, wonder what to do, and try to keep my heartbeat under control. Eventually, I open the passenger door. The dashboard chimes and I look behind me.

Dad lies in the gutter, coughing and clutching his stomach. Spit dangles from the corner of his mouth. 'Don't just stan' there gawpin'! Help me!' He holds out a pudgy hand that envelops mine. He almost pulls me down when he staggers up. I teeter on the balls of my feet and wonder if I shall land embarrassingly in his lap. My cracked ribs scream pain so loudly that I blink away tears. Fortunately Dad clambers up the side of the pickup with his other hand. He heaves his rear end onto the driver's bucket seat. Without a word, I follow him in. The door slams. The dashboard stops chiming.

Dad curses so loud I jump. I wonder if he is going to hit me, but he doesn't. Maybe Deputy Fincher's words have had an effect after all. He drives in silence back to the trailer.

We park up, get out, open the screen door, still in silence. Dad gets the door open and blunders inside, still coughing, still clutching his stomach. He tramps over the garbage on the floor, parks himself in his usual spot, and reaches for his phone.

I know what he's doing. He's calling Ken. And Ken will go off like a atom bomb. And he'll go after Deputy Fincher.

Deputy Fincher was trying to help me. But I don't think he realizes what he's done.

2.

Ken turns up forty minutes later. I hear the roar of his bike and the familiar fan of gravel under his tires outside. I hate that sound. I crouch behind the sofa when he bursts in. I don't want him to see me. I figure one life-threatening pounding from my psycho brother a day is enough. I sit

207

on a pile of crushed pizza boxes. A cockroach crawls over a moldy crust of Hawaiian. It scuttles over my foot, but I ignore it.

Ken is mad. Super mad. He yells and curses, jabs his finger at Dad, accuses him of being weak and not standing up for himself. He heaves a bookcase over, sending DVDs and magazines tumbling on top of the other trash. I make myself even smaller so he can't see me. *Nobody's gonna clean that up either.*

And *crash!* He punches a hole right through the partition wall screening the kitchen. He pulls his hand out, seems not to feel it. Not for the first time I wonder if my brother is some alien who doesn't feel pain. Most people, when they do something violent like knock over furniture or punch a hole in a wall, they calm down, anger spent. But Ken is not most people. Violence makes him worse, like a baby screaming rage at the world, spiraling up and up until it seems nothing will satisfy it. He screams at my Dad, but Ken's pride will not allow him to do nothing.

Seconds later, he barges out of the trailer, screaming that he is going to find Deputy Fincher and kill him.

And I'm scared. Because if Ken kills Deputy Fincher, it will be my fault.

I want to leave the trailer. I want to find Nathan, ask him what to do. Should I go after Ken? Should I try to warn Deputy Fincher? I feel like I have to do something, but I don't know what. I don't even know how far I'd get with a broken arm.

I'm halfway across the living room when I step on an old soda cup. It collapses beneath my foot with a *snap!*

Dad stirs. He looks up from *The Bold and the Beautiful.* 'Where do you think you're going?'

'Just going to find Nathan, maybe hang out at the 7Eleven.'

'You ain't goin' nowhere! You got a busted arm, and the police are watchin' my ev'ry move 'cos of you, you little dill weed. You want another whippin' today?'

I run back to my room, tears squeezing from my eyes. I slam the door, glare at all of Ken's junk, turn and kick the door, once, twice, three times. Dad yells at me to quit it, and I wonder if he's going to make good on his threat to whup me, but nothing is going to make him heave his backside off that sofa while *The Bold and the Beautiful* is on. I fling myself onto my mattress and gulp back tears.

I hear the TV chattering. I hear music playing, then ads. *Do you suffer with discoloration of the stool? Are you so embarrassed by the smell you don't like using the restrooms at work? I discovered PoopPerfect, a revolutionary new treatment that will banish embarrassment forever... Over fifty but still enjoying life? Worried about an affordable medical insurance that will follow you on vacation all over the continental US? Rest easy with FiveOhYes! Nobody over fifty refused... Find quality used cars at Chuck's Autos in downtown River Rapids. Also at locations in Williamson, Prestonburg and Pikeville. WV's own used car dealership...*

Then, *thump*, the bathroom door slams, and I hear the sound of pee hitting the bowl. I catch my breath, jump up, run into the living room and snatch up the phone. I do it before I can stop myself. I dial 911.

'Which service do you require?'

'Police.'

'This is the police. What is your emergency?'

'I need to speak to Deputy Fincher!'

'Your name, please?'

'I'm Daryl. I need to speak to Deputy Fincher.'

The sound of pee hitting the bowl stutters. Dad's bladder is nearly empty.

'How old are you, Daryl?'

'Please, please! I must speak to Deputy Fincher!'

'This line is for emergencies only.'

'This is an emergency! My brother is going to kill him! Why won't you let me speak to him?'

'I have a Deputy Johnson Fincher listed at River Rapids PD.'

'That's him! That's him!'

'I'm putting you through now, but please remember this line is for emergencies only.'

'It *is* an-'

But she's gone. The phone rings again. I hear Dad clear his throat and retch into the toilet. He won't wash his hands, he never does. Any second now, he will open the bathroom door.

The phone crackles.

'River Rapids Police Department.'

'I need to talk to Deputy Fincher!'

'Deputy Fincher is not at his desk right now. Can I take a message?'

The bathroom door opens, pushing cardboard toilet tubes, used towels and spilled Q-tips across the lino.

'Tell him Ken Epps is coming after him!' I whisper, and drop the phone into its cradle.

I turn and Dad stands in the bathroom doorway, staring at me. I stare at him, blink once, twice. How long has he been standing there? Did he see me use the phone?

'What're you starin' at?' he growls. 'Get me a beer.'

Gulping saliva and hardly daring to breathe, I pull a

Bud from the fridge. Dad crash lands in his chair like a stricken UFO. A plastic Walmart bag wraps itself around my foot and I nearly fall. The Bud slips from my fingers, but a stack of moldy plastic microwave trays breaks its fall and it doesn't smash. I wipe old lasagna from it and hope Dad won't notice. A fly lands on my nose as I hand Dad the beer. Another crawls through my hair.

'When're you gonna take the trash out?' Dad bellows. 'Stinks in here!'

I know better than to answer. I back away and make it to my room.

Ken doesn't return that night. I don't know if Deputy Johnson is still alive, or if Ken's been arrested.

I don't know if he's going to burst in in the middle of the night and kill me too. I jam a chair under the door handle. It won't stop him, but it will give me a second's warning.

3.

Monday, October 31ˢᵗ, 2011

It is still dark when I wake, but something is happening. I hear noises from the other end of the trailer, shouts and banging. It must be Ken, coming to finish me off. I squeeze into the furthest corner of my mattress, and pull the smelly blanket up to my eyes. My arm aches, aches, aches, as if somebody were stepping on it. And when I take deep breaths, my ribs hurt.

The door handle jiggles, but won't open because of the chair I jammed under it. Ken tells me to open the door. Why doesn't he just kick it open? Ken knocks. He asks me if I am in there. Then he pushes the door. The chair slides over his old issues of *Muscle and Fitness* magazines. I scream because I know this is it.

Only it's not Ken who enters the room. It's a woman, with a big face and big eyes.

'Daryl, isn't it?' she says. 'Don't be scared, Daryl. I'm here to help you.' She holds out her hand. I stare at it.

'My name's Clarisse,' she says. 'I'm with the police. We've come to take you somewhere nice. You come with me, okay?'

She reaches down toward me, but I am already in my corner and I can't get any further away. That's when I lose it. I stretch my mouth wide and I scream and scream and scream. The woman's eyes widen in panic, she says something about waiting outside, but I can barely hear her above the sound of my own screaming. Even after she's gone I keep screaming and screaming and screaming, because I can't think of any other thing I can do, not one, and you know what? Screaming helps. In some small measure, it truly helps.

I stop when my voice cracks, which could have been five minutes later or five hours later. The silence in the trailer lay heavy. No yelling. No TV. No cursing. No footsteps. No gurgling from the toilet. The trailer has never been so quiet.

I stand. I take deep breaths. I face the bedroom door. I grasp the handle. I open the door. I step into the corridor. I step over the trash. The trailer is silent and empty.

Except for the woman sitting in Dad's spot on the sofa.

'Hi, Daryl,' she says. 'I'm Clarisse. Do you feel better?'

I nod, but my throat is parched. The woman – Clarisse – seems to realize this because she stands and stumbles over the trash to the kitchen. She finds an old Dr Pepper fountain cup, rinses it and fills it with water. She passes it to me and I take deep gulps.

'Goodness, it's a bit of a mess in here, isn't it?' she says as she wobbles back to the sofa, feet tramping over old pizza boxes and Dad's used Budweiser cans. 'And unsanitary. I've seen flies, roaches. I wouldn't be surprised if there were rats in here somewhere.'

She wears a cardigan over a blouse with flowers on it and a long, brown skirt. She has a pearl necklace on, but I think they're fake. She's tall and wide and she reminds me of Brenda from the library. When she looks at me, her eyes are kind.

'Where's Dad?'

'He's at the police station,' she says. 'Your dad has been arrested, Daryl.'

She waits for me to say something, but I don't know what to say.

'Do you understand, Daryl? Your dad's been arrested because the police think he may have something to do with what happened to your mother.'

She pauses again, but I still can't think of what to say.

'He won't be coming back, Daryl, not for a long time. So we have to find somewhere else for you to live.'

Tears prick the corners of my eyes. Clarisse takes my hand. My first instinct is to pull away, but I don't.

'I know it's a shock, Daryl, but try not to be afraid. We'll look after you. I talked to your teacher, and she tells me your best friend is a boy called Nathan Dicken. Is that right?'

I blink. Slowly, I nod.

'Well, that's good news, Daryl. Because I telephoned

Nathan's mommy this morning and she says you can go live with them for a few days while we sort something out. That'll be nice, won't it?'

I nod again, because now I can see some good coming out of this mess. I like Nathan's mom. She's kind. She gives me ice cream. She's like moms are supposed to be. Many times I've dreamed of being Nathan's brother so she could be my mom too, and I could play with Nathan everyday. Nights when I've laid awake on my mattress, while Ken snores on the bed and Dad and Debra fight in front of the TV or grunt like animals when they go to bed together, that's what I've dreamed of. Being Nathan's brother. Having a proper mom and a proper brother. A proper dad. A proper family. Just like other kids.

So I look at Clarisse, and the knot of fear inside me stops growing. If she's telling the truth, maybe everything will be good after all. She helps me pack a case of clothes, and asks if there is anything I want to take with me. A cuddly toy? Photos? Special books or toys? I shake my head. There's nothing. She looks at me.

It's cold outside, so Clarisse fetches my coat. My breath clouds as I walk to her car. I pretend I'm smoking, holding two fingers to my lips and blowing smoke. I think it's funny, but Clarisse just looks at me like she's making a note in her mind of everything I say or do.

She opens the passenger door, helps me up and belts me in. She leans across me to push the belt buckle into the clip. Nobody has ever done that for me before. This car is big and smells of pine trees. The footwells are free of trash. No beer cans or fast food wrappers. No 32oz soda cups jammed in the cup holders, melted ice sloshing around inside. This car is clean and tidy.

Clarisse lands in the driver's seat with a little grunt. She pulls her seat belt around her and clicks it into place. She closes the door, adjusts the rearview mirror, inserts the key, starts the engine, moves the gear stick into place and disengages the hand brake. The car rolls gracefully forward. Before we reach the end of the drive, she is already signaling right. The car makes the turn smoothly.

And then we're rolling into town, and by the time I realize I should turn to look at my home one last time, it's already too late. And then I think I don't care anyway. I hate that place. I hate the memories. I hate Dad and Ken and Debra. I hate the trash. I don't care if I never see it again in my life.

Now I'm going to be Nathan's brother and life will be perfect.

We turn onto the Highway, passing the 7Eleven and the railing that Nathan and I used to swing from. The same 7Eleven where Fred once showed Nathan and me the last trace of my sister before she disappeared.

We pass the fast food outlets and malls on the edge of town: Chili's and Applebee's and Arby's. Taco Bell, Pizza Hut, Dairy Queen. We turn onto Cedar Drive, Nathan's road, following the same route I always take when I go visit him.

Clarisse pulls up on Nathan's driveway. From nowhere the thought pops into my head that maybe Nathan's mom has changed her mind and doesn't want me anymore. Maybe she thinks one son is enough. Maybe she's fed up of always taking care of me when I'm not even hers. My stomach lurches and I'm suddenly desperate to pee.

Clarisse pops my seat belt even though I could have done it myself. She leans across me and opens my door, even though I could have done that too. I slide out and follow her to the door. My knees are trembling and my bladder is bursting. She pushes the doorbell and I hear a jolly chime.

The door opens and Nathan's mom stands there. Nathan is behind her, peeking around. He gives me thumbs up.

'Daryl!' Nathan's mom says. 'I hear you're going to come live with us for a while! Isn't that wonderful?'

She gives me a squeeze. My heart thumps madly and my body freezes rigid. But she doesn't hurt me. She takes my bag from Clarisse and beckons us all inside.

'Why don't you boys go play while we adults go over boring details?' says Nathan's mom. 'You may even find some ice cream in the freezer.'

We don't need telling twice. We hop, jump and clatter down the stairs to the basement. Along with the freezer, the basement contains two old sofas, an old TV and Nathan's Playstation. Before long, bladders relieved, we have spoons of Ben and Jerry's in one hand and game controllers in the other. The trash and violence of the trailer seem like a long way distant, and I wonder if maybe at last I can allow myself to feel happy.

CHAPTER TWELVE
GEORGINA CAMPBELL AND
BARBARA BRUCHNER

1.

Wednesday October 26th, 2011

Barbara stared into her coffee mug and wondered if she would feel better by the time she got to the bottom of it. It wasn't quite seven in the morning yet, she sat in the kitchen with her back to the window and the darkness outside, and listened to her mother come slowly down the stairs, one careful step at a time. They had taken a taxi home from the medical center last night, arrived barely six hours ago, and she had hardly slept since. The last thing she needed was an argument with her mother right now, but she had a feeling that was exactly what was coming.

Georgina eased into the room, obviously still in considerable pain. She wore large sunglasses - ludicrous at this time of the morning - and the huge fake fur coat that Barbara hated but Georgina thought made her look sophisticated.

'Mom, what are you doing up so early? You should be in bed. You heard what the doctor said.'

'This is more important. I have to go to the police and make them listen.'

'Listen to what, exactly? You didn't kill Cristel Epps, mother!'

'I don't wish to discuss it any further, Barbara.'

Barbara made an exasperated squawking noise. 'Why won't you listen?! There's fresh coffee in the pot if you want it. Here, you sit, I'll do it.'

Georgina lowered herself onto a kitchen chair while Barbara poured coffee. She placed it in front of her mother on a coaster depicting an orchid (hers showed a rhododendron) complete with latin name.

Barbara took a deep breath and tried again. 'You can't go to the police and confess a crime based on a few bad dreams, mom! Do you even know how crazy that sounds?'

'I'm going as soon as I've finished this coffee, Barbara. With or without you. You can either drive me or I'll call a taxi. I need to talk to Deputy Fincher about the letters, anyway. And the phone call I received.'

Barbara could at least agree on that point. She reluctantly agreed to drive, on the basis that she would rather be there than not be there. Maybe she could limit the damage.

Barbara wasn't at all sure what time Deputy Fincher would arrive at the station in the morning, but Georgina would not countenance a delay. It was just past seven and still dark as they pulled away in Barbara's Honda. Georgina was uncomfortable and fidgety, crammed into the passenger bucket seat in her huge fur coat. They drove in silence along the largely deserted roads until they reached the freeway, headlights picking out the telegraph poles and the dense shrubbery along the edge of the road. Barbara realized her mother must have seen Cristel Epps somewhere about here. She had asked her mother about that morning back in August a number of times, but Georgina had never been very forthcoming about it. Perhap she felt she was being interviewed for the *River Rapids Recorder* instead of having a conversation with her daughter, and with a little stab of guilt, Barbara realized she would probably have been right. Anthony had been putting pressure on her to arrange an exclusive with Georgina for some time now, but Barbara had never felt able to ask. And what with the car accident, and this crazy idea she had got stuck in her head about Cristel Epps...

By the time Barbara pulled the Honda to a stop next to a meter outside the Police Department building, the sun was finally lightening the sky behind the bandshell on the Green. A desk clerk looked up as they entered and told them that, yes, Deputy Fincher had arrived, and yes, he would see them if they'd like to go through. Barbara helped her mother into the deputy's office and eased her into chair. She did not remove either her fur coat or her sunglasses. Barbara sat beside her, ready to jump in if Georgina started on any of this nonsense about her dreams.

'Good morning, ladies,' Deputy Fincher said. 'Can I offer you a cup of coffee?'

Georgina didn't even reply. Instead, she said, 'Deputy Fincher, I am here to confess! I did something to Cristel Epps!'

Barbara sighed audibly.

'What do you mean?' the deputy asked.

Barbara rapped the desk with her knuckles. 'Deputy Fincher, I'm afraid we're wasting your time. My mother hasn't been sleeping lately, and has convinced herself-'

'I have something to do with Cristel Epps' disappearance,' Georgina said. 'I just can't remember exactly what. I've been having dreams - visions - of a little girl drowning. God is trying to tell me something, Deputy, and it is my civic duty to come and tell you all I know!'

'Visions?'

'Yes, vivid visions, like I was really there. We're struggling in a river and I have... I have my hands around her neck.'

'Just a dream, mom, that's all! We've been over this! You haven't been yourself. You've been ill.' Barbara turned to Deputy Fincher. 'She even wrecked the car yesterday. She's lucky to be alive. She's overwrought, and I'm sorry for wasting your time like this.'

'It's not just me, Barbara. Somebody else knows too. Whoever sent those letters, they know what I did! Whoever it was called me yesterday. They know, Barbara! I can't ignore this!'

'Who called you yesterday?' asked Deputy Fincher.

'I don't know. They disguised their voice.'

'But you spoke to an actual person?'

'Yes, right before I called you.'

'Good, good. I'll check the phone records. We may be able to trace the number.'

'What about me?'

'You, Mrs Campbell?'

'Aren't you going to arrest me? Fling me into jail? Send agents to investigate me? I don't even have an alibi!'

'I'll certainly pursue every lead, Mrs Campbell. Thank

you for your frankness. If only all the citizens of River Rapids were so civic minded. In the meantime, I'd ask you not to leave town for the foreseeable future.'

Barbara hustled her mother out of there before anything worse happened. She had called Gerald that morning to explain that she would be late in, but didn't want to abuse his indulgence. *Not that he's paying me yet,* she thought ruefully. She drove her mother home. Georgina said very little. Barbara suggested she wait to see if the trace on the phone call would yield anything. Deputy Fincher had promised to call the service provider that very day. 'Try to get out of the house, mom,' she finished, as she pulled up. 'It's not good for you, staying inside all day. Go to the mall, a restaurant, something. Treat yourself.' Georgina pulled her fur coat tight around her and tottered up the front path.

The newsroom was quiet when Barbara arrived. Gerta Trupp was on the phone, talking about land prices to somebody. Annette Goodkind stared at her monitor, one hand on her mouse, organizing a front page layout. Gerald was a shadow behind the frosted glass of his office. Anthony was missing. Annette shrugged when she asked. 'Chasing a story somewhere,' she said.

Barbara sat at the desk she had made hers and called up a story she had started working on. A rash of missing cats in the Ryland Park area. Probably nothing interesting, and yet better than the unsubstantiated sightings of a bear washing itself in Clayton Creek. *Small towns*, Barbara ruminated. *Where would we be without them?*

Gerta Trupp put down the phone and groaned. 'Try getting a quote from City Hall about land values skyrocketing over by the bowling alley and the rumors flying around that the land has been earmarked for a new golf course. Amazing how many officials suddenly have nothing to say.'

'Better than missing mogs,' Barbara said. 'Anybody for coffee?' It was nearly nine thirty and she hadn't had coffee since she'd got up that morning. Definitely time for another. Gerta and Annette shook their heads, so Barbara shrugged and made her way to the coffee machine for a single cup.

Where was Anthony? She hadn't quite forgiven him for leaving her name off the Daryl Epps interview yesterday (and his cavalier attitude about the Epps boy, of course, that was bad too) but she found herself wanting to know what he was doing and what she was missing out on. He'd better not be out and about chasing some hot story while she kicked back here filling her time with missing cats and bad coffee.

She tried to restart work on her story, but after she had clicked the word count three times in less than five minutes, she admitted to herself that she really couldn't summon up enthusiasm for a few forgotten felines. She called Anthony. His phone rang once, twice, and then she heard his familiar ringtone emerge from his desk drawer. She opened the drawer, and there it was: his battered Nokia with her name in the call id. *Seriously? He didn't even take his phone with him?* She hung up, and was about to close the drawer when she saw a file tucked in there under his phone. It was faded, clearly old, and bore the words *Cold Case - Lori-Ann Judd (Aged 10).* A post-it note had been pasted to the cover, a note reading *Cristel Epps - relevant??!!* Barbara pulled the file out and opened it.

The file consisted of a number of clippings of old issues of the *Recorder*. Sixty years old, in fact. The clippings were all from the same week in May, 1951. The font was smaller and the copy arranged in narrower columns than Barbara was used to. Fewer pictures too. The largest article lead with the headline, *LOCAL GIRL, TEN, DROWNS*. Barbara scanned for details.

> *The body of ten year old Lori-Ann Judd was pulled from Clayton Creek yesterday after an afternoon swim with her friend ended in tragedy. Mother Ann Judd, 32, and father Jacob Judd, 34, are inconsolable. Says Jacob, 'We just can't understand it. Lori-Ann swam in Clayton Creek many times. She was a strong swimmer.'*

Barbara's attention flicked to another article, dated two days later.

> *WAS LORI-ANN'S DEATH REALLY AN ACCIDENT? New details have emerged regarding the death of local girl Lori-Ann Judd, who drowned in Clayton Creek at the weekend, casting doubt on the cause of death. A source at River Rapids Mortuary claims that Lori-Ann may have been held under the water. The Recorder understands that police have already questioned the only witness to Lori-Ann's untimely death, her friend and fellow swimmer, Georgina Lovell, also ten.*

Barbara dropped the file and staggered against the desk. It scraped across the floor an inch or two. Annette looked up. 'You good? What's that you've got?'

Barbara quickly picked up the file and jammed the clippings back together. 'Nothing. Just an old file from the archives. It's nothing.' She made her way back to her desk, conscious of Annette's eyes on her back the whole way. In the safety of her work station, she opened the file again.

Nineteen fifty-one. Her mother would indeed have been ten years old at the time. Living in the same old house on Columbia Road, going to River Rapids Elementary, living much the same life as Barbara herself had lived some thirty years later. Only Barbara had never been allowed to swim in Clayton Creek.

There was another clipping. This one was smaller, just half a column and from page five. *NO CHARGES BROUGHT IN LORI-ANN CASE.*

> *Judge rules death by misadventure. Police have decided not to proceed with Lori-Ann case. Sheriff Philips today said, 'We are satisfied that the tragic death of Lori-Ann Judd was a terrible accident. We must now allow the Judd family to grieve in private. My sympathies go to Lori-Ann's family and friends at this difficult time.'*
>
> *However, Jacob Judd said, 'Lori-Ann was a strong swimmer and no way would she have drowned in Clayton Creek. The truth is being covered up.' Lori-Ann's friend, Georgina Lovell, the only witness to events last Saturday, remains out of sight at home.*

Her parents declined to comment when we attempted to contact them.

Barbara closed the file and took deep breaths to try to calm her heart. Her head was beginning to ache. Had her mother been involved in the death of her best friend when she was a kid? The articles certainly seemed to imply she had something to do with it. But her mother was no murderer! The idea of it was crazy! Her own mother! The woman who had loved her, provided for her, always been there for her, raised her as well as she could. Georgina could not perhaps claim the title of World's Best Mother, but Barbara knew of many who were worse. Her childhood, at least until her teens, when she and Georgina had begun to butt heads, had been a largely happy one. How could the woman who loomed large in all her memories be a murderer? Barbara just couldn't take it in. She felt tears spring to her eyes and quickly ran for the restroom.

The restroom was tiny, ill-equipped, and smelled of chemical air freshener, but at least she was alone. Tears flowed freely, and the one thought circling her brain was: *My whole life has been a lie!*

And then the tears were out. And she looked at herself in the mirror above the handbasin and her face hardened. This latest blow would not finish her. She had survived the collapse of her marriage, she had picked herself up when her life in DC had fallen apart. Whatever dark secrets her mother had hidden from her, nothing else had changed.

But there was one thing she wanted to know. Why had Anthony had the file in his drawer?

She wiped her face, smoothed her hair, stood tall, and left the restroom.

2.

Georgina felt she was in a dream. One of those frustration dreams when everybody around you disregarded everything you said and nothing you wanted to do worked out. Why would nobody take her seriously? She was just a crazy old lady imagining things, somebody to humor and patronize because she was losing her marbles, poor thing. She could practically hear Barbara say it. *She's not sleeping, she's overwrought, let me take care of her.*

One thing Barbara *had* said was get out of the house. Don't stay trapped inside. And that was advice Georgina wanted to follow. The house was getting to her again. The walls were looming over her, the shelves of china teapots looked as though they would topple over her head at any moment. She wanted to get out, but she had no car. Well then, the only thing she could do was walk.

She couldn't remember the last time she had walked down the path and onto the sidewalk, except perhaps the last time she had visited Janice across the street, and she hadn't visited her for a while now, not since all this business with Cristel Epps had begun. Her driveway was empty for the first time in years - even Barbara's Honda was gone - and the wide space outside seemed alien and wrong. Still, she pulled her fur coat around her, because it was October and she had to expect the weather to be cold, and walked along the sidewalk beside Columbia Avenue. The street seemed different from this perspective, unframed by a windshield, somehow bigger and taller. She noticed things she had never noticed before, like the aspidistra in the window of number fourteen, the fact that number twenty's guttering was broken, and number twenty-eight had added an extension to the side of the house. How had she not noticed that before?

At the end of the street, she turned right onto Queensway. Ahead was the row of stores she always passed in the car. A liquor store, a print shop, a clothes store supplying 'NY fashions at WV prices', a pet store. How many times had she passed these places and never once stopped? She stopped now, outside the window of the pet store, looked in at the rabbits and guinea pigs in cages, the choice of dog leashes and gourmet pet foods on offer. A hamster spared her a look and burrowed under sawdust.

Further on, she took a left into an unfamiliar street. She had lived in this little town her whole life, how could any street be unfamiliar? But it was. She walked past tidy little bungalows in their own plots, some with kiddies' tricycles abandoned on the lawn, some with rusting vehicles in lean-to carports. Nobody was about. Most of the drapes were drawn. Everybody at work or school, Georgina thought.

She was getting tired. Breath rasped in her throat. By the time she reached the end of the street, she needed to sit down. She found a bus stop and lowered herself onto the hard, concrete bench. The back of the bench displayed an advert for Pepsi, faded with age. She took deep breaths and rubbed her aching thighs. Maybe she ought to head back. Back to her favorite armchair, get some coffee brewing. Put on a DVD. One of those genteel British shows she liked so much. *Midsomer Murders*, or that one about the two old ladies who fought crime. She didn't know how they summoned the energy to fight crime. Hard to catch criminals when you had to sit on bus stop benches for a rest every five minutes.

At some point, the bus pulled up with a hiss of brakes. The doors burst open and a portly man with a huge mustache covering an equally huge toothy mouth looked at her. 'Can I take you anywhere today, ma'am?'

'I used to dream of visiting New York,' she said.

'A little off my route, I'm afraid.'

'Well. I guess I'll just sit here awhile and rest my legs.'

'You go right ahead. And have yourself a great day.'

The bus hissed again and off it went. Georgina watched it turn the corner and disappear from view. So that was it. She was an old lady resting her legs at a bus stop. How had that happened? Old age had snuck up and overtaken her at some point and she hadn't even noticed. The street around her - she didn't even know its name - when had it been built? The homes were no longer modern, but none of this had been here when she was a child. Perhaps twenty-five years ago. When the world was a little less complicated.

She had been disappointed when Barbara had moved to Washington DC. She hadn't understood what the city could offer that River Rapids couldn't. How could anyone prefer a busy, noisy city over a small town where everything was familiar and safe? But maybe Barbara had been right. Maybe leaving the confines of River Rapids had been the right thing after all. Maybe Georgina should have done the same. Her life would sure have turned out differently. Georgina Lovell would never have met Ardal Campbell for a start. And for all his faults, Ardal had been a good husband. He'd never made demands on her, despite the many she made on him. He'd indulged her whims and fancies. Like the time she'd wanted a boat so they could go on sailing vacations (which they had done precisely once, after which the boat had sat on blocks on the driveway for six years before they'd finally gotten rid of it). Or when she'd taken up knitting and insisted they both wear identical sweaters for several months. Or the British detective shows. Or the china teapots. What other man than Ardal would have put up with her?

No, she couldn't complain about her adult life. It was her childhood that had been difficult. The only child of dispassionate, distant parents, who'd been content to leave her to make her own way in life. She had gotten so used to having everything how she wanted it, she found making friends very difficult. In fact, she had had only one true friend as a child, and the friendship had ended suddenly. The girl - her name had long since vanished into the misty past - left town, or fell ill, or something. And nobody had wanted to be her friend after that. Her mother had become even more distant, treating Georgina as little more than an obstruction. The fact that Georgina wasn't wanted had been plain. Was that why she clashed so much with Barbara? An attempt not to repeat her own mother's mistakes. A shrink would no doubt say so.

Surprising that she had turned out so well-adjusted, all things considered. She put that down to Ardal's influence. And her faith, of course. No, she couldn't complain. Not really.

A chill wind made her shiver. She suddenly realized how cold the concrete bench was beneath her buttocks. How long had she been sitting here? With a shock, she realized she had no idea. With a second shock, she realized she had no idea how to get home either.

The sun cast long shadows. The street was empty. Before she knew what was happening, panic overtook her. Her breathing shortened to gasps, her heart fluttered in her chest. With trembling fingers she reached for her phone and speed dialed her daughter.

3.

Anthony returned to the newsroom mid afternoon. His open necked shirt, perfectly tousled hair and handsome grin was more than she could bear and she threw the file at him. It thudded against his chest and fell to the floor, shedding papers.

'When were you going to tell me about that, you two-faced liar?'

Annette looked up. Gerta put her phone down. Gerald appeared in his doorway.

Anthony had the grace to look shamefaced.

'So what were you doing, huh? Investigating my mom? Dredging up the distant past so you can get your name on another byline?'

'Look, Barbara, I didn't... it wasn't...'

'You're a piece of work, Tony, you know that?'

Her phone rang. She grabbed it from her desk. 'Mom? This really isn't a good time. I'll call you b-What? Slow down. You did what? Where are you? Well, can you see a street sign? Come on, mom, there must be something! Okay, fine. Just stay where you are, I'm on my way.'

She took up her bag and keys, glanced at Gerald. 'I've got to go. Sorry, Gerald, but my mom's not well. She's lost herself somewhere, I've got to go find her.'

She shoved Anthony to one side and ran out of the newsroom. She hurried to the end of the block and turned right onto Robarts. Her car was parked just ahead. The sun had already sunk below the roofs of the buildings opposite, casting the sidewalk into chilly shadow. Barbara found herself shivering as she started the ignition. Winter was just around the corner, she could feel it. Hardly surprising with Halloween less than a week away. She pulled away suddenly, causing a honk of protest from a pickup right behind. She waved an apologetic hand.

She wasn't even sure exactly where her mother was, but she surely couldn't have walked far from home. The plan was to cruise around for awhile, phone her for more details if necessary. Find her before it got too dark and cold. She headed back toward Columbia Avenue, all the time scanning the sidewalks for anybody who could feasibly be her mother. Along Quaker Mill Lane, across the junction with Grand where Georgina had wrapped her Nissan round a bus stop just yesterday - was it really just yesterday? Barbara sometimes felt like she was living two lives at once at the moment. She turned right onto the highway, leaving the downtown area behind. Now she was in the land of the fast food joint. Both sides of the highway were lined with McDonald's outlets, Subway, Pizza Hut, Burger King, Taco Bell, Quizno's Subs, each tucked away in their own building, each surrounded by a parking lot and a drive-thru fairway. The crouching buildings, all similar in design, reminded Barbara of scarab beetles in desert sands. Now where had that disturbing image come from? Even though the sun had not yet quite slipped behind the horizon, each beetle-like building was brightly lit and attractive, rows of windows showing busy uniformed workers rushing about inside. *Maybe they were the true beetles,* Barbara thought, and then told herself to keep her mind on finding her mother.

She wouldn't be here, that much she was sure of. Mom would never be seen dead in Taco Bell.

A couple of blocks further on and banks and offices replaced the restaurants. Barbara turned right by the Virginian Bank and cruised up and down Columbia Avenue. She even stopped off briefly at the house to check if Georgina had made it back after all. Finding the place empty, she hopped back in the car. Where would she go? If her mother wanted to get out of the house and was on foot, where would she go? Barbara turned right at the end of the street, passing a row of stores including a liquor store and a pet store. She must have gone this way. Must have headed into the newer part of town that she didn't know.

Was this what her mother was capable of now? Unable to be trusted driving, wandering the streets aimlessly when walking. This whole Cristel Epps thing had really got to her. And now this other girl too. Her childhood best friend drowning in Clayton Creek. Maybe it was just as well Barbara had returned home from Washington DC. Her mother needed her now in ways she had never needed her before.

And there she was. Sitting on a concrete bus stop bench, fur coat pulled around her, un-made up eyes scared and red. Hair windswept and lopsided. Two or three months ago she would never have been seen out of doors like that. Just two or three months ago, she had stood tall and poised, with not a hair out of place. Barbara felt a stab of yearning for the old Georgina as she pulled the Honda to a stop. She hugged her, helped her into the car, drove her home. Made coffee. Ran her mother a bath.

When Georgina reappeared downstairs, she looked better. More her old self. Her hair was back in its usual bouffant style and a little mascara made her face look less drawn. 'You must think me a foolish old woman,' she said. 'I don't know what I was thinking.'

Barbara shook her head. 'You've had a tough time recently, mom.' She poured her mother another cup of coffee. 'May I ask you something, mom?'

'Of course, my dear. What is it?'

'Have you heard the name Lori-Ann Judd?'

For a second or two, Barbara wondered if her mother had heard. Then her eyes darted away, looked back at her. She frowned, looked like she was about to yell, closed her mouth, shook her head, and finally said.'

'No, I don't believe I have.'

'She was your best friend, mom. Way back when you were a kid. You don't remember her?'

Georgina turned her back, rummaged in a drawer.

'I don't remember the name at all. You must be mistaken.'

'I'm not mistaken. She died when you were small. Drowned in Clayton Creek. You must remember. You were the only one who saw what happened.'

'Don't tell me what I do and don't remember, young lady! I'm positive I've never heard the name! Where did you get all this from? Somebody filling your head with lies? Making you call your own mom a liar?'

'I'm not the liar here, mom! You do remember, don't you? Because she's the one your dreams are about, isn't she? You're not dreaming about Cristel Epps at all. You're dreaming of Lori-Ann Judd and what happened to her sixty years ago! You spent sixty years trying to forget, but this thing with Cristel Epps has brought it all up again!'

'I don't want to talk about it.'

Matthew Link

'I bet you don't! But why, mom? What are you hiding?'

'I will not be questioned by my own daughter, Barbara. And you mention that name again, you will no longer be welcome in my home. I trust that is clearly understood.'

She left the room. Barbara heard her climb the stairs, heard her bedroom door close. She released a huge breath and shook her head. Why was it every time she and her mother tried to talk, they ended up fighting? But she was sure she was right. Georgina's dreams were about what happened at Clayton Creek with Lori-Ann Judd back in 1951. And the threatening letters? None of them had mentioned Cristel Epps by name. She was convinced the letters, and the phone call, referred to Lori-Ann too. Somebody had found out Georgina's secret.

And there was only one person it could be. The letter writer had to be Anthony Cryer.

CHAPTER THIRTEEN
JOHNSON FINCHER

1.

Monday October 24th, 2011

By the end of October, everybody seemed to have forgotten Cristel Epps. The papers were full of Halloween and the recent election of Earl Ray Tomblin as Governor of West Virginia, and what that would mean for the hard-working people of River Rapids, and the opening of a brand new Sonic Drive-in Restaurant at the Cedar Creek Mall. Nobody was interested any longer in a little girl who had disappeared two months ago. She would likely never be found and people wanted their news to have an ending, preferably happy.

Questions were still occasionally being asked about the competency of the RRPD, and of Sheriff Millstone and Deputy Sheriff Fincher in particular, but although the investigation into Cristel Epps' disappearance and her mother's murder had not reached a satisfactory conclusion, town bosses also found they could not pinpoint any moment when either Sheriff Millstone or Deputy Fincher had conspicuously failed in their respective duties. Gradually, the frequency of complaints dropped, especially when the *West Virginian* and *River Rapids Recorder* found they were struggling to justify their position of support of Donald Epps. Supporting an unemployed redneck who probably neglected his children in his unsubstantiated claims about fine, upstanding officers of the law with hitherto exemplary records was not tenable in the long term. So they quietly dropped the whole thing.

'I still don't see what I could have done different,' Johnson said in bed a week before Halloween. Susan walked in from the bathroom, showered and dressed. She sat at the dresser and stared wide-eyed at her reflection. Johnson didn't like talking about work at home, but this time he just needed his wife to tell him that he'd done good.

'You did everything you could,' she said on cue. 'Everybody knows that. Including Bill Millstone.'

'Not the DA.'

'Even the DA. If they were going to fire you, they would have done it by now. Just don't stuff up again, that's all.'

That wasn't the reassurance he was looking for.

'It's the kid I feel sorry for,' Johnson said. 'Daryl. Stuck in that trailer. What kind of life is that? He doesn't deserve it. He's a good kid.'

Susan rummaged in her make up box. 'So phone the city. If he's in danger. You have a duty.'

'Mmm. But I can't prove he's in danger. And I have to tread very carefully where the Epps family is concerned.'

Millie screamed from her room. 'You'd better get up

if you don't want to be late,' Susan said and went to tend to her daughter.

Johnson spent the day plowing through paperwork. Georgina Campbell's threatening letters still sat in his in-tray, but she had reported no further arrivals so they had lost priority. He was sure the writer was some bitter and twisted loner who had read in the *Recorder* or somewhere that Georgina had been the last person to see Cristel Epps alive, and decided to pick on her to vent some hatred. Johnson pictured some spotty faced kid who spent his life parked in front of a computer talking to strangers in chatrooms, locked away behind permanently closed drapes. Or maybe a hardened old crone, spitting venom at random strangers just to bring some danger and excitement to her dried up life.

At five o'clock, Carole Jeffrey called over from her desk. 'Word just in,' she said. 'Daryl Epps has just been admitted to River Rapids Medical Center. He's been badly beaten.'

Johnson closed his eyes and shook his head. 'Dad or brother?'

'Anyone's guess at this point. My money's on the brother. Thought you'd like to know.'

'Thanks, Carole. I'll get over there.'

The RR Medical Center was three blocks away and one over. Less than ten minutes later, Johnson parked the Crown Victoria as close to the main entrance as possible and hurried inside. The thought that Donald Epps could be here had crossed his mind, but he wasn't sure what steps he should or could take if they were to run into each other. After all, he was Deputy Sheriff of River Rapids County and had every right to visit the Medical Center. On the other hand, a public confrontation with Donald Epps was something he'd rather avoid just now.

Daryl lay in bed, face puffy and bruised and his arm attached to a splint. A nurse walked in and out but nobody else was there. Johnson found himself releasing a sigh of relief that he didn't know he'd been holding.

He sat next to Daryl and smiled. 'How you doing, kiddo?'

Daryl didn't smile back. He looked away.

'What happened?' Johnson said.

At first, Johnson thought Daryl was going to ignore him, but then he said, 'Two guys beat up on me.'

'Who were they, Daryl?'

'I don't know.'

'Was your brother one of them?'

Daryl's eyes fixed on the doorway behind Johnson.

Donald Epps stood nervously in the doorway, clearly desperate for a cigarette, and probably contemplating lighting up in the hospital. Johnson clenched his fists. He felt his fingernails dig into his palms.

Susan regularly told Johnson that 'control freakery' constituted a significant part of his character, and he was quite sure she was right. It was one of the reasons why he made a good police officer. He liked to think he could make a positive change in the world around him and the lives of the people within it, even if that world were only a small town in West Virginia. And yet here in front of him was a nine year old boy whom Johnson seemed to be powerless to keep safe. Fire burned in his belly at the sight of Daryl's bruised face and he would have liked nothing more than to take it out on the useless cretin of a father standing in the doorway. A so-called father who cared more about his next cigarette than he did the welfare of his own son.

And then Donald Epps saw him and completely lost his chips. Red in the face, he ordered Johnson away from his son.

'I'm here on official police business, Mr Epps.'

'This ain't the business of the police!'

'It is when I have serious concerns about the well-being of a nine year old child. This is not the first time Daryl has suffered suspicious injury, Mr Epps.'

'Are you saying I'm a bad father? I don't care who you are, get your filthy pig hands away from my boy!'

Johnson stepped right up to Donald Epps' face and said under his breath, 'What do you care? Deadbeat loser like you cares for nobody but yourself. You'd rather he were dead, wouldn't you? Isn't that what you want? You want to beat him to death and do away with him like you did his sister?'

In the moment of silence that followed, Johnson wondered if he had gone too far. The wretched fire in his belly when he couldn't control something, once again. He stepped away from Donald Epps and the moment broke.

'Help!' Donald Epps yelled. 'Help! This man wants to hurt me! Help! Help!' Footsteps approached in the corridor.

'I'm coming after you, Donald Epps,' Johnson said. 'You better make sure you always look behind. You make one wrong move, I'll be there. I'll personally make sure you can never hurt Daryl again.'

With one last sidelong glance at Daryl's wide, bruised eyes, Johnson hurried from the room. He almost bumped into an orderly on the way out. The young, stocky guy backed off when Johnson flashed his badge. 'Nothing to see,' Johnson said. 'Mr Epps is just a little worked up.'

He returned to his paperwork, but he couldn't get the image of Daryl's bruised face out of his head. He got up, wandered around, tidied the mess room, and felt guilty that he wasn't already on his way home to spend the evening with his family. Finally, he strode out of the building, jumped into the Crown Victoria and pulled noisily onto Main Street.

It was getting dark as he roared along Quaker Mill Lane. He wanted to put the siren on and really exercise the engine, but he was already on thin ice with the Sheriff. Probably best not.

Without quite realizing what he was doing, he pulled onto the Highway and found himself signaling to turn at the 7Eleven. As the 7Eleven disappeared behind him, he realized he was driving toward the Epps trailer. And the instant he realized that, he also realized that the pickup a short distance ahead was Donald Epps' pickup.

Johnson shook his head. Almost as though it were meant to happen. *Is that you, God? Or just a coincidence?*

The blue and red lights went on.

Johnson was adamant that when he pulled Donald Epps over, he had no intention of hurting him. He was sure he hadn't thought that far ahead. Maybe he had some vague intention of inconveniencing Donald Epps. Perhaps reminding him that Johnson was on his case, never far behind. Certainly not threatening him and punching him in the stomach.

But when he saw Daryl sitting in the passenger seat, arm in a sling and face black and blue, whatever it was that had been building up in him over the whole day, snapped. His control freakery took over, as Susan would say, and within moments, Donald Epps lay gasping and doubled over on the tarmac.

Johnson whispered in his ear, stalked off to the Crown Victoria and roared away.

As soon as he was out of sight of the Epps' pickup, he started to shake. He pulled over and took deep breaths.

What had he been thinking? He wasn't the sort of cop who resorted to intimidation tactics. That wasn't his way at all. If Donald Epps complained, he could lose his job. Could even face criminal charges himself. He had let his emotions overcome him, and wasn't that precisely what no cop should ever do? All his training, all his experience taught him that the one thing you never do is lose your cool. No matter how much provocation, *you never lose your cool.* And yet here he was acting like a schoolyard bully.

But he deserved it, a voice somewhere inside him said. *And trash like Donald Epps, violence is all they respond to.*

But no. He didn't think that way. He was better than that. The people of River Rapids deserved better than that from their law enforcement officers.

Relax, Johnson. Nobody saw. Epps won't complain, and nobody will believe him if he does. You got away with it.

Yeah, but getting away with it doesn't make it right. You know who thinks it does? Toddlers and criminals.

It's late. You shouldn't be out here. You should be at home with your wife and daughter.

Johnson performed a wide U-turn and went home.

He arrived in time to read Millie a bedtime story: *The Three Little Pigs* this time. He sat on Millie's Disney duvet, at the end of her bed, halfway between a doleful Dumbo and a manic Minnie. The room was full of her toys, some stacked neatly on shelves like the Barbie dolls house and the My Little Ponies, others still scattered over the carpet like her cuddly Hippo and the *My First Bible* Susan had got her for her fourth birthday. Johnson picked it up and lay it on the bedside table.

He had hoped she would be asleep by the time Big Bad Wolf fell down the chimney, but her eyes were still wide and unblinking.

'What happens when you lock up the last bad guy, Daddy?'

'What do you mean, Cinnamon Bun?'

'When only good guys are left will you always be here with mommy and me?'

'Well, it doesn't work like that, baby. Bad guys and good guys are only in stories. Like the Big Bad Wolf and the piggies. In the real world, things are different.'

'I thought you caught the bad guys?'

'I do, darling. But sometimes bad guys do good things too. And sometimes good guys do bad things. Everybody makes mistakes from time to time.'

Millie shook her head.

'You don't?'

Millie shook her head again.

'Well, you must be a very special little girl, then. Even Daddy makes mistakes sometimes.'

Millie was still staring at him and Johnson found himself saying. 'Daddy made a mistake today.'

'What mistake, Daddy?'

Johnson took Millie's little hand in his. His daughter's head lay on her pillow, hair fanned out like a halo, and maybe she was right. Maybe she had never made a mistake. He could think of no purer picture of innocence right now.

'I hurt somebody, baby. I got angry and I hurt somebody and I wish I didn't.'

'Are you sorry, Daddy?'

'Yes, Cinnamon Bun, I am.'

'Then all you have to do is ask Jesus for forgiveness. Mommy says. And Jesus will always forgive you, even if it's really bad.'

Johnson squeezed her hand.

'Thank you, baby. Mommy's right. Will you help me?'

'It's easy, Daddy. Just close your eyes. Go on, close your eyes. And say, *Dear Jesus, I'm sorry for hurting somebody.* Say it, Daddy.'

'Dear Jesus, I'm sorry for hurting somebody.'

'Amen.'

'Amen.'

'And now it's all gone, Daddy.'

Johnson wiped a tear from his cheek and kissed his daughter on the forehead. 'Thank you, Millie. I love you, Cinnamon Bun.'

'I love you, Daddy.'

Her left her curled up and went to find Susan downstairs. She was pouring coffee in the kitchen and offered him one. 'How was work?' she asked.

He shook his head. 'Did nothing useful. You know that sort of day? I should have come home earlier. Sorry, Susan.'

'What for?'

'I don't know. For mixing up my priorities, I guess. Just a feeling recently that things are getting on top of me.'

'You're finally letting go of that Cristel Epps business, that's all. And about time too. It was horrible, Johnson, but it wasn't your fault, you know? None of it. You did everything you could.'

'Time to move on, eh?'

'That's right. That's exactly right. Listen to what God's telling you. Move on, leave the responsibility behind.'

Before Johnson could reply, the phone rang.

'Thought you'd like to know we have Ken Epps in custody,' Carole Jeffrey said. 'He burst in here threatening to kill you. Claims you attacked his pa, or something. Slugged Phil Logan a good one before we got the cuffs on him.'

Johnson felt his heart thumping, and he knew why. Guilt. Guilt, because he knew he had done something wrong, but didn't know if he wanted to get away with it or not.

'What's he saying now?'

'The Epps kid? Cooling his jets in the cell. Periodically yelling obscenities, you know the sort of thing.'

'Look out for him. The kid's dangerous. Practically killed his little brother today.'

'A night in the cells will do for him. One odd thing: just before the meathead rocked up, we had a call. A kid warning that Ken Epps was on his way to kill you. A little boy, by the sound of it. Reckon it was the kid brother?'

'Has to be. Thanks, Carole. See you tomorrow.'

'Day off. See you Wednesday.'

'Will do.'

Susan looked at him as he replaced the receiver. 'Okay?'

'Yeah, fine.'

The mysterious caller had to be Daryl Epps. Who else

could it be? So the kid did care. Maybe he was getting somewhere after all.

2.

Tuesday October 25th, 2011

Johnson's first call out, shortly before nine in the morning, was to a small, one-level residence on Euclid, where a woman had started her day by hitting her husband upside the head with a fry pan. A fry pan containing two half-cooked eggs, over easy and all ready for toast. Johnson had found the husband sitting against the oven nursing a huge lump over his left eye, face bloody, fragments of egg distributed over the linoleum. His wife was fussing over him, dabbing his face with a kitchen towel, offering him a mug of his favorite coffee, massively penitent and swearing that it would never happen again, he had just said something snarky about her latest purchases at *Clayton Creek Fashions* over at the mall, and she had just seen red and just lost it. He could understand that, right? She didn't *mean* it. And the husband had waved it all away, asked Johnson what man *didn't* like a bit of fire in his woman, and apologized for wasting his time. Johnson left, making a little wager with himself that he would be back at this address before the end of the week.

A suspected break in at a house on Appalachian Way and a reported prowler in the garden of the residential home for the elderly over on Vanderbilt (which turned out to be the new gardener - freshly arrived from Mexico) filled up the rest of the day until Johnson heard of a traffic accident on Quaker Mill Lane. Apparently, a Nissan had gone into a bus stop at the junction with Grand Avenue. Still, Phil Logan could deal with that. He needed some traffic accident practice.

'We had a call for you this afternoon,' Jan Creevy, subbing for Carole Jeffrey, said, when he got back to the station. 'Georgina Campbell. Wouldn't leave a message, but said will call back.'

'Okay, thanks, Jan,' Johnson said, and felt guilty that he hadn't made much progress with the Campbell woman's threatening letters. He'd get back to her in the morning.

The rest of the day was mostly given over to Bill Millstone's ongoing feud with Gerald Sumner, editor of the *River Rapids Recorder*. According to Bill, Gerald had wanted the Sheriff's job way back in the day. Bill had got it instead and Gerald had never forgotten the fact. Sounded like there was more to it, but Johnson had never dared ask. Bill summoned him into his office late that afternoon and brandished an advance copy of the latest edition of the *Recorder*. *MISSING GIRL'S BROTHER: I MISS CRISTEL*, read the headline. Johnson groaned. Just when he'd been daring to hope the media circus over the Cristel Epps disappearance was on the wane.

Sheriff Millstone theatrically thumped the copy with a forefinger and read, '"Has the River Rapids Police Department forgotten the heartache caused by their failure to solve the disappearance of this little boy's sister? Little Daryl Epps, just nine years old, will never forget, even if Sheriff Bill Millstone and his Keystone Kops have." Keystone Kops, Johnson! That's what they're calling us!' He peered at the byline. '"Special correspondent Anthony Cryer," the little snot! Gerald Sumner's gone too far this time! We'll see what he has to say when I sic Mayor Vance on the seat of his pants!'

Later on his way home to his family, Johnson found Bill Millstone's problems faded in importance. He kept thinking of when he'd pulled Donald Epps out of his pickup, punched him in the stomach, and left him gasping on the tarmac. In front of his son.

3.

Wednesday October 26th, 2011

Johnson had only been in the office for half an hour, and was still gingerly sipping his way through his first coffee, when Georgina Campbell and her daughter walked into the station and asked to speak to him. Quickly tidying his desk, he summoned them in, and invited them to take a seat. Georgina Campbell was heavily wrapped in a (probably fake) fur coat. Even with the large sunglasses perched on her nose, Johnson could see bruising on her face. She walked stiffly and sat slowly. She was clearly in some pain. Johnson wondered what had happened.

Georgina's daughter - Barbara, wasn't it? - sat beside her, brows drawn down over her eyes, lips pursed.

'Good morning, ladies. Can I offer you a cup of coffee?'

Barbara shook her head and Georgina ignored him completely, instead proclaiming, 'Deputy Fincher, I am here to confess! I did something to Cristel Epps!'

Johnson blinked and took another sip of his coffee. He'd been expecting a demand to know what was being done about her threatening letters.

'What do you mean?' he asked.

247

Barbara rapped the desk with her knuckles. 'Deputy Fincher, I'm afraid we're wasting your time. My mother hasn't been sleeping lately, and has convinced herself-'

'I have something to do with Cristel Epps' disappearance,' Georgina said. 'I just can't remember exactly what. I've been having dreams - visions - of a little girl drowning. God is trying to tell me something, Deputy, and it is my civic duty to come and tell you all I know!'

'Visions?'

'Yes, vivid visions, like I was really there. We're struggling in a river and I have... I have my hands around her neck.'

'Just a dream, mom, that's all! We've been over this! You haven't been yourself. You've been ill.' Barbara turned to Johnson. 'She even wrecked the car yesterday. She's lucky to be alive. She's overwrought, and I'm sorry for wasting your time like this.'

'It's not just me, Barbara. Somebody else knows too. Whoever sent those letters, they know what I did! Whoever it was called me yesterday. They know, Barbara! I can't ignore this!'

'Who called you yesterday?' asked Johnson.

'I don't know. They disguised their voice.'

'But you spoke to an actual person?'

'Yes, right before I called you.'

'Good, good. I'll check the phone records. We may be able to trace the number.'

'What about me?'

'You, Mrs Campbell?'

'Aren't you going to arrest me? Fling me into jail? Send agents to investigate me? I don't even have an alibi!'

'I'll certainly pursue every lead, Mrs Campbell. Thank

you for your frankness. If only all the citizens of River Rapids were so civic minded. In the meantime, I'd ask you not to leave town for the foreseeable future.'

When his visitors had gone, Johnson leaned back in his chair and finished his coffee. He had that nagging feeling that he was missing something. Not the first time he had felt it since Cristel Epps had disappeared, and probably not the last either. Georgina was clearly not a credible suspect, but she *had* been the last person to see Cristel alive. She couldn't account for her movements on August 20th and claimed convenient memory loss. *And* there was this business with the threatening letters and now the phone call.

Well, that was something he could take action on. Find the exact time the call had been made to Georgina Campbell's home and put a trace on it. With any luck, he would find himself a suspect somewhat more credible than Georgina Campbell herself...

CHAPTER FOURTEEN
GEORGINA CAMPBELL AND
BARBARA BRUCHNER

1.

Friday, October 28th, 2011

Barbara hadn't been back to the *Recorder* newsroom since she had left early to find her mother on Wednesday. She had phoned Gerald and told him that her mother was ill and she was going to take a couple of days off to look after her. And, she figured, since he doesn't actually pay me, he can hardly say no. *In fact, let's see how they get on without me for a day or two. If Gerald really wants me to return, we can open negotiations on a starting salary.* And, of course, it meant she didn't have to face Anthony Cryer for a few days. But, she thought, as she idly flicked through one of her mother's *House and Garden* magazines on the sofa, staying at home with Georgina all day was perhaps not the good idea she had initially thought. After all, getting out of the house and out from under her mom's feet was one of the reasons why she had approached the paper in the first place.

But it's only for a couple of days, she thought, *and I need a break from the paper just as much.* Specially after she had created something of a scene in the newsroom on Wednesday.

Feeling suddenly irritated by the perfect homes on view in the magazine, she tossed it on the coffee table and thought about taking the car to Clayton Creek Mall. She could treat herself to a new pair of shoes to replace the pair she had ruined chasing through the mud after Daryl Epps. Maybe even a cup of coffee and a cupcake at that new coffee shop right there that she had been hearing good things about. She could take mom. Do her good to get out of the house, and in the neutral environment of the coffee shop, she could even bring up the tricky subject of Lori-Ann Judd again.

Barbara hadn't dared to mention the name for the last two days. Instead, she had tiptoed around her mother, carefully avoiding any mention of Wednesday's conversation for fear of another fight. But she couldn't avoid it for ever, and neither could Georgina. Sooner or later, Georgina would have to talk about what happened that day sixty years ago when her best friend hadn't returned from a swim in Clayton Creek. Barbara meant to have the truth. She was only waiting for the right time, and maybe the new coffee shop would be the right place. Her mom would not start yelling in public, Barbara was sure of that.

Georgina was in the kitchen, chopping vegetables for the casserole she was preparing for dinner. Barbara could hear the sound of the knife against the chopping board - *thud, thud, thud* - and the occasional splash of water from the faucet.

The other thing Barbara hadn't done anything about was her suspicion that Anthony Cryer was the writer of the threatening letters and phone call Georgina had received. Barbara had thought long and hard about Tuesday and the time her mom had received the call - had it really only been three days ago? - and had tried to remember if Anthony had been in the newsroom at that time. Could he have slipped out to make the call? She didn't think he had, but she couldn't swear to it. He could have nipped to the restroom and made the call from there. Wouldn't have taken long. It was possible, but Barbara couldn't understand why he would do it. What could he possibly gain from threatening to expose a secret her mom had kept for sixty years? If he was planning to blackmail her, he was taking his time. He hadn't even made a demand yet.

And all Anthony thought about was his career anyway. Thought he was the new young hotshot reporter on his way to the big East Coast dailies. How would blackmailing an old lady in a backcountry town advance his career? Anthony wouldn't be that stupid.

And yet who else could it be? Nobody else knew about what had happened to a little girl, killed in a swimming accident, sixty years ago. Back before Obama and 9/11, before *Challenger*, Watergate, Vietnam and Neil Armstrong. Even before JFK and Cuba. Back when America was still innocent, when the world was a larger but friendlier place. Who would remember that? Only the hotshot young reporter who stumbled on it in the newspaper archives when searching for cases involving missing girls. It *had* to be Anthony.

Georgina had finished chopping. Pots and pans clattered from the kitchen. Barbara had to get out of here and she wasn't ready for the Big Conversation with her mother. She yelled, 'Just going out for a while, mom,' and was out of the door before her mother could protest.

The first major frost of the winter had left patches of ice on her windshield, some still clinging on in the corners. She rummaged in the glove box until she found a scraper wedged in at the back. The ice peeled off the window in slivers. The Honda started on the third attempt. By the time she pulled out of Columbia Avenue onto the Highway, the engine was humming, the heater whirring, and the remaining crystals of ice were dribbling down the windshield to collect in the gutter by the wipers. At the stop light with Quaker Mill Road, her phone rang.

'Deputy Fincher, this is Barbara Bruchner. What can I do for you?'

'Good morning, Mrs Bruchner, just wanted to let you know we've made an arrest regarding the threatening letters and phone call your mother received.'

'You have? That's great news! Who is it? What happened?'

She took a breath, waiting to hear the name *Anthony Cryer.*

'We were able to trace the call made to your mother's landline on Tuesday. The call was placed from a payphone on Main Street.'

So it was Anthony. He must have slipped out of the newsroom and made the call from the payphone down the street.

'We cross-referenced the time with footage from a CCTV camera mounted across the street for traffic control purposes, and we were able to identify the caller as she left the booth.'

Wait, what? 'She? Did you say 'she', deputy?'

'That's right. And I believe you know her, Mrs Bruchner. The caller was Annette Goodkind.'

2.

Barbara pulled the Honda into the feeder lane to turn left onto Quaker Mill Lane. The new coffee shop in Clayton Creek Mall could wait. Despite what she had said to Gerald, she was going into work. She turned onto Robarts Street and within a block the road narrowed and storefronts appeared at the roadside. She passed Frank's Gym and Harry's Mercantile, cruised past Kelly's Diner and the *Recorder* offices, parking curbside just off Main. She pulled the door open and hurried inside, ignoring the tinkling of the bell.

Annette's desk was empty. Anthony was there, talking to Gerta. They looked up when she burst in.

'Barbara, hi,' Tony said, nervously.

'I guess you've heard,' said Gerta.

'Yeah, I... Annette?'

'Deputy Fincher was here couple hours ago. Took Annette away. Gerald was fuming. Doubtless thinking of his next stinging editorial. We couldn't believe it!'

'I found the file on Annette's desk,' Tony said. 'Was going to tell you but... Well, I didn't know what to make of it. Guess I was kind of hoping it would just go away.'

'I owe you an apology, Tony.'

He shook his head.

'But why? Why would Annette want to threaten my mom?'

'Because she's a nutcase. Who knows what goes

through the heads of people like her? Gerald thinks she must have looked through the archives for cases similar to Cristel Epps and ran across it. Thought she could make a bit extra on the side maybe.'

'He says that if she comes back, she's fired,' Gerta put in.

'And he wants to see you,' Tony said. He sidled up to her and gave her a nudge. 'This could be your big break, kiddo!'

She rolled her eyes at him and knocked on Gerald's office door. She hadn't even sat in the chair he pointed at before he said, 'So you can start on Monday, right? Full salary. Health insurance. All the benefits in the *Recorder's* not inconsiderable employee package?'

She told him she'd think about it.

3.

Georgina had finished chopping vegetables and had started preparing the casserole when she heard Barbara yell something about going out and the door slammed. Georgina let out a breath she hadn't realized she'd been holding. Barbara didn't mean to do it, but her presence always seemed to prevent Georgina thinking clearly. Something about her daughter being in such close proximity.

Georgina sank into her favorite armchair in the living room. For once she ignored the china teapots and the box sets of detective shows. She leaned back and closed her eyes.

Lori-Ann Judd, Barbara had said. Where had she even heard that name? Georgina hadn't thought about

Lori-Ann Judd in more than half a century. She had tidied that whole incident away so successfully she had forgotten the whole thing. No, not just forgotten. She had *suppressed* it. Acted like it had never happened. A fine piece of doublethink, rewriting history to such an extent she had even believed it herself.

Lori-Ann Judd. Just those words explained so much. All her dreams of drowning for a start. The girl in the water with her. The girl who wasn't Cristel Epps at all. Even the threatening letters and the phone call. They hadn't been referring to Cristel Epps either. Somebody had found out what had happened sixty years ago. And that made everything so much easier. Now she knew exactly what to do.

She called a taxi.

Less than twenty minutes later she handed over a twenty dollar bill and stepped onto the sidewalk outside Our Lady of the Sacred Heart Roman Catholic church. The church looked much as it had the last time she had been here, which Georgina was shocked to admit, was more than ten years ago. The building, although built in the nineteen-forties, adhered closely to the European cathedral style, complete with flying buttresses, which seemed somewhat grand for River Rapids. Tall gables supported a high cross that reached up into the white cloud as if trying to touch God Himself.

Ten years ago, the priest had been one Father Donnelly, but the board outside gave the name of Father Graveney. Georgina wondered what had become of Father Donnelly. Maybe God had called him home. She wondered how long she had before He did the same for her and whether He would be pleased to see her when He did.

I still have time to set things straight, she thought.

At first she thought the church was locked, but the doors opened when she leaned heavily on them. Inside, weak sunlight filtered through stained glass windows and lighted columns of dust. Incense fragranced the air. Two steps inside and the peace and stillness brought tears to her eyes. She had forgotten how comforting God's presence was. Why had she stopped coming here? When had she decided she could do without God? She walked past the rows of pews with their cushions to kneel on and their plastic covered Bibles to the confessional booths along the side wall. She entered a booth and bowed her head before the outline of the priest on the other side of the grille.

'Forgive me, Father,' she said. 'For I have sinned in the eyes of God.'

4.

Barbara had celebrated her new job with Tony, Gerta, and a Kelly's Famous Burger with All the Trimmings, and then they had repaired to the Funky Monky Bar two blocks down Main, where they had sunk nine cocktails between them.

Emerging onto the sidewalk shortly after midnight, Barbara realized she was too drunk to drive. The knowledge floored her for a moment. Until she rummaged through her bag for her cellphone and dialed a taxi. 'I can get the car when I come to my new job on Monday!' she cried, triumphantly, and her companions cheered. When the cab arrived, she bade tearful goodbyes and promised to see them at work on Monday.

In the back of the cab she realized how tired she was. She was jolted out of a doze when the cab turned onto Columbia and the driver asked her where she wanted to get out. She paid him, and standing on the sidewalk, she noticed a light was still on in the living room. Had Georgina fallen asleep in front of the TV? Wouldn't be the first time.

But when she entered the house, the TV was off, and her mother sat in her favorite armchair with a mug of coffee in one hand. Barbara suddenly felt guilty, as if she were a teenager caught coming home late and drunk. She decided to get in first.

'Did you hear the good news, mom? They've got the threatening letter writer!'

'Yes, Deputy Fincher phoned when I was out. He left a message on the machine. Would you sit, Barbara? There's something I need to talk to you about.'

'You went out again? Without your car? Mom, I thought we had decided that was a bad idea.'

'I took a taxi. I knew exactly what I was doing. Please, sit down. This is important.'

Barbara sat on the sofa opposite her mother.

'I want to tell you about Lori-Ann Judd, and an angry, spoilt little girl called Georgina Lovell.'

The tiredness drained from Barbara suddenly. She listened to her mother speak.

'You never knew your grandmother, Barbara, so you'll have to trust me when I tell you that she was a hard woman. My mother didn't love me or want me. I was an accident she had to live with. She was cold and unfeeling and never once showed affection for me. I'm sure a psychiatrist will happily tell you all about the damage this does to a child, but back then it was a fact of life for me. I'm telling you this not as an excuse for what I did, but because it helps explain it. Maybe it explains why I never made friends as a child. Why, even now, I know almost nobody in this town, not properly.'

She stopped. Barbara realized she was crying. The dim light from the reading lamp had hidden how upset her mother was. Barbara couldn't remember the last time she had seen her mother cry. Georgina flicked the tears from her lids, took a deep breath.

'Lori-Ann Judd was the only girl from school I used to spend time with. We played together, shared toys. We had these old fashioned dolls, we used to play with those for hours. I still have some of them upstairs.'

Barbara remembered her mother waking her in the middle of the night, moving old toys, the night after she had returned to River Rapids.

'People said we were best friends, Lori-Ann and I, but we weren't. Behind the smiles, I hated her and she hated me. And this day, this day in 1951 when we decided to go swim in Clayton Creek, I seriously don't think I've ever felt such hatred for another human being in my life. You know what it's like when you're ten. When every emotion hits the extreme. When you ricochet from joy to despair and back in the space of seconds. My mom had spanked me that morning for finishing the milk and leaving none for her mid morning coffee. She called me worthless and ungrateful. I wish I never had you, she said. And then I ran out of the house, found Lori-Ann, and we went to the creek. And Lori-Ann showed me a new painting set she had been given, packed full of brushes and paints and pencils, every color of the rainbow.'

She flicked more tears away, took another shuddering breath.

'And you know what she said to me, Barbara? She said, Your mom gave me this. Your mom said she loves me more than she loves you. I wish Georgina was more like you, that's what she said!'

'Mom...'

'I know! I know she was making it up. She was just saying spiteful things, whatever she knew would hurt me. I know that, Barbara. But I saw red. And when we were in that water, I put my hands on her shoulders and I pushed her under. All the way. And I kept her there. I didn't mean to hurt her, Barbara! I swear to you. I swear before God, all I meant to do was scare her. To stop her saying those spiteful things. But suddenly she stopped moving. She stopped moving and I thought she was playing and I dragged her out, and I begged her to stop it. And finally, I ran.'

Tears fell freely now. Great shuddering gasps.

'They said it was an accident. Had to be. Just a tragic accident. One of those things. Nothing anybody could have done. And time passed. And people forgot. And it was like it never happened. But I did it, Barbara! It was me! I killed that little girl!'

Barbara ran over to her mother and wrapped her in her arms. She squeezed her and hugged her and rocked her and they cried together.

CHAPTER FIFTEEN
JOHNSON FINCHER

1.

Friday October 28th, 2011

When Johnson got to work on Friday morning, he found a sticky note right in the middle of his computer monitor. *Call Jim at AT&T.* Johnson knew what this was about. The trace on the nuisance call Georgina Campbell had received. Sure enough, when he returned Jim's call, Jim (Johnson vaguely recognized him as somebody he used to hang out with at high school) very helpfully supplied the information that the phone call had been placed from public booth number 133452, located on the corner of Main and Robarts. 'Just about ten feet exactly from the front door of Kelly's Diner,' he said, cheerily. Johnson thanked him for his help.

He had expected that the call would have been made from a public payphone. It took a special kind of nuisance caller to make the call from his own phone. Usually, this was where the lead dried up, because it was impossible to prove who had made the call. *But...* This payphone was right there on Main Street. It was just possible one of the downtown stores caught the phone on their CCTV. Or even the traffic cameras. If they could cross-reference the video footage with the known time that the call was placed... It was worth checking out. Johnson sent Phil Logan to investigate.

A little less than two hours later, Phil placed a VHS cassette on Johnson's desk. 'Traffic cam footage. The payphone's right there.'

'And you got video footage from Traffic and Highways in less than two hours? I'm impressed, Phil. They've been known to drag their feet for days.'

'Let's just say Marnie in the office likes a man in uniform,' Phil said. He wiggled his eyebrows and wandered off.

Johnson inserted the cassette into the machine.

Five minutes later, he knocked on Sheriff Millstone's office door. The Sheriff was staring at an Excel spreadsheet, brow furrowed. 'Give me some good news, Johnson,' he said.

Johnson handed him a screenshot of the traffic cam video covering the junction of Main and Robarts. In the corner of the picture a woman was stepping away from a public payphone booth.

'Annette Goodkind, of the *River Rapids Recorder*, having just made a nuisance call to Georgina Campbell. More than likely, she's the threatening letter writer too.'

The Sheriff leaned back in his chair and shook his head. 'You're sure? No cockup potential this time?'

'Not this time, Bill. Evidence is right there. This callbox. Time matches within seconds.'

'*The Recorder,* eh? Well, that's just fine and dandy,

ain't it? Gerald Sumner needs taking down a peg or two, the number of times his little rag's put the boot into this police department. Get down there right now and make the arrest, Johnson.'

'Sure thing, Sheriff.'

Johnson took his Crown Victoria. The *Recorder* offices may have been just three blocks away, but it wouldn't do for an officer of the law to walk in off the street. Had to maintain appearances. He took Phil Logan with him for that very reason. He parked directly outside the *Recorder* offices and strode confidently through the entrance with Phil right behind him. A young guy working at a desk near the door looked up and jumped to his feet.

'Deputy Fincher, isn't it? What can we do for you? Would you care to make a statement about progress on the Cristel Epps case?'

Johnson ignored him and instead approached Annette Goodkind's desk. 'Annette Goodkind?'

'That's right.'

'Would you come with us to the precinct, please?'

'Why? What's this about?'

Gerald's office door opened. His bulky form filled the doorway. 'What's going on, Deputy Fincher? What are you doing here?'

'I'm here to take Ms Goodkind in for questioning, Mr Sumner. I'm afraid she will have to come with us.'

'Why?'

'I'm not at liberty to divulge that information, Mr Sumner.'

'You'll divulge that information pretty doggone quicksmart, sonny, or I'll be making a call to Mayor Vance quicker than you can scurry back to that precinct of yours.'

'Ms Goodkind is suspected of sending threatening letters and making nuisance phone calls, Mr Sumner. And I suggest you phone a lawyer before making that call to the Mayor. You may just need one.'

Without a word, Annette Goodkind snatched up her bag and followed Johnson and Phil outside to the Crown Victoria. They helped her into the back seat and pulled away. Johnson felt oddly satisfied driving the three blocks back to the station. Gerald Sumner and his cronies at the *Recorder* had wasted no time bringing Johnson's competence into question after Cristel Epps had disappeared. Johnson had tried not to take it personally, but when he was named in the paper, it was hard not to. And at last, perhaps just for a few seconds, he'd succeeded in wiping Sumner's smirk away.

He pulled up in the parking lot and led Annette Goodkind into the station. He took her into an interview room and bade her sit.

'How well do you know Georgina Campbell, Ms Goodkind?'

Annette shrugged. 'I don't know her at all.'

'But you know who she is, right? You know where she lives. You know her daughter, right? After all, Barbara Bruchner works at your very newspaper. Isn't that correct?'

'Yes, that's correct.'

'And you know that Georgina Campbell was the last person to see Cristel Epps before she disappeared?'

'Yes.'

'So why did you send her threatening letters?'

'Do you know who Lori-Ann Judd is, Deputy?'

'Enlighten me.'

'You should check your files, Deputy. Look under *unsolved cases*. Sixty years ago, Georgina Campbell killed her childhood friend. Lori-Ann was ten years old. And she got away with it. You think that's coincidence? She killed Lori-Ann and she killed Cristel Epps. She must have.'

'I don't follow. In what way are the two cases connected?'

'Georgina Campbell is the connection. And thanks to you, she's going to get away with it again. Isn't she? Two months on and you're still no closer to finding out what happened to Cristel Epps, are you?'

'There's nothing to suggest that Georgina Campbell had anything to do with Cristel's disappearance.'

'Then what about Lori-Ann Judd? Doesn't she deserve justice?'

'How did you plan to hurt Ms Campbell?'

'I just wanted to scare her. Make her fear for her life, just like she did to Lori-Ann, and likely Cristel too. Let her know somebody's onto her.'

'Did you plan to blackmail her?'

'Yeah. I guess. She should pay for what she's done.'

'Do you have any concrete evidence linking Georgina Campbell either to the death of Lori-Ann Judd or the disappearance of Cristel Epps?'

Annette Goodkind said nothing.

Johnson left the room. He found Phil Logan, told him to book Annette Goodkind for threatening behavior, and sat wearily at his desk. Annette Goodkind was right about one thing. He was no closer to finding out what had happened to Cristel Epps two months ago. And now this lead too had ended in a dead end. He had no more leads to follow. What else could he do? Would Cristel Epps really end up consigned to the *unsolved crimes* file? If she did, he would turn in his badge. He knew that much.

But for now, he could call Barbara Bruchner and Georgina Campbell to give them some good news. And God knew any good news was welcome right now.

2.

Later that evening, before he headed home for the day, Johnson pulled the police file on Lori-Ann Judd. He skim read the details. The judge at the time had ruled the little girl's death as accidental, and Johnson had no reason to think otherwise. Not unless new evidence came to light.

It was quite possible that Georgina had had something to do with the death. But it was sixty years ago. A lot of time had passed. Lives had been lived and lost. Perhaps this was one wound that time and forgiveness could heal.

Johnson closed his eyes. *God, if Georgina has anything to forgive, please forgive her.*

After all, he too had done things he needed forgiveness for. Who hadn't? He thought again of his fist hitting Donald Epps in the stomach. Of the out of control anger he had felt while was he was doing it.

Yes, God. Please forgive Georgina, and while You're at it, forgive me too.

3.

Sunday October 30th, 2011

Every day Johnson wondered if he had gotten away with his assault on Donald Epps. And he worried about the safety of Daryl Epps. He had already failed to protect one of the neglected Epps kids, and he couldn't bear the thought of failing another. Ken Epps had been released on the Tuesday, having cooled down from seeking blood to making schoolboy threats. Johnson kept a look out for him, but he seemed to be keeping a low profile, probably because he was planning something. Whatever it was, it could wait. The rest of Friday and Saturday had trickled away dealing with a disturbance at Funky Monky Bar downtown, two or three domestic call outs, and an attempted runner from the Sleepy Nite Motel. Usual stuff for a small town.

And by Sunday, Donald Epps still hadn't filed a complaint. Johnson began to breathe easier.

Mid afternoon Sunday, while watching *Sesame Street* reruns with Millie, the phone rang again.

'Hi, Johnson, this is Jeanette Schwartz. Got something for you.'

Johnson's heart beat fast, because phone calls that began like this had broken open difficult cases before.

'Little bit of out of the box thinking, because nobody likes boxes. Had a look at Daryl Epps' blood sample the folks at the Medical Center took when he was brought in last week. Compared it with Yvonne Epps' blood. Did a bit of reverse engineering jiggery pokery. Long and short is, I managed to isolate Donald Epps' DNA. You know, son minus mother equals father. Kind of thing. In Layman's. And – drum roll please – it matches the blood found on Yvonne's body.'

Johnson couldn't prevent the grin spreading over his face.

'Jeanette, you beauty!'

'Are you objectifying me, Johnson?'

'Too right I am! If I could kiss you down the phone, I would!'

4.

Monday October 31st, 2011

5am and it was still dark. Johnson knew black lines ringed his eyes, but he could catch up on sleep after Don Epps had been arrested for the murder of his wife, Yvonne. For now a black Starbucks would have to do. Two of them better still.

Phil Logan sat in the driver's seat of River Rapids PD's one and only Special Service Vehicle, an aging van with two benches lining the walls in back. Back there right now sat Joe Longfellow and Gilly Dwight, two part time officers here to make up the numbers and provide support. In case Donald Epps resisted. Or his elder son got involved. And in the driver's seat of a Nissan in the next parking spot sat Clarisse Bevan, representing the city and tasked with keeping Daryl Epps safe.

The SSV was parked in the 7Eleven parking lot awaiting the go signal from Bill Millstone, safely ensconced in the command center at the station. Also known as Carole's desk, Johnson thought.

Phil Logan looked at the bright lights of the 7Eleven. 'They have good donuts in there,' he said. 'And right now I wouldn't say no to a machine made coffee.'

'Forget it, Phil.' If Phil ran in for a donut and coffee, the go signal would come. Sure as houses. And Johnson was taking no chances of stuffing this up. Not for a donut and coffee. 'Should have come prepared like I did,' he said, and indicated the two Starbucks cups lined up on the dash.

Phil continued to stare longingly at the coffee machine behind the 7Eleven window.

'Everybody doing okay?' Johnson asked, and received a chorus of grunts in reply, which he took as a good sign.

Johnson picked up a radio from the dash. 'Clarisse, you clear about staying out here until we secure the place?'

Clarisse Bevan's voice floated from the radio, from the car three feet away. 'Civilians keep out. I gotcha, Deputy.'

The call came as the sun began to lighten the sky in the east. Phil would have had plenty of time to gulp back machine-made coffee and devour a donut. But those were the breaks. He'd have to function without caffeine and sugar after all. He pulled the SSV out of the parking lot, and roared along County Road Six like an angry bull. Johnson was surprised how much speed the ungainly SSV could pick up, even if it did rattle in protest. Clarisse's Nissan struggled to keep up.

They swept into the Epps' drive, fanning gravel. The tires had barely halted before Johnson's police regulation boots hit the ground. He hammered on the screen door, practically tearing it from its hinges, Phil, Joe and Gilly right behind him.

'Police!' he bellowed. 'Open up!'

Without waiting, he made room for Phil to kick the door with a mighty swing, practiced for years on the football field at River Rapids High. The door splintered around the lock and shuddered inwards, slamming into something behind. A smell of garbage hit Johnson's nostrils. Phil and Joe covered their noses. Gilly muttered, 'What *is* that?'

Johnson was already inside, stomping over a layer of trash. Food packaging and crushed beer cans mostly. Trash lay piled over every surface in the living room and the kitchen, the biggest pile a mountain balanced next to the recliner opposite the TV. Johnson's mouth dropped open. The trailer had never exactly been clean, but this was by far the worst he had ever seen it. What sort of lazy slob could live like this?

The sort of lazy slob who was probably asleep in the very next room right now. Johnson tramped his way across the garbage, keen to retain the element of surprise. Phil, Joe and Gilly followed, gazing around themselves in shock.

Johnson slammed open the door of the bedroom. Donald Epps lay like a beached fish on a bed almost lost in a sea of trash. He pulled himself up, blinking, muttering a string of barely connected curse words. His wobbly, hairy belly spilled over the waistband of a pair of stained and holey Y-fronts.

'Police!' Johnson yelled. 'Donald Epps, you are under arrest for the murder of Yvonne Epps. You have the right to remain silent, but anything you do say may be used against you in a court of law. You have the right to an attorney. If you cannot afford one, one will be appointed for you. Do you understand?'

But anything else Johnson said was drowned under of a torrent of curse words and orders to get out of his house. Johnson motioned Phil forward.

'Get dressed, Mr Epps,' Phil said, 'or we'll take you to the station as you are.'

Leaving Phil to cuff the prisoner, Johnson checked the rest of the trailer. The door of the back bedroom wouldn't open more than an inch. Looked as though a chair had been wedged against the handle. Johnson thought about bursting it open, but if Daryl were inside, he didn't want to freak the kid out.

'Daryl? Are you there? It's Deputy Fincher. The police, Daryl. If you're there, open the door.'

No reply. Nothing happened. But Johnson was sure he could hear scared breathing from beyond.

'Daryl? I want to say thank you for phoning to warn me last week. That was very brave of you.'

Still nothing. He shook his head. Leave Clarisse to deal with Daryl. That's what she was trained to do. The important thing was that Ken Epps was not present. Spending the night at his girlfriend's perhaps.

Donald had pulled on a grubby T-shirt with *River Rapids County Fair 2002* written on it, and a pair of shorts. Phil marched him out to the SSV.

'This place is disgusting,' said Gilly, covering her nose. 'Can't be sanitary. Got to be roaches everywhere. Probably even rats. What sort of person could live like this?'

'No place for a kid,' Joe said. 'Fire department saw this, they'd condemn the place.'

'Go tell Clarisse she can come in, will you? I think Daryl's in the back room.'

Joe followed Phil out.

'There's mold in here too,' Gilly said. 'Somewhere. I can smell it.' She shivered. 'People, eh? Just can't understand 'em.'

Clarisse appeared at the door. She wrinkled her nose at the mess and looked dubiously at her shoes.

'Seen anything like this before?' asked Gilly.

'More than you'd think. Unfortunately. At least we're getting poor Daryl out.'

'I'm pretty sure he's in back,' Johnson said. 'We'll have to leave you to it, if you don't mind. Gotta get his dad back safe.'

'No worries. I'll check in with you later.'

Johnson led Joe and Gilly outside to the SSV. Joe and Gilly stepped into the back and sat either side of the prisoner. Phil slid into the driver's seat with Johnson beside him. The SSV bumped onto County Road Six. Johnson watched telegraph poles flash past, wires swooping from one to another to another. It was still a few minutes to six. The whole thing had taken less than an hour.

The roads were clear at this hour. In moments, they turned onto the highway at the 7Eleven, passed Walmart and Dollarite and their eerily empty parking lots, past the *Sleepy Nite Motel* where a solitary, plump guy loaded a suitcase into the trunk of an old Buick outside unit 6, and then Phil hung a right onto Quaker Mill Lane and headed downtown. Shortly after five minutes later, the SSV pulled to a halt in the station parking lot.

While Phil booked in the prisoner, Johnson went to see Sheriff Millstone.

'We got him. No trouble. Already called the attorney. Should be here in half an hour.'

'You can make this stick, right, Johnson? We've got to be tighter than bark on a tree on this one, right? This goes belly up, neither you nor I'll walk away in a straight line. Got that?'

'Got it.'

'Just think of your pension, Johnson. Because, basically, this guy is it.'

Donald Epps only spent a few minutes in the cells. By the time all the forms were filled out, his brief was pulling up in the parking lot out front. She was in her fifties, skinny enough that her collar bone protruded above her neckline, draped thinly with blotchy skin. She had heavily-styled blonde hair, the color way too smooth and uniform to be natural. She wore high-heeled strappy shoes, a skirt that clung tightly to her thighs, and a cream jacket over a white blouse. And her name was Jean Brody. Johnson knew that because he had dealt with her before on a number of cases. He also knew that she could be difficult with the police, especially in controversial cases like this one. Bill Millstone was right. He could not afford for this to go belly up.

Jean Brody sat beside her client. Johnson sat opposite with Phil by his side, and checked that the tape was rolling.

'Why did you kill your wife, Donald?' Johnson asked.

'I didn't.'

'We have hard evidence that you did. Where did you hide her body before you dumped it in Jefferson's Wood?'

'I didn't.'

'Was Debra Faulkner involved? Was it her idea or yours?'

'I don't know what you're talking about.'

'We have your DNA on Yvonne's body, Donald. There's no point denying it.'

'Since you've brought up DNA, Deputy,' said Jean Brody, 'perhaps you can tell us where you got it?'

'It was found on the body of Yvonne Epps.'

'But how do you know it is my client's?'

'It has been comprehensively matched.'

'Yes, but with what, Deputy? Have you taken a DNA sample from my client without his consent?'

'No, Ms Brody, of course not. The source of the match must remain confidential for now.'

Johnson felt the interview getting away from him. He needed to regain control, and straight away. He felt that familiar feeling of helplessness ignite within him. Control freakery, as Susan put it. He could hear her voice somewhere in his head. *You always get mad if you feel you're not in control, Johnson.* And his own voice, as if in response. *Whatever you do, do not lose your cool.*

'Where's Cristel, Mr Epps?' Johnson asked.

'I don't know.'

'Is she still alive?'

'I don't know. If she is, it's no thanks to you.'

'It's been two months now. If she's dead, where have you hidden the body?'

Donald Epps leaned back in his chair, so far that for one delicious moment, Johnson thought he would topple over and land on his rump. Instead, he placed a huge smarmy grin on his face and said, 'This really eats you up, don't it, Deputy? You stuffed up bad an' everyone knows it. One little girl relying on you, 'an you let her down. Reminds you of Millie, don't she?'

'How do you know about Millie?' Johnson caught Phil Logan's sideways glance at him. *Don't do it. Don't respond to him. Don't let him talk about YOU. You're losing control of the interview again.*

'I know all about you, Deputy Johnson Fincher. Made it my business to know all about the useless cop who failed my little girl. You think you got it all made, wife and daughter, comfy little life. Perfect family, pillar o' the community. But we know different, don' we, you and me? We know what you're really capable of!'

Jean Brody leaned forward. 'What's going on here? What are you alluding to, Mr Epps?'

'He knows,' said Donald Epps, with a grin on his face so infuriating that Johnson wanted to reach calmly across the table and punch that face so that it could never grin again. Fortunately, Jean Brody requested a break so she could consult with her client, and Johnson didn't get the opportunity.

Round back of the station, where the squad cars and SSV were kept, Johnson took a deep breath of chilly air. A line of scrappy, spindly trees extended beyond the perimeter, choked with old Coke bottles and Walmart bags, until the ground was lost beneath tangled undergrowth. *Perfect place to hide a body,* Johnson thought. *Right next to the police station, where nobody would think to look for it. And everyday the killer would pass by, snickering at how clever he was and how stupid the police were.*

Big Phil Logan stood next to him. 'Times like this I wish I smoked,' he said. 'So what was he on about in there?'

'Nothing, Phil. Just the usual lies, trying to squirm off the hook. You know, not once has he asked about Daryl. His own son, doesn't give a rat's fart. You got a kid, don't you?'

'Little boy. Eighteen months.'

'You'd give your life for him, right?'

'In a second.'

'You know what pushes my buttons the most about that piece of horse pucky in there? People are scared because of him, that's what. Small town like this, people scare easy. One kid goes missing, the streets are empty. The good folks of River Rapids are living in fear because of him, and I can't do a thing about it.'

'Maybe you can now. If we can get this to stick.'

Back inside, Jean Brody waited with pursed lips. 'He won't talk to me,' she said. 'Only you. This has a bad smell

277

all over it, Deputy Fincher. If you've interfered with my client in any way, you can be sure you won't have heard the last of it.'

Johnson ignored her, and entered the interview room.

'What is it, Mr Epps?'

'Can anybody hear us? Any hidden cameras?'

'No, Mr Epps, the tape is off and there are no hidden cameras. What do you want?'

'You get me outta here and I won't mention what happened last week.'

'I don't know what you mean, Mr Epps. What happened last week?'

'You won't be so smug when you've got a complaint round your neck. What you did to me was illegal!'

'What I did to you, Mr Epps, was considerably less than you deserve. You got anything else to say?'

'Too right I do! I'll tell 'em you assaulted me! I'll tell 'em you pulled me over, beat me up and left me for dead on the side of the road!'

'You're a murderer, Mr Epps, and you're going down for what you did. Nobody would ever believe you, and they wouldn't care if they did. They'll be lining up round the block to thank me for putting away a piece of scum like you.'

'You think you're so much better'n anyone, don't you, Deputy? You were just the same at high school.'

'High school?'

'I bet you don't even remember, do ya? Mr Popular. Had it all sewn up, even back then. Future mapped out, all planned. We were in the same class.'

'We were?'

'You ain't changed at all. Still smug and self-righteous. Didn't even know I existed, right?'

He was right. Johnson didn't remember him. But then he didn't remember a lot of people he went to school with, and just then he didn't feel like feeling guilty.

'Shall we ask Miss Brody back in?' he said.

Donald Epps sucked his teeth and turned away.

By mid afternoon, Donald Epps was back in the cells. The interview had taken most of the day, but they had gotten nowhere. Donald Epps had steadfastly refused to make any admissions, about his wife or his daughter, and Jean Brody had made frequent references to the source of the DNA evidence, until finally Johnson had called a halt on the proceedings.

Now he sat at his desk and rubbed his eyes. Jean Brody was clearly not going to leave this DNA issue alone, and although Don Epps was languishing in the cells right now, there was every possibility that he wouldn't be there much longer. *Tighter than bark on a tree,* Sheriff Millstone had said, but this one was turning slippery on him already.

And this is your career on the line, Johnny-boy. If you want to stay Deputy Sheriff of this burg, you better pull your finger out of your backside.

Self-righteous, Donald Epps had called him. Smug, too.

'Phil, come here a moment,' he said.

Phil Logan glanced around as if he were being watched, and wandered over to Johnson's desk. He tried to sit on the edge of it nonchalantly and failed miserably.

Johnson leaned into him. 'This DNA provenance issue, he could walk over that. We need to sew this up and fast. A scumbag like Don Epps cannot be clean. I want all records checked, every county in the frickin' state, as far back as we've been taking DNA samples. Somebody must have one on file somewhere. Get on to Virginia, Kentucky, Ohio, heck, get on to the FBI in DC if you have to.'

'Got it,' Phil said and wandered away.

Outside, the sky was darkening. Girls dressed as witches and boys dressed as ghosts already walked the streets, dragging baskets of candy as they passed the station. Johnson saw a gaggle of preschoolers with moms in tow chattering excitedly as they trooped up and down the sidewalks off Main Street. Many would be on their way to the Halloween Scare-fest due to start shortly at the bandstand on the Town Green... which reminded Johnson that he was expected to put in an appearance that evening. Bill Millstone was very keen on what he called 'PR opportunities', and chances to mingle with the townspeople were few. Still, Susan and Millie would also be there, so he could combine work and family for once.

And, truth be told, he was looking forward to putting Donald Epps to the back of his mind.

He left with Phil Logan shortly after five, with a promise from the Sheriff that he would, 'follow on after he had taken care of some things'. Johnson and Phil took a squad car and parked it on the edge of the green, all to increase their visibility and presence. The Green was already filling up with families, but, Johnson noticed that parents were keeping their children very close to hand. No packs of school kids ran hither and thither as Johnson expected. He remembered what he had said to Phil about the townspeople living in fear.

A local band had set up on the bandstand and were

playing covers of the latest pop songs. Johnson recognized none of them.

The homeowners around the green, some of the wealthiest citizens in town, had spared no expense in decorating their houses for the holiday. Although they never acknowledged it, he knew the families around here attempted to outdo each other. This year's most impressive display probably belonged to number six. It was certainly the most ostentatious. The house was a big, old townhouse – worth close to a million bucks in Johnson's humble view – and covered with an enormous gray web from front door to chimney pots. A huge, trembling spider perched outside the second floor windows, legs twitching and eyes flashing. Made the skeletons dangling from the tree in number four's front yard and the pumpkins on the stoops look outclassed. Still, number four could always get their own back in a couple of months' time at Christmas.

Johnson caught a whiff of baking potatoes coming from a stall to the side of the bandstand. A concession van had parked up and dealt burgers, dogs, funnel cakes and cotton candy. Kids shrieked as they tumbled down a giant, inflatable slide. Over there, a clown made balloon animals, and over there a line of kids waited to have their faces painted until they looked like princesses, Batman, or tigers.

This, right here, is what small town life should be like, thought Johnson. The whole community, pulling together, having fun, living the American dream.

If only you had solved the mystery of the missing girl, Johnson, then this picture would be complete.

And then Millie ran up to him, screaming '*Daddy!*'

and jumping into his arms, and Susan was right behind, and he squeezed his daughter tight. She sat on his hip and tried to cram a giant lollipop into her mouth.

'It's Cinnamon Bun, the prettiest girl in town!' he said. 'And she's up way past her bedtime, what a naughty girl!'

'Silly daddy! Is Halloween!'

'Did you go trick or treating?'

'Yes!'

'Did you get lots of candy?'

'Yes!'

'Are you going to eat it all at once?'

'Yes!'

'Are you going to get fat?'

'Yes! No! Daddy!'

He put her down and she ran toward the inflatable slide.

'Stay close, honey!' called Susan.

'She'll be fine,' Johnson said.

'I know. Just... Better safe than sorry.'

Johnson nodded. He didn't say anything, and neither did Susan, but they both knew what they were leaving unsaid. A couple of months ago, Susan would have been happy for Millie to run around here by herself. The town green, heart of downtown, was safe. Everybody knew that. But not now. Things had changed. *And Donald Epps has done this*, Johnson thought.

Phil Logan was letting kids try on his hat, over by the concession van. Doing his bit for PR. Reassuring the public. The Sheriff would be pleased.

Rick Vance, Mayor of River Rapids, stepped onto the bandstand and cleared his throat to a blare of feedback. His big, bushy beard and perfect gleaming smile reminded

Johnson of Santa Claus and David Letterman both at the same time.

'Ladies and gentlemen, boys and girls, welcome to River Rapids' annual Halloween Scare-fest twenty eleven!'

A ripple of applause circled the crowd.

'I hope you are ready for an evening of family fun, with maybe a few good clean scares thrown in too! This is Halloween after all!'

Some polite chuckles.

'We have an evening of music, fun and entertainment lined up for you, courtesy of the River Rapids City Municipal Department and our good friend Chuck Moynahan at Chuck's Autos, the first stop for a used car. Well, folks, let's start the ball rolling with a bang!'

And as if the whole thing had been carefully rehearsed – which, of course, it had been, Johnson was sure – the first firework rocketed high and starburst above them. The good townspeople of River Rapids did exactly what was required of them and let out an *ooooooh* of wonder and delight. Rick Vance stepped down from the bandstand, grinning broadly, confident that he had just secured a further term in office. More rockets screamed into the sky, exploding into colorful galaxies and universes above.

Johnson glanced down and saw Ken Epps loitering in the space between the inflatable slide and the concession van. He wore his usual uniform of sweatpants and sleeveless muscle shirt, designed to show off his biceps. The kid didn't seem to feel the cold. From one of those prodigious arms hung a stick thin girl who also didn't seem to feel the cold, dressed in a tight skirt that barely covered her, and a thin, tight top designed to emphasize not her arms, but other parts of her anatomy. Had to be Ken's girl – Hayley, was it? Johnson remembered interviewing her shortly after Cristel had disappeared. Also hanging back in the shadows by the concession van was Ken's buddy. Dale, Johnson remembered. Another musclehead, pumped up on protein shakes and steroids more than likely. Dale stood uncomfortably behind Ken and Hayley, brows heavy. Johnson wondered what was creeping his cheese. *Being the third wheel, perhaps. No girl of his own.* Johnson couldn't bring himself to feel sorry for him. Instead, he spoke into his radio.

'Heads up, Phil. Ken Epps and his buddies are here. Keep an eye open for trouble.'

'Gotcha.'

Where was the Sheriff? Bill had promised to put in an appearance, but had yet to show. Suddenly, Johnson felt uneasy, as though the night were beginning to run away from him. He realized that Susan had stopped watching the fireworks and was now watching him.

'What's wrong, Johnson?'

'Nothing, nothing. Just want the evening to pass off without trouble.'

'You think there'll be trouble?'

'I don't know. Maybe you should take Millie home.'

'If you think that's best.'

But Millie, of course, had gone.

'She was standing right there!' Susan said. 'Next to the slide! Five seconds ago!'

Panic rose inside Johnson and threatened to choke him. *Please God, no! No! No! Take me, not her! Take me instead!*

'She can't be far, Johnson! She was standing right there! Right there!'

The space between the inflatable slide and the concession van was empty. Ken Epps and his buddies had gone.

Johnson was already running toward the inflatable slide, eyes scanning the kids on it. None looked like Millie. What was she wearing? What had Millie been wearing? He had seen her just seconds before and he couldn't remember what she was wearing. He was a *cop!* He was trained to be observant! And he couldn't remember what his own daughter was wearing! Had it been her puffy red jacket? Or the green duffle coat? She had been holding something. What was it? What had she been holding?

He reached for his radio. 'Phil, Millie's gone missing! Check the woods, Phil. She was right here seconds ago, she can't have gone far. My Millie! Holding a giant lolly!'

'On it, Johnson!'

Johnson saw Phil running on the other side of the green, running toward the strip of woodland that ran down a small valley to the Conway River, one of the rivers that gave the town its name. A gravel path ran along a number of shallow rapids down there, and was a popular nature walk during the summer. Now, however, the end of October and after dark, it would be deserted. Johnson pictured Millie falling into the Conway and being swept away in the rapids. The sound of his own breathing filled his brain. He couldn't think...

Somebody was calling his name.

'Johnson! Johnson!'

Susan. It was Susan's voice. She stood in front of him, holding Millie's hand.

'Johnson, it's okay. She's here. She'd wandered over to the face painting, that's all.'

The red puffy jacket, that's what she was wearing. Of course it was. The red puffy jacket and the giant lolly. Johnson felt strength drain from his knees. The *River Rapids Recorder* would not print the headline *NOW INCOMPETENT DEPUTY LOSES OWN DAUGHTER* after all. Johnson swept her up and hugged her tight.

'Take her home, Susan. Please. Keep her safe.'

'Come home as soon as you can, Johnson. Okay? Promise me.'

'I will. As soon as I can get away.'

He watched them walk away, hand in hand, to the Subaru parked a short way up the hill. He watched Susan strap Millie into the kiddie seat in back, and drive down to the stop light on Main. The light changed, Susan took a left, and she was gone.

The fireworks had ended and the band returned to stage. Soon they were cranking out some Britney Spears tune. Or Katy whatsername. Somebody. Johnson saw Sheriff Millstone pull up and let out a deep breath. Events were moving back under control. Maybe the evening would pass without incident after all.

The space between the inflatable slide and the concession van was still empty. Where were Ken Epps and his minions hiding?

His radio crackled.

'Johnson, you there?'

'I'm here, Phil. Panic over, we got her. You can make your way back.'

'Relieved to hear it, Johnson, but I can't come back just yet. In fact, you'd better join me here.'

'Why, what's going on, Phil?'

'Johnson, I... I think I've found Cristel Epps.'

CHAPTER SIXTEEN
DARYL EPPS

Friday November 4th, 2011

Nathan says he only agreed to play Batman versus Superman because I like superheroes. He says they're lame because they all have big muscles and contribute to the belief that might is always right. He says they add to the growing problem that men and boys now feel a superhero physique is the best and only way for a man to be and any man who looks different is weak and inadequate and barely masculine at all. And they wear silly costumes.

I say that is easy for you to say, being the strongest boy in Fourth Grade. He likes this and agrees to play even though he says make believe is for babies. I'm Batman. He's Superman. He creates his base in some shoe boxes under his bed. I make do with a cave fashioned from a pajama top slung on the floor.

All goes fine, until Batman, obviously, wins.

I have been living with Nathan for five days now. The first night was awesome. Nathan's mom (she wants me to call her Elizabeth but I can't) set up a cot bed for me on the floor of Nathan's room, squeezed in between the shelves of junk Nathan calls his scientific equipment (bits of old VCRs, a motor from his mom's old vacuum cleaner, old radios, stuff like that), and his collection of sci-fi books (Isaac Asimov, Ray Bradbury and other old-sounding names I've never heard of). That first night we couldn't stop laughing. Something about sleepovers makes them screamingly funny, but don't ask me what because I won't be able to tell you. Probably something to do with them being the most exciting thing ever! There we were in our pajamas! About to sleep in the same room! All night! We giggled into the late hours until Nathan's mom got cross and threatened to sit in there with us until we were asleep. After that, we whispered about school, Amelia, the stars, and whether Mr Bresham knew that hairs grew out of his nostrils until tiredness overtook us.

We woke together, dressed together, ate together, went to school together, came home together. And it was great.

Until Batman beat Superman.

'No way, man!' Nathan says. 'Batman is just a man! No way would he beat Superman! Superman comes from another planet and has all these powers, like super strength!'

'I thought you said super powers are lame!'

'They are, but they still beat Batman!'

'You're just sore you've lost.'

'And who decides I've lost? You? Yeah, that's convenient. That's not how wars are won!'

'I got into your base.'

'You threw Batman in there when I wasn't ready! A stupid, plastic figure! How is that fair?'

'It is fair!'

'Fine, take the stupid thing.' He throws the Superman

figure at me. It bounces off my shoulder and hurts. 'And get out of my bedroom.'

'What? No.'

'It's my room.'

'It's my room too.'

'No, it isn't. It's my room and I said get out!'

I kick over Batman's cave, throw the stupid, plastic figure at Nathan, and run from the room, slamming the door behind me. I'm shocked by how many tears pump from my eyes. I have no idea where to go, so I thump down the stairs, taking three at a time, and run into the living room, where Clarisse Bevan looks up and says, 'Hi there, Daryl, how are things going?' from behind a mug of coffee.

I stop, I look around, I wonder if she has come to take me back to Dad and Debra and Ken. I flick the tears from my eyes. My heart pounds. Now Batman seems so unimportant.

Nathan's mom sits in the other armchair with another mug. 'What happened, Daryl? You and Nathan mad with each other?'

She glances at Clarisse. Her rolled eyes say *Boys!*

Clarisse says, 'I have some bad news for you, Daryl. I think you should sit.'

I obey because I can't think of what else to do. I know what she is going to say. She'll say that I can't stay with Nathan any more. Nathan's mom and dad only want one boy, and I have to go back to the trailer. I know it.

Clarisse leans across and puts her hand on my knee. I want to pull away but I don't.

'I wanted to tell you before you saw it on the news. The police found your sister. I'm so sorry, Daryl, but she didn't make it.'

289

The silence in the room reminds me of the silence in the classroom when we have a test. The sort of silence when nobody wants to be there. I don't know what to do. Am I expected to cry? Should I burst into uncontrollable sobs like they do on TV?

All I seem able to do is stare at the corner of the room behind Clarisse, where, framed on the wall, the words, *God, grant me the courage to change the things I can, the serenity to accept the things I can't, and the wisdom to tell the difference,* are posted above a picture of a cute puppy chewing a bone.

'It's a shock,' says Nathan's mom suddenly, 'of course it is. You must feel terrible. You need anything, you tell me, you hear? We're all here for you, Daryl.'

I mumble something which I think is thanks. I know I should feel sad, but Cristel's been gone for weeks and I can't feel sad on cue. If anything I feel happy because I don't have to go back to Dad and the trailer after all. And then I feel guilty for feeling happy. And then I feel sad because I feel guilty.

I ask if I can see her because I can't think of anything else to say. Nathan's mom looks at Clarisse again.

'I don't think so, Daryl,' Clarisse says. 'That wouldn't be right. You can always say your goodbyes at the funeral.'

Nathan comes down the stairs in time to hear what she said. He comes to a stop with wide eyes. His mom says, 'Daryl's just had some bad news, Nathan. I hope you two didn't have a big fight.'

Nathan shakes his head and holds out his hand. I shake it and follow him out of the room, eager to take the excuse to leave. Why do adults have to be so weird about everything? Okay, so Cristel is dead for sure, but I guessed as much a long time ago, and standing around feeling awkward won't help any.

Nathan yells something about going out and I follow him to our secret hideout. We crawl through the tunnel of foliage to the clearing. Just peeking through the spaces between the leaves is the roof of Nathan's house, but we are far enough away to feel safe.

I sit there, blinking.

'They find your sister?'

I nod.

'I'm sorry, man.'

I nod.

'You should put this in the chest.' He hands me a telescopic aerial.

'What is it?'

'Latest military hardware. What the army use to spy on Bin Laden.'

'No it isn't.'

'Swear it. Remember that army convoy drove through town last week? Fell from a jeep. Had to trade Jeff Bowles two girly mags 'cos he saw it first.'

'Girly mags? Where'd you get them?'

'You know Jeff's brother, Greg? He has a newspaper route. He filches the old mags before they go in the incinerator.'

'Wait. You traded this from Jeff for girly mags from his own brother?'

'Wheeling and dealing, my friend. One thing you have to learn in life. There is always a way to get what you want. You wanna put this in or not?'

I can't help smiling and shaking my head. I take the latest army aerial, which can probably detect signals from

Mars or the depths of the ocean, or anyplace really, and put it in the treasure chest with the flattened pennies and the ostrich feather and the sword and the dinosaur bone.

We sit in silence for a while, neither of us afraid of it, enjoying the peace. Only a chilly November wind disturbs the stillness.

'What do you think happened to her?' Nathan asks at last.

'Taken by aliens,' I say. 'Taken to their spaceship to become their princess. To us she's been gone a couple of months, but to her it's been a lifetime. She lived in a huge golden palace of domes and minarets and she ate oysters and Turkish Delight whenever she wanted it. And she had servants who looked after her and cleaned up her mess, and a huge room with a bed with a roof and her own bathroom. And she lived happily ever after.'

Friday, November 11th, 2011

The funeral is today. I still don't know how I should feel or what I should do. Maybe I should try to cry. Nathan's mom comes into the room and says, 'Time to get up, boys. Breakfast in ten minutes.'

I get up and dressed without thinking much, and that suits me fine. Today, all I have to do is stand in the right place and look sad, which must be something I can do.

We eat Cheerios in a subdued silence, uncomfortable in black pants and white shirts. The drive to the cemetery is short. Nathan sits next to me in the back seat, but we don't say much. I wonder if Dad and Ken will be there and hope they aren't. We park at the side of the road next to the hearse. The road to the cemetery is narrow and bumpy and full of cars. I have never seen it so busy. People stand in groups and watch us as we drive by. Who are they? Why are they here? I don't know.

When I step out of the car, people rush forward, yelling at me, holding microphones and cameras. *Daryl, how do you feel, Daryl? What's it like losing a mother and a sister, Daryl? Have you said your goodbyes to your sister, Daryl? Have you anything to say to your father and brother, Daryl? Daryl? Daryl? Daryl?* Nathan's mom and dad step in front of them. Nathan's dad curses and tells them all to go away. And then suddenly, as if from nowhere, Clarisse stands in front of me. She puts her arm around my shoulders and leads me through a wrought iron arch with *River Rapids Cemetery* written on it.

The cemetery is small and overgrown, but the view across the valley to the main part of town is huge and wide. I want to go over there all alone and get lost somewhere in that view. If only I could jump in the blink of an eye, to the opposite hill where sheep chew the grass. It will be calm and peaceful over there, with nobody asking questions or putting their arm around my shoulders. Or perhaps, down there, on Main Street, browsing through the old comic store and maybe finding an early super rare Superman. Or down there, swinging on the rail outside the 7Eleven on the corner of County Road Six and Highway 32, the place where mom definitely did not hitch a ride to California or Illinois in a truck, because she was dead by then. Or perhaps over there, in the cannery, which you can't quite see because Jefferson's Wood is in the way, hanging out with Nathan and Amelia. Any of those places would do.

Anywhere but right here, right now.

I didn't go to mom's funeral. I don't even know what

they did. All I know is that they cremated her because the body was too old to be buried. That's what Clarisse told me anyway. Dad wasn't there because he was in jail. Ken didn't care. Nathan's mom and dad didn't feel they knew my mom well enough to go to her funeral. And I was too young to go alone, of course. So I guess it was just the priest, all alone. He must have felt stupid speaking to an empty room. I think he must have skipped bits and pretended he done them. That's what I would have done.

Clarisse still has her arm around my shoulders. Her arm is hot and heavy and I can feel her sweat against my neck. I want to fling her arm off and run away. But then I see Dad and Ken standing outside the chapel.

They've let Dad out of jail just so he can come to the funeral. A big policeman stands at his elbow. I wonder why he's allowed to come to Cristel's funeral but not mom's. Perhaps he didn't want to come to mom's. And everybody thinks he murdered her anyway. Standing as far away from the policeman as he can get, there's Ken. I can see he doesn't want to be here. He probably thinks people will think he killed Cristel if he doesn't come. He is wearing another of those tight muscle vests, because he doesn't have anything else. At least this one is black and has sleeves.

I don't want to see them. I don't want them to see me. I stop walking.

Clarisse knows why. She likely expected this.

'It's fine, Daryl, honey,' she says. 'You don't have to talk to them. You don't even have to say hello if you don't want to. And I'll be right by your side the whole time. You're safe, okay?'

I know perfectly well there's no way a fat lady like

Clarisse can keep me safe from Ken if he wants to hurt me. But what can he do when there are so many people around, right? There are even TV cameras down by the gate. If Ken attacked me, he'd be on the WVTV news before he'd even started his evening workout.

My heart begins to pound, but I look away and keep walking. Keep walking right into the chapel.

We sit near the front where I can't see Dad or Ken. But all through the service, I can feel their eyes against the back of my head like lasers. I feel like a damsel-in-distress tied to an operating table while a red beam comes closer and closer. I stare at the tiny coffin resting on trestles ahead and concentrate on breathing slowly. I wish Nathan were sitting next to me, but he's with his mom and dad across the aisle.

The priest talks about a life tragically cut short and a world that failed an innocent six year old. He hopes that maybe young Cristel can finally find peace. We say amen and sing a hymn about Jesus' love for little children. Then men in suits lift the coffin onto their shoulders and take it outside.

We follow the coffin out and as I turn, my eye catches Ken's. My heart thumps a crazy beat, fear pumping through it. I think of his fist plowing into my face on the side of the road, waking up in hospital, convinced that my own brother wants me dead. Ken grins at me and draws his thumb across his throat. My knees feel weak and I nearly fall.

Clarisse takes my arm. 'Poor love,' she says.

Outside, we stand by a freshly dug grave and watch the men in suits lower the coffin into the hole on ropes. Dad and Ken stand opposite me and I know they stare at me the whole time, but I don't dare look up and see them. I feel that they could kill me simply by eye contact. I picture myself dropping dead at my sister's funeral and the headline in the *River Rapids Recorder* the next day. Several times I am on the verge of throwing off Clarisse's arm and running away, disappearing through the cemetery and into the woods where nobody can find me. I could live like a wild man in the woods, wearing skins and eating nuts and berries. But I know I would never survive. I would starve within a week. I never ran away from Dad and Ken for the same reason. I'm just not tough enough to look after myself.

I bet Nathan could. I bet he could live like Tarzan in the jungle. I bet he'd enjoy it.

At last the funeral is over and we walk back along the path to the cars. I can't walk fast enough. Dad is bundled into a police car and is taken away. I watch Ken mount his motorbike and roar away with a fan of gravel and as much noise as possible. Before he lowers his helmet, he stares at me and another shock of fear shudders down my spine.

I hear cameras clicking and whirring, but they are kept back this time close to the fence. Seconds later, I am sitting next to Nathan in the back of his car, his parents in the front. Clarisse's head appears at the window.

'All over now, Daryl,' she says. 'Best forget all about it. Think of it as a new start. School on Monday!'

She waves to Nathan's mom, and we're on our way. As we leave the cemetery behind us, I wonder if she's right. Is it all over? It doesn't seem over to me. Not at all.

Nobody says anything as we drive back to Nathan's house. His dad stares at the road ahead. His mom looks out of the passenger window and winds a strand of hair around her fingers. I've seen Amelia do that sometimes. I get bored of the silence and poke Nathan in the ribs. He yelps, squirms, and pokes me back. Twice. I stifle a yell, which makes me laugh, so I stifle that too. This sets Nathan off too.

'What's going on back there?' Nathan's mom says.

'Nothing,' says Nathan, and pokes me again. I wriggle out of his way and we both stifle smirks.

Nathan's mom shakes her head. 'We just buried his sister,' she says to Nathan's dad. 'Kids.'

By the time we pull into the drive, Nathan and I are gasping to get out and run. We hare into the back yard, yelling and shoving each other. We fool around for a while, play a bit of soccer, tell stupid jokes.

'Your mom's so fat, if she were a dinosaur, she'd be a Jellosaurus Rex!' yells Nathan and rolls on the grass.

'Your mom's so fat, her cereal bowl comes with a lifeguard!' I yell back, and we both scream hysterically.

'Your mom's so fat, when she went to McDonald's, they called Wendy's for backup!' he yells, doubled over, until something smashes inside the house.

We stop laughing and sit up. 'Mom?' Nathan murmurs.

He's on his feet, running toward the house, and I'm right behind him. We step silently through the back door, into the kitchen. The house seems quiet, so quiet that my heart starts thumping again. The familiar sensation of fear courses through my blood, and maybe I should have listened to the warning, because standing there in the porch is Ken. Nathan's dad blocks his way into the house, and Nathan's mom stares at a brick and shards of glass on the floor. Cold wind blows the net curtains through the hole in the window.

'Get off my property or I call the police,' Nathan's dad yells.

'I know he's in here,' Ken yells. He's still wearing the black muscle vest he had at the funeral and I realize he must have followed us.

And then, of course, he sees me.

The sight of me seems to enrage him. From nowhere, he sucker punches Nathan's dad, who crumples to the floor without a sound. Nathan's mom screams and covers her mouth. Ken shoves her aside as though she weren't even there.

I am frozen to the spot. I cannot move. Terror roots me to the floor like a gazelle in front of a train.

Until Nathan screams, 'Run!' in my face and gives me a shove that very nearly floors me too. Then I am flying, back through the kitchen, through the back door, through the back yard, through the narrow tunnel to our hideout. I crouch behind the treasure chest, clutching my knees and rocking. 'Please God, please God, please God, please God...'

Deep down, some part of me wonders what Ken is doing to Nathan right now, but really, shamefully, I can barely think of anything other than staying here, staying hidden, and praying that Ken won't find me.

'What do you think you're doing, Daryl?' Ken yells, suddenly, and he seems so close, so very close. Standing somewhere in Nathan's back yard. Can he see me through the chinks in the bushes? 'What do you think you're doing? Think you can turn your back on your family? Family don't go away that easy, shrimp. Think you're better than us, don't yer? Me and Dad, you think you're so much better. Well, think again, shrimp. Think again while I tear your lungs out.'

I curl up tighter, bury my head between my knees.

Tears squeeze from the corners of my eyes. ' Please God, please God, please God...'

The pounding of my heart seems to drown out Ken's words. I strain to hear. He seems to have finished ranting. I hear him curse under his breath. I hear the sound of his lighter as he flicks it – once, twice, three times. Ken calls himself a fitness fanatic, but he's not. He wouldn't smoke or use drugs if he were. No, he spends hours at the gym building himself up so he can threaten people. It suddenly occurs to me right now that my big brother is no better than a schoolyard bully.

Only, he really will kill me if he finds me.

I hear sirens coming closer. Ken curses again and slings his cigarette away. It comes to rest not far from me, in the soil under the rhododendrons. I can see the cylinder of ash smoldering on the end and the words written around the filter. By the time Deputy Fincher and two other cops emerge from the kitchen, Ken has run through the shrubs into Jefferson's Wood.

I look up from my hiding place behind the treasure chest.

I don't want to come out even now. But when I hear Nathan calling my name, and see the shiner around his left eye where Ken punched him, I have no choice. As we enter the house, paramedics load the still semi-conscious form of Nathan's dad into the back of an ambulance.

This is my fault. Ken is my brother. He came here because of me. This has all happened because of me.

Deputy Fincher speaks into his shoulder-mounted radio. 'I'm putting an APB out on Ken Epps, that's Kennedy Epps. White male, sixteen years old. Approach with caution. He is dangerous. I want him brought in ASAP.'

I sit on the sofa, eyes wide, staring at the picture on the wall of the cute puppy chewing a bone. The words speak of courage, serenity and wisdom, but all I feel is emptiness right now.

CHAPTER SEVENTEEN
JOHNSON FINCHER

1.

Monday October 31st, 2011

Cristel Epps – who else could it be? – lay face down on a muddy patch of river bank, her head in the water and her hair floating out like sun rays. Johnson was glad he couldn't see her face because he was sure the sight would have haunted his nightmares for the rest of his life. Seeing her little, pudgy hands tied behind her back with duct tape was bad enough. She wore a set of faded Disney Princesses pajamas that were clearly too small for her.

Johnson thought of Millie's bedspread, sitting on it and reading her Dr Suess or *The Three Little Pigs* and he felt sick all over again.

'Phil, go get the Sheriff and tell the Mayor Halloween's over for this year and he'll have to send everybody home.'

Without a word, Phil turned and scrambled up the thorny bank toward the Town Green.

And suddenly, the only sound Johnson could hear was the gentle gurgling of the Conway River. If he listened hard, he could just hear something singing in the high boughs above him. *The calm before the storm*, he thought.

He didn't want to look at the tiny body half afloat before him, but it tugged at the corners of his eyes like a hook. His gaze fell on Cristel Epps' tiny body and he thought of Millie, and he wept. Suddenly and uncontrollably, in this moment of silence, he wept. *I'm sorry, God. As a human being, I'm sorry for yet another atrocity.*

Phil reappeared at the top of the bank and Johnson hastily rubbed away the tears.

'Mayor's not happy,' he said. 'Said he's not canceling Halloween on the say-so of a... er, well...'

'Spit it out, Phil.'

'Well, on the say-so of a Deputy Sheriff of questionable competence. His words. Sorry.'

'You can tell Mayor Vance he's welcome to move his backside down here and take a look at this body. If he doesn't mind spraying the funnel cake he's been cramming down his throat all evening down the front of his expensive suit. And you can use those exact words.'

Phil looked sheepish. 'Sheriff Millstone's dealing with it.'

Johnson was already taking deep breaths to prevent any funnel cake spraying incidents happening to him. Thank God he had sent Susan and Millie home earlier.

Moments later Sheriff Millstone appeared at the top of the bank. He turned away when he saw what lay at the bottom.

'I've pulled in Joe Longfellow and Gilly Dwight to clear the crowd,' he said. 'Forensics are on their way.'

Minutes later the area was crawling with people and the calm before the storm was undoubtedly over.

Johnson stood back as crime scene tape was stretched from tree to tree and a tent was erected over the body. He fought the urge to yell at everybody. He wanted them to back off and have a little respect and leave the little girl in peace. Above all, he wanted to shout, *Don't you dare treat this as yet another crime scene! Don't make this just another day like all the others! This one is different, don't you understand that?* But then he squashed his feelings away because he knew he would stand a much greater chance of bringing the killer to justice if he worked methodically and emotionlessly. *Methodically and emotionlessly, got that, Johnson?*

Somebody trooped up to him in a forensics suit and goggles. It was only when she spoke that Johnson realized it was Jeanette Schwartz.

'She hasn't been here long. A day or two at the most. Killed somewhere else, but I guess you knew that. The duct tape around her wrists and ankles is interesting.'

'It is?'

'Duct tape's not all the same, you know. All sorts of fiber patterns show up under analysis. Match it with tape in a suspect's possession, you've got compelling forensic evidence right there.'

'Good to know.'

She ambled off, careful where she stepped. Sheriff Millstone gingerly slid sideways down the river bank, coming to a halt with a grunt.

'I want this kept quiet for now,' the Sheriff said. 'We don't want a circus. Get some space to make headway on this before we release it to the press. This is the opportunity we need to restore a little faith in the RRPD.'

A spark of anger surged along Johnson's arms and

legs. 'A little girl is dead, Bill. I wouldn't call it any kind of opportunity.'

Sheriff Millstone's eyes narrowed. He looked at Johnson as if he were regarding a zoo animal. 'I'll take it from here, Johnson. You can cut along home.'

'I'm fine, I can stay longer...'

'Go home. Rest. Come back full of ideas tomorrow, and we'll crack this case.'

Johnson nodded and started to climb the steep bank.

'And, Johnson?'

He stopped and looked back.

'Just you make sure you look after that little girl of yours.'

2.

Tuesday November 1st, 2011

Seconds after Johnson reached his desk, Phil Logan perched his rear on the edge of it. He held out a wad of paper.

'Thought you'd appreciate some good news, boss.'

Johnson took the papers and flicked through them.

'Is this what I think it is?'

'Yup, all the way from Lewis County, Ohio. Donald Epps was involved in a bar fight in a roadhouse out that way, three years ago. Arrested and held on related charges for two days. DNA sample taken as routine.'

A huge grin curled onto Johnson's face. 'Then we've got him! We've tied him to his dead wife's body! He killed her and we can prove it! Jean Brody can shove her technicalities where the birds don't sing!'

Phil was grinning too. 'Up all night chasing that!'

'I'll stand you a stiff one, Phil! Heck, I'll stand you ten! In fact, you can get on to Jean Brody right now and tell her we're charging her client with first degree homicide. That'll wipe the smile off her face.'

An hour later, Johnson sat opposite Donald Epps in the interview room. Jean Brody sat next to her client, cheeks pinched and lips pursed. Johnson started the tape rolling.

'You don't get out much, do you, Mr Epps?' Johnson said.

'What?'

'When was the last time you got out, do you think? And I don't mean a beer run to the 7Eleven. I mean, when was the last time you took a vacation? Got out of town?'

'What the...?'

'Three years ago, maybe? September of 2008? Let me jog your memory. Weekend trip to Lewis County, Ohio. Got into a bar fight. Glassed some poor dude and spent two nights in the cells, any of this ringing bells?'

'Get to the point, Deputy,' said Jean Brody, but Johnson could see from her face that she had figured out where this was going. And that look, right there, was the first time Johnson had felt good since this whole sorry mess had started.

'The Lewis County Sheriff's Department were very helpful and sent us your DNA as soon as we contacted them.'

Johnson saw sweat appear on Donald Epps' brow and that was the second time Johnson felt good. So good. He leaned forward and said, 'We can tie you to your wife's dead body, Donald. Your blood is under her fingernails.

Fought back, did she? What did she do? Hit you? Punched you in the nose, maybe? Cut your lip? Scratched you with those nails?'

Jean Brody stared out of the window, her long neck and bony shoulders angled away from her client. She had clearly given him up for a lost cause.

'Why did you do it, Donald? I've been trying to figure that out. Care to enlighten us?'

Johnson couldn't catch Donald's eye, but he saw a bead of sweat run down the man's forehead into his eye.

'I'll tell you what I think happened, Donald, how about that? I think you met Debra Faulkner. And suddenly Yvonne was in the way, wasn't she? You didn't want to be married anymore. You could have divorced her, but that was expensive and you'd have been stuck with alimony for three kids. You could never have afforded that, could you, Donald? You'd have had to get a job, and all those days of guzzling beer in front of the TV would have been over. No, simpler just to kill her. Was Debra in on it, Don? Did she help you?'

Donald stared at the tabletop. Sweat ran down his face but he said nothing.

'I think she did, Donald. Yvonne was in Debra's apartment, wasn't she? The carpet fibers prove that. I think you got Yvonne to go to Debra's apartment on some pretext. Talk things out, maybe. Then you strangled her with electrical wire. She clawed you while you were choking the life out of her, didn't she? Caught you in the face, arm maybe. Drew blood. Then what? Left her there for a while. I bet Debra wasn't happy about that, but where else could she go? The police would be all over your trailer for a while. Couldn't put her there. So you waited until the fuss had died down. Waited until everybody assumed she'd left you, skipped town, run off with some trucker. Then you dumped the body in Jefferson's Woods, deep where it would never be found. How am I doing, Don?'

Donald Epps still stared at the table. Jean Brody still stared out of the window.

'And you know what, Donald? If we hadn't been searching for your daughter, we probably never would have found your wife. Kinda ironic, that. Could have got away with it, if only you'd left your daughter alone.'

Jean Brody suddenly snapped to attention. 'Can we take a break?'

'I don't think so, Ms Brody.'

'We're done here, Deputy Fincher.'

'No, Ms Brody, we're not done. It's not your day today, Donald. Because, you know what? We've found your daughter too.'

'What?' Jean Brody blurted.

Donald Epps raised his head. 'You've found Cristel?'

'Why was I not told of this?' Jean Brody barked.

'Cristel's body was found bound with tape floating in the Conway River,' said Johnson. 'We're going to need you to make a formal identification, Donald, but we know it's her.'

'You're lying,' said Donald Epps.

'Did you do to her what you did to her mother, Donald? Kept her body hidden somewhere until the fuss died down and then dumped it where you thought it would never be found?'

'No, I...'

'Why'd you kill her, Donald? One less mouth to feed, is that all it was? One less distraction from your TV screen?'

'No, I didn't...'

'What DNA will we find on her, Donald, do you think? More of your blood, maybe? Did she fight back like her mother did, Donald? No probably not. She was only six years old, wasn't she?'

'I didn't touch her! I did nothing!'

'You'd love us to believe that, Donald.'

'Listen, you gotta believe me. I didn't touch Cristel! Yes, okay, Yvonne, that was me, but Cristel, no!'

Three people were yelling at once. Jean Brody yelled, 'Mr Epps, I strongly advise you to say not another word!' clearly trying to drown her client's confession. Johnson yelled, 'Just to be clear, Donald, are you saying you did murder your wife?' Donald Epps yelled, 'I never touched a hair on Cristel's head!' Jean Brody yelled, 'Deputy Fincher, I demand a recess! I need to speak to my client in private!' Johnson yelled, 'I don't think so, Ms Brody, your client just confessed to first degree homicide! We have it right here on the tape!'

And suddenly there was silence. Johnson could hear the tape reels revolving.

'To be clear, Mr Epps, are you confessing to the murder of your wife, Yvonne Epps?'

Donald Epps did not raise his eyes from the table, but he said, 'I killed Yvonne, but I didn't kill Cristel.'

'Did Debra Faulkner help you kill your wife, Mr Epps?'

'No.'

'Who else was involved, Mr Epps?'

Donald said nothing.

Johnson took a deep breath and said, 'Mr Epps, we need you to identify the body. Now may be a good time to make the identification. Then we can talk about who murdered your daughter.'

'I don't...'

'It was you or somebody you know, Mr Epps. We'll take it from there, shall we?'

3.

Johnson reached home on time and enjoyed the look on Susan's face when he walked through the front door. Millie was in the living room watching Dora the Explorer while Susan folded laundry in the kitchen.

'From the look on your face, you've had a good day,' she said.

'Donald Epps confessed to the murder of his wife,' said Johnson.

They spent the evening cuddled up on the sofa after Millie had gone to bed, watching *The Late Show.*

4.

Friday November 11ᵗʰ, 2011

Johnson had heard somebody say that in policing you are only as good as your last arrest. As he pulled the Crown Victoria onto Main and nosed toward the parking lot in front of the precinct, he wondered whether the poor numpty who came up with it had a boss riding his tail too.

A week had passed since Donald Epps had confessed to the murder of his wife, Yvonne, and the congratulations had already dried up. One case solved, but another was pending, and this was the one everybody – Sheriff Millstone, Mayor Bob Vance, the DA, the *River Rapids Recorder,* the good townspeople of River Rapids, everybody – wanted a cut-and-dried solution to. They wanted to know exactly who to blame for the abduction and murder of Cristel Epps so that they could convince themselves that this was just a blip in the history of their town, and everything would now return to normal.

But eleven days after Cristel's body had been discovered floating in the Conway, Johnson was no closer to finding the killer. Although he would have loved to pin a double murder on Donald Epps, Johnson was convinced that Donald really did not have anything to do with it. A week and a half of strenuous denials of involvement was persuasive. And no sniff of a motive could be found. Johnson was sure that the answer lay in an area he hadn't thought of yet. Something he had overlooked. Something that, as Sherlock Holmes had probably said, lay right under his nose but he just couldn't see it.

Bringing the Crown Victoria to a halt in his parking bay, Johnson killed the engine and leaned back in his bucket seat for a moment. He knew as soon as he stepped foot into that station, Bill Millstone would be on his back, demanding to know what leads were being pursued and what progress was being made.

Worse, today was Cristel's funeral, and the papers would be desperate for some new morsel to lead with.

Johnson leaned back and rubbed his eyes. He needed a vacation. He should book some leave and take Susan and Millie somewhere nice. The Ozarks or the Tetons. Maybe even Florida if he could afford it. Just as soon as all this was over.

The first thing Bill Millstone said to him when he stepped into the station was that he didn't want Johnson to go to the funeral.

'Won't it look odd if I'm not there?' Johnson said, knowing that the Sheriff was never one to miss a PR opportunity. 'What will it look like if there's no police presence?'

'Phil Logan's going in your place, Johnson. Given your history with the Epps family, I think we need to show a little sensitivity on this one. Phil will take custody of Donald Epps while he's there.'

'You're letting Donald Epps go to the funeral? He's a confessed killer!'

'He's also the father of a murdered child, Johnson. A child whose murderer is still at large, thanks to us. Like I say, sensitivity. I'm not giving Gerald Sumner over at the *Recorder* another chance to crucify us.'

Johnson wanted to protest further, but knew it was pointless. On matters to do with the press or the media, Bill Millstone was immovable. Johnson sat at his desk and opened the case file, just as he did every morning. He liked to review the case at the start of every day. Not only did it mean he knew it inside out, but sometimes, just sometimes, something new would pop out at him. Something he had missed before. Something maybe right under his nose.

He watched the blurry black and white CCTV footage of Cristel passing the 7Eleven. He freeze-framed the vehicle that seemed to follow her slowly along the street. Many times he had stared at this image, trying to catch a glimpse of whoever was driving, until his eyes lost focus and the picture was nothing more than random pixels. He reviewed interview statements from Donald Epps, Daryl Epps, Ken Epps and Debra Faulkner. Even the witness statement from Georgina Campbell, and her weird pseudo-confession based on her dreams. Visions, she had called them. Just imagine if the *Recorder* got hold of that. At least he could depend on Barbara Bruchner's silence on that one.

After re-reading all the statements, he kept circling back to one question. What had Cristel been doing on the Highway? Had she been taken there? But Georgina Campbell had said that the girl was alone when she had seen her. Had she left the Epps' trailer voluntarily? But why would she leave at six in the morning? Unless she had been running away. But if she had decided to run away from home, why that morning? And what had happened to her after she had passed the 7Eleven?

Johnson had pondered these questions many times in the months since August 20th, but without more information he couldn't answer them. The circumstances surrounding Cristel's abduction and murder were still frustratingly beyond reach.

And now he wasn't even allowed to attend the funeral. Johnson felt like getting up from his desk, walking out of the station and driving up to the cemetery right then and there, forget Bill Millstone and his stupid sensitivity.

Johnson took a deep breath and tried to unwind. *Let go of the control freakery, Johnson*, as Susan would say. Of course, he knew that Bill Millstone was under a great deal of pressure too, and was simply passing it downwards. His own position was up for review before long, and Bill had no intention of passing on the position of Sheriff of River Rapids any time soon. Johnson tucked his legs under his computer and settled down to some hard thinking. Carole Jeffrey dropped off a cream cheese bagel sometime around lunchtime and tried to engage him in light-hearted small talk about Thanksgiving plans. After thirty seconds of attempting to explain why the family couldn't go to her sister's in Wisconsin this year, she gave up and wandered away. Shortly after lunch, Phil Logan returned with Donald Epps. He reported that although both Daryl and Ken Epps had been present, the funeral had passed without trouble. Donald was returned to his cell. Johnson felt childishly disappointed, as though trouble at the funeral would have justified his wish to be there. Now, it looked as though Sheriff Millstone's arbitrary decision had been the right call.

Sometime that afternoon, Carole called him from the dispatch desk to report a home invasion in progress. 'Call just in. The address is where Daryl Epps is staying,' she said. 'Sounds like his brother's turned up.'

Feeling absurdly pleased that he had a reason to leave his desk, Johnson ordered Phil Logan and Joe Longfellow to follow him, and they ran out to the the parking lot. Seconds later, the Crown Victoria screeched onto Main, sirens wailing and lights flashing. Traffic clogged the junction with Euclid, causing Johnson to come to a halt, sirens chirping, behind a Nissan and a Subaru.

'Come on, move yourselves!' he yelled, leaning on the horn. The vehicles moved unhurriedly to one side, and Johnson roared through, ignoring the stop light and speed bumps, taking the corner onto Quaker Mill Lane at nearly 50 mph.

The squad car pulled up outside the Dickens' detached Californian a little over six minutes later.

Mrs Dicken stood in the door, eyes wide with fear, tears bubbling. 'He attacked Martin! My husband, Martin! Right here in our own house!'

A man lay semiconscious on the floor, his nose leaking red.

'Did you call an ambulance?' asked Johnson. 'Ma'm! Is an ambulance on the way?'

'Yes, yes, I called them. They're coming.'

'Where did he go?'

'This way,' she said and led the police officers through the house, past a scared-looking boy with a puffy eye, to the back yard.

'He's after Daryl,' Mrs Dicken said. 'He entered the woods, what, less than a minute ago.'

The end of the Dickens' back yard bordered dense woodland. *Probably another offshoot of Jefferson's Woods,* Johnson thought. A narrow trail wound between dense shrubbery. 'Get after him,' Johnson ordered Phil and Joe, 'but be careful. He's dangerous.'

'Where's Daryl?' he asked Mrs Dicken.

'I.. I don't know!'

The boy with the puffy eye, a kid Johnson recognized from the time Daryl and his buddies had rocked up to the station to tell him about CCTV footage, ran to the end of the yard and yelled, 'Daryl! You there? Come out, he's gone!'

Johnson realized his heart was beating loudly in the moments it took Daryl to emerge from the woodland. For a handful of seconds there, it looked like they had another missing child on their hands. Johnson could all too easily imagine the media circus that would ensue if it emerged that Cristel Epps' brother had now gone missing. He breathed again when the boy appeared amid the undergrowth and stepped into the backyard. He was pale and trembling, face covered with tears, clearly terrified.

At the sound of an ambulance pulling up outside, Mrs

Dicken disappeared into the house. Johnson spoke into his radio. 'I'm putting an APB out on Ken Epps, that's Kennedy Epps. White male, sixteen years old. Approach with caution. He is dangerous. I want him brought in ASAP.' He knelt before the two boys and said, 'You're safe now, boys. Everything's going to be okay. Let's go indoors.'

Paramedics were loading Mr Dicken into the back of the ambulance as they entered the house. The Dicken kid – Nathan, wasn't it? – looked like he would burst into tears any moment.

'I'm going to the hospital,' Mrs Dicken declared.

'Leave the boys with me,' Johnson said. 'I'll call Clarisse Bevan.'

The ambulance departed and suddenly the house seemed so quiet. The boys sat on the edge of the sofa, backs rigid, arms by their sides, ready to spring up and run if they had to. Johnson wondered if he should offer them a drink or something to eat, but decided to leave such things to Clarisse Bevan. He knew Carole would have already called her. She should be on her way by now.

The boys tensed when they heard footsteps approaching, but it was only Phil Logan and Joe Longfellow. Phil shook his head. 'It's a warren in there,' he said, apologetically.

'I've put out an APB,' Johnson said. 'We'll find him, and we'll put him in jail.' This last was said for Daryl's benefit. The boy perched on the edge of the sofa, jumping at every sound. *He must think Ken will be back to kill him,* Johnson thought, and felt a familiar surge of anger build within him. Another resident of River Rapids who didn't feel safe. Another citizen who didn't trust the police department to protect him.

A car pulled up outside. Through the window, Johnson saw Clarisse Bevan ease herself from the driver's seat of her Nissan. She stood on the sidewalk for a moment, adjusted her glasses, straightened her beige-colored jacket, and walked up the path to the door. Phil went to open it.

'You poor darlings!' she said as she entered the room. 'You must be frightened half to death! He must have followed you back from the funeral. Well, you can't stay here. You come along with me and we'll find you somewhere to go for the night while we sort something out.'

Both boys went with her. *Poor kids, being passed around like dirty dollar bills,* Johnson thought. He had thought about offering his home for the night, but he didn't know what Susan would say. Or Sheriff Millstone. Best to leave it to Clarisse. She had procedures to follow for just this sort of thing. Clarisse put the boys in the back seat of her car, fussed about belting them up, and finally eased herself into the recently vacated driver's seat. The Nissan pulled away and was gone.

Phil and Joe were already making their way to the door, but Johnson said, 'What do we know about Ken Epps? He wants to kill his brother, maybe he killed his sister.'

'He has an alibi for the day Cristel disappeared,' said Phil, 'and it checks out.'

'What about his girlfriend – what's her name – Hayley?'

'We took a statement, but we didn't bring her in formally.'

'Let's do it. I want to talk to her.'

He was missing something, Johnson knew that. And although this wasn't it, maybe he had taken a step closer.

5.

Saturday, November 12th, 2011

The loud ringing of phone beside the bed pulled Johnson rudely into the new day. The digital clock read *06:17*. 'Tell them to go away,' Susan mumbled into her pillow. 'Don't they know it's the weekend?'

Johnson picked up the receiver, dropped it, and picked it up again. It was Karen Shriebner, who handled the night shift dispatches.

'Thought you'd want to know,' she said. 'Clarisse Bevan was involved in a car accident late last night. She was only found this morning. Hospital says she's in a bad way, touch and go whether she'll wake up.'

Johnson struggled to press sleep out of his eyes. 'Was anybody with her?'

'Apparently not.'

'Well, get on to the Dickens. Make sure the boys are all right.'

'Already done it. She wasn't happy at being woken this early on a Saturday, but she says everybody there is fine.'

'Okay, great, fine. Let me know if anything changes, Karen.'

'Sure thing. Enjoy your day off.'

Johnson lay back on the pillow. He would love to enjoy his day off. Now dare he hope the phone hadn't woken... The bedroom door eased open and admitted a tiny, wide-eyed face. 'Mom, Dad, hungry! Want Cheerios!'

Johnson sighed as Millie padded into the room.

6.

The weather had certainly taken a chilly turn over the last few days. Johnson sat on a bench in Ryland's Park and watched wind whip the treetops in the valley below. Susan sat beside him, smiling at Millie, who was attempting to roll down the hillside like a log, but instead kept landing in a heap. They were all cozily wrapped in heavy winter coats, scarves and gloves. Millie had a beanie with a pink pompom jammed over her ears. The wind still stung Johnson's face, but he enjoyed the sharpness of it. Helped distract him from feelings of guilt over not going into work that morning. *But, he told himself, he hadn't had a day off in nearly a month, and he couldn't do much all the while Ken Epps and his girlfriend were missing anyway.* No, he was determined to spend quality time with his family and feel good about it.

'Judy's thinking of applying for the waitressing job at Kelly's Diner,' Susan said. 'I think it'll be good for her. Get her out and about a bit more. I've been taking Millie over there sometimes, just to cheer her up, you know, and it's done her the world of good. And Millie gets on so well with her little one, Rosie. It's like they're sisters, it really is. I wish you could see them together.'

Ryland's Park was a municipal space on a hilltop to the north of town. George Ryland had been a local benefactor sometime after the Civil War, Johnson wasn't sure exactly. There was also the Ryland Wing of the River Rapids County Museum downtown and the Ryland Cup awarded to whichever High School won the football tournament every year. The park was a wild and windswept spot, a suitable contrast to the dark and dense Jefferson's Wood and to the landscaped orderliness of the Town Green. This time of year the place was usually full of dads flying kites with their sons. Today it seemed strangely empty. One kite fluttered just over the crest of the hill, but other than that, Johnson and his family were alone.

'I know none of this means much to you, Johnson, but you could at least fake an interest.'

'Sorry. Judy's getting a new job?'

'Waiting tables at Kelly's. Thinking about it. You know what she's like, though. When it comes down to it.'

The kite was getting closer. It was a Batman kite, in the shape of the Batman symbol of a bat in silhouette, although Johnson always saw it as a mouth crammed with oddly-shaped teeth. Suddenly, watching that ominous black shape flutter near, Johnson shivered. Its owner crested the hill and ran into view: a boy of maybe seven or eight years, wrapped up warm just like Millie only without the pink pompom. He stopped suddenly when he saw people, as if unsure what to do or where to go. His father's voice yelled up the hill after him.

'David, I said wait for me! You know what I said about running off! You want some paedo to take you away and kill you, huh?'

Susan stopped speaking at the interruption. A man crested the hill, in his thirties, wrapped in a Parka, Blue Jays cap pulled low over his eyes. He was breathing heavily from climbing the hill, but still found breath enough to yell at his small son. He stopped suddenly when he saw Johnson and Susan. He eyed them suspiciously and grabbed his boy's hand.

'You run off again and we're going home,' he hissed. He pulled the Batman kite savagely from the sky and thrust it at his son.

'Think you're staring at?' he yelled at Johnson.

Johnson hadn't realized he had been staring. He had been watching the father's anxiety, thinking that River Rapids shouldn't be like this. River Rapids should be a friendly, safe, nurturing environment, where people didn't panic if their children dropped out of sight for a second. And this was all because of Cristel Epps and his failure to find her killer.

The man's barked accusation caught him off guard. He stammered something.

'You keep your eyes on your own kid, you hear?!'

'Hey, there's no need for that,' Susan said. 'Let's just enjoy the park.'

The man looked like he was about to leave when he looked closer at Johnson.

'Wait, you're that cop. You couldn't even find the sicko who did it. This is your fault! You know that right? If you did your job, we wouldn't have a child-killer loose in this town!'

Susan stood suddenly. 'You don't have a clue what you're talking about. Johnson breaks his back for this town so dill weeds like you can take your snotty kids to the park. Maybe you should try thanking him one day!'

The man blinked at her. He opened his mouth to yell right back but Johnson got to his feet and he seemed to think better of it.

'Come on, Johnson,' Susan said, 'let's go.' She called for Millie and they made their way downhill to the parking lot. Johnson looked back once and the man and his son had gone.

As Susan strapped Millie into her seat, she said, 'You okay, Johnson? You know that's garbage, right?'

'Yeah, I know.'

'I mean it, Johnson. I know what you're like. How everything's got to be perfect. But River Rapids isn't perfect. People aren't perfect. There'll always be idiots in this life. You driving?'

Johnson drove. Down Ryland Drive, past the Presbyterian Church, past the cemetery where Cristel Epps had been buried the previous day. Every cop in the county was on the lookout for either Ken Epps or his girlfriend, Hayley Kramer, but so far they hadn't surfaced. Probably gone to ground somewhere after the assault on Martin Dicken. Odds were they were together, on the run like Bonnie and Clyde, holed up at some motel a couple of towns over. Johnson was confident they wouldn't stay off the grid for long. It was only a matter of time before Ken got into another fight, for one thing. Ken's buddy, Dale Everett, had been spotted on Jubilee Avenue where he lived with his mom, but he was keeping his head down and so far there had been no reason to suspect that he knew where his gym-buddy and his girlfriend were. Both Phil Logan and Carole Jeffrey were under strict instructions to call if anything developed, but Johnson hoped they didn't. Just for once, he wanted a day with his family, uninterrupted by Epps family drama.

By the time they sat around the TV that evening, watching *America's Got Talent* on catch up with plates of tuna pasta bake on their laps, the kite guy at the park was long forgotten. After three reruns of *Two and a Half Men* (which Johnson never found funny, but Susan loved), Johnson took a reluctant Millie up to bed. He helped her into her pajamas and tucked her in, with Sandra the Panda in the crook of an elbow. By the time he had finished *Where The Wild Things Are* she was asleep. An afternoon flying a kite in the park was more than enough for a four year old, it seemed. Leaving the bedroom door ajar and the landing light on, Johnson tiptoed down the stairs.

He and Susan cuddled up on the sofa, half watching some late night comedy and Johnson didn't think of Cristel Epps once.

7.

Sunday, November 13th, 2011

The phone rang moments after Johnson reached his desk. It was Jeannette Schwartz, and she only rang if she had good news.

'The tape around Cristel's wrists,' she said. 'We put it through every test we've got. It has a distinctive chemical profile. Acid levels, absorbency, elasticity, yadda, yadda, you name it. We matched it to a brand called TapeTac, which is – drum roll, please – sold in only three outlets in the whole of River Rapids County. Harry's Mercantile, downtown River Rapids, 24HR EZ-MART, Clayton Creek Mall, River Rapids, and Frampton General Store, Frampton. You're welcome, Johnson. I haven't forgotten you owe me a drink.'

'Jeannette, you're worth your weight in gold.'

'Cheeky sod. Bet you say that to all the big girls.'

Harry McCarthy, owner and proprietor of Harry's Mercantile just down the road from where Johnson was sitting at that precise moment, guiltily admitted that the CCTV camera he had mounted in the corner of his store near the door was in fact a dummy, but would Johnson please keep that fact quiet because, for obvious reasons, he didn't want it spreading around town. He also admitted that he didn't keep full records of who bought what in his store, especially something as innocuous as a roll of TapeTac tape, because if he did, he'd spend his entire day filling out logs rather than doing anything important like completing his tax return, and anyway customers didn't like it if they had to give their personal details every time they made a purchase. Larger, more dangerous items, like chainsaws and BB guns were a different matter, of course. That went without saying.

Johnson thanked him, asked him to call should he happen to remember who may have bought TapeTac tape from him approximately three months ago, and hung up.

First one a bust.

Frampton was a small town a little over ten miles away, out near the county line. It was too small to possess its own police force and technically came under RRPD jurisdiction, not that Johnson ever needed to go out there.

Gray Judson, owner of the Frampton General Store answered the phone with a sleepy, 'Yup?'

Johnson explained who he was and what he wanted.

'I'd love to help you, Sheriff,' said Gray in a tone of voice that suggested just the opposite. 'But we don't believe in spyin' on folks over here in Frampton. Folks want to buy tape it ain't nobody's business but theirs.'

'Are you telling me you don't have CCTV, Mr Judson?'

'That there's exactly what I'm telling you, Sheriff.'

'Thank you for your cooperation,' Johnson said. He hung up, making a mental note to go and visit Mr Gray Judson of the Frampton General Store very soon.

Second one a bust. That left the 24HR EZ-MART out at Clayton Creek Mall. And maybe he should go visit that one. Johnson knew the manager over there, one Sheila Grant, and he could count on her cooperation.

8.

The Clayton Creek Mall had been built in 1985 on vacant land adjacent to the Clayton River to the south of town. The first mall in town, it had occasioned much excitement when it opened. Johnson had been a kid at the time, but he remembered his mother telling him that 'it was like southern California had come to West Virginia.' For a while they had shopped nowhere else, much to the consternation of downtown business owners.

These days downtown had rallied and the Clayton Creek Mall was looking a little shabby. The enormous parking lot had developed cracks and most of the name chains had moved out to the newer River Rapids Center on the other side of town, replaced by dollar stores, goodwill stores and thrift stores. *Clayton Creek Fashion* was still selling 'fashion items for the elder lady', many of which looked unchanged probably since the place had opened. Johnson couldn't imagine the kind of woman who would shop there. He knew Susan wouldn't go near the place. The anchor store, and the only outlet that still seemed to be doing good business, was the River Rapids outlet of the discount store 24HR EZ-MART.

Johnson pulled the Crown Victoria into one of six empty handicapped parking bays. Privileges of being a cop, he thought as he killed the engine and made his way along the sidewalk to the store entrance. The handicapped bays had been added at the insistence of the city council, but Johnson had never seen any of them in use. Occasionally they brought in a little revenue through fines when somebody parked in one without a handicapped sticker. The rest of the enormous parking lot fronting the huge, one floor building was maybe half full. Posters advertizing special offers on soda and 2-for-1 promotions on microwave dinners filled the wall space. A Red Box DVD rental machine stood to one side of the Main Entrance, a line of shopping carts on the other. A skinny guy with spots speckling the area around his mouth wore the bright yellow EZ-MART T-shirt and busied himself pulling the final wayward shopping trolleys into the stack.

Johnson stopped after the first set of automatic doors and spotted a camera hanging from the ceiling. It was one of those little ones housed in a dome and a red light blinked somewhere inside. It didn't look like a dummy. Johnson walked past the plastic bag recycling skip and the Dr Pepper vending machine and through another set of automatic doors into the store proper.

Nearly thirty years ago, it probably had been impressive. A huge warehouse-like space divided into aisles containing anything a modern housewife (or husband, Johnson thought) could possibly need. He could imagine the difference the EZ-MART would have made to the lives of the fair citizens of River Rapids, WV, back in the eighties. Now the polished concrete floor and harsh strip lighting looked dated, the lack of fresh produce was very noticeable, and the sheer number and size of dangling signs proclaiming the latest discounts in vibrant explosions of color was almost overwhelming. These days the store very much catered for the families at the lower end of River Rapids' range of income.

Johnson walked behind the checkout toward Sheila Grant's office, conscious of the eyes of the shoppers on him every step of the way. He wondered if they too recognized him from the papers or the TV, and if any of them blamed him for the recent tragic events in River Rapids, as the guy in the park clearly did. This time, however, nobody confronted him.

Johnson noticed the very obvious cameras on poles trained on every checkout, clearly intended as deterrents too, and hoped that they had been switched on and recording. Anybody buying tape in here could hardly have avoided appearing on video.

Sheila Grant emerged from her office as Johnson approached. She was cheerful and short and one of those people who never seemed to change. She'd had the same bob cut, the same slightly crooked front tooth, the same faded tattoo of a rose on her right forearm for decades. She'd been manager of EZ-MART for decades too and seemed to enjoy her job just as much now as she did when a teenage Johnson Fincher used to hang out here. In fact, she had chased him and his buddies away once or twice when they had been causing a nuisance, a fact he was sure she had not forgotten. Right now, however, she was smiling that crooked smile of hers and holding out her hand. Johnson shook it.

'Deputy Fincher, welcome to EZ-MART, River Rapids' number one superstore! What can I do to help you today?'

'Hi there, Sheila, hoping you might have some CCTV I could look at.'

She took him into her office, a small windowless cubby that looked more like a den than a manager's office. She sat at a cluttered desk mostly taken up by a massive, ancient PC and a cluster of coffee cups. She motioned him to sit on a chair. 'Just move the boxes,' she said.

He transferred a number of boxes of papers to the floor and sat.

'I'm looking for somebody who may have bought a roll of TapeTac tape sometime before August 20,' he said.

'TapeTac, eh? I gotcha. Aisle nine. Yellow logo. Prefer Scotch myself. Doesn't tear so easy.' She started clicking the mouse. 'May just have exactly what you need, Deputy. This new system head office introduced last year. Pain in the sit-upon, makes everything run slow, but if we're lucky...' A list of times and dates appeared on the screen. 'There! The moon must be in conjunction with Mars or something. Every time we sold a roll of TapeTac in August this year.'

Johnson blinked. 'Wow. I'm impressed. Don't suppose you have the names and addresses of the purchasers?'

'Fraid not. Not unless they purchased an item at the same time that must be registered by law. But, with a few clicks of the mouse, we can cross reference the dates, times, and checkout locations with the CCTV footage.'

'You can do that?'

'Of course! Twenty-first century now, hon! And EZ-MART is committed to keeping its stores at the forefront of modern technology. If the computer cooperates, that is.'

It took a while, but Johnson found he was not in a hurry. He was pleased to get out from behind his desk, away from Sheriff Millstone's scrutiny, and Sheila Grant was so effortlessly personable that Johnson was perfectly happy to spend a little time with her. In the line of duty, of course.

Twelve rolls of TapeTac had been sold in the period

between August 1 and 20. Johnson suggested starting at the most recent and working backward. Sheila clicked on the CCTV archives, stored as compressed video files on the chain's main servers and accessible via encrypted internet connection, Sheila proudly informed him. A window opened showing one of the checkouts that Johnson had recently walked past, the image clearly taken by one of the cameras he had spotted. The image was low quality but good enough to make out what was happening. Three people waited in line, others walked by pushing carts. A time code ticked by in the bottom right corner. Johnson was pleased to see that the cameras were mounted close enough for the faces of the customers to be clearly visible. This time, a man in his fifties wearing a wife-beater and a baseball cap placed a roll of TapeTac, a pair of scissors and a six pack of beers on the conveyer. For a second, Johnson thought it was Donald Epps, but no.

'Well, whattaya know,' said Sheila. 'It works.'

'Next one, Sheila,' Johnson said.

Johnson spent the next two hours looking at footage in Sheila's office. She showed him how to do it and left him there. He was aware that he didn't really know who he was looking for, and that whoever it was could easily have bought tape from Harry's Mercantile, or even gone out to Frampton to get it.

But then, suddenly, after two hours, he spotted a face he recognized. He freeze-framed the image. Four thirty-five pm on August 2nd. Caught right there, buying a roll of TapeTac, the very same roll of tape that would be used to secure Cristel Epps' wrists and ankles some eighteen days later. A face he recognized, but not at all a face he expected.

CHAPTER EIGHTEEN
DARYL EPPS

1.

Friday November 11th, 2011

Clarisse Bevan has given me some paper and pencils but I haven't used them. Coloring is for babies and I'm too scared anyway. Nathan sits next to me. Somebody came to look at his black eye a while back. Nobody has spoken to us since.

We sit in the corridor of the building that Clarisse works in. It's a few blocks from downtown, near the dentist that mom used to take me to. Before Dad killed her. Clarisse says that Dad has admitted killing mom. This means he'll be in jail for years, and somebody else will have to look after me. I think she hopes Nathan's mom will do it.

People rush past, looking important. Phones ring. Printers print. Computers click.

'Sorry about your eye,' I say.

'Are you kidding?' says Nathan. 'It's cool! Just wait 'til the kids at school see it. Coolest thing ever.'

I smirk. First funny thing since the *your momma* jokes. At least Nathan's still my friend. Even if I did put his dad in hospital.

I'm getting bored, but I'm also scared. Down the corridor, I see the reception desk and the glass doors to the street. What's to stop Ken walking through those doors, past the reception desk, along this corridor, and killing me? None of these women walking past in their skirts and heels, none of these men walking past in their shirts and ties, none of them could stop him. I keep glancing at the glass doors, and every time I do, I expect to see Ken's hulking outline against the sunshine, on his way to kill me, punching out everybody who tries to stop him like Arnie in *Terminator 2*. Not even Nathan could stop him.

'Mom?' Nathan says.

He too looks at the glass doors at the end of the corridor and my heart lurches in my chest. But no, it's not Ken. It's Nathan's mom. She talks to the receptionist and walks toward us. She looks pale, and her lips are pushed together. She ignores me and crouches beside Nathan.

'Daddy's going to be okay, honey,' she says. 'They're keeping him in overnight just to be sure, but he'll be home tomorrow. You wait there for a moment. I just need to talk to Mrs Bevan.'

She knocks on Clarisse's office door even though it is already open. I hear Clarisse say, 'Mrs Dicken, please come in. How is your husband?' But then Nathan's mom shuts the door and I can't hear any more.

She's not inside for long. Soon the door opens and she comes out. She takes Nathan's hand.

'Come on, Nathan, we're going home.'

As she passes me, she says, 'I'm sorry, Daryl,' and then

they are off, along the corridor, past the reception desk, through the glass doors into the street outside. Nathan has time only to say goodbye to me with his eyes.

Then I am alone. Clarisse's office door closes again. She must have closed it from the inside. I can hear a murmuring voice, like she's on the phone, but I can't hear the words.

I pick up a piece of paper from the pile she has left me, and tear it slowly into strips.

2.

I sit outside Clarisse Bevan's office for a long time. I stare at the wall and wonder what will happen to me. I don't know what Nathan's mom meant when she said sorry to me, but I can guess. My stomach growls but nobody gives me food. I guess they're all too busy answering phones and going to the printer. I need the toilet but I don't know where the restroom is.

At last, the office door opens and Clarisse beckons me inside. 'Goodness, you must be famished,' she says. 'Let me see what I can get you from the machine down the hall.'

She disappears for a while and I think about just getting up, walking out of the office, along the corridor, past reception and through the glass doors. It'd be easy. Nobody takes notice of a kid unless they're yelling or running. Just walk calmly out of the building and nobody would give a rat's tail. SuperDaryl could do it. SuperDaryl and his powers of invisibility could do this in a second.

One thing stops me. I have no place to go.

Clarisse walks back in, carrying a Snickers and a cardboard cup of water. She puts them on the desk in front of me. I tear the wrapper off the Snickers and munch it in three bites.

'I have good news and bad news, Daryl,' Clarisse says. 'Mrs Dicken says she doesn't want you living with them anymore. I'm sorry, but she says they were attacked in their own home and she doesn't want to be scared. She has to put her own fam-. Well. Anyway. You'll still see Nathan at school, won't you? It's disappointing, but these things happen. And I'm afraid I just can't find another place for you at the moment. We don't have a whole lot of places open in the county, and what with one thing and another... Anyway, the good news is... Well, I guess, you'll just have to come home with me for a few days. I've squared it with Child Protection Services, and... well, you have to go somewhere, don't you? I'm sure it will be fine.'

It is getting dark when she leads me out of the building to where her old fashioned car waits in the parking lot. She holds bags of binders and files which she dumps in the trunk, all the while talking about her spare room and her nephew who sleeps there when he comes to stay and how I should meet him because she's sure we would get along famously, but then again, second thoughts, maybe it's best if we don't meet because, well, you know, but I'm sure he won't mind you sleeping in his room for a few days, and on and on she goes. She opens the back door and guides me in and fastens the seat belt, and the whole time I am trying not to cry. I try not to think about the fact that first my mom abandoned me, and then my sister, and my dad and my brother, and then my girlfriend, and now my best friend has gone. I try not to think that I am left with no-one.

Clarisse slides her bulk behind the wheel, checks her

mirrors – side and rear view – clicks her seat belt into place, wiggles her bottom, looks under the dashboard to find the pedals, and finally turns the ignition key. The engine purrs into life, Clarisse turns on the headlamps, even though it is not fully dark yet, looks behind her, checks the mirrors again – side and rear view – and pulls slowly from her parking spot.

She drives slowly to the parking lot exit and she hums while she drives. No tune I recognize. Probably something from before I was born. It's like she's forgotten I'm back here.

We turn onto Main Street. A few blocks ahead the stop signs become stop lights and downtown proper begins. The Police Station is there. The Firehouse. The Courthouse. Kelly's Diner. Two blocks beyond that, Main Street skirts Town Green with its bandshell and gentle slope down to the woods along the Clayton River. Clarisse's car crawls along, block by block, stopping at every stop light.

Then we leave downtown behind. I realize that I have no idea where Clarisse lives. I don't know where she is taking me. I don't know what I will find when we arrive. I don't even know if she is married, or whether she lives alone. I pull my knees up so my feet rest on the seat. Tears gather in the corners of my eyes, but I quickly blink them back. I will not cry. I am too old to cry. I empty my thoughts and watch the town slide by beyond the windows.

The street lights are on now. The last of the day's light slips away in the west. The lights stop at the edge of town and the road disappears as though we have reached the end of the world. The headlamps are on but the darkness eats the feeble yellow light. For some reason, I think of Dad sitting in his spot on the couch cramming Hawaiian pizza into his mouth, *The Bold and the Beautiful* on the TV.

The road is empty of traffic now. Beyond the curb, cornfields quickly fade into nothing. I can see a moon hanging brightly, but no stars. Not a single one.

'Won't be long now,' Clarisse says suddenly, and I jump. 'Nearly home.'

At that moment, a bright headlamp reflects from the rear view mirror into my eyes. I put up a hand to block it out. Clarisse is doing the same thing. 'Shoot!' she says. 'Dip that light, can't you?'

Somebody is driving right up close behind us. Hardly surprising when Clarisse drives so slowly.

'Okay, okay!' Clarisse grumbles. 'Go around me if you must! Why are people always in such a hurry?'

She drives right over to the edge of the road, leaving plenty of space for the guy behind to pass her. Instead, he moves over too.

'Come on then, if that's what you want,' says Clarisse and she clicks her tongue.

There is only one light behind us. I realize that it must be a motorbike. And only one person I know drives a motorbike. Suddenly, mind-numbing fear blooms in my head again. I feel like I am going to be sick. I start to shiver.

The light swoops toward us, filling the back window like a UFO. Clarisse releases a scream.

'The maniac! Is he trying to kill us?'

The car wobbles as the right front wheel skips off the tarmac and back on again. My head smacks painfully against the window, but my heart is beating so fast that I barely notice.

The motorbike accelerates to the left of us. My brain finds time to wonder what will happen if we meet a vehicle coming the other way. The scary sound of a Harley engine revving and revving is so loud it blocks my thoughts and seems to enter my ribcage, bouncing around my heart. I gulp back saliva, my hands grip the seat back in front of me.

Clarisse says a word I can't believe she even knows and loses control of the car. The Nissan bumps off the road and nose dives into a ditch. Clarisse screams, there is a wet *thwack*ing sound, my head rebounds off the roof, and then silence.

The car creaks.

It leans forward like it's about to throw itself off a cliff. My backside tries to slide from the seat. Only the belt keeps me still.

The door next to me bursts open. Ken reaches in and twists my T-shirt in his fist. He hauls me right out of the seat belt and slings me onto the gravel at the side of the road. I scrape my palms painfully against it, sure that I would see blood if I dared to take my eyes from my brother long enough to look.

One thing I do see as I am hauled from the back bench seat is Clarisse slumped over the wheel, a nasty wound on her forehead where she headbutted the windshield. She looks dead.

'Hiya, runt,' Ken hisses in my face. 'Thought you could get away, didn't ya? You're going nowhere, pal, except back home where you belong.'

He climbs back onto his Harley and slings me across his knees like a sack of trash. He turns, leaving tire marks on the tarmac, and soon we are rolling back into town. I can't see much more than the road surface whizzing past just inches away. I daren't struggle in case he drops me and the ground churns up my face. I daren't do or say anything for fear of what he will do to me. I'm surprised he hasn't killed me already.

A lifetime later we finally turn off the road and onto gravel again, and I realize where we are. I'm back at the trailer, the one place I dared hope I would never see again. Ken brings the bike to a halt and throws me onto the ground.

'It's your fault Dad's in jail,' he says. 'It's your fault the cops are after me. You've ruined this family, you know that? A pathetic little snot like you. Well, you're gonna pay for what you've done.'

The trailer is dark. If it weren't for the moonlight, I would not be able to see the looming window of the living room or the broken bits of vehicles left in the grass. Or the remains of one of Cristel's dolls lying squished in the dirt. Ken yanks me to my feet and pushes me toward the screen door.

The living room stinks. If possible, it smells worse than when I was last here. I wonder if another dead body has been stashed behind the sofa or stuffed into the fridge, and then I realize that I can't see either the sofa or the fridge. Both have disappeared beneath a towering pile of trash so tall that I imagine it toppling any moment and burying me alive under half eaten pizza and empty beer cans. In the corner of my eye I see movement and think, *This is it, crushed to death by falling trash, can't be worse than being killed by my psycho meathead brother, can it?* and then realize that the movement is actually a rat slithering down the pile.

I cough and retch.

Ken is just about to say something when a thumping noise comes from his room further down the trailer. His room and mine. He clenches his fist and picks his way over the trash toward the door. Slowly, carefully, I follow, hoping that SuperDaryl turns on his powers of invisibility right about now.

Ken is a few steps from the bedroom door when it opens. Hayley stands there with a sheet wrapped around her and her arm across her chest. She is clearly naked under the sheet. And some part of me recognizes the sheet as the one bunched up on Ken's bed for months. Same stains for one thing.

'Hi, honey,' she says. She's sweating. Her eyes are wide and imploring.

'What... Hayley?' Ken mutters. 'What are you doing here?'

'I've been waiting for you, honey. Waiting for you to come home.'

He pushes past her and opens the bedroom door. Dale stands stark naked in the bedroom, eyes buggy with panic.

Nobody moves. You know when you fall off your bike and scrape your knees over the tarmac, there's always that precious moment of calm before the pain kicks in? You lie there in the road after face-planting and you're still not quite sure what happened. And then you suck in air, fill your lungs and howl until you feel better. Well, this is like that. A precious moment of calm. And the last any of us would enjoy for more than two days.

So, for those not keeping up: My nutcase brother Ken just found his girlfriend in bed with his best friend. In Ken's own bed. Ouch. That's gotta hurt. Absurdly, I feel a pang of sympathy for my brother.

Ken doesn't need my sympathy. He flings Hayley into

a corner with one swipe, covers the distance to Dale with two strides, and punches Dale in the mouth. Dale just has time to say, 'Look, Ken, buddy...' before his jaw collapses.

Dale drops, smacking his head against the corner of Ken's bed. Ken pulls his shirt off, tearing it in the process, and flings it to one side, and that's the moment when fear explodes within me, so much fear that I cannot move, nor think, nor do anything but close my eyes as my brother picks up one of his dumbbells and swings it at his best friend's head.

I hear a sickening *thud*.

Then the air is silent and thick.

Until I realize Hayley is sobbing.

Ken stands in the doorway, chest heaving, sweat dripping over his muscles and collecting in the waistband of his pants. His eyes are dead, his face calm. He walks past Hayley. She screams, but he just takes her arm in the hand that isn't holding the dumbbell and drags her into the living room. He throws her down on a pile of trash on the couch. She sits there, sobbing, clutching the sheet and pulling it ever tighter around her.

I follow automatically, unable to think of anything else to do, and sit beside her uncomfortably on a pile of crushed Pabst cans.

Ken wordlessly sits on the same chair he always used to sit on when he watched football games with Dad. The dumbbell is still in his fist. Ken starts to do bicep curls with it. His enormous biceps bulge and straighten, bulge and straighten, like he's in training for a contest.

I don't know how long we sit there, too terrified to move or speak, but it is a long time. I feel like these are the final minutes of my life ticking away. Soon Ken will kill us too. I am certain of this. A rat darts past Hayley's leg. She squeals, and then clamps her hand over her mouth, wide eyes fixed on Ken. But Ken simply transfers the dumbbell to his other arm and continues his bicep curls.

And still we sit in silence.

The smell of garbage is overpowering. I watch a cockroach emerge from a Pringles tube and scuttle across what remains of the carpet. I watch it disappear into a tiny space between a half-empty package of mac and cheese TV dinner and a crushed Coke Zero bottle. I wonder why Ken doesn't try to get away on his Harley, zoom off into the night before the cops come and find the dead body in the bedroom. Or maybe they'll find three bodies by then. Has he given up? Does he think running is futile? No, that's not Ken's style at all. He's not running because he thinks he's unstoppable. He thinks not even the police can touch him. He thinks he can do anything because he's strong.

And he's bug-eyed crazy, of course.

Back to the first arm. Bulge, straighten, bulge, straighten. Just how big can a sixteen year old get? His face and chest are soaked with sweat, some of it drying into a crust by now. His hair is slick with it.

Finally, he puts the dumbbell down. He stretches and flexes. Then he stands and walks slowly toward the couch where Hayley and I sit. Hayley screams. My throat is too dry to make more than a whimper.

Ken takes my hand in his. His huge hand engulfs mine. He runs his fingers gently over my fingers, pushing his big, thick fingers between mine and clasping my hand within his.

Then he squeezes. Pain explodes along my arm and I pass out.

3.

I regain semi-consciousness when I hear Hayley screaming. Weak daylight filters through the dirty windows. Is it morning already? Ken, now wearing only a stained and worn pair of underpants, has pulled away the sheet Hayley had wrapped around her and he's hurting her. Her screams hurt my ears so bad I fall asleep again.

4.

Ken is asleep now. Passed out with his head on the table. His hair is soaked, flattened against his forehead. His skin glistens with sweat. Hayley is spread-eagled on the couch. She is either dead or unconscious, I can't tell.

5.

My own stomach growls and wakes me. It's dark outside again. I realize I have no idea of the time, or even the day. Hayley, covered in cuts and bruises, still lies on the sofa. I think she's dead. Ken, half naked and clutching a bread knife, is still sprawled asleep across a pile of garbage on the table. I think about moving. I think about darting to the door and wrenching it open and running screaming into the night. Or at the very least, scraping together some food from the leftovers on the floor to satisfy the craving in my stomach. Just a mouthful of water from the tap.

But each time I think about it, I picture what will happen. I picture Ken rousing to life and cutting me into pieces with his knife. I picture him squeezing my hand into a pulp. And I don't move. And I try to vanish into the floor, as if I could seep away just by wishing hard enough.

At last, mercifully, I pass out again.

6.

Next time I wake, I find a few drops of Pepsi in the bottom of a bottle. Without waking Ken, I shake them into my mouth with the fingers that I can still move. The drops taste like golden water. I cram half a slice of pizza into my mouth. I barely notice the green spores of mold along the edges. I start to cough and smother my face with the sleeve of my unbroken arm, terrified that I will wake Ken. Eventually, consciousness drifts away. *Please God, the next time I wake, let me be in heaven.*

CHAPTER NINETEEN
JOHNSON FINCHER

1.

Sunday, November 13th, 2011

On his way back from Sheila Grant's EZ-MART, Johnson remembered to call the River Rapids Medical Center for news of Clarisse Bevan's condition. The doctor reported that she had stabilized, but was still unconscious. She had been unconscious for more than thirty-six hours now, probably owing to the head trauma she had received when her car had gone off the road into a ditch, which Johnson took to be med-speak for hitting her head on the windshield. As soon as she showed signs of waking, he'd call.

Johnson pulled the Crown Victoria into the parking lot, and seconds later, knocked on Sheriff Millstone's door.

'Johnson,' Bill Millstone said, 'we are sure there's nothing more to this car wreck, aren't we? Just a coincidence Clarisse Bevan drove into the ditch?'

'Seems that way, Sheriff. Of course, we haven't spoken to her about it yet. She's still unconscious.'

'Never comfortable around coincidence, Johnson. Coincidences play havoc with my gut. I always find you dig deep enough and nothing is ever a coincidence.'

'The doc at the RR Medical Center is gonna call as soon as Clarisse is awake. I'll speak to her just as soon as possible.'

'Awesome. Anything else for me?'

Johnson was unable to keep a wide grin cracking open his face as he laid a tiny memory stick on the Sheriff's desk.

'CCTV footage from EZ-MART. All there in black and white. Hayley Kramer buying a roll of TapeTac tape, the exact same make used to bind Cristel's wrists and ankles.'

'Ken Epps' girlfriend?'

'The very same.'

'So you're thinking she's in on it? She helped her boyfriend kill his kid sister?'

'Looks that way. We may even be able to argue premeditation.'

'She could be buying tape for any number of reasons.'

'Just eighteen days before Cristel's disappearance? The very same make of tape, sold in only three stores in the whole county? That's a heck of a coincidence, Sheriff.'

'Don't I know it,' Bill Millstone said, patting his curvy gut. 'It's still not conclusive.'

'But it's convincing. Juries have convicted on less.'

'What about motive?'

'God knows, Bill. Family like that, they don't even need a motive. Because she was too whiny. Because they had no babysitter. Because they were too selfish to look after her. Because her teacher was asking too many questions about home life. Could be anything.'

Bill shook his head. 'We need more, Johnson.'

'But, I...'

'We need more, and you know it. Did Ken kill his sister? How much was Hayley involved? How premeditated was it? And doesn't the meathead have an alibi anyway? How does that square up?'

Johnson nodded. It was true. Ken claimed to have been at Frank's Gym the night Cristel went missing and there was videotape and more than a dozen witnesses to prove it. And although it was possible that Ken Epps had been involved with Cristel's disappearance early the next morning, the likelihood was low. The Sheriff was right. Johnson hated to admit it, but they did need more. And there was no way Johnson was risking the killer walking away from this one. Not this one, not this time. He would just have to keep digging.

He plugged the memory stick into the USB port of his desktop and spent most of the afternoon playing back the footage frame by frame. Even though the picture was grainy and black and white, Johnson felt that he was getting to know that corner of EZ-MART very well indeed. In the foreground, the conveyor carried items past the checkout girl, a podgy teenager with her hair tied roughly into a ponytail and a button reading, *Hi! My name's Trish! Tell me how I can help you!* Just behind Trish was another checkout. To one side, Johnson could see a bench outside the entrance to the restrooms and a board on the wall with *Community Notices – Make Sure Your Notice is Noticed!* written on it. People walked by pushing carts and dragging children.

Johnson watched Hayley Kramer approach the checkout. She placed a packet of peanut M&Ms, a large pair of scissors, and the familiar package of a roll of TapeTac tape on the conveyor. Trish scanned the items and dumped them in a plastic bag. Hayley handed over cash. Trish popped the cash drawer and handed back a number of coins. Hayley picked up the plastic bag and walked past the *Community Notices* board and the bench beside the entrance to the restrooms, and suddenly she was gone from the picture.

The video file ended. Johnson clicked on another that showed the store entrance and parking lot. He watched Hayley walk past the Red Box DVD rental machine and the plastic bag recycling bin. With just a cursory glance for approaching vehicles, she stepped off the sidewalk and walked out of shot.

The screen went blank.

Hayley must have got into a car and driven off and eighteen days later wound her recent purchase of TapeTac tape around Cristel Epps' wrists and ankles. But did she do it alone? Or with Ken Epps? And if the brother were there, was she acting under duress?

As Sheriff Millstone said, it wasn't enough.

Carole Jeffrey called across the room. 'Johnson, I've got Doctor Fredriksen on the line for you.'

'Who?'

'From the Medical Center. You wanted him to call you?'

'Oh, right. I'll take it here.'

He picked up the phone. 'Doctor Fredriksen, this is Deputy Fincher. How's Clarisse?'

'Thought you'd want to know, Deputy, she woke up half an hour ago. Seems to be doing fine.'

'Can I talk to her?'

'Only if it's life or death, Deputy. She's sleeping normally right now and really shouldn't be disturbed.'

'Did she say anything? Like if another vehicle was involved?' Bill Millstone's gut didn't like coincidence, and Johnson was beginning to feel that way too.

'No, nothing like that. She just wanted to know if Daryl were okay. That mean anything to you, Deputy?'

'Daryl? Yes, he's a kid she's looking after. He's fine, he's safe at home.'

'At home? Oh, fine. Because she seemed to think he was in the car with her.'

'No, no, he's safe at his foster... She thought he was in the car?'

'That's what she said.'

Johnson felt a heavy dread spiral up from his gut. His heart thumped madly and he suddenly found breathing difficult. *No, no, please God...*

'L... listen, doctor, stay by the phone. I may need to get back to you.'

He slammed down the receiver. He picked it up again, and stared at the number pad. He needed... he needed... *What on Earth did he need?*

'Carole! Carole, I need the number of the place where Daryl Epps has been staying. What's the name...? Dicken! Carole, help me out here!'

Carole threw him an odd look, but she was already clicking away at her computer. 'It's ringing!' she said, and Johnson snatched up the receiver again.

The dial tone buzzed in his ear... once... twice... three times. *Be at home. Please God be at home. Be at home and answer the phone.*

The dial tone clicked and stopped. 'Hi?' It was Mrs Dicken.

'Oh, er... Hi there, Mrs Dicken, this is Deputy Fincher.'

'Hi, Deputy. What can I do for you?'

'Er... Well, I just wanted to make sure you're all okay.'

'Oh, well, we're all kinda shaken up, but anybody would be after being attacked in their own home like that. It's the sort of thing you read about happening, but you never think it will happen to you, you know?'

'And the boys? They're okay?'

'Nathan's got a nasty black eye, but the doctor says he just needs to rest it and let it heal by itself. I think he rather likes it, truth be told! Boys, eh? Thinks it makes him look cool! Martin's back from the hospital. Doctor says he's got to rest, signed him off for at least a week. Says he can catch up on some TV! He never did see the end of *Lost*! He's as bad as Nathan!'

'And... and Daryl?'

'Daryl?'

'Yes, is he okay?'

There was a silence. Johnson was just about to repeat the question when Mrs Dicken said, stiffly, 'Daryl doesn't live here anymore, Deputy. I know it's not his fault, but trouble seems to follow him around, and when my own family are attacked, well, I have to put them first.'

The spiral of dread reached Johnson's heart and gripped it tight.

'So you haven't seen Daryl since...'

'Since I left him with Clarisse Bevan late Friday night.'

'Thank you, Mrs Dicken.'

Johnson put the phone down.

Daryl Epps had been missing for two days.

Bill Millstone instantly ordered Johnson to take as many officers as he could get out to the Epps' trailer. Joe Longfellow, Gilly Dwight and Phil Logan were ready to go. Charlie Hound and Oliver Finch, two part-timers, were called in from their weekend and instructed to meet Johnson on site.

Less than ten minutes after the call from Doctor Fredriksen came in, Johnson's Crown Victoria bumped over the ramp onto Main Street, lights flashing and sirens blaring. Darkness had fallen without Johnson noticing, and the businesses on Main Street were beginning to close for the evening, those who had bothered to open at all on a Sunday. Harry McCarthy was pulling the shutters down over the display windows of the Mercantile, and the lights were already off in the used book store. Kelly's was still open, several tables filled with couples enjoying burgers or teenagers sipping root beer floats. Heads turned as two squad cars screamed by, heading up the hill toward Quaker Mill Lane, but Johnson scarcely noticed. He could think of nothing but Daryl Epps' scared, pinched face and the fact that he had failed that kid yet again.

Two days! Two whole days at the mercy of his psychotic, violent brother. In all likelihood, Daryl was lying dead somewhere inside that trash heap of a trailer right now. Or maybe he was somewhere else, spirited away where he wouldn't be found for months. Dumped in Jefferson's Woods, maybe, like his mom and his sister.

And you know what, Johnson, if the kid is dead, that will be on you. Because you promised to protect him. And you let him down.

349

Johnson pumped the accelerator.

They turned onto County Road Six at the 7Eleven. The built up area of River Rapids quickly fell into rural isolation. Electrical cables looped between dim lampposts. Trees loomed in dark outlines against a moonlit sky. Phil Logan sat silently in the passenger seat. Johnson flicked off the flashers and the sirens. So did the car behind.

They pulled silently to a stop outside the Epps' trailer and gathered on the grass verge. Johnson drew his sidearm, the Glock 22 that had rested against his hip since he had started in the RRPD. Without a word, he led the way along the side of the gravel path and up to the trailer. The main picture window at the front of the trailer was dark. He wondered if Ken Epps was in there, keeping watch in the darkness. Was he armed? Had he already seen them coming? Maybe he was taking aim right now. Johnson swallowed back the saliva that gathered in his throat and ignored the thumping of his heart.

And then he glimpsed a figure in the window and his heart leaped into his mouth. He motioned his fellow officers into the shadows and crept closer to the window on bended knees. His knees cracked, and he had a moment to think that he was getting too old for this sort of thing. Should be thinking about a desk job by now, like the Sheriff. Something Susan wholeheartedly supported.

He dragged his thoughts back on point and risked a glance through the window at close range.

Ken Epps sat at a trash-strewn table, apparently asleep. He was almost naked and covered in sweat.

And behind him on the sofa, asleep or dead, were Hayley Kramer and Daryl.

Maybe Johnson had made a sound as he stood looking in the window. Maybe one of the other officers scraped a shoe on the gravel or sniffed or cleared his throat. Or maybe it was the sheer force of hatred in Johnson's gaze. Whatever caused Ken to start awake at that moment and grasp a bread knife in his fingers, it also caused Johnson's heart to pump faster and send adrenalin surging through his body. Without thinking, he brought up the Glock 22 and shot Ken right through the window.

The bullet lodged exactly where Johnson expected it to: in the meat around Ken Epps' left shoulder. Even before the shards had finished falling from the window frame, Phil Logan had shoulder charged the door and burst it open.

Howling with pain, Ken Epps punched Phil in the mouth. Phil went down hard.

Through the shattered window, Johnson saw Daryl open his eyes. The kid was still alive. *Thank you God.*

Ken Epps slashed at Joe Longfellow with the bread knife, cutting through Joe's uniform shirt and opening a red line on his arm. Joe tried to grab the weapon, but his hands slipped and slipped again on the sheen of sweat covering Ken's skin. Ken fought like a wild animal, naked, bloody and feral. Johnson, still on the stoop outside the trailer, tried to get through the door, but mounds of garbage blocked him. He caught confused glimpses of Ken's muscular arms swinging violently, of his teeth bared in a snarl. He smelled the salt tang of blood on the air.

Joe finally managed to grab the arm holding the knife, but only when Gilly Dwight, Charlie Hound and Oliver Finch piled on could they subdue him enough to snap cuffs on. Even then, Ken caught Oliver on the nose with a nasty head butt.

While Ken Epps was dragged to the lead squad car, Johnson picked his way over the carpet of Pizza Hut boxes and Taco Bell wrappers to where Daryl sat curled on the couch. The boy was pale, skinny and terrified. He had clearly been eating rancid leftovers to stay alive.

And all because Johnson had failed to protect him.

Johnson couldn't prevent tears squeezing from his eyes as he called out to God.

2.

Hayley Kramer had been slashed, presumably by the bread knife, forty-two times across the face, arms and abdomen. She was taken to the River Rapids Medical Center, and later transferred to Charleston. She needed more than five hundred stitches and would bear the scars of the attack, physically and emotionally, for the rest of her life.

Daryl Epps was badly undernourished and dehydrated, and had suffered a shattered hand. His hand was set in plaster at the River Rapids Medical Center, where he was kept in for observation for two nights. This handily gave Clarisse Bevan's superiors at child services two days to find somewhere for him to go. Daryl's bed was two doors down from Clarisse's.

Dale Everett was found battered to death in a bedroom in the Epps' trailer. The body was sent to Jeanette Schwartz for autopsy.

Ken Epps was thrown into a cell at the RRPD Police Station.

3.

Even a month on, Hayley Kramer looked a mess. She sat in the interview room, chewing at sleeves pulled down over her hands. The ends of the sleeves were ragged and stained with saliva. Tangled strands of hair had worked loose from a colorless band. A dirty sticking plaster covered a cut on her face. Another cut had healed into a red line across her chin. She kept her head tilted away.

Jean Brody sat beside her, professional in her trademark pant suit, saying nothing. Bill Millstone was present, but he was letting Johnson take the lead.

'So how long had you been seeing Dale Everett behind Ken's back?' asked Johnson.

He wondered if Hayley were going to maintain a sullen silence, but then he saw the tears collecting in the corners of her eyes and she began talking. The tears, the injuries, the apparent contrition, Johnson thought he should feel sorry for her. But he couldn't. He just couldn't.

'I don't know. A long time.' Her voice was quiet, shuddering, punctuated with sniffs and silences. 'But not all the time. We would go weeks without seeing each other, and then we'd get together twice in a week.'

'And you thought Ken would never find out?'

'He'd kill us if he found out. That was kinda the point. We liked the danger, you know?'

'You liked the danger. And that's why you and Dale had sex in Ken's own room, his own bed?'

Hayley said nothing. She looked at the wall and wiped her nose with the back of her hand.

'Let's go back a few months to August 20ᵗʰ. Late evening. Donald Epps was out with Debra. Ken was at the gym. Daryl was at a sleepover with his buddy Nathan. You and Dale take the opportunity to break into the Epps' trailer for a bit of dangerous fumbling in Ken's bed.'

'We didn't break in. The door was always unlocked.'

'But you forgot about Cristel, right? Left home alone.'

Hayley sniffed and covered her eyes. 'She walked right in, caught us right at it. I thought maybe she didn't know what she was seeing, she was only six! But Dale was terrified. One word to Ken and he'd kill us. So he threatened her.'

'What did he say?'

'He said he would kill her like he had killed her mom.'

Johnson glanced at Sheriff Millstone. 'You're saying that Dale Everett killed Yvonne Epps?'

'I don't know if he killed her. I know he helped dump the body. But he told Cristel that he had killed her mother and would kill her too if she told anybody about us. And if she didn't believe him, he even told her where he had dumped her mom's body in Jefferson's Wood.'

'Then what happened?'

'She went back to her room, and we...'

'Continued from where you left off?'

Hayley said nothing.

'How long before you realized Cristel had left the trailer?'

'Not long. Ten minutes, maybe twenty.'

'She'd gone to find her mom, hadn't she? Taken herself off late at night to find her mom's body in Jefferson's Wood.'

Hayley nodded. 'Dale went mental. Convinced himself that she would tell everybody, that Ken would find out. He said we had to find her.'

'So you followed her?'

'We took Dale's car. Spotted her near the 7Eleven. Followed her for a while. Dale was yelling, saying we had to do something, we had to take care of this problem. I tried to get him to leave her alone, I did! I told him! She's six years old, she doesn't know what she saw, and even if she did tell, no-one believes a six year old, right? But he'd told her about her mom's body. If he'd only kept his mouth shut...' Suddenly, she looked up from the wall, made eye contact with Johnson. 'I tried to stop him, but he wouldn't listen.'

'So Dale Everett killed Cristel?'

Hayley sniffed, drew her hand across her nose, sobbed and looked away again. 'We parked up. By the time we'd caught up with her she'd made it as far as the highway. Dale... he... dragged her into the woods, tied her up with tape... and...'

'And he strangled a six year old girl.'

Hayley nodded silently.

'Where did you take the body?'

'He buried her in the crawlspace under his place until the fuss had died down. But he was terrified. He thought you were getting closer. Expected you to turn up on his stoop any day with a warrant to search the place. So he dumped her in the Conway River. Figured once she had been found, interest would finally die away.'

4.

There was no way of telling just how involved Hayley was in the murder of Cristel Epps. Had she purchased the roll of tape knowing full well what she intended to do with

355

it, or was its presence in Dale's car a coincidence like she claimed? In the end, it really didn't matter. Hayley Kramer was charged, along with the late Dale Everett, with the murder of Cristel Epps. The case was tried in the River Rapids Courthouse and the jury deliberated for only three hours before returning a guilty verdict. Judge Hilary Fentiman gave Hayley Kramer a life sentence behind bars.

Kennedy Epps went on trial one month later, charged with the murder of Dale Everett and several counts of assault, including assault on his kid brother. The jury needed only two hours to determine his guilt and the same judge who had presided over the Hayley Kramer trial gave an identical sentence.

Hayley Kramer and Kennedy Epps would be very old indeed when they were released from jail, if indeed they were released at all. And Judge Hilary was very insistent that their status as juveniles was in no way to be held in their favor. 'These despicable young people thought nothing about perpetrating the most heinous of crimes,' she said, 'and deserve not a shred of leniency due to their youth.' And not a shred did they receive.

Finally, Donald Epps went on trial for the murder of Yvonne Epps. His taped confession and the forensic evidence linking him to the body of his wife was more than enough for a jury to reach a guilty verdict, despite Hayley Kramer's claim that Dale Everett had confessed to the same murder. 'Although Dale Everett may have had a hand in the disposal of the body,' the prosecuting counsel summed up, 'the evidence proves beyond all doubt that Donald Epps was the one who committed the deed.'

Donald Epps also received a life sentence.

5.

Sunday January 15th, 2012

Millie pulled faces all through the sermon. She stuck out her tongue, she stretched her mouth with her fingers, she rolled her eyes up and down and she pushed up her nose. She didn't seem to be doing it at anybody in particular, although if Pastor Freddy had seen it whilst elaborating on the importance of righteousness, he may have been somewhat disconcerted. No, she seemed to be doing it for the sheer joy of doing it, in which case, Johnson was perfectly happy for her to continue. Pastor Freddy was nearly done in any case. At least, Johnson hoped he was nearly done. The morning was wearing on and he was looking forward to a nice Sunday lunch.

His eyes wandered to where Daryl sat with Nathan Dicken and his family. The Dickens had been irregular attendees for some time but had started coming more frequently recently. Johnson knew this because Susan had mentioned it. Mr Dicken – Martin, wasn't it? – seemed to have recovered from Ken Epps' attack without permanent ill effects. He sat wrapped in a woolly sweater, engrossed in the sermon. His wife – whose name Johnson could never remember, and it was way too late to ask now – sat beside him, arm around Nathan, who seemed to be playing some sort of kicking game with Daryl, to which she seemed miraculously oblivious. There was a family safe and sound again, who had escaped the turmoil caused by the Epps family. And over there, sitting alone, was Barbara Bruchner. She too had started attending recently. Apparently, her mother had resumed attendance at the Catholic church downtown, Our Lady of the Sacred Heart, but Barbara had wanted to strike out on her own. Her new paid job at the *Recorder* had resulted in more balanced coverage of RRPD activities in the newspaper. Something Bill Millstone approved of.

The congregation had definitely grown in recent weeks. The holiday season, despite some brutally cold snowstorms, had helped to lift spirits in River Rapids, and Johnson hoped that the recent arrests had contributed. The people of River Rapids were starting to feel that life was returning to normal, and their little town really was the nice place to live that they had always hoped it was. And maybe he could take a little part of the credit for that.

Pastor Freddy came to an end and everybody stood to sing *Amazing Grace*. Mrs Dicken realized what her son and his buddy were doing and glared until they stopped. Millie had finally stopped pulling faces and was attempting to discover how far up her nose she could insert her finger. Susan spotted what she was up to and pulled her finger out, embarrassingly glancing around to see if anybody had noticed. The instant Susan turned away, the finger was returned to its former position.

After the service, Johnson found time to walk up to Mrs Dicken and thank her for reconsidering and taking Daryl in again. She huffed a little, embarrassed.

'Of course I had to reconsider,' she said. 'After you had taken care of that vicious young man, Deputy. I just couldn't bear to think of Daryl having nowhere to go. Of course, we know it won't be forever. Just until child services can find a more permanent solution. And Daryl knows that too.'

'Nevertheless, thank you.'

6.

That afternoon, they went sledding in Ryland Park. The snow wasn't really deep enough to make a first rate sledding track, but Millie didn't care at all. She sailed down the hill on her little wooden sled, squealing in delight. Susan had a go, with Millie balanced between her knees, and Johnson took photos. He already knew which one would be his new Facebook picture. And he was pretty sure there were one or two others Susan would want to frame and put on the sideboard.

Plenty of others had also had the idea of spending their Sunday afternoon sledding in the park. The whole place was busy, especially the area around the slopes. For the second time that day, Johnson felt a glow of warmth. The fog of fear that had hung over the town since last summer really was lifting. And maybe he had a little something to do with that.

Millie giggled with pleasure as Susan pushed off once again from the top of the hill. It seemed sledding really didn't ever get old when you're four. An unbidden smile lifted Johnson's face.

Daylight was already beginning to fade. The gusting wind had taken on a fresher sting. Soon they would have to head home to their cozy living room and settle in to dinner – Susan had promised pizza and ice cream today – in front of the TV. Susan loved to watch *Oprah* and they both loved those reality shows on the Travel Channel about terrible hotels that needed a makeover.

But right now – in these final moments of the dying day – Johnson scooped up his family as the sled spun to a halt, and held them close.

ABOUT THE AUTHOR

Matthew Link is a Christian writer currently living in Cairo, Egypt, where he teaches English at a British/American International School. He was born in the south of England and has lived in London, in Washington DC, and in Bogota, Colombia. He has published a number of novels and short story collections with the aim of telling good, exciting stories that glorify God and present Christianity positively.